KINNDRAILL:

A WHITE KNIGHT SAGA

OSBORNE B NCUBE

DEDICATION.

TO THE BRAVE SOULS WHO DARE TO TREAD THE SHADOWED PATHS, TO CONFRONT THE DARKNESS WITHIN AND WITHOUT, AND TO EMBRACE THE ALLURE OF THE UNKNOWN. THIS BOOK IS DEDICATED TO THOSE WHO FIND BEAUTY IN THE MACABRE, SOLACE IN THE EERIE WHISPERS OF THE NIGHT AND STRENGTH IN THE DEPTHS OF THEIR FEARS. MY ITS PAGES BE A BEACON IN THE ABYSS, GUIDING YOU THROUGH THE LABYRINTH OF DARKNESS TO THE LIES BEYOND.

CONTENTS

A WHITE KNIGHT SAGA

Prologue

On the fourteenth year after the world ravished its lands for power stood an elegant beauty drenched in golden locks. Staring out of her cottage, reminiscing on her past equally in both the good and bad. Amid the wheat, moves the young boys as they dance in the art of fighting breaking their mother's joyful trance.

"Eros! Alexander!" She shouts. "What do you think you're doing? how will your sister feel seeing her big brothers act like animals?"

With a hint of a smile, Alexander whispered. "She only stopped us because you were losing. For the two hundredth time."
As usual to his temper, he took the bait screaming in hysteria. He was a young boy no older than seven and Alexander knew how to push his buttons. Even with the crowd of his sister and pet running circles around them he continued to argue and stomp his feet.
As the screaming, laughing and barking continued Alexander could see a small vain on Eros's neck enlarge and his eyes turning red by each passing moment. Unable to hold back, Alex adds to the teasing, pushing his golden curls out of the way, closing his ears and letting out an exaggerated laugh.

"You're shaking," Alex mocks. "You will end up making yourself ill if you continue."
The fiasco continued until their mother, hand gripping her long-pleated dress stepped out of their small home.
"Alex. I see, you have too much freedom." She added pulling the cheeks of Eros. "Look how small he is, at least let him have a weapon." The dog barked loud enough to break the tension and falling into the trap Alex picked up a nearby stick praising their dog Fargo as if he suggested.

Adira let Eros go pushing him to grab the object. Then he
swung with such intent it shocked even Adira and forced Alex
to jump back on instinct. Unwilling to accept the shock his
younger brother gave to him he shrugged. "Look ma, we have a
Milo in the making. I guess I can't hold back." He mockingly
added stretching his limbs readying himself to attack.
The shock had settled and as Eros's frustration grew from being
unable to hit his brother, Adira grabbed him by the shoulders,
kneeling to his eye level petting his head and drying his tears.
"Come, my big strong man. Look at your sister, you have to
protect her whilst your brother is at camp." Adira pat down her
son's shoulders echoing a warm smile all the way. "If you cry
over something so simple how is Fanisse supposed to react?"
As she pointed at her glowing daughter. "Look at her, she needs
her big strong bother to protect that smile till she can do it herself."
Eros started to perk up, whilst Alex tried to sneak away hoping
to get away with his crimes "Don't take another step or you will
be doing double the work young man" Adira said with her back
turned to Alex.
With daylight still hugging the lands, Alex dragged Eros along
to his weekly hunt. This was his last before going to camp and
he wanted his younger brother to learn to ease his mother burden.
Eros kicking and screaming. "I don't want to!" he shouted, loud
enough to scare the birds away.
Alex started to whistle as he dragged his brother along. "If you
want hairs on your chest this is what you have to do."
"That's dumb, I don't even eat meat why do I have to do it?"
"Because mum Fanisse and Fargo do," Alex adds. "Now I'm
only teaching you just in case you decide to help out around the
house one day."

The trip ended as they entered a small forest not too far from their home, where they saw rabbits playing and deer grazing. Alex started to get lower to the ground, scanning his pray holding his brother close to him to not make any noise. He pulled the bow back tightening his muscles, and after a small breath let loose an arrow whizzing through the hind leg of a deer. The noise snaped the animals to attention. Quickly they scatter in all directions. "Let's go brother!" shouts Alex as he sprints after them.

Eros too scared to walk back alone followed quickly. "Look for footprints" Alex commands, as each one of the footsteps from the animals leave a fresh crisp mark for them to follow. Finally, they catch up to the injured deer, tired struggling to limp away. Alex with a sorrowful look in his eye pulls his bow back once again.

"Do we have to kill it?" Eros desperately asked. "Look if we let it go, we can still eat potatoes and such."

"You are not wrong, but his death will feed us for weeks, give us pelt to sell, bones to crush and turn into medicine. All of him will be used, just like us when we die. Our body will be used by the earth, feeding the grass that will one day feed another deer."

Confused Eros looked down. "Why are you telling me this," he muttered under his breath.

Alexander forced a smile on his lips before releasing his arrow killing the deer. "Teaching you a lesson that father taught me when I was younger than you. In this world, the strong will always trample on the weak. But it is the duty of the strong to respect the weak even in death," he said as he approached the corpse of the deer.

Following closely Eros took a misstep quickly falling on his back. Seeing this Alex Laughed as he reached out his hand to help his brother up.

With the day ending, the family as small as it is dysfunctional sit around the table as they begin to eat. Eros immediately indulged eating more than he could. But even with the table laced with delicacies including meat he still avoided it, preferring the bread, washing it down with milk. Fanisse and Fargo did not care much though playing with their food throwing it in the air annoying their mother.

"Enough!" she said. "If you don't stop acting like an animal you will both sleep outside today!"

Though she stopped Alex chuckled under his breath knowing whatever his sister did Adira could never stay mad at her. She was the spitting image of Eros' father Ivan after all. However, as everyone continued to eat talking about their day Adira stopped admiring her small family.

she looked down at her deer bone scratching it. "You are leaving by the beginning of next week, right?"

"Yes, on at the break of dawn."

"Good at least I get to see you off. On that day Eros will be looking after his sister for the first time."

"Why?" Alex asked

"I have to go into the city to trade remember." The mention of the city drives energy into Eros and Fanisse as they start to bombard their mother begging and pleading to her to bring them along into Utopia. A city that laid in the middle of a torn continent where the north flourished with power. Filled to the brim with powerful beings who could control the very earth we walk on. Then the south, ravaged with war from several clans trying to control lands and three major countries of Zen, Nero and Pocasis locked in constant war.

The peaceful days pass, with Alex teaching all that he can to his little brother before he must disappear for three years.

As the week comes to an end the duo of Eros and Fanisse stop trying so hard to convince their mother and instead start coming up with a cunning plan of their own to visit Utopia until Alex catches them in the act.

"Why do you want to go into such a busy area? Trust me it's not the kind little ones like you two would like." He says, only to be further intrigued by the smirks of his little sibling. Fanisse finally speaks. Her words jumbled but still powerful, nonetheless. Talking about how their favourite entertainer 'Charlie the clown' will be performing and giving away the new toys. With such passion Alex is unable to control himself as he starts hysterically laugh holding his belly and wiping his tears.

"I wish I could take you, but I can't...go for it, but promise me any sign of trouble you find mum at the trader's guild. OK?" He says with the two siblings responding with glimmering smiles.

On the morning of Sunday, the carriage arrived to take Alex to the camp, his peers sitting shouting for him to get in. But as he tries to sprint to the carriage, he is quickly embraced by his mother viciously kissing him. As his peers looking on Obnoxiously laughing, Embarrassment filled Alex.

After a while, he managed to wiggle away and ran into the carriage before his mum could grasp him again. The noise went unnoticed as it alerted the rest of the family who came out screaming, laughing and barking, as they chanted their sweet goodbyes to Alex.

As the carriage starts to drive away, Adira with her hand on her chest and a smile on her face proudly proclaim to the rest of her children "your brother is on his way to being one of the men in uniform who protects these lands."

"I will be the best Galient," Eros shouts. "Just wait till I turn ten, I will break every record you get in the camp!"

With Fanisse unable to hold back her excitement, jumping and shouting, "me too!". And Fargo close by barking in agreement. Later gathering the food onto a wagon double the size of its kind Adira comforts her kids with the knowledge that she would return by nightfall. Promising them that next time she would gladly take them into the city. They calmly acknowledge this offer with a nod. The sun beaming in the middle of the morning, Adira takes off leaving her kids behind, who immediately begin to will their plan into motion.

Fanisse slowly starts to feel guilty for lying to their mother and with the guilt clearly showing on her face, Eros desperately trying to keep this going stands as tall shouting. "Don't worry big brother will protect you remember that!" these simple words quickly jolt Fanisse into a better mood.

"I'm not worried," she says enthusiastically. "If we got into trouble mum can find us, she always does!".

So, the plan continues and on the dirt road to the city marches the kids and the dog in unison. Eros takes the lead with a blade of wheat in his hand flaunting it and pretending to be a captain of the Galients. Fanisse behind him with her head held high singing songs of the brave and Fargo tailing both barking in tune with the singing. The high moral of this sweet moment does not last as hours go pass and with the sun getting hotter the kids are seen dragging their feet, panting for water.

" I want...go home now!" shouts Fanisse clearly tired of this fiasco.

"We are almost there..." Eros replies. "Remember Charlie ok. We might miss most of the show, but we will see the best part." At the trader's guild a lively place. Hours of Haggling through the noise to determine the price of the goods brought by Adira finally seems to come to an end with the bitter Trader Khan submitting to the will of Adira.

Adira filled with confidence, crosses her arms and legs sitting back and accepting victory. "Ten thousand Cuni, it is then, old friend."

It was strange to see Khan Cave to such a price for only two tons of Flour and a couple of pelts. A few months' pay gone simply because he was tired of arguing with her. Adira then leaned forward in her stola and began to sign over ownership of the goods she brought in, whilst continuing to mock Khan, only for the fat old man to reply with quips of his own.

Star gazed with the scenery. Fanisse and Eros finally Standing at the gates are quickly brought back to reality as a large man flaunting a ginger beard and blond short hair dressed in the blue and red uniform of the Galients approached them, towering over the kids as if he were a giant.

"Eros, Fanisse what are you doing here on your own without your mother?" The man asks only to get silence from the kids. "Even you Fargo, I'm disappointed in you." He adds as Fargo hides his shameful face under his paw.

"Don't worry Nad, we came to surprise mum! she's at the Trader's Guild, right? right, Fanisse?" Eros calmly adds to the continuous nods of his sibling and dog. Amused Nad stops trying to harass them and simply tells them to be careful before letting them into the city.

Loud screams of merchants trying to sell their goods, Galients, soldiers meant to be responsible, getting drunk crying over lost bets. A city, known for the poor and rich walking hand in hand. Eros, Fanisse and Fargo once again filled with energy start the run through the city carefree. Running past stands located infront of Victorian houses. Stands that are built on the banks of rivers clear as mirrors, which ran through a bed of jewel-encrusted stones. Under the many white marble bridges that hold the world of Utopia together.

In the blinding joy, Eros is hit back into reality when he collides with a man dropping him on his back.

"Hey, watch where you're going " Fanisse shouts instantly going to her brother's defence. The tall, hooded man crouched to the kids' eye levels revealing a pale almost ghost-like face with

unnaturally bright silver hair. He goes to grab Eros' hand noticing it had just sustained a small injury from the fall.
"I'm sorry I'll be more careful from now on," the man says before letting go of a now fully healed hand. Astounded the kids
start visibly wondering how this man did that. Until a woman
looking almost like the man's clone peeks her head over his
shoulder. "Brother we should be going now."
The strange couple still bouncing through Eros' mind minutes
after the event. Locks him deep in thought before a loud,
"Move!" is shouted by a force of Galients rushing towards the
main gate.
'*War is a gift from the goddess, maybe for her own entertainment... who
knows*' thinks Nad as he gazes upon foreign banners spanning as
far as the eye can see. "Fools I tell you, attacking Galients in
such an obvious way!" says one of the guards marching back
into the city walls.
"I guess," Nad said. "As soon as the last person gets behind the
gate, close it and arm the walls ready to lose at any moment."
An ominous feeling starts to rise as the army like statues stood
on top of the hilltop waiting, giving the Galients a chance to
ready themselves. Finally, at the peak of the wall, Nad stood
dormant, observing the strangeness of the enemy. Whilst the
eagerness of the rest of the Galients begins to show as they start
hoping, almost praying for an attack. No sooner after the Galients had gathered on top of the wall like fans to a stadium, a
solitary mounted knight dressed in full white and silver armour
treads forward towards the city's gates. dragging a steel spear
hanging off his fingers.
"Look, Corporal, they want a duel," jokingly says one of the
Galients. Only to add to Nad's curiosity pushing him to rush
back down to the gate instantly demanding to his superiors that
he fights this rouge knight.

Minutes pass and as the knight calmly waits close to the gate. Stomps on the ground begin ringing through the air as if they were thunder. Getting louder by each second until the solitary Nad steps out with his sword and shield in the air basking in the victory that is yet to come with an audience chanting his name. "You have a date with destiny today boy!" shouts Nad getting closer to the knight. The knight seemingly tired of the bravado finally dismounts from his White steed and through his helmet his eye travels up the body of Nad until he sees his face, "you're one short knight you know" Nad exclaims as he stands chest to face with this Knight.

With no response again Nad smirks before swinging his sword downward as if to chop the head of an animal only to miss and break the ground beneath his feet. The crowd roars at this showcase of strength and Nad being overly confident begins to bask in the glory forgetting of the danger only to be brutality reminded with a slash across his face. this drops his joyful aura as he starts to repeatedly pressure the enemy at hand with brutal swings, knocking the Knight off balance with each attack. Until one connects ripping the Knight's helmet apart, "a child?" Nad quietly questions reviling a boy in the clothes of a man. This stunning moment stops Nad in his tracks but a shock to the chest quickly wakes him back up.

He starts to gaze down and sees part of the spear deep into his heart, he looks back up seeing for the first time what the child truly is. A person with eyes that sank deep, seemingly bottomless. He looked at the child as if he were staring at the abyss. Now filled with more sorrow than dread Nad falls to his side and with his body hitting the ground. The silence screams so loud that you would not be at fault for not hearing the loud cries of the populace in the city.

Before Nad's death, residing at the middle the city, the Goddess' cathedral watches over the people and at the peak of the

Cathedral stood nine hooded figures overlooking Utopia. They continued taking in the sites until the one who stood in the middle raised his hand and with a deep almost hypnotic voice commanded. "Remember stick to the plan... no mercy."
With those few words, the rest of the figures seemingly vanish from his presence and then he proceeds to slap the ground he stood on. The air stills, before an earthquake, erupts in the area sinking the nearby buildings into the ground, parting the rivers and killing many nearby. The city gets quickly launched into a panic. Scared, Eros immediately grabs his sister's hand and starts running away.
"You're hurting me!" shouts Fanisse as her hand is getting squeezed, ignoring this Eros continues to pace through the panicked crowd looking for somewhere where safe to hide. When he quickly notices an old woman signalling for them to come inside. But before starting to move forward one of the hooded attackers drops between them.
Trapped Eros squeals. "Please don't kill us..."
This oddly works, with the hooded figure's bright red eyes quickly glancing at them before continuing its job by spreading its arms apart like a cross. Inhaling an ungodly amount of air then releasing an explosion of air across the area, immediately sending the kids flying and levelling a mass amount of land.
"Another one..." says Adira, looking to the east of the town.
"Shouldn't... we run Adira?" Ask a cowering Khan hunched over, hiding behind her.
Amused by Khan's reaction, she puts her hand on top of the balding man trying to calm him down. Only to leap back barely avoiding an attack from the silver-haired pale-skinned woman.
"Good reflexes" the woman compliments.
"Thanks" Adira responded.

"Now who are you?" The woman questioned before launching silver chains from her robes towards Adira only to be swatted away like bugs.

Startled yet curious the silver-haired woman's eyes shine brighter as they gaze at Adira trying to fathom her power. But the site of the disgusting amount of Will emitting from her immediately pushes the woman to vomit.

"Are you afraid?" a smug Adira asks, slowly raising her hand, but in abrupt fashion, the silver-haired woman immediately retreats. Unsatisfied, Adira tells Khan to get to a safe place and immediately rushes towards the mysterious woman.

Over at the walls, the invaders start scaling the walls. In a panic, few of the Galients try to retreat the people to a safer area whilst the rest desperately shoot waves of arrows down trying to stop the invaders climbing. Through this hell, the sun suddenly disappears, and with eyes snapping towards the sky, the civilians stop.

"This is a dream, right?" ask a young, impoverished man staring along with others.

Baffled, scared and mesmerised, the people stand enchanted as they ogle upon the image of a giant towering over many of the buildings. "Goddess Sen, please protect us..." drops a woman praying.

"it's moving," says one of the Galients. When with one swipe from the giant's hand sends all those near flying in the air and all the buildings crumbling under the pressure.

"Captain Basil! your orders?" shouts a young recruit trailing behind at a balding old man.

"Containment...primary mission, don't lose the wall, secondary evacuate the civilians to the underground!" orders Basil.

As he walks out of the plaza ready for battle, holding the handle of his sabre by his right and putting on his glasses with his left hand. Taking loud, proud strides forward he thinks, how foolish they must be wanting to challenge the Worlds Government. But before finishing his thoughts, an ominous presence is felt to the back of him, and he immediately slashes his sword at it only to see a mile of corpses where his men used to stand.

"Good afternoon, Captain Basil... I'm afraid I'll have to borrow you for a minute," says a tall figure with such a paralyzing presence, Basil stands is frozen in fear.

In one flow of motion, Basil's head is grabbed and then slammed into the middle of what was once the cathedral but now, just a pile of rocks.

"What?" a dazed Basil asked.

"Teleportation my friend" responds the figure stepping back towards his accomplices.

"Who are you, people?"

"I'm No one important. Now Captain please open the door," The silver-haired pale man politely answers pointing at a basement door.

Realizing the danger these people possess, the captain drops on his hands and knees, Basil starts to plead and warn them of the backlash of what they are trying to do only for it to fall on deaf ears.

With the world of Utopia crumbling around him. Eros laid on his back, directing his eyes at a sky without a cloud in sight. At peace only for the sound of his dog's bark alerting him to the situation at hand. Scared, he sits up only to witness his dog kicked passed his face.

"Fargo!" screams his sister jolting Eros to act.

In a moment's notice, he starts running towards the still Fargo, gripping his sister's hand as hard as he can, cradling Fargo like a baby and blitzing forward as fast as their little legs can take them. Then stopped at a bridge as on the other side a wall of the invaders stood, slaughtering the people of Utopia. Upon seeing this the energy is drained from Eros's eyes. With fate not giving them a chance to relax, a rouge arrow flaps towards the kids when Eros in a moment of foresight drops his dog and pushes his sister over the edge of the bridge.

Trapped between the hooded monster exploding everything in his path and an army slaughtering the residence. Eros jumps off the bridge following his sister whilst crying as he leaves Fargo behind.

As the day turns into dusk the chaos still proceeds, the land now red with blood, filled with the dead and drowning in un-ending screams. Eros drags his sister from the bed of the river. Now at the far eastern point of the city surrounded by rubble. A distorted Fanisse glaring at the ground on her hands and knees completely consumed by fear asks, "Fargo is dead... are we next Eros?".

"No!" Eros shouts.

Trying to protect his sister from this harsh reality he pastes a massive smile and tells her that all they need to do is find their mother and they will be fine. With this reassurance creeping up Fanisse she finally shows her radiant smile. When a powerful force-lands next to them bouncing them off the ground and as they land Eros snaps his head around, for then his eyes to climb up this gargantuan monster. Only to be disrupted by an inaudi-ble sound it echo's from where its head would be located.

After it finishes mimicking the sound of whales it uses its sec-ond foot to try and squash the bugs that are Eros and Fanisse only to barely miss. Instead, the force from the stomps sends them wheeling into the air crashing Eros' entire left side into nearby rubble of a wall and Fanisse bouncing past the edge of the river and colliding with a window of a bar.

Thinking of them as dead the monster walks away to continue its destruction. Again, defying fate Eros maintains conscious-ness watching the monster plod away.

"Fanisse..." he whispers before lifting himself up. "Wake up...mum...we have to get to mum."
he keeps talking inching towards his sister who has yet to move, "wake up please..." he squeals with a tear starting to roll down his face. With each agonizing step, he finally reaches his sister dropping to his knees as swells of tears and blood drip from his face. Shaking, terrified he reaches with his right hand towards his sister when an acute sound comes from her and an immediate sigh of relief escapes Eros. Moments pass as he slowly picks up his sister.
"Hold on tight we...going home..." Eros says as he carries his little sister on his back. But before even taking a single step an illumination of red grabs his attention as the sky now loss of its innocent blue and filled with bodies trying to swim out. It would not be too different from what one would see at the gates of hell.
Half-conscious and mesmerized Eros begins to drag his crippled self forward, towards the centre of the city whilst talking to his sister, limp after limp over the destroyed land and dead bodies. Finally, as he inches closer, the sky returns to its innocent blue. Eros, moving on instinct walks past the screams for help and the horrors left on the land unfazed.
"We are almost...there," he says to no response from Fanisse. As time passes Eros reaches the edge to the centre and finally, after scaling through the rubble he makes it to the middle of the city. Where the Land stood near empty...barren even...
It looked strange as one person laid in the middle of this land with arms spread and a club being gripped by one of their hands. Eros without fear limped towards this person and as he got close enough one-word slips from his mouth before collapsing, "Mum?".

Elizabeth

As the second morning dawned, the invaders advanced through the Pangea's lands as quickly as they could. Many joyful of the loot they acquired including Drominic as he took strides through the lands counting each of his gold coins. After a short phase of soft whistling, his eye is drawn to his ally only feet away.

"That kid will have you running for your money soon Al'Gadrood," he says. "I think all that muscle is slowing you down..." even when he tries his hardest to ignore the fool, the blatant mockery visibly upsets Al'Gadrood.

Drominic's endless chatter continues to further irritate Al'Gadrood. With the sun getting hotter and sweat starting to drip from his skull, his mind begins to focus on escaping. Only for him to notice a small pond not too far ahead. *'Thank G'al'* he thinks right before he pushes Drominic into the bed of water. Laughter ensures, filling Drominic with embarrassment and in response Drominic trots forward immediately grabbing Al'Gadrood by the collar.

"You wish to fight me now? Mr bow and arrow?" mockingly asks Al'Gadrood as he mirrors his taller half's actions.

Now surrounded by a crowd pressuring the two to start fighting, a small mercenary boy runs in between and with few words ends the squabble. taking them with him towards the front of these mercenaries. As they begrudgingly reach the front a horn is sounded halting the army to rest.

"Our payment is here" proclaims Elizabeth. "So enough with your childishness and accompany me."

Drominic quickly salutes, "yes Lizzie," before shielding his eyes from the gold of Elizabeth's armour. Her hair did no favours for her either, bright red, tumbling over her shoulders. She was a hard person to ignore. They looked like a circus act as they moved forward. Drominic and Al'Gadrood arguing close by and a silver-haired boy by Elizabeth's side obediently walking, griping his lance.

Noticing the boy, Drominic leans over to Al'Gadrood asking "does that kid ever smile?" prompting a timid snicker from Al'Gadrood.

"It can laugh!" shouts Drominic continuing his quick remarks towards the boy.

Elizabeth, hearing these two, leans over to the boy and with a foreign tongue. "Ignore them little Isaac".

"It's Lancer!" The boy shouts in the common tongue.

A gentle laugh from Elizabeth ignites, trying to calm the situation. "Ok, Lancer, I'll remember that for next time." She says before stroking the boy's hair.

"Honestly, do you think they're fucking?" Drominic softly whispers to Al'Gadrood.

"What no! he barely has hair on his balls."

"I mean we just saw a giant spawn out of nowhere stranger things happen. All I'm saying is id fuck her, wouldn't you?" an unfazed Drominic asks.

Before Al'Gadrood could respond the shaft of a lance was already firmly pressed on Drominic's neck. With his cold dead eyes, Lancer's command finally made Drominic silent for the rest of the trip. Ending their journey, they see in the distance two trees planted on top of a small hill "almost couldn't tell the difference between the tree and him" says Elizabeth as she dismounts from her old steed.

"What hell did he just escape from with that many bandages?" responds Al'Gadrood. As they get closer the man finally speaks in an ominous tone "The mission failed." A cold silence seeps through the air and fearing betrayal the feral Lancer pounces forward for an attack only for Elizabeth's command to stop him.

"Calm down Isaac, I doubt only one of them would come if there was a betrayal" she exclaims.

Understanding the situation, the man nods in response. "a warrior should not do transitions. But my brothers need to rest. You completed your part of the mission. So, enjoy. Your spoils" he adds as he presents a chest. Finished with his task he begins to limp into the distance.

Elizabeth who had been born a sordes looked down upon by bastards and slaves. Sickly throughout her youth, trapped with her mother in a small, impoverished village south of Zen. She gazed on to her salvation with a pile of gold coins dripping off the edge of the chest, her mother's dream, her dream finally at reach. With a smile touching each corner of her face she stands and with a fist to her heart, screaming "Praise G'AL! for his glory and bounty!" and with this infectious mood, Elizabeth quickly rides with her small group to the rest of the camp. With the shimmering gold flooding with light and like moths, their attention grasped.

"Today as G'AL rose from the ashes, the band of the White Knights burns, and the White Knight Kingdom rises!" proudly proclaims Elizabeth holding her sword in the sky.

"All hail the Queen!" shouts a lone soldier in the crowd and like sheep, the rest follow the chant in unison. The night of celebration continues and as Elizabeth stands in the outskirts overseeing the camp with a mug of ale in her hand and a grin on her face, she sees a drunk Al'Gadrood stumble towards her. He was of faith, like his father before him. G'AL much like the people from the north was the god he worshipped, a benevolent god who would bow to those who fell in battle. So, for him to be this intoxicated not praying or preparing for battle stunned Elizabeth for a moment. However, as this fleeting moment passed Elizabeth once again gazed at the camp with flickering lights of fires and roars of joy in front of her.

"You see those, all those lights, each man with a dream of a better life, a life away from war, all those lights together brighten mine and my mother's dream for a kingdom where all those dreams can become a reality." Out of respect, Al'Gadrood stands back letting Elizabeth be swallowed by the atmosphere. "Tomorrow, we travel to Lumina..." she adds before sitting on the grass.

"Dafrak's lands?" asks a cautious Al'Gadrood.

"Are you afraid?"

"A little, more cautious really..." He admitted. "His too unpredictable, unhinged why trust him?"

Elizabeth smirked, "He's also smart and after seeing what I bring to the table he will be swayed to an agreement."

The great horde of the White Knights began their travels the next morning to one of the small towns that border the Republic of Pocasis. One of the small towns that no clansman dared to raid or conquer. One of the small towns that proudly draped their banners for all to see. Commonly known for many names, the land of thieves, villain's paradise, land for the lost. Lumina the city of the sordes was the heartland for all clans in the south who wanted trade.

The week's journey continued as they cross through the Beasts' territories and burn the banners of smaller clans that dared challenge them. The sound of the screeching horn halts the White Knights at the gates of Lumina and once again Elizabeth with her three companions march alone into the city.

Contrast to belief, the people immediately give Elizabeth a hero's welcome she was one of their own after all, a sordes who had defied fate and rose her mercenary group to the peak in the west. With each person gazing fondly at the angel that rode before them, Drominic starts looks around at this odd set of circumstances "Hey big guy, did you know that boss was this popular?" he asks.

"Her mother as you know built a powerful mercenary group of sordes that even the officials of Zen began to fear. Then when she took power, she added to it bringing it to this point. A small army of unwavering loyalty..." Al'Gadrood proudly responds. The group eventually approach the black iron. A tavern that is commonly known in the underworld for dealings regarding the western corner. But before signalling for a stop the sound of glass smashing and laughter exploding grabs their attention as they see a slender young commoner stand from the rubble, brush off the glass from his clothes and saunter into the distance.

"Dismount!" Elizabeth commands.

The four companions pour through the doors of the tavern expecting attention but received none. As the residents continued drinking themselves under the table, smoking at the corners, betting on whose arms were stronger.

"This might be the first time in a while boss has been ignored" Drominic stated.

Al'Gadrood, quickly responds. "Ignored. Does that strike to close to home?" prompting Elizabeth into a quick laugh and even pasting a small smirk on Lancer's face.

The moment passes and a soft whistle so sharp it cuts the air in the room, freezing everyone, grabbing their attention. The whistling gets louder by each note until a tall man with a small lady to his side approaches the edge of the second floor. Doused in leather, fair and handsome with long black hair and dark sideburns to match.

He leans over the edge whistling his soft tune uninterrupted and unending until unable to hold his tongue Drominic speaks up.

"You're calm to say that twenty thousand men just came knocking at your gates."

Strange as it seemed for someone to interrupt Dafrak he seemed unbothered at this notion. This irritates Drominic to the point of mocking Dafrak in front of his men, "good thing we came for a friendly chat or well be fucking your women in the ass right now."

"Enough!" shouted Elizabeth trying to deescalate the situation. Dafrak finally spoke in a calm tone. "Lizzie conqueror of Utopia, leader of the White knights... a pleasure to meet you."

"I'm here for business, I need weapons, armour and food my army. Clearly, you know that it's growing fast." she quickly chimes in.

Dafrak, pointed at the bar bellow him. "Let's get to know each other before we talk business."

"Not yet," Elizabeth said. "Not until I know this will lead somewhere beneficial for both of us."

"A pity, my drinks are imported from E's lands."

"The east," Elizabeth responded softly. "So, the rumours are true, you are doing business with that psychopath." This matter left a bad taste in her mouth. Everyone in the underworld knew of E, but they also knew how untrustworthy he was. For someone like Dafrak to do business with him, why would he risk so much? she pondered.

"Well, business with his people. Yes," Dafrak corrected.

"Enough!" Elizabeth shouted, losing patience in this conversation. "Do you not want my money!?"

This simple flow of words gravitated to the surrounding audience grabbing attention, even that of a little lady that stood beside Dafrak.

"Don't mind the angry woman sweet pea go back to your room I'll deal with this" he says sending her off in his calm piercing voice. "Rose what a sweet girl. You know her mother works all day and most of the night... I mean since the brother decided to get himself captured that is...shame really. I already put out the orders for what you need, so don't disappoint me now Elizabeth..." finished with what he had to say Dafrak strolls off down the hall whistling away.

Eros

Still bearing the heavy scars of the recent attack the people desperately dig through the rubble trying to salvage anything of value. The days became less favourable, with the silence of Pangea people quickly turned. They turned to their Goddess following the preachers and nuns. They turned to what's left of the military hoping for safety and stability. With the underworld seeping through the surface.

In Eros' long sleep, three shadows loom in the horizon, one of his dog, one of his sister, one of his mother. With each step, they travel further away from him "where is everyone going?" Eros asks, "mum? Fanisse? Fargo?" he adds to no response other than the unbreaking distance. fearful, Eros begins to run towards them getting no closer.

"Stop, wait for me!" he shouts, "please don't go."

Drenched in sweat, he woke up as if sleep had become a dangerous thing. His heart sprinted and his thoughts confused. His eyes dry from crying flicked everywhere trying to adjust. He sat up dragging his feet off the edge of the bed, stretching his limbs though feeling pain at every moment. He looked down watching his legs dangle above the hard stone floor, "Fanisse" he softly whispered.

"he's finally awake!" shouts a nun.

"Praise the goddess, our prayers were answered" another response joyfully.

"Fanisse, Mum," Eros says holding his head in pain, to only the concern of the nuns' faces shown to him. An older nun kneels before Eros only managing to say " the goddess chose you..." before being choked up by her words.

"It was the will of the goddess that we found you still breathing," enthusiastically says one of the younger nuns and as she continued a brutal realization dawned on him. With the noises slowly turning to static he throws himself off the bed, stands, holding his left arm he starts to limp away. The nurses and nuns beg for him to stop walking, but he ignores this and continues to the door.

Once pushing it open images of his family start appearing and with disorientation and unwillingness, he forces his crippling body to run. He Ran as fast as he can through the destroyed districts, doused with dread, drowning in poverty. Until he reaches the middle of the city and on a bridge that separates the north from the south he finally collapses on his back staring at the clouds in the sky as they start to weep on him.

A heavy night loomed over Eros as he came to terms of his new reality, a world without his beloved sister, his powerful mother, his loyal dog and his brother miles from him for years. Upon returning, Eros sits in the corner and watches the world pass by, disconnecting himself from everyone unable to gain the strength to try and survive any longer. Night and day pass by him, as he moves through this still world. With grey in his eyes, he sees a red apple fly onto his lap waking him from his daze.

"Eat kid," says a joyful girl maybe twice his age poured in her dungarees with her dreads covering most of her face but her smile radiating like a ray of sunshine.

"No."

"No?" she repeated back confused. "Even now there are people who refuse food. Anyway, Names' Sarrah... and you are?"

"..."

"Don't speak, much do you? that's ok I like to talk, where are you from? if here then that's rough. If you want to come with me that's fine. We have a small group, but we protect each other."

The cold silence beginning to fill the room, Sarrah took this opportunity to leave Eros alone with a few words of encouragement. Which at first seem to not have a single effect on the Eros. But after a while and with hunger taking over, he quickly consumed his apple. Finished he dried his tears revealing a more determined face.

He then lifted his broken body up, moved towards the outside, the fresh air lets him think for the first time in a while. Immediately, he begins to ask the people where the traders did their business, thinking it would be the best place to gather money and with the information gathered he starts to hobble towards the trading area gathering as much information of his surroundings as he could. From opportunists taking advantage of the situation selling familiar goods back to their original owners to remaining homes being turned into pubs for those to drown their sorrows in.

He pressed forward almost convinced that his plan would work. After a long walk, he comes face to face with the traders, took a breath and began to beg for whatever they could offer. A few days pass and like a stray cat he arrives, the traders give him what they can from food to copper coins.

"He's back again..." a bitter beggar mutters with under his breath.

After gathering what he could like clockwork Eros heads back to the church past a familiar face who waves him goodbye.

"Why are we here," Raijin asked polishing his blade. He swung it forward pointing the tip towards Eros, before glancing at Sarrah.

"To make sure he's safe." She chimed in. "You know, he sorts of reminds me of you, just shorter, and a lot frien-"

"No!" Raijin snapped at her. "Look at him. Pathetic. Weak body, begging all day people like him should do themselves a favour and die."

"You're a mean one Ry Ry."

"I don't care. Anyway, this is a waste of time," He reminded her. "We have a mission."

"Since when does the wonder child follow orders?" She mockingly asked.

"I'm not but Kaza's plans work so why not listen." He added before jumping off the ledge shoving his blade through his belt and scratching the dirt of his thick black afro. This day was un-naturally hot as the pair moved on to complete their mission, Raijin already sweating through his grey top, but Sarrah enjoys the sun's rays rubbing the ebony of her skin.

At the north-west point of Utopia, a club-footed man with a hat that reached the heavens screamed his name to his subordi-nates, "I am Barak!" Shouting to them about being unable to handle two children day after day. A nun not far off was on her way to the church to help, on her way she took a few minutes to pray to the Goddess when she finished, took a few more to dry her tears. Whilst doing so Barak had finished scolding his men. He had worked up a sweat and decided to take a few minutes to relax. Whilst he was doing so the nun took a step outside carrying a bag of bread and fruit, standing outside as her usual carriage was late on this day.

The Coachman had stopped at a house that had recently turned into a pub, drinking himself almost under the table, loudly com-plaining about the lack of help from the Pangea's Government. Whilst this was happening Barak had started to take a stroll with a few of his trusted men leaving the base for the first time. Af-ter the drunk Coachman had finally arrived, he started to drive the Nun to the church. Then a man ran in front stopping the carriage in its place holding an odd combination of items. Sweating. "Piss off!" the Coachman shouted angering the nun who began to loudly pray. Whilst the nun's voice had risen higher, Barak had finished his walk and decided to sit down near a bench, talking to his men about his ambitions of taking all off Utopia.

Whilst Barak was relaxing the Coachman had had enough of the nun and began threatening her, reaching his hand out to her whilst shouting. The nun unimpressed threw at apple something that had become a commodity at the Coachman hitting him on the head but allowing him to catch it. Raising his spirit and continuing to drive all the faster whilst loudly eating the apple. Whilst a man high on leaves started dancing in the road briefly grabbing Barak's attention, "Move off the road you fool," he mockingly shouts. The addict smiled as he saw Barak and started pulling out coins from his undergarments rushing towards him. Whilst the Coachman seeing the fool in the road went to pull his horses to a stop. A rouge orange thrown from the nun and hit the back of his head forcing him to lose his grip and fall forward.

Swerving the carriage and sending it flying to its side as it bounces off his body. The crash heard by many as they snapped their heads to the damage. A few moments pass and a nun's hand reaches out forcing many from both sides of the road to rush towards the carriage. Many except the few on one side of the road Raijin and Sarrah who had just turned a corner and on the other Barak and his men watching on.

Raijin quickly tapped Sarrah on the arm. "That's Barak, right?" Sarrah turned her head silenced by the coincidence. "I think so..." she muttered.

"I'm going to get him," Raijin confidently said.

Sarrah pastes a crooked smile on her face. "Moving without Kaza's command. Wow. So, only a few opponents, I go high you go low?"

"No. You stay here," Raijin said softly.

"What?"

"You stay here!" He commanded with a stern tone.

Though talking their eyes never flickering away from Barak. The space between them was empty as a crowd was focused on making sure the nun was safe and healthy. Barak's men's weapons were drawn, all heavy and hard to swing freely. Two in front had swords, and two in the back where calm with one leaning on a harmer and the other with his arms crossed smiling. Raijin was banking on them making a mistake, "four" he muttered as he counted his opponents.

The sand flew across them as the sun was at it its peak. They stood like statues until Sarrah broke the silent stare down by taking a few steps forward. Immediately stopped by the blade of Raijin acting like a guard to a private ball. Then as they bounced their feet off the ground, Barak's men ran forward leaving a joyful smirk on Raijin's face. The first swung his sword aiming to take Raijin's head but horribly missing, as Raijin, much smaller, got even closer to the ground pouncing behind the man and slashing the back of his knee. As the man dropped to his knees, another swung his sword, but Raijin unfazed parried the blow holding his sword at an angle allowing for the enemy's weapon to slide off.

Quickly, he slashed the man's neck, then flipped his blade pointing it to his person, and impales the first opponent, on the neck as he was trying to pick up his own blade. Barak started to get drenched through his suite, "Kill him!" he shouts.

"Whoever kills him, gets a million Cuni." He added shaking as he pointed his finger.

A gust of wind suddenly hit Raijin, sending him flying to his original starting point only to be comfortably caught by Sarrah.

Their world opened as a crowd was cheering for them to continue.

"You are strong. Extraordinarily strong, now I understand the Milo comparisons. Then again on missions together you just disappear. Leaving me by my poor lonely self. Never witnessing your power," she said, pouting. "But you are now fighting an elemental. So big sis will help you out, save your few tricks for another time."

"I'll kill you!" Raijin snapped. "If you get involved, you become my enemy and I will kill you!" he emphasised.

He stopped. looking at his new elemental opponent, looking at his blade collecting dust below him, looking at Barak laughing through his fat stomach. Building in frustration. Only enough for a few seconds, he thinks as strings of light flowed from his body, dancing around him. Making the sound of chirping birds as he rushed forward, cracking the ground beneath his feet.

"Lightning Elemental..." Barak said softly, frozen by fear. The man who had just pushed Raijin away stands unfazed, pushing a ball of air towards Raijin. However, like a grasshopper, Raijin jumped above the ball of wind and kicked the man in the face. Then as he lands his eyes flick above seeing the man disoriented, then flicking his eyes below seeing his blade in reach he quickly grabbed it shoving it through the man's chest. As the man dropped on his back Raijin stood tall, taking short breaths no longer covered in lightning. He tries as he must to take a second to breathe but he notices a hammer from the last guard inching closer to his skull only to be stopped by a single punch from Sarrah.

"At least pay attention Ry Ry."

The comment had struck him as the vein on his neck grew bigger, he grits his teeth as he jumped slashing the last opponent's neck.

Raijin scanned Sarrah up and down, as he quickly cleaned his blade. When finished he turned around strutting towards Barak.

"Your strength is unnatural. I can't tell yet where you fall. A witch. Someone who can control their aura greatly. Or an elemental, Earth or water." He spoke.

"Unnatural?" Sarrah responded softly. "If that's how you see me, I guess that explains why you didn't do anything to my involvement. What did you say again 'I will kill you' right?"

Raijin still grinding his teeth decided to ignore this as he started to run towards Barak.

Barak started to take a few steps back begging. "Please don't! I can give you whatever you want. Money? Land? Women? just name it and it's yours."

Almost silenced by frustration, Raijin ignored these pleas for mercy and impaled a fleeing Barak on his back.

As Barak struggled for air, the crowd began to grow louder some celebrating and some screaming in anger. Raijin looked around panting, he pulled his blade out and started to walk towards the carriage. biting into a half-eaten apple.

"Barak is dead," he said. "This land now belongs to us the misfits. All those who wish to challenge us, know this. You are challenging the next greatest swordsman! so prepare to die."

Later as they started walking back to the base a joyful Raijin asked. "Why, do you care for him Sarrah? Really?"

"I like him, he's cute, like a puppy unlike you. Grumpy."

"Weak like one as well," Raijin muttered.

Before responding Sarrah notices two beggars walking past and starts to follow skipping along the way.

"Now, now Raijin that's not how you make friends come let's see what these lovely people want with my little puppy," she adds.

Playing to their game, the beggars attack Eros kicking him away and taking his belongings before leaving an empty threat "stay away from our spot, boy!" they shout as they laugh and count their earnings. Down on the floor, Eros grasps the ground below him "give it back" he says to the laughter of the beggars. "Give it back!"

My money Eros thinks before rushing into them blinded by tears. One of the beggars punts him away laughing with his friend as Eros' body rag-dolled away.

"Give it back..." Eros said again as he lifted his beaten body back up.

"You want to die boy?" the beggar says as he is walking back to Eros.

Eros, shaking as he struggled to stay standing up balled up his fist looking at it. *'What am I doing? why am I still fighting for a few coins? what would Alex do right now?'* He thinks finally coming down as a smile, creeps onto his face.

"Is that all you got?" he asked wiping the blood from his nose. A slow faint clap starts to get louder by each second, as Eros looked and saw Sarrah approaching wiping a fake tear and as she started shaking her head in approval. A beggar runs at Sarrah being immediately knocked out by a left hook from her, then Raijin quick as ever appeared from behind her slashing the second's throat. Eros immediately looked down, and each time he heard the final squeal of each beggar his body shook.

"All for a few coppers" Sarrah sighs as she collects her bounty.

"Lift your head boy!" Raijin shouts looking at Eros cleaning his blade.

"Calm down Raijin, his not built like you he actually has feelings for life. You heartless monster." Sarrah adds as she hops over the dying bodies handing the money back to Eros.

"So little pup, why are you collecting coins?" she asks as she crouches.

"Rumours. Rumour is there is a man who is planning to take us out of here. But he needs money."

"Ok well pup, get some rest well help you get out of here to-morrow," she adds. Receiving an innocent smile from Eros.

"Eros, my name is Eros Amyntas Senesto."

Their conversation ends and as the light fades from the world, a more confident Eros returns to his church, laying in the back unable to calm his mind. And as dawn breaks, Eros steps back outside the church as he sees a familiar face relaxing chatting away to her friend. She notices Eros at the corner of her eye and signals him to follow close by through the dark corners of the city until they reach their unimpressive destination.

A small lodge seemingly out of place compared to the rest of the buildings that surrounded the area. Seemingly put together with anything solid they looked more similar that the lone lodge.

Then upon touching the handle of the door, Sarrah pulls Eros to the side, narrowly avoiding a fair-skinned boy flying through the door, landing on his back. Dazed the boy sat up brushing his fingers through his thick black hair smiling from ear to ear.

"Damn, you got a lot stronger Raijin!" he shouts.

"Hey, can you train me?" he asks as he dusts himself off while listening to Raijin blustering in his victory.

"What's happening..." Eros squeals brimming with confusion.

"Raijin being Raijin and Mr muscles over there just encouraging him" quickly replies Sarrah as she drags Eros closer to the group revelling the full cast of misfits.

a slender boy reading chapters from the past uninterested in his surroundings and Raijin more animalistic than boy as he tries to assert his dominance flexing from the high of his victory.

"What brings you here so early?" asks Kaza as he embraces Sarrah.

"Customer!" Raijin shouts from the back of the room.

"Does he only have one tone of voice" Kaza wonders but quickly moves on as he starts to stare down the timid boy blending in with the wall. "And what does this customer want?"

"Same as the rest of us Kaza, freedom from this place!" says Raijin.

A smirk from Kaza appears "One hundred Cuni then!" he shouts. "that's a thousand of copper coins in the old trade boy." Raijin seemingly being the new middleman turns his head sending Eros off to collect the money. As soon as he exits Raijin shouts "Our plan is to leave this place... not die protecting trash like that!".

"Was that directed to me?" asks Sarrah directing a Piercing stare to Raijin.

"We are beyond that, only a day and more people are joining us. We have become rich and powerful. Utopia is for the taking," Bored with the situation Kaza takes his leave. "Either way we leave in a month. Spreading our power, building trade. securing Utopia from the outside in. So, it doesn't mean much to me about the boy."

Raijin and Sarrah's stare breaks as they both decide to go rest for the remainder of the day.

Sarrah with a troublesome aura found herself gliding towards Eros the next morning, "you have one-month pup" she adds before throwing another apple for Eros to eat. Upon catching it she sits next to him and starts rambling about nothing, but with words flowing through her calm tone, Eros's ears tingled at the slight hint of a foreign accent come from her mouth. Though in the world that Eros grew in, different accents were commonplace. This one stood out to him forcing him to ask where she was from to her surprise. She acknowledges Eros' decipher and responds simply with Gevana city that grows on forever in height.

"But they say it's just a constant warzone..." Eros adds innocently to the dismay of Sarrah who pets his head as she gets up to leave.

"Go get your money I'll be back tomorrow to see how you did."

"Why are you getting so attached to him so quickly?" Jon asks as he lingers out of the dark.

"Glasses!" Sarrah shouts joyfully taking him under her wing as she walks past the crowd. "I'm just being nice to our new ally."

"Train him then or he'll die the second we get past the wall..." the meek Jon mumbles as he travels alongside Sarrah towards the wall. Finally, after a short walk, they reach the wall to see the other side of their city, now looking more alien by each glare. Fences in every corner guards patrolling relentlessly and people moving aimlessly as if they were zombies.

"So that's the better half, right?" Sarrah says, smirking with her thin finger pointed towards the secured zone of the Galients. The empty chatter carries on till night where the rain begins to cover the area, " you should cover your head... Don't want to be sick, do you?" says Jon. "It's fine, its only water right" quickly responds Sarrah.

As she sits there, she is quick to remember her land. Where the rain was calm. Almost hugging you like a mother. It made her remember the days of her blissful youth hearing her friends' laughter as she ran through the streets. she remembered the sand beneath her feet how it would carry her, making sure she did not slip and how the slow boy Mula would eat anything given to him entertaining them for hours.

"Time to go" Jon speaks breaking her from her peaceful state, they quickly reach the shed only to be greeted by Raijin, who seemed to be training his blade, dancing it through the raindrops. Noticing this Sarrah grabs Jon's shoulder stopping him from interrupting, "here it comes..." she whispers before an arrow of lightning hits Raijin in full force sending shivers down both the bystanders. Upon stopping Raijin opens his eyes which now had a glow of blue so bright it could blind the unprepared.

"Borrowed power looks so cool..." she whispers again.

"Borrowed?" asks a confused Jon to no response.

"Your eyes look so beautiful in that form Ry Ry," says Sarrah as she enthusiastically steps towards Raijin.

"Huh? My eyes look manly!" he quickly responds as he briskly stomps past Sarrah.

"Too bad they're not constantly, like that" she adds seemingly unaffecting him.

As Raijin walks around the corner, he immediately loses control of his breath and grasps his chest trying to compose himself. When he finally catches his breath, he punches the wall next to him out of frustration and then continues to stomp away. He soon finds himself at the church and hears Eros panting close by. As he looks at him, he sees this meek boy swinging a stick back and forward in the rain. He sniggers, immediately zapping towards Eros, scaring him to the point where he dropped to the ground.

"I always wondered, why people were so weak," he says with a stern tone. "When I realised it's because I'm amazing. I am destined for greatness and everyone else is destined for nothing, just side characters to my story."

"Why are you telling me this?"

Raijin smiled. "Because from the second I noticed you, I hated you. You are the weakest most unimportant character in my story. Yet you can't disappear from my site."

"Hated me?" Eros replied softly. "You stood up for me against Kaza though..."

"No, I didn't, you were just convenient for me to show Kaza who is in charge. But I think your usefulness is over. You should probably kill yourself, save yourself the pain."

Eros angered, stood up rushing towards Raijin. Though feeling the difference in strength, he still swung his arm completely missing and being taken down. Time begins to pass quickly, each day Eros begun to get stronger, constantly challenge Raijin when he saw him but failing just as quick. In passing, moments begin to mix with the group more learning as much as he can, from learning the sleight of hand from Sarrah as they travelled back and forward from the lodge and the church.

To relaxing with Jon under trees away from the world. "I always see you reading that old book," Eros chimed in.

Jon lets out a small chuckle. "Old. He says. These are the works of a great Philosopher, lost in time. Leang Zhue later known as 'Shadow'. A world breaker who fought for the Sun kingdom." Huffing Eros spoke up. "How did you manage to get that? works of devils!"

"Maybe. But what he spoke I agree with," he said. "He talks about anger and revenge. Anger is like the edge of a cliff. One can look over at the unending darkness at the edge of the cliff but must be careful not to be consumed by it. One if not careful can fall off the cliff never to rise again."

Eros scratched his head. "I don't understand but seems complicated. What about revenge?"

A striking statement, which Jon only paid attention too because of the conviction in Eros' voice, "Those who seek it are doomed to be devoured." He quickly adds closing his book and laying his head on the tree behind him taking a mid-afternoon sleep.

At every waking moment between hanging out with Sarrah and Jon Eros would find the hiding Raijin and challenge him to a duel. Loosing quickly and gaining a wound as a memento. Until one day during heavy rain, Raijin had grown tired of Eros finally spoke up.

"Every time, you come here to disturb me and won't die! why?" Eros smiles through his wounds. "Revenge for belittling me!"

"Revenge? what did I do to you?" Confused Raijin asked.

"You told me to kill myself," Eros added. "I want you to apologise and I will keep doing this until you lose and are forced to apologise."

"I remember now, why should I say sorry for speaking the truth? you should apologise for being weak. You Utopians should be getting stronger fuelled by the idea of avenging your people. But all you do is cry and complain!"

Eros stood up and smiled with a cracked tooth. "I can't bring them back. But I can find my brother. They would want me to continue, follow a dream or something at least I think they would."

Begrudgingly Raijin turned around walking away, "I'm done, continue living I don't care anymore," he adds.

As the weeks pass and the day is drawn closer Kaza is stopped from one of his tales of the world outside the west. As Raijin returns to the shed, calmer and composed only to be greeted by animosity from Kaza.

"What is it?" asked Raijin.

"Three and half weeks Raijin! where did you disappear off to... did you even get information on the other side!" quickly responds Kaza growing in impatience.

"A rotation of four guards each shift of eight hours, one of which is doing extra work to help his family, he has a young boy, that's his weak spot expose that and we enter the south without any problems," responds Raijin now with his arms crossed gazing at Kaza without breaking eye contact.

"Boys come down, clearly we have everything, power, intel and a distraction" Adds Sarrah trying to ease the tension. To alight snicker from Raijin.

"Something funny?" Asked Kaza, standing clearly offended.

"No nothing she's just speaking the truth one more night and I won't have to look at you anymore, but if you beg I might be willing to take you as my underling" Raijin adds.

At nights end the group start to exit all noticing the timid Eros waiting like a patient dog in front of their shed holding a brown sack. With confidence brimming from him.

"Good luck kid," says Sarrah as she walks away whilst Raijin just glares at him following behind. "Come in kid," Kaza says Loud enough for Eros to Hear. He grabs the bag opens it to see copper coins almost overflowing and without breaking contact with them he says, "meet us near the most east bridge when the sun goes down, your job is to distract the front guards, then when the signal goes off you come running as fast as you can ok?".

"Ok! do I need a weapon?"

"No that would just slow you down, I'll give you mine when we reach the outside. I have to go back for a few trips anyway."

Eros nods in agreeance. Brimming with excitement as within a day his true journey could start. Within a day he will be on his way to his brother wherever he is.

The next day Sarrah walks into the street, already looking at her best with her dreadlocks tied up, showing her tanned skin more clearly. Although grown into a small frame, her baggy clothes hid it well. Just down the road a sight to see as the logical Jon kneeled on the floor praying for protection from the Goddess, dressed in tight fitted cloths dark in colour. With a bow and arrow close by him ready to hide under the dark moonlight supporting his friends from the distance. Kaza close by, swinging his sword aimlessly ready for the worst, Raijin away from everyone, meditating under a tree before opening his bright blue eyes. Then Eros staring blankly into space trying to focus on the mission despite his mind replaying the worst day of his life, trying to put doubt in him. Filling him with regret.

Apollo

Hours pass, a cluster of Knights on the back of horses, ride across the distant fields drenched in white and silver armour with blue trimmings and white capes to match. Knights no more than a thousand marched onward, protecting a horse-drawn carriage that was covered in rare jewellery and solid gold paint. A man at the head of this march in the same armour but without a helmet, allowing his short blond hair to feel the cool breeze of the summer air.

"Boy, how long until we reach this Utopia?" he asks the squire to his left.

"We will reach by nightfall" The square responds coldly. The Lord of this group yawns bored out of his mind mutters for there to be beautiful women at least before continuing his journey forward.

"It's time," Kaza says standing at the destination watching the sun disappear from his eyes, patiently he waits as his group of misfits gather one by one and lastly Eros slouched, walks towards them to the joy of Sarrah "I'll see you on the other side boys!" she shouts to a powerful resounding roar from everyone else.

The plan begins as Eros walks towards one of the guards with his arms up, to no one's surprise his meek presents manages to tug at the heartstrings of the guard who for only moments leaves his post giving the rest a chance to invade, using the dark they make it through most of the southern part of the city and with only Galients patrolling the streets it's made even easier. Then without warning a bell rings, the shock of being caught runs through the group with Kaza's shout breaking their trance "Fuck, run!" he shouts.

Raijin quickly responds "Wait!"

"Wait?"

He starts moving away back to the direction of the border, "wait to die?" Kaza desperately asks as he starts walking back, a small argument of what to do breaks out as their personalities clash, but at the end, the stubbornness of Kaza prevails and they start running back with their tails tucked between their legs.

As they make it back to the gate, two guards stood there arguing with each other and as the group got closer, they hear a conversation surrounded by the disappearance of a boy.

"He escaped, that means he's going to the other side..." Kaza says.

In amusement a smile breaks out from Sarrah's face "the plan is back on I guess" she says stretching her legs before running towards the crumbling wall at the edge of the city. "Giving up is for the weak..." Raijin says quickly following Sarrah, "let's not fall behind Glasses" Kaza responds and follows behind with Jon.

So close yet so far away, the band of misfits travels through the dark corners of the city most heading towards the edge where they think freedom lies. At the wall, the gates open, and a line of Galients stand in salute as the Knights enter Utopia.

"That's him, the scum prince, Apollo Vassellet" a Galient whispers.

"Wasn't he a Head-Captain, what's he doing here?" asks another, quickly silenced by the raised hand of Apollo.

"Sir, why are you stopping us here?" asks the squire but to only one response.

"My sword give it to me" Apollo demands, to the quick but confused response of the Square giving the weapon to Apollo. As He grabs his sword, with a smirk and a strong grip he smacks his feet into his horse forcing the animal to dash forward until he gets in the vision of the group slowing down to a halt.

He smiles cracking the corners of his cheeks. "Here is me thinking my stay here would be boring," he says as he starts moving comfortably towards the group, still with his sword sheathed and in his right hand.

He charges forward once more and, in a panic, Sarrah jumps forward getting into a stance and moving the ground beneath Apollo, knocking his horse off balance sending it tumbling down with him still on. Only for him to quickly jump off the horse and comfortably land in front of it. "Sarrah!" shouts Eros as he comes sprinting towards the group holding his hands up ready to fight by them.

"Good kid..." Sarrah whispers finding it hard to hide her joy of Eros returning.

"Injuring the hand of the goddess' trusty steed. That's brave of you, now I have to arrest you," Apollo says as he calmly strolls from the dust. Before lunging forward with his sword pointing towards the kids only for Sarrah to tense her muscles as she digs her fingers into the ground slashing the broken ground towards Apollo. Who effortlessly bats the pieces out of the way using the sheath of his sword.

"Sarrah stand back!" shouts Kaza as he launches forward with his sword firmly in his hands, "Glasses cover me!" he shouts again as he goes in for a swing which again is effortlessly dodged, and proceeds hit across the head by Apollo's scabbards dropping him to the ground dazed. Then a rogue arrow flies towards Apollo which he catches inches from his face, he drops the arrow and blocks a surprise attack from Raijin "the screaming birds, a lightning elemental how annoying" Apollo says as he jumps back.

"Earth elemental, lightning elemental how fun... I guess I should introduce myself like a warrior then, my name is Apollo Vassellet, Prince of the Vassell Isles, First of his name, Head Cap... Guard of the Knights of the Hand." He adds with enthusiasm.

Giving the group the Knight's salute pointing his sword to the air with his right hand and placing his left behind his back. After finishing his speech, he points his sword's hilt to his chest and the point towards most of the group.

"You...you forgot scum in your little speech" faint voice echoes in the air, changing the mood of Apollo who quickly passes towards Kaza punting him as hard as he could and then stomping on his face repeatedly until everyone else starts to rush forward. Then, suddenly they stop.

"What is this?" Jon asks aiming his bow towards Apollo.

"It's like I'm being crushed by the air" stutters Raijin.

"I can't move..." responds a terrified Sarrah.

"Did you not wonder how I found you so quickly? when these idiot guards didn't even know you existed, well to put it simply I located your aura or bloodlust or will or whatever you want to call it. You Elementals... always thinking because of physical power you are above humans, forgetting the gift the goddess blessed us all with," says Apollo as he turns his head.

"You feel it don't you, something that overwhelms you, your instincts telling you to run as far as you can, but your body not responding," He adds before placing the tip of his swords upon Kaza's neck. Only for his rage to be broken by Eros, slowly stepping forward, each step mesmerising Apollo to the point of joy. "Too bad the guards are coming," Apollo says. As Predicted, the guards appear around the corner running towards him.

"A bunch of criminals where in the area I stopped them," Apollo says before walking back to his calm steed back on all fours.

He jumps on its back and rides back to the rest of the knights, the second he gets out of vision, Jon drops having wet himself Raijin stands in crushing silence feeling a weight. The weight of a pathetic performance. Sarrah quickly runs towards Kaza who now lies unconscious in a pool of his own blood and Eros close by, starts to vomit violently as he finally calms down.

Apollo arrives back at the knights and finally orders them to move forward and just as quickly as they move, they arrive at the captain tent not far from the main gate. There fifty Galients stood in formation, the acting captain begins to move forward. "Acting district captain Azual. Sir!" He shouts as he salutes the knights who dismount parting in the middle allowing the Vassellet family to move through. With the head of the family, Madas Vassellet dressed in white and gold robes that covered his body neck to toe and the simple crown of the Vassille isles which seemed like an interlocking of branches and leaves but made of gold metal comfortably placed on his head. His wife Hestia the Queen of the isles wearing a long tunic of a similar pattern with long straight blond hair and pale skin. finally, their youngest daughter Gaia, resembling the father the most with high spirit, wearing a ranger's outfit with curly orange hair like her fathers.

They reach the front of the knights to the salutes of the Galients.

"Father... this is the captain in charge," says Apollo.

"It's Archbishop Vassellet...knight" responds Madas to the clear frustration of Apollo.

Though annoyed Apollo responds appropriately "yes Lord Vassellet".

Madas satisfied turns back towards the Galients simply saying praise the Goddess to their joyful response. As morning breaks the word of Heathens coming to Utopia spreads and the will of the archbishop has come to save everyone. The Galient forces along with the thousand Knights move into the rest of the city quickly silencing heathens and capturing criminals, all men of age quickly armed and turned into town's guard, the women and meek going out the gates in droves to farm the fields outside Utopia.

"Hours... it took them hours to fix this city. When your pockets run deep its simple to solve problems I guess," says Azual as he watches in shock as the city suddenly runs like a well-oiled machine.

Time slowly passes by, and the purging of evil continues in the city as criminals who plagued the city, when captured are lined up to be beheaded with the archbishop praying to the Goddess for their souls, one by one they drop but with no one cheering only praying silently. This continued Day after day with the Ark Bishop being slowly turned into a Hero in Utopia's eyes. Until One day he passed his son quickly ignoring him and charging past.

"You, there Knight, how are our prisoners holding up... I mean it has been just about a month and all" Apollo asked a nearby guard.

"Well, enough my lord, though one is at death's door". This did not surprise Apollo though, as the holding cells were just hollow cubes of concrete, with the only light coming from the rays of the sun. A place meant to break you.

Whoever designed these prison cells did not just build them but put pure hatred into the design. Each room could barely hold one cellmate, but it was uncommon to see them lumped together like livestock.

"How many do we have in those cells now?"

"Just over Hundred ser!"

"Bring them."

In the middle of the prison yard under the scorching sun, all hundred prisoners stood in formation, watching a Vassell

Knight standing Infront of them and Apollo approaching from the distance.

"Due to new information, soon we will conduct an attack on the wastelands, establish a base and hunt down every single person involved in the invasion of Utopia." Apollo spoke as he gulped a mug of ale. "You hundred will be the frontlines, thus we need you at your best."

"So, stand at point soldiers from this day till the attack you will be trained by me Ser Eugene Greger!" Shouted the young Knight to the amusement of Apollo.

Ser Eugene annoyed by the meekness of the soldiers he had been given started to pace back and forward abruptly stopping Infront of one. "Name?"

"Beltramino…"

"Too long, who's the inbred fool who gave you that name?" Ser Eugene interrupted.

"My mother?" Beltramino questioned.

Ser Eugene stepped closer. "Bart, you shall be the dog that howls when he sees the enemy bark for me Bart."

"Bark…"

Ser Eugene stepped towards another prisoner. "What's your name?"

"Gi…"

"WHAT?!"

"Gi…"

"What?!"

"Gi…"

"He can't speak you shall be retard; everyone he shall be called retard from now on." Ser Eugene commanded. Again, he stepped towards another prisoner. "Who told you, you can look at me boy!" He shouts as Raijin stares him down. With no response Ser Eugene inches closer to Raijin as he starts to draw his blade. Until Sarrah yawned Loud enough for everyone to hear.

"I'm sorry, am I boring you?" Ser Eugene asked as his eyes slowly turned towards Sarrah.

"It's ok I'm just tired."

"I see would you like to go rest, maybe some food?" Ser Eugene said before pointing his finger towards Kaza. "You, cyclops go get some food for the young lady."

"Don't worry about it ill just eat when you finish this thing." Sarrah said laughingly to the amusement of Apollo but to the rage filled confusion of Ser Eugene.

Alexander

Tucking in his shirt in, late to the morning assembly. Alexander races there. As he arrives a frown falls on his face, as he sticks out from the crowd of cadets.

"I hope the punishment humiliating this time" he mutters as he awkwardly stumbles past everyone to get to his unit.

Alex's back shivered whilst standing in attention as he could feel the drill sergeant's glare.

"Looks like Alex is fucked..." whispers AL'lioe a short in stature bald boy with brimming muscles.

"Wonder what will happen this time?" says Caesar the comically opposite to AL'lioe as he stood closer to the heavens.

"Hope your arse has healed from last time" responds Ava, "take your role as number one seriously and stop the clownish behaviour" she commands.

"Galients of the future, protectors of our Free World, stand in attention to the District Chancellor Damien Anemoi" The Drill Sargent announces still staring at Alexander.

The mere mention of the name 'Anemoi' sends chills down the Cadets' spines. A family of myths and legends that commanded fear. Each Cadet watching the District Chancellor walk up to centre stage could feel from his presence alone. This man was strong.

Finally standing in front of the Cadets he took a heavy breath, before quickly fixing his tie. In a calm noble voice, he commands the cadets to attention, allowing them to gaze upon a contradiction, as this man with a giant's aura stood slender and shorter than some his age, stylish haircut being combed by the wind and a young face accompanied by sunken dead eyes. Monotoned and seemingly uninterested he spoke "As District Chancellor, I have been given the duty to protect these lands, along with all other Chancellors and above. However, I have failed all of you as of two and half months ago, Utopia, a city that has stood unpenetrated for a thousand years, fell in the hands of new powerful clans one of which call themselves 'The White Knights'...."

As he continued his speech, Alex's head dropped quickly. "Two and a half months..."

"What?" Ava quickly replies turning towards Alex. Ava stood bewildered as she gazed upon a foreign expression on Alex. "Calm down...Alex" she whispered.

"Two and a half months and we hear about it now!" Alex screams angered to the point of tears.

"Cadet, hold your tongue towards your superior!" shouts the drill-Sergeant.

"Leaked information would have been catastrophic for Pangea, we had to keep it silent but worry not help should have arrived by now," Damien yet again responds softly.

With Alex's Knuckles turning white from clenching his fist too hard and gritting his teeth in effort to remain silent. And his gaze exuded animosity that was like acid. Seeing This alongside his face turning red Ava put her hand on his shoulder.

"They will instantly kill you if you move from this spot. Even if by some miracle you reach the Chancellor, you could feal it as, well, right?" Ava said as she desperately tried to calm Alex down. "That man would cut you down before you even blinked so think about your next action Alex."

Alex laughed. "I'm just kidding…" He whispered his blood started to drip from his clenched fist.

"Sergeant, Punish the outspoken boy appropriately, then bring him to me tomorrow." Damien Anemoi commanded before walking away.

With the first leaf of fall landing on the ground morning dawned and a splash of cold water is what woke Alex up from his small cage "time to go," one of the Galients commands to silent compliance by Alex. With the Galients standing by each side of Alex pondering scenarios of what is going to happen his mood starts to soar. While the rest of his companies had just risen to stand in front of their beds ready for another day's training Alex had found himself standing steps away from Chancellor Damien. The Man Looked called as he clenched his hands together, gazing up at Alex. *'Did I make a mistake?'* Damien thinks as he stood from behind his desk. *'Most people would not know what this kid awakened, not even the Drill Sergeant could tell beyond simple bloodlust.'* He continued pondering as he walked closer to Alex.

"Leave us..." commanded the Chancellor. Watching the Galients salute and leave the office, the Chancellor glanced back at Alex.

"what's your name?" he asked.

"Alexander sir!" Alex responds with the addition of a salute.

"Just Alexander?" Damien asked as he stepped back grabbing the Cadet's file and sifting through it.

"Alexander of Utopia?" questioned Damien, "are you a Bastard?"

"I trust that would be listed in my records as well sir" Alex responds with a sly look in his eye. Failing to impress Damien as his eyes start to be heavy with boredom.

 Paused for a moment Damien Yawned. "State your rank." without skipping a beat Alex smiled. "Unit C 177 Rank one, Alexander of Utopia sir!"

The chancellor sat quipped by interest. "A Rank one bastard? what an overachiever we have".

"Thank you."

Unannounced a blade scrapes past the cheek of Alex planting itself firmly on the wall right behind him. But even with blood dripping by his cheek Alex did not react, seemingly frozen in fear just from Damien's changed gaze. With eyes now as sharp as a predator Damien lifts himself up by his hands.

"Let us have a bet, if you can strike me within the hour, I will let you go home immediately. If not, you will be trained by me without any complaints, for about the entirety of my stay at this camp".

A small laugh breaks from Alex who immediately launches at Damian but as quick as he tries to attack fate for him is sealed as within the hour, he stands exhausted and defeated being unable to land a single hit. '*Who could have trained him*' wonders Damian, as he stares down a defeated Alex.

"Rest up tomorrow you will be my new apprentice" Damien adds.

As dawn breaks Ava emotionless stands above an unconscious Alex, "you got even further" she whispers before kicking him awake.

"I've been asked to come to get you" exclaims Ava with a bitter taste in her mouth, confused and dazed Alex looks around to see he is laying in front of the building he was brought to the day prior.

"Get me? where are you taking me?" Alex says as he sits up, layered with a perky expression. "A date maybe?" he mockingly adds before the ever-serious Ava turns her back to him asking him to follow behind.

Still tired Alex struggles to get up but quickly hides it with short jogs towards Ava and as he reaches her, he locks his hands behind his head and seemingly skips forward with a slight whistle under his breath, "you're awfully different from before" she adds to the disappearance of his whistle.

"My mom is strong, she'll protect my siblings, I'm sure she wouldn't want me to worry." Alex response with an unusually serious tone, taken back for a moment Ava nods in agreement. "I just have to believe that" he adds before letting his arms swing and putting on a smile. '*A beautiful lie*', Ava thinks as she sees a smile from Alex painted in sadness.

"Talk later" Alex adds as they arrive at the courtyard with only Damian standing there, waiting for battle. Alex aware of the situation quickly grabs a wooden sword nearby walking past his pears now turned audience and starts heading towards Damien.

"Leave!" commands Damien, which everyone does without a second thought.

Pouting Alex adds "I wanted an audience though" before twirling his sword.

The standoff continues for a few more moments before Alex flips his sword, balancing its tip at the edge of his finger and as he flips it back around, he mutters "victory or death huh..." before grabbing the handle tightly and launching towards Damian. Only to find himself staring at the clouds on his back,

"Is that all." Damien mocked before Alex jumped back on his feet. Again, rushing towards the Chancellor but this time instead of being sent flying he dodges the invisible attack forcing a smile on the chancellor's Face as he moved forward to exchange blows with Alexander.

this dance between master and student continues with days quickly turning to weeks. The bruises and cuts left on Alex's body become tattoos, leaving a reminder of his unending growth throughout. Finally, on the last day of Chancellor Damien's stay, he approaches a hunched over Alex, he hands him a cup of water.

"When I leave a few of you will come with me there is no point wasting you as Galients" Damien said glancing down at Alex.

In response Alex swallows the rest of cold water, "I'm, sorry but I refuse... I have to go back to find my family" he responds with a sombre look.

the Chancellor swore on his military Sigil. "They're safe. Adira Senesto, Fanisse Senesto, Eros Amyntas Senesto and even the dog... they're safe."

Though with a sceptical look Alex knew a man in the Chancellor's position would not swear on his Sigil so easily. He sighed knowing he was going to be doing more work. "I guess I have no choice..." He said as he stood in attention accepting the Chancellor's offer.

Dismissed and Hand on the chest, Alex limped away to relax waiting to departure with the Chancellor for wherever he wished for him to go, on the way back a small voice echoed in Alex's ear. Curious he begun to move towards the forest climbing over branches and sliding past the trees to see Ava kicking a tree repeatedly, whispering to her self-rising numbers and finally as if to motivate herself she says in a louder voice " if I can't do one hundred kicks, then... I'll do two hundred punches!".

"You'll injure yourself, doing that" sings Alex leaning over a tree playing with a stick.

Ava glances over, paused for a moment then spoke. "Go away Alex" she calmly says with a strange tone of flatness to her voice.

"Make me" Alex quickly responds mocking her with his smile. Then without hesitation, Ava launches forward surprising even Alex with her speed, forcing him to jump back but as he lands the pain sets in forcing his vision to be blurry only for a moment but long enough for Ava to close the distance "your breasts are too much of a distraction!" shouts Alex embarrassing her giving the opportunity for Alex to knock her off her feet with a swift kick to the face, but as she lands on her side Alex falls on his back unable to lift his weight up anymore.

"Fuck you..." she says.

"Just strategy," he quickly responds. "They're safe by the way..." he adds before grasping his chest again looking more in agony than before.

"Good," she responds before lifting herself up ashamed of losing once again. "One day I will beat you" she adds before lifting Alex's body and allowing him to lean on her on the way back. As the night passes until Alex wakes up in a fit of pain, "hey, fat boy" Alex says in a calm voice, AL'lioe unfazed continued to sit on him devouring an uncooked potato as if it were sugar. He turns his head to see Caesar and Ava staring him down looking concerned.

"The crew is all here I see" adds Alex before revealing a brimming smile.

"Today will be a fun day, the chancellor said he wants all year one classes lined up at the courtyard..." says Caesar fiddling with a string slowly trying to attach it to a wooden slab.

"So as our number one you can't be late or do anything stupid ok" adds AL'lioe still enjoying his potato.

"So today we are staying here to make sure you won't," responds Ava, with her eyes closed and her arms folded.

With the sun peeking from the clouds above them, the trainees poured into to the field in a river of blue and red pressed uniforms planting their feet into the ground as they stood line by line. The Drill Sergeant stood in front of all of them with cold eyes but a loud voice he shouts.

"Hand on your heart! and stand at attention to the Honourable District Chancellor Damien Anemoi!"

"Sir!" respond the Cadets.

Damien then took over from the Drill sergeant, and as he surveillance through the crowd, his only thought was how the Cadets' shoes would get dirty but as he opened his mouth again in his soft tone.

"A Cadet's training lasts three years. Then at the end of those three years they can select from a range of choices. First being part of the Galient Legionnaires, the strongest of all of us. Front line Warriors that hold our enemies back and are ready for war at any moment. Second being Galient Police, these would be stationed at their home villages or towns as they stand as the law order and first line of defence. Third would be the Navy route, specially trained for the sea. Only few passes the test to enter these branches. Finally, would be the path of a Chancellor, where only the best would be allowed to attempt.

Though two years early, I believe it's time. Today the best ten of you will be selected to be trained as royal Guards when your name is selected step forward," he said, stepping back and allowing the Drill sergeant to announce the names.

"Alexander!" and the rest of the students' part allowing the bruised Alex step forward with his head held high. Then the rest of the names were quickly announced.

"AL'lioe, Ava Dansu, Amadeus Jullian Caesar, Basil, Adonis, Icarus Homer, Kal Magus, Kal Orrin and Stavros" Commands the Drill Sergeant immediately dispersing the rest. "Be ready at the break of dawn, you leave not only as trainees but as guards to the District Chancellor!" he shouts.

casually striding back to their bunkers, the Kal brothers began conversing "the human. How strong is he?" asks the younger taller brother Orrin "doesn't matter brother after the training one of us two will be the so-called best" quickly answers the older yet smaller brother. They continue the conversation along with the rest of the ten chosen until they separate one last time before their long journey to the Vassille Isles.

Logan

"Golden lions, protectors of the Kingdom. Kings of Zen," says Ezekiel standing in the king's hall gazing at the empty thrown before him. "I have always admired their craftsmanship, but their pride is something else don't you think Obeh?" Ezekiel asks as he points to the ceiling doused in three hundred years of the Golden Lions' conquests.

"A mere butler speaks of pride while he stands in the middle of the throne room as if he himself is king, you are very intriguing my friend " responds Obeh with his hands firmly placed in his robes taking small steps into the throne room.

"Where are the guards kiel?" he asks to the odd emptiness around him.

"Still with the childish nicknames I see... well the princes are jousting, so I'm guessing with the princes." Responds Ezekiel edging closer to the throne.

"During a war, these boys decide to play around... seriously" quickly responds Obeh visibly frustrated.

"Be calm my fat friend before you have a heart attack. Since the attack on Utopia our borders have never been stronger, I mean with the Thousand Beasts seeming to be going into conflict with these new bloods what do they call them again?" Ask Ezekiel.

"The White Knight Kingdom" quickly responds Obeh.

"Well war is war breeds nothing but death and sooner or later it'll be at the lion's doorstep, and they don't seem ready" Obeh adds.

"War breeds power," Ezekiel interrupts as he grasps the edge of the throne. "In war, heroes are born, simple man become gods in an instant, the world is put into controlled chaos and in this chaos, even the mere ones among us can become kings" Ezekiel adds.

"Careful old friend some will think you're after the Golden Throne" Obeh concerned adds as he stares down Ezekiel.

"It is a beautiful throne, probably the most beautiful in the world, but beauty does not equal power, power is power, a throne such as this belongs to the lions, not me I belong by my prince's right hand... Now if you excuse me old friend" Ezekiel adds before exiting the Zen throne room. As Ezekiel steps out of the castle, he quickly locates his prince who is being armoured ready to joust and marches towards his side blending in naturally with the dozens of personal that move along with the prince.

"Why is our dear prince fighting this time?" asks Ezekiel.

"He and the elder prince had a squabble over a girl," quickly whispers one of the help. As quickly as Ezekiel arrived the prince had finished being armoured and upon stepping out from the shadows his golden armour shined even brighter. "Lion's crest firmly on his chest, brother sure is prideful even in his husky form," mocking says one of the princes sitting in the bleaches tanning his fair skin watching as the event unfolds. "I see even prince Andrew attended this" Ezekiel adds as he glances at the comfortable prince in the bleaches.

A meek square so small you could only view his rough, thick hair that almost like an unkept afro steps forward with a scroll almost as big as him and shouts as loud as he could. "Today we... witness the great lion, Second of his name, Hero of the battle of Bamier, Master General Prince Logan St.Louis the second! Crunch His foe Prince Pier St.Louis 'the White'!"

"Yes, older brother crunch him well!" Shouts Andrew as he starts hysterically laughing, quickly joined in by the Aristocrats watching this event. But to everyone's surprise, Prince Logan refuses to react as he steps forward and hops onto his horse holding his head high as he shuts his helmet and holds out his lance ready to attack. On the other side on a white steed with white amour and a golden cape sat proudly with his porcelain skin, matching his personality, devoid of life and warmth.

After a moment of silence, they launch towards each other lances forward and with all the determination in the world only for Logan to quickly find himself staring at the clouds dazed as his brother stands tall above him.

"You still have much to learn little brother, come back when you're stronger," says Pier as he dismounted his steed with a slight wince, with a grateful nod, he handed his lance to his younger brother, a squire.

"Brother!" Francis St.Louis exclaimed, smiling through the gabs of his teeth. He reached out to assist his brother, offering a steady hand to steady him as he removed his helmet. With practiced ease, the squire helped his brother shed the heavy armour, his touch gentle yet firm.

"Where is my father?" Pier roared towards the nearby maid.

"With... the queen mother sir" the maid quickly responds to then get the cold gaze of the prince.

"Which queen mother, woman?" again Pier asks but with slight frustration in his tone of voice. With the fear building up the maid quickly hides her face behind her hands repeating the third queen mother repeatedly and when she stops and looks around the prince had already disappeared from her site.

"Maybe next time big brother!" mockingly shouts Andrew as he takes his maidens returning to his room, leaving only the maids, butlers and help that stay around Logan.

"Master, your orders?" asks Ezekiel as he bows at the presents of Logan.

"If you ever embarrass me like that again squire, I will have your head" says Logan to his timid squire "now help me up I need a bath" he commands to the immediate reaction of his help.

In the castle Pier marches from room to room searching for his father until he enters the conference room to see his father humping one of the maids.

"Three wives, eight children and kingdom to rule and you still have time to mess around with common filth!" shouts Pier.

"Son! how can I help you?" quickly responds, the King as he sends the maid away.

"If the Crimson Lion where alive we would not be talking."

"He Lives my son, one of the soldiers holds that name now."

Pier sighed. "I meant the original, the strongest of all of us. My Uncle your brother."

"I cannot bring the dead back, now you only ever grace me with your presence if you want something." King Christiano roars as he smacks the table.

"The Thousand Beasts seem to be coming back to life, I want to secure our borders before it comes to that point." Pier spoke as he begun to pour some wine.

 Christiano Laughed. "Thousand Beasts are dead and gone. All that's left is a few that hide in the wastelands."

"What of this new Clan the White Knights."

"What of them?"

Pier stared his father down. "They conquered Utopia, not even the sun kingdom could manage such. Now there's constant rumours of their leader being a sordes, forcing the lower lifeforms in our streets to have life in them once again. And even if it's just Paranoia the idea of the unnatural disaster that is the Beasts coming back… does none of these things scare you, my king?"

"I fought before you were a sperm in my balls boy." Christiano says as he stands from his chair. "If you have so much fear crowned prince, go sort it then. So, speak what you want boy."

"I want to go to the front lines and lead; a lion is supposed to protect its pride not laze around like sloths" Commands Pier banging his fist on the table.

"Fine, as long as I stop being interrupted by you, I King Christiano St.Louis the fifth grant leadership of our armies to you my impatient son" responds King Christiano as he plops himself onto a chair nearby "is that all?" he adds.

"Logan has to come with me, of all the Lions he is the only one willing to fight" the now calmer Pier commands to his father.

Christiano pondered for a moment. "He is useless, so I see why not, however command of my armies, and being able to execute whatever plan you have in mind. That is a lot, when you return you will marry her then. That is my only condition."

Pier clenched his fist. "Fine."

Christiano snorted as he waved Pier away. "Call that maid back!" he shouted as Pier walked away.

Apollo

"Lord Apollo, news from mainland!" shouts one of the Knights, unceremoniously waking up Apollo in a blanket of empty mugs stinking of booze.

"What..." Apollo asks with his face still planted into the ground.

"On the journey back the District Chancellor Damien Anemoi was attacked by masked men with katanas" responds the Knight.

"I trust he enjoyed his journey then," mockingly responds Apollo as he sat up paying full attention.

With the thick moist smell emulating from Apollo, he stood, commanding the Knight to follow but almost stumbling over as he struggled to keep his balance. " So, we respond. Twice these vermin pocked us, so now we must retaliate I guess," Apollo said, rocking himself forward to the cells.

"They seem lively." Apollo said as he picked at one of the mass halls as the prisoners ate and enjoyed themselves.

"Upon your orders to treat them as soldiers, their moods have gone up sir."

"And the one swinging a rock attached to a sick?" Apollo asked glancing at Raijin in the distance.

The Knight looked uninterested as he quickly shrugged. However, given the opportunity he quickly asked Apollo on what he should do about the ill prisoners.

"Line them up within the hour, we have to announce the attack on our Chancellor after all." Apollo said with a cold look in his eye.

As Raijin was training, he saw Apollo stumbling into the yard with a chair in hand and as he reaches the furthest point the plops himself onto the chair and closing his eyes. Though short his slumber was quickly interrupted by the stumbling of the prisoners. Within minutes they were in formation waiting Apollo's orders.

He continued siting as he slowly opened his eyes and raising four fingers. "The Chancellor was attacked. Pangea will order a counterattack sooner than we expected. You are the scouting legion front line of the front line. You have the rest of the day off enjoy it."

Through his chapped lips, Kaza spoke up. "If we are successful in this mission grant us freedom."

Apollo though surprised smiled at this notion. "Is avenging your parents, friends, country... your people! is that not enough for you?"

"No."

Apollo scratched his head before standing up. "Who else wants what this frail looking man wants?" and too his surprise many lifted their hands in agreement.

Apollo thought back to his past has he put his hands behind his back, he lifted his head and smiled. "Would you die, if ordered?"

Jon saluted with his hand to his chest. "I would rather live, but I will fight to death if freedom was involved sir!"

Apollo's mood worsened. "Slave." He muttered before raising his hand to dismiss the prisoners before lowering it to point at Eros.

"You stay."

As the prisoners begun to walk away, Kaza leaned on Sarrah's shoulder as she took him into the mess hall. Jon and Raijin followed closely glancing back at Eros as they got further away.

"What's your name?" Apollo asked as he sat back down.

"Eros Senesto."

Apollo's eyes flicked up for a moment as he started to giggle.

"It's not wise to use your full name sometimes boy."

"I'll keep that in mind sir."

Apollo continued to glare at Eros as his mind wondered.

'Though light it's not even affecting him. I was right.' He thinks before smiling. "Who taught you how to withstand Will?"

Confused Eros quickly shook his head. "I don't know what that is sir."

Still curious Apollo blitzed forward punching Eros in the gut forcing the boy to vomit and pass out on the spot. "Shit," he said softly. "I didn't expect you to be that weak."

Apollo looked at him more clearly. Through his heavy eyes, he saw Eros as he was. Barely fitting into his clothes, barely any weight and. Pale skin, with flees jumping from the red of his hair.

"So many colours for hair, brown and red mixed everywhere.?" Apollo muttered. "I think my knights might have mistaken you for a sordes Eros Senesto. Must have been hard for you."

On the first day, Autumn settling in for the upcoming months, the gates had been open, and trade was beginning to thrive, whilst Eros laid unconscious on the ground with fresh wounds from what Apollo called training. On the seventh day, Eros continued being rag-dolled in the courtyard as Apollo released his anger, Kaza and the rest got stronger, having time to re-cover and proper meals did not go unnoticed on their bodies. By the fifteenth day Eros, all but a corpse laid there trying to grasp his breath whilst reports of many skirmishes just south of Utopia between the Beast Remnants and the White Knights be-gan to be commonplace.

On the twentieth day, Apollo dropped a hood on Eros com-manding him to follow.

"Do you hate me?" Apollo asked as he walked next to a hooded Eros.

Eros' eye snapped towards Apollo which did not go unnoticed.

"Still with life, that's good." Apollo interrupted before grabbing

Eros by the shoulder and pointing towards a group of Slaved Sordes as the cuddled in the corner.

"I brought you here for my own selfish desire." Apollo said.

"You are no sordes, maybe your ancestors where since you have some red in your hair, yet the first time I saw you in that prison you were treated like those people there."

"Is this part of some training?" Eros quickly asked.

"Some knights are here to collect you; I don't know why but it was on my father's request so I cannot refuse." Apollo quickly responded. And as he did so he firmly grasped on Eros's shoulder as the King started to appear from the distance.

"Look at them Eros. Can you tell me which one of them is free?" Apollo asked as his hand started to shake. "Not the slave or the King, it's the one who breaks their bondage."

Eros looked up at a clearly fearful Apollo. "What are you talking about?"

"Think of what keeps you alive, what keeps you moving." Apollo said before removing his hand and walking away from Eros as knights quickly tackled the boy.

On the final day, the blue tents stood at the edge of Utopia holding an army of barely trained soldiers about to go into war with the clans that held most of the west, Apollo walks into the head tent armoured and ready for battle to see his father sat there with the acting captain.

"Lord Vassellet, Captain Azual," says Apollo before sitting on the opposite chair.

"Head Knight, you're still alive, I thought all that drinking would have killed you by now" answers Madas with his fingers knotted together, resting on his stomach.

"Lord, with all due respect this is insanity, most of the men there are still unskilled. Sending them out to the wastelands will only lead to our demise," Apollo politely stated as he grabbed a cup of wine taking a small sip from it. It was cold and bitter-sweet but had a pleasant aftertaste.

"In truth with the recent attack on the Chancellor, an immediate reaction from Pangea is required, first Utopia now this, if we do not show our strength what power we hold will quickly perish," Madas said.

"I understand... so who will be taking lead? the captain?" Apollo asks as he politely sipped on his wine.

"No, you will."

"Though I am familiar with the lands, I did not train this army, or know these people. Moral from someone like me would not help my Lord." Apollo say as he tries to maintain composure whilst glancing to the corner.

"Years before, I would have listened to your advice, I mean imagine being blessed by the Goddess with abilities few men possess. A man that can stand on the same ground as an elemental, a man that is still attached to one of the most powerful families in the world, a man who still has a youthful body despite his growing age. And tell me, what have you done with all these blessings? other than bringing death, destruction and a stain to your family name. We have a chance a rare chance to show the world that the Vassellet name still means something, and for you to show that you were not a waste of seed that you continue to show yourself to be every single day. Now leave, you move in a few hours don't disappoint me... again" Madas swats him away from his tent leaving only him and Azual.

Over in the field ready for war, the group of misfits sit as they ponder what war will be like for them, with Kaza sitting watching as far as his eye can see, he reached out picking out a broken twig using it to clean his teeth.

"Don't worry we fought for years this is just another enemy is all." He speaks.

"It's not that, our little pup is still with him I wonder if he's ok?" Quickly responds Sarrah.

Kaza finally stood stretching his legs, "he is a misfit, maybe to them we are just a bunch of worthless thugs. But to us, we know that we fight to our last breath so his fine if not once we escape, I'll be sure to throw him a perfect funeral" he says.

"And how do you hope to do that again?" Jon asked as he checked his bow, aiming it into the field to make sure it was levelled.

"Simple, gather together all members of the misfits and run, fast and far!" Kaza replied with an enthusiastic smile on his face, still with a remark that once lit a fire in the belly of his comrades all Jon could see was a broken man with a missing eye.

"Raijin has been distant and silent since that day, you were blinded in one eye, Eros has not been seen since he left with Apollo. Only me and Sarrah have any right to say those words boss..." Jon said, "but if you make a move as your friend, I will move as well" he adds before hearing the hoard of footsteps from the Knights moving to the front lines.

Apollo riding in the front, in his magnificent armour, his squire riding closely to his left and Eros marching to his right, pale like a ghost with eyes dulled and hair thinned.

Kaza gritted his teeth. "Eros, what did they do to you. That curious look in his eyes... I didn't even notice it."

"They hurt my pup... that man Apollo... I will have his head"

Sarrah added with a cold stare towards Apollo.

"Move!" shouts captain Azual, "we follow the Knights stick close and follow the command of your squad leaders!".

Marching with the Knights, calmly riding in the front and half of their infantry barely knowing how to hold their weapons Kaza next to a familiar face goes to grab his shoulder only to be shrugged away. "In the battlefield, these little lines they have us in will break away so the misfits will meet up and move as one" he whispers to Raijin, who just continues to ignore him.

A few days pass and they reach the dead forest, a forest deprived of wildlife but known to be brimming with small clusters of small gangs that hide away from Beast territories and wait to attack anyone who dares to move through. A signal from Apollo is raised for all the solders to build a camp and rest before moving out. As the army starts to camp Apollo marches out on foot with a small squad of Knights, and Eros by his hip.

"Captain! I hope you can count to five for me!" shouts Apollo as he moves out confusing the captain for but a moment before

Azual move deeper into the camp to help his soldiers set up the tents.

Finally, after a short walk Apollo along with his men reach the edge of the forest, he rubs the ground grabbing a small bit of the sand. "Never thought I'd see the Dead Forest again. Well, I don't believe a bunch of devils will be hiding in here but can't be too sure." he says as he lets the sand flow through his hand "boy, go scout for a bit... if you find anything fire an arrow in the air and stay where you fired it from" he adds as he nudges Eros forward.

So, on command, Eros marched forward in the dusk with night falling, only five arrows in hand and a small knife attached to his waist, with only the objective in his mind. At last, after walking what seemed for miles, he reached an encampment filled with rugged men, half sleeping and the other half talking amongst themselves.

"It's been a few weeks since a merchant came through here" says one of the men starring into the sky.

"Well with the Beast Remnants fighting the White Knights, what do you expect" quickly replies another.

As Eros watches on he pulls his bow and arrow out lighting the arrow with some flint and launching it into the clouds, then sitting down as ordered waiting for Apollo to arrive. Enough time passes for the gang to change shifts but as one goes to wake one of his comrades up, a rouge arrow impales him through the neck, followed by several more, "enemy!" shouts one of the gang members but quickly realises it's too late as the Knights, light in armour rush into the camp slaughtering every-one there.

Eros standing there has his lifeless eyes are awakened by the shock before him, he turns his head to look away when he sees a girl not much older than him standing there deep in the forest in horror, they lock eyes. But with the girl's face first filled with fear, slowly turns to anger as she quickly turns to run deeper into the forest.

"Boy!" shouts Apollo breaking Eros' trance, "was that all of them?" he asks to the slow nod from Eros.

"Good, move the bodies, get the food ready lads!" shouts Apollo to the rest of his squad.

a short amount of time passes, and as Apollo's group eats, Apollo rips some meat from a hog and throws at Eros' direc-tion which Eros launches at like a wild animal, ripping it apart making a mess with his eyes wide open.

"I see, that's why his so obedient" says one of the Knights to the sad smirk from Apollo.

Under the chainmail, and the thick hide sweat was still drawing from Apollo's body, but knowing of the time limit and the open fights ahead he plastered on a smile draping confidence upon his Knights, looking far into the forest he whistled, and Eros dragged himself over. "Same again boy" he commands sending the youngling deeper into the forest alone. He kept his head down as he sprinted close to the ground avoiding the many twigs as each sound they made when broken would revive the heart of the forest and whatever laid there would swallow him hall singing the song of screams throughout the land. After a while as if a wall had appeared before him, Eros stopped as he saw a faint light in the distance, and with each step he took, the sounds of his next enemies started to bounce from the trees, and upon seeing a foreign skull swinging back and forward he immediately attached himself to a nearby bark of a tree.

Again, he prepares himself pulling his bow back pointing above the towers of the trees when a faint sound sends chills down his spine and sends his eyes flying as they attach themselves to each part of the forest until they lock with another. A figure masked by the night stood not too far away gaping a hole through Eros' skull with her gaze, a fear unlike another started chocking him and on impulse, he aimed his bow directly at the figure. His vision blurred and an icy sweat trickled down his palms, with only the flickers of light from a nearby fire giving the figure a human-like form, its feline eyes fixed on him, examining him. His eyes start to strain, his arms get heavy and although the voices in his head screamed for him to run or to kill his cowardness took over forcing him to lower his bow fearing the taking of another life above survival. In a world on their own, no noise could have entered their battle of wills but a snap from a twig as the figure steps forward blanks the mind of Eros and as he awakens yet again, he finds himself aiming at her. With the sweat dried out and his heart back in his chest, he looked calmer and more focused. Loud roars from the crowd pop the bubble of silence Eros was in ready to kill his face numbs as he pulls his shoulders back, only to be stopped as a rouge drunkard stumbled into the frame, vomiting and abruptly leaving back to his party.

As the disruption left Eros focused once again only to notice the silhouette smaller, vanishing from his site the further it went. Allowing the voices to scream once again 'What would happen if I let her leave if I let her go, will it be a mistake' He asks himself as his hands again begin to clam up, his heart escaping his chest but not long after the decision had been taken away from him as the figure disappeared from his site. A defeated sigh dibbled from his mouth, Eros once again places his back on the bark of the tree lighting an arrow and launching it into the sky, and soon after like the Valkyries Apollo and his men appear, moving in for the kill comfortably with sinister smirks on their faces. "Good job boy" a fleeting comment stated by Apollo as he walked past. The familiar song of swords started to play. And on completion without seemingly a break Apollo's hound is sent forward once again. He moved through the forest only hearing the of leaves and twigs as they crackle beneath his feet the vision of the figure occupied his mind its eyes carnivores but its shape so slender it almost looked fragile, the thought of this creature, drowned the bodies of the dead that had been traumatising Eros.

After the unending run, he noticed something strange, a light peeking through the cracks of the forest curious, he brushed past the trees, squeezing to the outside of the forest and he felt it, the air was warm, welcoming, wild. As he gazed upon this new world he thought if the goddess did exist this would be her backyard. The grass dancing with the wind, animals singing to the blackness of the night as it held the spotlight of the stars shining all the brighter, and the moon slashing over the land giving all before him, life. Run was the only thing in his mind when he witnessed this tranquillity, his blood warmed, his fingers clawed into the tree he had been holding onto and his toes dug into the ground with a sparkle in his eye, and a smile so foreign it hurt he sighed turned around and started walking back with his tail between his legs.

"I don't understand boss why he wouldn't run," asks one of the knights following Apollo closely.

"Because he has a little crush," quickly responds Apollo as he jumped over a broken tree.

With his men conversing a small figure in the distance quickly catches apollo's attention, he tries to focus on what it was but age having clearly dulled his eyes he rips a bow from the back of his squire. He pulls back the bow's string aiming for the figure's head and releases an arrow cutting through the woods barely missing the target.

"Looks like you missed boss, getting old are we" mocking responds one of the Knights.

"Maybe."

As the distance closes, the figure gets revealed as Eros dragging his feet towards the Knights, "set up camp we wait here for the rest of our lovely army" commands Apollo before setting alight to three arrows and launching them into the air.

"They should be here in the morning, rest up boys we are done here." He commands one last time before dropping on his back and watching the clear sky ready for sleep.

Enough time passes for everyone to be sound asleep, except one Knight as he stumbles across the camp finding a corner to relieve himself. But as it travels across the round a faint touch wakes Eros upon in fright, he looks down and upon realising starts to move position, a small snicker comes from the Knight before an arrow drills through his neck. Crucifying him onto the tree, as his life vanishes before the boy Eros falls onto his bottom and as he turns his head to warn others, the war cry of the enemy charging drowns all sounds and wakes the band of Knights in a fit of panic and as they scramble to arm them-selves.

One by one the enemy takes their lives. The strong still stood tall fighting them off in each moment, including Apollo as he cut through them as if they were paper, finding himself perched before Eros trembling on his hands and knees "boy, if you wish to live, I suggest you pick up a blade and soon". He gets a quick glance of Eros' face looking down at him as if he were garbage. A quick scan around showed his men falling, losing hope of winning and at that moment a glimpse of the Old Apollo appeared as he stood erect with his chest out, releasing his immense aura trembling those closest. Stopping the bloodshed for a moment as everyone became mesmerised by Apollo's presence, he took a deep breath and shouted to the heavens "Knights of the hand! you will stand and protect the will of the goddess! do not let heathens trample on Her name! Now fight till your bodies are no more!"

Simple words one would think, but enough to light fire bellies, and even with the battle continued crashing around them Apollo swung his sword relentlessly as if possessed by a berserker.

"It looks erratic and almost amateur like" comments a girl standing in the distance.

"But look he has not taken one hit and continues to slay our people, that is the style of our opponent," a masked man replied as he laid on the back of a beast.

During battle, the knights put a valiant effort to survive until one of the enemies. Dressed in thick leather and wool like the rest of his allies, and a missing a helmet allowing his short red hair to flow through the air as he rushes towards Eros, knocking him onto his back and holding him down by his neck. Panic sets in and instincts arise as Eros struggles pacing his eyes left and right to find anything to help him in this situation when suddenly beneath his old white t-shirt, around his waist supporting the rope that held his trousers up the blade, small and cold-pressed on his skin. His eyes dazed as he started to fade away.

As his vision narrowed the hard floor of dirt felt like a feathered bed, the sound of the battle all but vanished leaving only his heartbeat to sing him into the next life. The world slowed his eyes collapsed to the left of him, in a moment of delusion he thought of death coming for him as he peered at a snow-white beast with antlers as big as trees and a body to match, staring at him ready to carry him to the afterlife. The voices of his family echo in his ears and as his body numbs a faint smile slowly appears on his face.

"A child?" whispers the boy still holding Eros down, how unfortunate He thinks as he grasps his blade harder and swinging down to Eros' head.

However, as Eros opened his eyes, with only a vague cut and a drop of blood from him as his enemy's blade had impaled the ground instead, quickly followed by a vomit of blood painting Eros' face. The boy's hand loosens on Eros' neck and as he looks down only the handle of a blade can be seen. Coming to his senses a scream almost deafening comes roaring out of Eros' mouth as he pushes the boy off him, scrambling to the top and yanking the blade from his chest. A face full of panic Eros throws all of his might into the neck of his enemy. "Please, I have a-" shouts the boy as the blade digs through his throat, with blood gushing out, their eyes meet, unbreaking as the life fades from the boy. Eros falls off shaking with a down-pour of tears exploding from his face, all the food he had eaten on this day flooded onto the ground and suddenly as he lifts his head up to the sky he numbs, watching the peak of the trees wave at him.

A rouge sword is thrown into the air towards the fleeing ban-dits, "Come back I was only getting started!" shouts a Knight who stood bigger than his allies with a distinct white headband holding not only the Sigil of half the moon but his long hair from his face.

"Don't tempt them... " States Apollo as he fell on his back from exhaustion. Apollo quickly scans the Knight fixating his eyes on the headband "You fought well kid what's your name?" he asks. "Felix sir" quickly responds the Knight panting with his hands on his knees. Apollo reaches out his hand "help me up Felix the fight is not over yet". Apollo starts to drag his feet towards Eros stepping over the dead unfazed and as he reaches the boy, he attempts to reach out his hand before suddenly stopping. "don't think about it, you are already going to carry that weight... don't make it heavier."

This statement though vague brought Eros back to reality, with sharpness from his eyes glaring at Apollo, shaking Apollo for only a second but long enough for Eros to stand and walk to the back of the camp silent. "Ok boys, when we step out of here don't be surprised if there's an army waiting for us" He states. "Now rid of the bodies, we camp till the rest of the army arrives then we move forward." After some time, dawn breaks the morning shined bright, each member of the Knights sat looking at all directions refusing sleep from fear of another at-tack, suddenly an opera of feet thumping onto the ground, each second getting louder.

"Sir! the army is here!" shouts Felix with a joyful glint in his eye. Apollo groaned as his rest was disturbed.

"Fine, tell them not to stop we need to exit this forest before we camp the army. We need to establish higher ground before their main forces slaughter us with our hands in our pants." He groaned again stretching his back as he stood.

Tired he leaned towards Eros, with a stern look on his face "I'm not sure if you tuned into a statue or your meditation is incredible."

"I'm getting too old for this you know... I just hope I can go home after this campaign."

"You stand as the best Knight in the West sir," Felix said sheathing his sword. "I heard you where the luck of Vassille, tell me, sir, how many battles such as this have you fought at such a huge disadvantage."

Unbothered He shrugged, "a lot more than any prince should have."

"And you won all of them?"

"Like you said luck of Vassille." as the conversation carried on the rest of the knights moved several feet ahead of Apollo and Felix, keeping close to the ground with their eyes so strained they could almost pop from their skulls. However, the Captain novice in the art of war ran mindlessly towards Apollo who at this point was heavy in his steps talking to Felix as if they were old friends. Finally, as they reached the edge of the forest, a Knight in front held his hand high signalling for a stop.

"I always hated that name you know, 'Luck of the Vassilles' all it did, in the end, was cause me pain and suffering, but again and again it followed me even now as that Knight soils himself hoping no one would notice. But you all believe in victory as long as I'm with you... again we must test fate" Apollo added as he travelled to the front only to see an image all too familiar even with different colours. Death itself laid before his eyes, a sea of heathens standing ready for battle waiting for Apollo and his allies to make the mistake of stepping out of the forest.

"What do we do sir?" asks Felix gripping his blade as hard as he could.

"Pray..." answers Apollo with a defeated smile on his face. "We can't stand still, or they will grind us slowly till we all perish, we can't retreat because their scouts would signal an attack by their full might, so our only choice is to run into their blades, and they know this far too well."

He begins to scan the area, losing hope by each look as men barely armoured stood before him waiting on his bacon call. He reaches for his blade and whips it out in such a manner he had hoped all would see, he took a deep breath and screamed for all to hear "Prepare to attack! we cannot let these heathens do as they please on the goddess's lands! Lay your bodies in her name and arise at the gates of paradise as she welcomes you home with open arms!"

A deafening silence quickly follows as the masses stood there confused at how to react when a warrior scream from Felix breaks it shocking all those to follow like sheep and a roar of screams echoes through the forest. And like the first drop of rain a rouge arrow flies past Apollo's face and as he looks up arrows so vast in numbers, they blot out the sun, "Shields up! use the trees as covers!" screamed Apollo, as he and his allies had found themselves pinned in one position, holding out the fury of the arrows. Behind his unending smile, he glanced at Eros hiding underneath a wooden shield and muttered. "Looks like it's about time we test out my luck."

The second the arrows slow, Apollo, launches forward followed closely by his allies. A familiar hand reaches out to Eros "you can find that shaggy brown hair in any battlefield, come, you can tell me about it after" Sarrah promised. "Now keep that dagger close to your heart, stick close to your friends. let us be the heroes little pup."

Surprised by the kind words from Sarrah, Eros perked himself up. "Where is everyone else?" he asked.

Sarrah pasted on her signature smile. "they're close."

As the battle raged on and the sounds of swords smacking together and the screams of the people filled this once-majestic field, the misfits one by one came together with little words but large gestures they came to fight as one once again. With Sarrah providing an offensive attack and Jon covering her with a fury of arrows, Kaza commanding small tactics to his allies and Raijin itching to get to the front lines. Until, as if a bird, Felix flies through the air with his body barely clinging together, A boisterous laugh grabbed the attention of everyone nearby. Especially Raijin as his eyes lit up when he got a glance at the sharp black spikes of hair peeking above the rest, the blood tipped golden harmer swinging wildly, and a beast not of this world watching over the battlefield.

"The white stags" whispers Raijin as his joy took over, forcing him to slither past his allies to the front lines to get a clear view of several members of the thousand Beasts. And towering above everyone in the field impossible to ignore stood Folke 'the troll' with tree trunks for legs, broad shoulders and thick chest to match, nearly twice the size of a bear, his shear frame blocked the sun from the allies, basking a lot of them into the shadow of the troll. Then without warning another swing ir-rupted into the ground sending several soldiers flying into the air, revealing Apollo close by, almost drooling with anticipation, his eyes pace left to right "nine of the white stags stand before me what a joyful occasion... I take your heads to father and my name will finally be clean!" he proclaims before rushing head-first into the enemy swinging wildly but missing just as equally. However, occasionally, a man is shown the limit of his power when a greater force appears toying with his life's work like it was nothing and at this moment Apollo felt the crushing blow of an opponent such as this, a singular punch from a member of the Stags Gustav a simple man to look at but bared enough power crush the ribs of Apollo knocking him unconscious. Gustav stands ready to kill Apollo when the slight sound of chirping birds grabs his attention as a boy in mid-air stood eye to eye with the troll, and within moments a fury of attacks emerge onto the troll with one breaking through his defences. But only impaling him through the hand and as the blade slides through his palm, Folke locks his fist onto Raijin's hand and

launches him into the air, before stepping back ready to bash Raijin away with his hammer when he is close enough. And as fate had it, once on target Folke swung his great Hammer, but quickly breaking out in laughter as Raijin slips past it.
"Did you see that! He dodged the swing in mid-air!" he screams. But as one of his own goes in to kill Raijin he swats him away killing him immediately "Don't interrupt… the boy just needs to get his footing. Here boy your blade" he quickly adds pulling the blade out of his hand and throwing it to the feet of Raijin. Not wanting to look weak Raijin stands, grabbing his blade and launching again towards Folke only for the troll's speed to catch him off guard as he is immediately pinned to the ground "Good try b-" before finishing this sentence another blade impales him through the eye. "Let him go you bastard!" screams Kaza shaking uncontrollably, but Folke shoulder badges Kaza out of the way and throws Raijin into him as if he weighed nothing. "Two injuries... I'm impressed what are your names, boys. For even after death no one can ever forget the people who managed to injure The Troll this much!" Folke announces with a massive grin on his face and a small blade pocking out of his eye. The fun is suddenly stopped as the sound of the horn is

blown causing the allies to retreat into the forest with their tails between their legs.

"That was fun but time to leave boys!" shouts a joyful Folke.

"Annoying that we can't just wipe them out" Gustav groaned with his back to them.

"Careful now, those where direct orders from the King, now we can get back to him and finish these pesky White Knights," Holger said fully armoured with a spiked helmet on standing by his brothers and sisters in arms.

from the short distance, Eros turns his head with Raijin's body balancing on him to see an overjoyed giant waving them good-bye "Let's do this again soon!" shouts the giant as his voice lightens the greater the distance. The army treads back through the forest taking half a day and the remainder of their resources to emerge from the other side to the archbishop and remaining Knights who stood by him. With their heads low the mass of soldiers bloody and broken walk-in line through the first camp carrying their injured friends and some who have deceased back to Utopia. Madas unimpressed is filled with crippling disap-pointment as he sees his son carried through, unconscious. A painful aura nested in the march back as Madas rode in front plain in the face, through the crowds of shame. Finally, he reached his Villa immediately ordering masses of food to be collected from the farms.

"I refuse to let the name Vassellet to be a joke, because of one piece of trash" he explains to a confused crowd, "send for our armies, as soon as they arrive a campaign not seen in years will take place, with my one true heir Hermes."

"Are you sure?" The queen added as her eyes had grown wide from this idea. It was strange for her to see her husband enraged, but she had a feeling though feeble that this would be a bad idea.

"Hestia, my dear wife," he says trying to calm down. "If we do not do this the entire world will think of us of our family as weak. We are beyond just accepting defeat; the world is watching woman. The loser will never be able to rise again. I'm sure of that!"

"Calm yourself," Hestia said. "I can see why you would be scared or angry. But please sleep on this, pulling our forces out of our country even with the Pangean military base there is not a smart idea. We will only see thousands of our young men die. We do not know these lands, the enemy and most of our soldiers have never had a battle. You forget they came after the war." She quickly signalled some of the slave girls to escort

Madas out. Living in a war-torn land had its benefits she thought as she let out a slight smile.

Madas quickly disappeared from the slaves, heading to his basement alone. A room filled with devices made to cause people pain. Then a girl tied to the back of the room, struggling to stay awake with her back bare, still red from wounds facing Madas. Calmly Madas removed his clothes grabbing a whip and moving forward. The screech could be heard throughout the house, as Hestia quickly held their daughter Gaia's ears shut pretending to rub her skull.

Elizabeth

News like the wind travelled fast in this world if not monitored and within a few days, the news of victory over Pangea quickly spread throughout the forces of the Thousand Beasts and beyond, lighting a fire in their hearts unseen before. All those close by to the Beasts' castle gathered, filling the great Hall of Zalius, a place hazed with mist and smoke, where the cold air sang through the halls. Its grey stone draped with the Banners of the Beasts, Red, black, and orange in colour with the heads of a hound that once guarded these very gates many aeons ago. Drums start to play with fires being lit all around and ale being served to them, music roars on throughout the night with everyone getting more drunk by the minute, roughhousing to test their strength and singing along to the music of the old world.

In its third hour, the doors creak open, and a man hugged by his fur waltz in grabbing the nearest ale and chugging it as quickly as he could, each step he took opened the sea of the Beasts finally he reaches the throne already occupied by another entertaining a lady. He nods at him "Halvor it's good to see you have not changed even after all these years." Halvor, growing in rage groans at the man before quickly looking away from him. Curious, the man turns around to see a silent room, a silence that caressed his skin as the people standing there fixed their gazes at him gripping their weapons harder by the second. "Gina my old friend you still looked beautiful even after five years," he says with an enthusiastic smile on his face. "Gjurd, monster how have you gotten bigger, people how has he gotten bigger!" he adds with his hands wide open hoping for a response.

"I see, I deserve this, I am your king, but I left how dare I come back let alone stand as your leader again right?"

"It appears that I'm not welcome anymore," he quickly he unsheathes his sword "we follow the old Gods, so you know how this works if you want to rule you have to kill me" he carries on pointing the handle of his blade towards the audience asking each if they want to be King, "Gina do you want to be the leader of these great people? come on just push the blade into my heart... no?"

"Gjurd just one big swing and you will be King...no?"

"Halvor this is your chance, your only chance... do it, go on, do it, finish off your infamous rival... no?"

"No one wants to be King? no?! so long live the King!"

He again scans the area, seeing several heads nod he raises his sword. "Shall we show the world why the Beasts are still as dangerous as the time of Zalius' rule?" The Beasts start to make small noises of agreeance," then drink, fuck and eat for tomorrow the awakened Beasts bare their teeth!" finished the Beasts lifted their mugs to the sky as they screamed to a scream so loud it pierced through the walls.

In a field not too far in the distance, the White Knights camp enjoying their recent victories, Drominic bored of the parting travels through avoiding the stragglers that have recently joined looking at their untamed ways as they enjoy the food, wine and women provided by the White Knights. "I'm all for parting but these sordes know how to ruin a good time" Drominic mumbles as he walks into the Queen's tent quickly met by numerous members of aristocrats, who saw the rise of the Queen, latched onto her like leaches.

"Your highness best we talk things over with the Thousand Beasts tomorrow because further conflict will strain your resources and their sheer numbers when together will wipe you out within a day."

Another quickly chimes in "Yes, we have won many skirmishes, but they have yet to declare war and look what they did to Vassille soldiers not but a few days ago.

Lachlan Gungadad lightly laughed holding his pot belly, "not only that Elizabeth you want to make movements in the Lion's sleeping grounds do you not think you are overestimating your abilities, what if in tomorrow's meeting they announce war, we support you, but we fear the Beasts and their World Breaker level of power."

But with the negatives came positives as those who believed in the queen presented her accolades believing she would win at the end. The arguments uncontrollable continue till Elizabeth bored steps out of the tent meeting up with Drominic as he smoked staring at the sky by the spine of the tent.

"They are right about one thing Lizzie... your obsession with Zen is making you do one too many moves," Drominic said. He glanced over at Elizabeth and to his surprise she looked unfazed by the situation.

"Unless a response from the Beasts is what you wanted." Finally, as Drominic finished his smoke Elizabeth tightened the strap on her armour and cracked her neck. "Believe me Drominic, I do not make light moves but our friends inside have a right to worry. Though, after tomorrow they will see why I deserve the Zen's throne."

"I hear you princess, but how? have you got some sort of contract with some sort of deity to achieve impossible things?"

"When G'AL chooses you, it would be blasphemy not to show your faith to him," Elizabeth quickly responded with a confident glint in her eye. "Whether they decide to fight us or not we have already proven to their King our power."

Drominic finished, stood and start to walk away. " I piss on these gods. All I know is I followed your mother now I follow you if there is gold, food and pussy at the end of this tunnel just tell me where to aim princess."

Mass panic in the hall of the Lions as the King sits on his throne silent "The beasts have gone mad challenging the World and winning, what would happen if they decided to stretch their borders... they can do what they want now!" Princess Marguerite shouts into the crowd slightly stretching her corset as it barely held her stomach in.

"What of the trade deals with them, will they drag us into war to continue it?" shouted one of the Wealthy in the back and with the continued noise rising the King finally spoke up.

"My subjects I hear your turmoil but do not worry I have already made movements to this situation. As we speak a large recruitment drive is being put in place to send solders to our borders in case a call to arms, Aid will be sent to Utopia as soon as I can give the order to do so. Thus, for now, my people let us go back to the festivities as The Lion's renaissance has yet to finish!"

With the Fall winds in full blast, the sails bulged out carrying the flag of Pangea with it. A ship draped in blue and red, far from modern but the price choice of Chancellor Damien. She was called Queen Annabelle's voyage, named after his mother. as it rocked back and forward, a crewmember rushed past a seasick Alex, and a tired Ava petting him on the back, and as he rushes through the cabins, he finds himself banging on the door of Chancellor Damien. The door swings open to an unimpressed Chancellor but as the crewmate hands him a newspaper from a carrier bird and as he unrolls it, he sees the headline, changing his mood completely. He proceeds to grab the crewmate by the collar "send word to the Vassille Isles, I want the armies on ships to the mainland immediately!" he shouts.

"But sir a Chancellor cannot order armed forces..." the fearful crewmate quickly responds with his eyes closed.

"You are right, then send a request from the District Chancellor to the acting King of Vassille for his direct involvement against the Beasts."

The Day of the meeting arrives and as both sides travel towards each other tensions start to rise and panic from those who could not fight becomes visible. The barbaric horde's voices get stronger the closer they get to each other a swarm of cavalrymen ride with their war cries echoing through the sky encircling themselves upon Elizabeth and her small band of allies. Finally, the spectacle stops as dozens of Beasts stood opposite dozens of White Knights. Elizabeth still unfazed steps forward and the King of the beasts does the same shocking everyone with his unimpressive stature.

"That's the legendary King of Beasts?" Gungadad adds in his confusion.

"Many even those in his ranks have never seen him but I can tell just from his aura that man is not for the faint of heart" Al'Gadrood adds with veins popping out of his head and grasping his blade as hard as he could.

"The Thousand Beast King Gulbrand the Great." Says Elizabeth with a sly smile on her face.

"Queen of The White Knights and Mother of sordes. Seems we both know of each other, so there is no point of pretending."

A site no one would expect as Elizabeth flipped her cape, and proceeded to bend the Knee, confused Gulbrand began to fill with rage "do you think this is a joke?" he says as his voice rises, changing the air as frost grew on the tips of the grass strands sending a coldness, a type of coldness that rapped around the bones, freezing many in their footsteps sending members from both sides, one by one to fall to the feet of the King, many bleeding and some forming in the mouths.

Vividly angry Gulbrand out of character shouts "you killed my brothers, my sisters, laid waste to my lands, disrupted my trade but worst of all forced me to bare my fangs after years of peace!"

"Now you bend the knee asking to join? me? you either have realised what trouble you are in, or your insanity precedes you."

"If you stay calm you will live!" shouts Drominic standing, stationary stone-faced with his hands shaking uncontrollably.

Suddenly the pressure fades, as a smile from Gulbrand "Drominic is that you? how are you still alive" asks Gulbrand as if reunited with an old friend. "Are you here to join the Thousand Beasts if so come over here, you can even have what your soul always wants, all the gold and women you want!" he shouts once again with a joyful tint in his voice.

However, Drominic loyal to his Queen shakes his head in refusal, "I do enjoy seeing you arrive, because you always manage to cause a lot of damage..." but with this response, Elizabeth and the ones closest to Gulbrand notice his tone of voice, as it was unusual for him to speak in such a serious manner.

Gulbrand, once again scans the people before him noting down in his head all those who were still erect, he points his finger towards Elizabeth "you follow her?" to a unified nod from the current audience.

"Then sure why not... welcome to the family!" he shouts approaching Elizabeth with his arms wide open ready to embrace, with his own men of those who were still conscious, confused by the response from their king, with even some like Halvor visibly upset.

The path back through the meadow was silent. Though it had been a cold fall the grass was still thick and lush as it rustled in the breeze one would marvel at mother nature at this moment, but all eyes were on Elizabeth. Little did she care though as she walked like a swan with grace and confidence looking forward with her usual allies close by.

"Silver hair and crystal eyes, the boy there do you think he is one of the survivors from that one island that disappeared during the war?" curiously asks Gjurd leaning close to Halvor. Hearing this Lancer shouts in his mother tongue confusing the masses that were close by, he sighs and repeats his words in the common tongue "that was a lie from you people."

"Pay no attention to them, Lancer, they are ignorant of the truth in the world," with a stern tone Al'Gadrood says loud enough for everyone to hear.

Not too far in the back of the pack as Gulbrand whistled a soft tune he suddenly stopped his melody as he saw Gina approaching with a concerned look on her face. Without hesitation, she asked: "Sir, how did the stags know about the attack? "

Gulbrand smirked. "I have my ways."

"If you knew, would it not been wiser to hide?" Gina asked.

"You do know they will come with an even larger force next

time. They may even call for the G'AL'Rodinia Empire. Please don't let me think these actions are that of a man losing his mind."

"Even with our major differences. Tell me what is the one thing all primitive life forms have in common?" Gulbrand grinned almost mockingly as he asked.

"Fear. For a while, the tides have been changing for the Beasts, we have lost land, some have fallen, smaller clans do not believe in our strength anymore and yet there is still infighting and conspiracies whilst the world around us is closing in. So, let me ask you this, what is the best way to unite people?"

"A greater threat" answers Gina almost baffled with her King's mindset.

"Don't worry though, our victory is inevitable because Pangea cannot afford a large-scale war at the present moment."

"How can you be so sure?" Gina asked quietly.

"Weeks or even months it took them to aid the people from their pride and joy that was Utopia, evidence enough that their economy is just hanging by a string at the moment, and that's just one thing. I predict less than one hundred thousand soldiers will do battle with us, and when we win, they will be forced to recognise us as a Military strength putting heathens like us on the same level as their precious Yin Clan and E's band of psychopaths."

As they continued to converse the vision of their Castle strengthens in the foreground as it laid there like an old man, moss clung to its side and its walls crumbling. No longer the glory it once was each step took into it left a painful noise that if it could talk, you'd beg for deafness. As the audience poured in the drums start to bang and the music gets louder by the second. Before long, the music was as loud as thunder everyone be it the Beasts or the White Knights melted into the beat and drowned themselves in alcohol. Hours in with half the people sleeping or enjoying each other company and the other half drinking as if they would not wake up the following morning, Elizabeth seeing an opportunity, slipped to the outside rubbing her arms to keep warm but seemed at peace as the pure blackness of night was a blanket of comfort.

as she travelled around the grounds, listening to the hazy sounds coming from within a whistle breaks her concentration. As she scanned the area squinting her eyes as hard as she could, a man who looked old even for his age stumbled out of the shadows rocking back and forth. At first, she believed years of

drinking had robbed him of his youth, but as the man's scars reflected off the light of the moon, she knew it was far worse.

"You seem to be drunker than most of the people inside" Elizabeth jokingly says to a simple response of a groan from Halvor
as he stepped closer.

As she looked up, she smiled at the brawny man dribbling over
his beard buried under the fur that was his clothes, as he got
mere inches from her, she again went to speak but was stopped
by his hand grasping her neck.

"I could kill you," he said. " I am stronger, faster and more dangerous than you, but you stand there mocking me with that
gaze, joking as if we were friends. As if we were equals?"

The harsh scent of drink reeked all over Halvor. She could see
him struggling to keep his balance, her composure told a different story to her body as every ounce of her was screaming to
escape, fearing for her life as if a predator stood before her
about to rip her apart.

"You could, and no one would blame you," Elizabeth said
softly. "I would at least like to know who killed me."

Halvor groaned. "Halvor the bloodhound, prince of the Thousand Beasts." He smiled. "The next King of the Beasts."

Elizabeth grabbed his hand, loosening the hold on her neck. "The old gods do not follow the line of monarchy, if one wants to be King then they have to kill the King and who would oppose you? you stood in his place for years right?"

Halvor fumbled backwards letting Elizabeth go and vanishing into the dark once again. Once out of sight she took heavy breaths, her legs were nimble and weak at this point as she took steps back into the protection of the castle. When she thought she was safe she massaged some life back into her neck and walking through the halls she heard the sound of battle, and when she approached, she saw an all so familiar scene, perfectly choreographed as Lancer and Al'Gadrood danced the art of battle in a large pathway.

"One day their sacrifice will be all the more worth it," she said softly, before laying down pillowing the wall next to her.

The morning after Elizabeth is woken by a cold chill breezing past her, she swallowed the cold air stretching herself when the first sound was not of the wood creaking or the birds chirping but of an impact of two bodies, when she lifted her head, she saw the boys still fighting. They stopped in that frozen second between the fight their eyes flickered uncontrollably. Each banking on the other to have an opening, to make a mistake.

"Enough boys, I don't want to see you killing each other, now do I." She struggled to hide her joy even turning her back to them. "Lancer, go rest, you can continue this training tomorrow."

"Yes, my queen," Lancer responded as he walked away from the conflict.

"I can still go." Al'Gadrood chimes in smiling endlessly.

"Strange how after a full night of fighting the Elemental is on his Knee whilst the Human stands tall. I guess with his skill now, soon no one, not even an elemental could stand against him, and fortunately for him, time... is on his side." Gulbrand adds sitting above them, eyes blood red, slumped over the second story.

"I'm sorry for being a boring shit right now but usually I'm never this sober just got interested in a rare talent is all." Gulbrand softly added. "So, don't mind me I'm going to find me some ale to get me back in shape!" he shouted before disappearing into the background.

Apollo

Somewhere in the stone maze of Utopia, laid Apollo. Upon waking from his long sleep, his heart and lungs expanded, his eyes still glassy and heavy with tiredness. For a fleeting moment, he felt at peace as his eyes greeted the sunshine peeking from the window. The second to return was his ears, as a thump to the ground grabbed his attention slowly and reluctantly turning his head, he saw a young girl, possibly a nurse run out of the room leaving only him and another Knight on opposite sides. He rubbed his hands on his face and sat up dragging his feet off the bed, stretching his arms and yawning.

"They were too organised." He softly said. "Unless you are in-sane even the idea of Pangean forces coming for you would cripple moral." He added, then paused for a second before his eyes brightened and as his head snapped towards the knight. The Knight hung his head in shame.

"I see..."

Soon, he let his feet hit the cold floor rubbing the palms of his hands on his knees in an attempt to wake his weakened mus-cles. "One hit.," he mumbled under his breath before a herd of Knights rammed in quickly surrounding him in silence.

No words were spoken but Apollo knew what was happening. "Bring me my armour," he said. "I will step out as a Knight proudly, even in defeat."

One of the Knights quickly chimed in, "We are short on time Apollo, please wear this." To a nod from Apollo, as he grabbed the feeble fabric of his woollen clothing, took off his dressing gown and poured himself into the clothes of peasants. He dragged his feet towards the door still carrying the fatigue from his previous battle. As he slowly stepped out, for the first time without the goggles of alcohol he could feel the life brimming in the streets, hymns of the goddess being sung all over, he could see the joy in the faces of people as they traverse to their jobs or nails being hit by others rebuilding the city.

As quickly as he marvelled a carriage appeared whisking him away to his destination, the Villa. As it got closer, Apollo noticed the ominous site of his own Knights standing in line with dread plastered on their faces. The carriage finally stopped, and his mind drew many conclusions: what if this were his execution, what if he would be stripped of his title again, what if his father would again humiliate him, as he did so many years ago. The fear sank into him as the thought of the past repeating itself ran in through his head. But with no choice, he stepped into the hall. The site all so familiar as again his father stood at the end of the hall and all those who had power stood erect, avoiding eye contact with him. A crooked smirk came to his face, as he seemed to embrace another downfall.

Madas joyless cupped Apollo's shoulders before stepping back. "Your name, your title, your past and present failures have all been stripped. " He took a heavy breath before continuing. "Gather the sword of the Goddess as it shall protect you, gather clothes that will keep you warm throughout the winter and gather those who dare to move beside you."

Madas smiled nervously, struggling to finish his speech. "As of present under the Goddess' watchful eye, I... I Archbishop and King of Vassille Isles Madas Ceidious Vassellet second of his name Here by banish Apollo Amadas Vassellet first and last of his name, to never as long as our name holds the crown be able to use the given names, Apollo and Vassellet under the watchful eye of the Goddess." He echoed. "Second, as of the sun setting, you are to never be able to enter the lands under her protection, including the Vassille Isles."

"Please don't do this... father, my sister I can prove to you I can bring glory to the name again," Apollo said as he struggled to hold back tears.

"As this is the banishment of royalty, any who wish to oppose speak now" Madas commands to the uncomfortable silence of the Audience.

"Mother please" he cries out to his mother for the second time in his life for help. But as she turns her head to leave the simple words begging her to stop travel softly out of his mouth. Crushing him where he stood, head hung in shame he turned around to walk out of the villa grabbing A Galient and taking the sword on his waist. "Sword of the goddess remember," he said bitterly as he walked out of the villa.

"Knight!" he shouts to those by the gate. "At sunset, I want all those who want glory, freedom or money to meet me by the gates!" he adds before swiftly walking past them back into the carriage. With the world still and grey in his eyes, Apollo stumbled towards the gates as the sunset. greeted by those who wanted glory and money thieves, rapists, murderers and heathens. Then those who wanted freedom, the slaves not even desirable by Madas to keep. Hundreds of stood before him but as he scanned the area, not a single Knight, even those who would laugh and drink with him stood in this line-up. Apollo let out a short sigh before grasping the handle of his new weapon.

"We Travel to the lands of the Beasts," Apollo said. His words were heavy with sorrow. "I promise you riches and glory and those in the collars I promise you freedom."

On the march out, Apollo scanned the map knowing within the week, he would be launched in the world of unending war and an aimless path, with its end for the men that follow him would be death but for him he hoped differently he hoped to bathe in the bathhouses of Vassille, to stand before his Father once more as a Vassellet.

"The Troll," he said softly crushing the map in his hand.

Four solders smaller than others squeezed through to the front of the march. "How much a bath and a good meal could change someone," Apollo says as he looks at Eros now with shorter hair and holes sworn shut on his clothes. The walk, tiresome without any breaks, through the deeps of the darkness of night, till the sun rose and the forest was mere feet from them. Finally, as he looks behind him at his men panting and rubbing their soles Apollo signals a break.

"At midday, we march to the other side," he says. before going to relax at the edge of the camp, reading the map given to him over and over again, as his eyes get heavy, the sound of steel clashing shakes him awake full of energy as he stands flickering around to locate the noise when he sees, Eros and Raijin training, the site amuses him as he is reminded of him and his brother Hermes as they would challenge each other on a daily basis to see who was stronger.

However, the call of sleep forces him to pass out only to be woken up at dusk by again the sound of swords clashing, those this time as he looked it was a rouge mercenary from his camp duelling with Eros, further amused he approached immediately commanding the mercenary back to the camp to get everyone ready to move and unsheathing his sword offering a duel to Eros.

"Since when do you like swords boy."

"I don't." Eros groaned as he passed around Apollo. "But I don't want to die either."

Eros then charges in with a blank look on his face. "With that look, it's hard to tell if your even alive," Apollo mockingly commented as he bounced Eros' attacks off him.

"Who do you think the enemy is?" Apollo adds as he glanced passed Eros but quickly shrugging and laughing as he walked away.

An hour passes and as the sun sets and the winds change, getting colder by the second, this band of undesirables match aimlessly into the forest, passing through however unlike the first time whether it be fatigue or a lack of fighting spirit they took their time in the forest resting often. Each day Apollo would watch Eros train for hours on end till his hands would bleed raw and harden, forming a layer of thick skin on his palms. On the third day, they made it out of the forest, with no heathen in site but the endless grass blowing in the wind.

By the end of the first week, they had already started to live off the land with their mouths cracking from the cold, and chilled to the bone with complaints starting to rise from the group. However, unlike the others, Eros and Raijin did not complain as in any free time they trained with each other or alone. Until finally in a village close by, the flags of the Stags and the Banners of the Beasts were planted proudly for those to see.

"Eros, aim for the kidney then the neck, it's a faster kill" Apollo softly says. Before turning around to the rest of his men "time to eat boys!" he shouts leading the charge into the village with the song of swords raging louder. Soon after a celebration followed, the land laid quiet, now a graveyard for the unburied but those who had won could not care less and ravished the lands of its food and its people.

"That woman she's being dragged by her hair!" shouts Eros. Kaza begrudgingly pulled Eros closer "Do you want to die?" he asked letting that statement hang there for a moment. "Good now continue swinging your sword, our next opponents might not be so easy." The festive continues as chatter between the slaves lightens the mood, as each talk about what they wished to do once they are free, "what will you do Eros?" asks Kaza.

"I don't know yet, I hope to see my brother again," Eros answered coldly swinging his sword back and forward.

Eros

A few more of these attacks made over the next coming days gave this small band, some infamy. When one day as they sat joyful off another victory, Apollo falling to his old ways drank alongside his men. Whilst Eros and the rest of the slaves camped further way.

"If we did not have these collars on, this would be a fun adventure," Kaza says.

Sarrah nodded. "If I remember, this was what we were going to do. Yes, priority was to get trade into Utopia that you controlled. But for the rest of us, it was the adventure. The adventure home, the adventure to find a brother, the adventure to become the strongest swordsman."

"I'm going to take Fokle's head and then I'm going to become the strongest swordsman," Raijin added viciously swinging his blade. "And what type of adventure is this, we've been moving around like headless chickens."

"If I remember correctly Kaza was the one who blinded him saving your life," Jon adds with a slight smirk on his face. Raijin, silenced moved away from the slaves starting to do push ups in the corner, gritting his teeth as he does.

As the day goes on, an arrow flying past and landing in the middle of the two groups snaps them back to attention. "Shield wall!" shouts apollo, leading his men into protection. He looks behind to see if the arrow hit anyone as the shields get closer to his body. "Arrows ready! Loose!" He commands opening the top of the shield wall as they return fire into the distance. The rampage of the White stags appears as they run almost feral into Apollo's shields, "Hold!" he screams as both sides impact into each other. "Open!" he shouts again opening the were most impacted making the enemy lose footing killing all those who fell before him.

He looks at Eros and his group, "Misfits, bring me their leader's head." He commands once more. As the misfits, few in number moved around the crowd of white stags, Eros cleaned his blade once more. They had all become used to the idea of being the assassination group that had one goal of taking the leader out whilst Apollo and the bulk of his army pushed through the enemy's ranks.

On the other side, their captain held strong commanding them to continue pushing forward as he stood on higher ground watching the fight more clearly. When the sound of someone screaming in pain hits his ear. He sees one of his own fall revealing Eros stood behind.

"A child?" he questions quickly shrugging it off by ordering arrows loose on Eros. Used to the fight Eros grit his teeth picking up a shield and accepts being pinned down by a fury of arrows. The second the arrows slow Eros shouts, "Move out!" as Raijin appears from behind the shield using his lightning to gain speed. "Don't ever order me again!" he shouts running towards the White stag captain.

Raijin rushed forward counting ten enemies in front of him. The first tries to swing his sword at him but Raijin's speed is far too great as he cuts the enemy's hand still holding the blade. Then in the same momentum makes quick work of the following Five gliding and slashing past them as if they were butter. He struts forward with a smile so wide it touched his ears. "Is that it, the great stags I even used my lightning on you!"

He then pounces forward killing the remaining three leaving only the captain, who strangely did not seem fazed as he drew a spear out. He points it at them.

"My people, value these moments more than battle itself. In these moments, your true strength is shown. The old gods can sit and watch as we entertain them. Come young warrior show me your resolve!" The captain shouts rushing forward to Raijin. It seemed more like a dance than a battle as neither could reach their target, Raijin starting to slow down in his movements as the strains on his body grew, then he loses balance and falls rolling over to his knee. Taking advantage, the captain strikes at him barely being parried away. At that moment Raijin felt a sharp pain in his arm feeling the strength of the monster that stood before him. He knew he was fighting someone strong and grew even happier, before being drowned in anger as the small frame of Eros appears behind the captain slashing at the back of his knee forcing him to jump away. As he lands, he sends a wave of the ground at them but Raijin seeing red ignores even his pain and rushes forward. As the man tries to react to his Pitbull running at him the sharp pain of his wound stops him and gets him impaled by Raijin's blade.

"You were an Earth Elemental! Yet you didn't use that on me?" Raijin shouts as he stabs the man again. Killing him. He goes for another but is suddenly stopped by Eros, screaming "Enough!"

"Enough? Enough he says. Shut your fucking mouth!" Puzzled Eros slowly approached him. "What's your problem we won."

"You are my problem," Raijin adds. "Like a parasite always there, why did you get involved I would have won on my own. I'm the swordsman, not you. You are just a powerless distraction!"

They continue to squabble but are stopped as their collars tighten forcing them to drop to their knees gasping for air. "We won, now we drink. I don't like seeing you boys fighting each other you know that." Apollo says as he loosens the collars allowing them to breathe.

Alexander

For Alex, writing letters home was the most difficult thing since the attack he had sent a few to his home. But lack of response had weighed on his mind. It made him suffer, it made him vulnerable at times, talking to them whether it was one-sided or not kept him going. To remind him that he was fighting for a better life for him and his family. After he finished writing, he stepped out of his room, whistling as usual as he travelled to the barracks without a care in the world.

"Again!" Sir Oslad Nabbie commands with his sharp voice.

"I can't do this anymore." cries a noble teenager, as he struggles to do any more push ups.

"Late again Bastard, ten laps!" Oslad shouts as Alex cracks a smile running past the other Cadets doing what seemed to be his daily runs since joining this Academy. It was beautiful he thought, though he had seen it more than a dozen times the scenery of this Academy was the pride of the Vassilles, white marble buildings and stairs dug into the ground as if they were naturally there to begin with. Prisoners working as slaves for the time of their crimes tending to nature and fields as far as the eye could see.

As off returning from his first lap Oslad waves him back in line. Oslad groaned. "Soon a gathering of some of Pangea' most influential people will be happening. This is all I have to present? You are all worthless far too weak to be training in the ranks of royal guards! Tomorrow I will cut this group in half so I can at least I can salvage something from you worthless maggots!" shouts Sir Oslad Nabbie. The day carries on the same, as what seemed to be endless push ups and sparring carried forward. The time for the next class came sending all those into euphoric joy.

They enter their classroom still wearing their armour, it felt warm and welcoming, a salvation from the slave driver that was Oslad. As they sat in what felt like pillows, their teacher a woman of similar age began their lesson, talking to deaf ears.

"Right class today we will learn about the battle of Garash commonly known as God's end and the tactics used by our government to triumph over Zalius and his empire of the 'chosen' people." The class continued, but only a few were paying attention as Alex concentrated on the watch above waiting for it. Finally, as the bell rang Alex jumped from his chair joyful for the end of the day.

free for the remainder of the day he took his chest plate off stretching his shoulders and preferring to holding his armour than wear it even in this cold weather. As he walked towards the barracks, he noticed something at the corner of his eye, immediately putting a smirk on his face.

"Which do you think will survive the final selection?" Asks Damien as he steps out from the shadows.

Oslad smiled seeing an old friend. "A few if not all the ones you brought, the top draw would probably be the young lady and the blond boy they might even be beyond Royal Guards and could take the examination for Statesmen instead bringing them directly under your Command, Damien."

"Being a fighter is only one path to Chancellor, there are many ways to my job, but it does put a smile on my face that the one I trained would be staying close by, when I get promoted, I will know my position now will be in safe hands."

The night felt by many from the camp was filled with dread and despair each wondering, if they had achieved enough to continue on this perfect track to their future whilst those, who came to this world with a silver spoon, looked all the more comfortable, sleeping as soundly as children. When Alex burst through the doors with a bright smile on his face waking up all the Cadets in there.

"What's this fool doing now?" Basil asked as he rubbed his eyes.

"Probably one of his childish pranks." Junia a fair skin female cadet added as she put on her glasses.

As they finished speculating Alex pulled out two bottles of fine wine from inside his jacket. Seeing this Stavros jumped out of his bed running towards and eventually putting Alex on his shoulders as he took a gulp of wine. "Bow to our new King, the great Alexander!" He shouts as the rest of the cadets joined in celebration. "Alex! Alex! Alex!" they all screamed so loud disturbing Ava as she stopped training to listen in to the Idiotic shouts of her pears.

The time until the final selection became a little easier and as the day came each of the cadets in line in pressed uniforms and bags to their side. As today would change their lives forever. Each name said, salutes holding back their tears as they grab their bags leaving the Academy. At the end of a gruelling hour, only twenty Royal Guard trainees remained. Oslad smiled joyful of the remainders, "now that the useless limb has been cut off, tell me Royal Guards what is your end goal in this the Goddess' great military."

"Serve, protect and show the lost souls the way!" shouts the cadets with their right hands firmly cupped over their left breasts. Oslad, Unconvinced by Alex's words inched over towards him with his hands behind his back stretching his grey suit and with eyes like an owl as he gazed at Alex, "Tell me, bastard, a man such as yourself surely does not care about serving and protecting."

"What do you really want to accomplish Royal Guard?" he asks calmer but more terrifying.

"Grand Chancellor, so I can control laws and such giving my family name pride and ensuring change happens on all the lands under the Goddess' watchful eye."

"Tell me the truth."

"I just did."

"No. You told me a script now tell me what Alexander wants not what he thinks he should want."

"I don't know," Alexander says softly. "But I know if I had the chance, I would make actual change, bring laws that would help people like me, not ones that only feed the rich and pamper the wealthy under the eye of our almighty Goddess!"

A comment so controversial the staff and guards on duty stood surprised what they heard, even his own allies from the camp stunned by his response.

"Good I hope you achieve such an interesting goal one day recruit now back in line!" shouts the Drill sergeant. After a brief moment of silence, training continued but something began to be noticeable not just by Alex but other cadets, that the Sergeant had started to refer to him as a Cadet rather than a simply a bastard. Finally, the sunsets and another day of training ended.

Alex and Ava walk back side by side, Ava uncomfortable pulls splinters from her palms.

"Even with gloves, and clashing swords made of wood you still find a way to go over the top," Alex mockingly comments proceeding to a short chase around the grounds till, a roaring sounds from guards catches their attention and as they sneak past the woods, into the grazing fields of the horses they see Guards throwing coins and gossiping with each other, this, however, does not keep their attention to long as they quickly return to the dorms.

The next morning Alex and Ava spar Heavy with curiosity getting Oslad's Attention, "what is it? why are you two so mature today?" he asks with a sharp tone.

"Nothing important just Guards betting on horses" Ava adds to a burst of short laughter from Oslad. Now it was strange for such noises to come from him making the young cadets all the more curious, joyful Oslad announces the day's lesson, "If anyone manages to complete this test, they will immediately be put forward for Statesmen training," Commands Oslad with a mischievous smirk plastered on his face as he drags his oblivious students to the grazing area of the horses.

As they get closer a horse unlike any other laying down eating it's hey, "Meet the Arki, a breed thought to have been lost in history. He, however, is the last of his kind, first to be found in a thousand years, many come to the Vassille Isles to marvel at its beauty" says Oslad. And he was not wrong the beast was bigger than any other horse of its kind to the point calling it a horse would seem like an insult, its coat shining in glistering gold, its eyes so white one would think it was blind. "Now your test is to try and tame it!"

All twenty of the students with bravado marched in full force towards the beast thinking this would be an easier task than first thought. But immediately all stopped as a cold breeze wrapped around their ankles. Feeling as if in quicksand they tried their best to drag themselves forward. Again, as they got closer the beast lifted its head, and as its eyes focused on the cadets, an aura unlike any other emulated from it, with a cold wind that wanted nothing more than to announce its arrival, blowing with such a powerful passion most of the students fell to their knees struggling for breath.

Apart from two, Ava and Alex who both stood erect taking heavy steps forward with their fists clenched thinking they had taken the brunt of this creature's power. But troubled the horse

Neighs with a tone so deep that the force of its wind became so great concrete and skin cut the same, forcing Ava to fall holding her chest in tremendous pain. With even their bones freezing Alex, refused to bend the knee to this animal, and took even heavier strides with veins popping from his skull, his eyes strained and his body shaking uncontrollably. Noticing Alex approaching the beast had had enough of this defiant human and stood on all four of its legs letting out its full Aura, showing its might causing Alex to hold his chest tight as he slipped in and out of consciousness to the point blood started dripping from his eyes.

"Alert the Guards!" shouts Oslad concerned for his students. "Cadet kneel!" he shouts to Alex, who seemed to refuse but in reality, he had been deafened by this beast's aura at this point. With the silence surrounding him, Alex, given time to think, came to a realisation no one else could, this untameable beast would let out its aura whenever approached.

"You are afraid," he said softly, as he slowly reached his hand out. One stroke to the beast's face made its aura vanish, stunning the rushed guards who had just arrived to see a spectacle as one boy stood caressing the face of the untameable beast.

"Who is he?" asks one of the Guards.

"Alexander" Oslad answers softly.

Logan

"The land that changed the war to our favour." Ezekiel looked further. "The land that gave you your title my prince," he says referring to Logan as they stare into the outskirts of Bamier.

"You would think the people here would raise a toast to your name every day," Pier replied with a slanted smirk on his face. "Maybe you need to liberate them a few more times."

Logan groaned with frustration, "They're late," he said. Hundreds of lions stood at the edge of the village watching over the land waiting on the other houses. "Lords and Ladies are different from warrior princes, they need more time to get ready after all."

"Sires, the Lords of house petal and house Falco have arrived and more can be seen in the distance!" The young squire said, dripping in sweat, desperately trying to control his breathing. As the lions march down into the village, Pier notices the whispers all including his brother's name he smiles noting of a hero's welcome for his brother, after all the lands he was riding on were the same ones he stayed to defend till the last man.

"Lion, squires, the help, you will stay out here. Only me and my brother will meet with these great leaders." Pier went on. "Even if it breaks down at that point, I have the hero Logan to fight by my side. Right?"

"It's no time for jokes brother."

"Really? no. Why would you take those below us so seriously?" Slowly getting frustrated Logan hurried forward forcing a chuckle from Pier. As they reach the meeting place, Logan thinks that even in a land ravished by years of war the bar, seemed untouched a cornerstone that has only seen peace. Pier caught up, rested his hand on the rough of the door and pushed, revealing lords and ladies of Zen, Nero and Pocasis. Even the representation of the eunuchs and the trader's guild did not go unseen.

"I'm glad you could see this brother, some of the most powerful people in our three kingdoms in one room. can you feel it? the crushing pressure?" he softly asks as he steps over the splinters on the floor waving away all those who followed but his brother.

Two chairs are pulled out squealing as though they were a warning. As they sat an overwhelming silence begins to bear its head only crushed by Pier's simple words. "Sir Favier Petal of house Petal, Sir Hugo Falco of house Falco, Sir Velentin Piere of house Rose, Lady Marie St.Justine of House Petram, Father

Alec O'Caron and all the other Lords and ladies that came from our kingdom and the other two, thank you for attending this meeting."

"Our ancestors would be proud today, one hundred years of conflict and yet we sit being civil." Sir Favier replied. "However, as you might have noticed we all have lands to govern. Why have you brought us here Pier?"

A cup of wine is passed over to Pier and as he takes a sip warming his chest with its fruity aftertaste. No one dared to disturb Pier as he drank after all the Sigil on his chest carried the weight of the Lions and each other Lords and ladies in this room had felt its bite at one point or another.

"This has to do with the Beasts does it not?" Hugo added shaking his leg as his frustration grew.

Finished with his drink Pier finally put the cup down on the plank of wood balanced on two drums of ale, the residence would call a table.

"Yes," Pier said with a stern tone. "The Beasts have shown their fangs by defying the strongest empire in the world. Then to add insult to injury, they recruit their own Enemies and the attackers of Utopia the White Knights to their ranks. With these recent events, Pangea is sure to make a move unmatched since the great war and we the Lions have decided to ally with them, now I ask you, Lords and Ladies, to put aside our differences and ally together to take care of the growing threat of the Beasts."

By the end of the speech, silence befalls the room, broken by a mocking slow clap comes from Velentin a man with scars to bare from the many battles he has fought with the Lions.

"Pier the White Lion. I piss on your proposition and instead offer you an escape from the kindness of my heart." He stands to smack the Table grinning through his shaggy beard.

"Everyone here has fought the Lions at one point or another, correct? so instead of listening to this boy, why not join hands and wipe the Lions now. I mean you have clearly shown us that you are desperate."

He quickly raises his hand clouded in confidence. "Who here wishes for the Lions to subjugate, and their lands handed to us?"

Velentin leaked a smile taking comfort in this small revenge on the Lions. All those in attendance silenced by his bravado are thrown into shock as Lady Marie and Sir Hugo slowly raised their hands shortly followed by Father Alec immediately, unifying both the counties of Nero and Pocasis in a matter of seconds.

It was unlike him to be outplayed in such a way; the sheer shock muted him from responding forcing his brother to finally speak his peace. He put his hand forward, grabbing everyone's attention with the shine from his golden coating.

Logan was never much use in talking, having used his past accolades as his power he let others with more confidence do it for him. Too weak, too fearful, too green is a way most would describe the prince. So, while he had managed to grab the people's attention, his brother knew not much could come from Logan. "Please listen to my brother." He spoke. "Please listen," he added again quickly falling into repetition.

"Speak boy, we have little time to waste" Lachlan Gungadad quickly chimed in revealing his presence from the background. "Yes, your right."

"Good you were saying about your brother?"

"Yes, yes. My brother is right if we do not join hands and put our differences aside for now and the Beasts come to our borders, whether it be Zen Nero or Pocasis they will destroy us, but -" before finishing his sentence Valentin's boisterous laugh forces him to be silent. "Cut the head and the fucking Beast dies." Valentin confidently adds he folds his arms sitting back down one last time.

"I will take care of Halvor myself then we will take care of Zen."

Lachlan's fascination grew as he came to the realisation that those in attendance, did not realise the return of Gulbrand. When he first came here his intention was to harbour a trade deal with the Lions as commanded by Elizabeth, but now with this information, he knew it could quickly turn in favour of the White Knights.

"If you are certain about crossing the border and testing your strength against the Lions, then we welcome it," Pier now calmer said with fortitude.

"I am, little cub," Valentin replied standing alongside his new allies. "Next time we meet will be the last time you breathe the air of this beautiful world. Do me a favour, enjoy these next few weeks indulge, paint, hell spread your seed if you wish."

Lachlan, almost drunk with joy grinned as he watched several Lords and Ladies leave beside Valentin. "Imagine, Eunuchs that literary gave their body to the Goddess siding with her very enemy. That is the level of hate they hold for you."

As Lachlan and the remaining Lords and Ladies laughed, Pier sat there gulping another cup of wine grinding his teeth slowly showing more frustration to his peers. Logan one of the two not entertained by the outcome of the meeting could no longer hold back his emotions.

"They mock us!"

"Only the Lions, I believe" Lachlan quickly replied. Sending the audience into nervous laughter. Finished being belittled, Pier quickly carried himself out of the building, soon followed by his brother and the rest of their allies, all going separate ways to ready themselves.

"A trader in a meeting of Lords, how intriguing," Ezekiel chimes in stopping Lachlan as he tried to vanish in the background.

"Trade, when an opportunity comes you know," Lachlan said with an unhesitating tone.

"I don't but that's why you are rich and I'm poor."

"Well," Lachlan giggles. "We all have to start somewhere." Ezekiel smiled. "I agree. What sort of trade do you do? maybe our countrymen would be able to provide."

"Spices."

"No slaves?"

"No."

"Very Nobel you are trader worthy to look up too," Ezekiel adds putting a subtle smile on Lachlan's face. "But with our country being launched back to war, I fear the crown cannot withstand the storm this time."

"Don't worry, Lions are infamous for their military strength."

"I suppose. Well, I must catch up to my prince, good luck in your jewel trade."

"Thank you."

Soon Night falls and as the birds are sent to the capitals warning of the impending attack, the brothers lay in their tents unable to sleep knowing what's to come. Again, for the second time in their lives, they will have to fight a war with no end in sight. Logan stepped out of his tent, stretching his tights. It was early, twilight had melted away but there was no light yet over the horizon. The drum of rain droplets hitting the ground echoed in his ear, he shouted for his squire as he began running through the camp. Eventually going past his brother's tent, crisp and clean, perfect like him, Logan thought as his eyes wandered past it. "Sir, the prince is still asleep" the squire mumbled. "Should we wake him?" he softly asked.

"He's not asleep his probably already out training," Logan said. Panting with every word. "Now don't drop my blade!"

"Yes, sir!"

However, Pier laid slummed to the side of his desk, an empty bottle dripping on his leg. But as the sound of his brother screaming peaked through his ears, his eyes dragged open to the sight of the Lion's Sigil. He opened his day with a sip of wine, sitting back down on his chair looking at the map that covered the borders of his land. His fingers were numbed from the cold air and his neck was sore, and as he looked upon his bed thinking of nothing but sleep, he knew his presence was needed among his men.

The third prince, Philip had seen a bird fly to the castle at the break of dawn, and immediately got ready. But despite standing in a crisp suit, perfectly tailored in silk not found in the west, the man inside could barely hold the rotting hatred of his siblings, knowing he could never hold the crown. A prince third in the birth of his siblings, but the name bastard followed him closely at every angle.

"Oh, my lord the King wishes for your presence," One of the guards said from the far end of the hallway, bowing.

The prince strode towards the King's hall, wearing all his favourites. Each time he knew he would be called in, he would glide in making no sound at all, and would always see the blank face of the king caressing his hands.

"Father?" He gently asked. "Are my brothers dead?"

"Nothing of sort," King Christiano quickly replied, with his head hung and tone sombre, "Much worse my son."

A rare moment for the Kingdom of Zen when both the King and the Playboy prince both stood silent, serious. From his memory, this was the first time he had been called son. Philip Bewildered took a step back, opening his eyes for the first time, for once the aura of King disappeared from his father and he could see him as he was, a man. A man who had avoided all the bad of the world, a man who had never felt the weight of responsibility that came with the crown. Surely there was some bravely on the inside Philip thought. But without Philip's Uncle to lead the armies as he did in the past, he could see fear and acceptance of defeat in his King's eyes. "The stalemate ended. I see."

"Well then fuck Pangea and the Beasts we have bigger issues now."

A nervous smile touched Christiano's lips. "I've already sent word to Chancellor Damien that we will join in the war efforts and sent a large amount of crop to Utopia."

"Then address your people, winter will be hard this year."

"I will," Christiano answers with a smile. "As the third oldest you have a duty to protect your family in these times my son, whilst your brothers fight in the front lines you must help keep morale on home ground."

"I will father, as best as I can."

Elizabeth

As Twilight ended, the frost of dawn ravished through the Castle of the Beasts, Elizabeth hugged herself for warmth, pulling away from the balcony ending her watch of her men training. One her own came closer laying a blanket over her. "The meeting ended. Another war between them I believe. Their general leading the Lions is Pier the white."

"What? are they not scared of the Beasts anymore?" Elizabeth asked. Staring at the rising sun as it basked her skin with warmth.

The man sniffed, raising his voice slightly. "Even better my queen, they believe Halvor is still leading the Beasts, and Velentin has made it clear that he will assassinate him soon." He said as he smiled from ear to ear.

"I see," she replied. "Now if you will excuse me, I need to get ready, 'The King' is throwing another party later."

The Ale slowed down, the winds got hasher, the people started to grow in boredom, days had passed, and each time Elizabeth would brush her long red hair giving it a slight glow when held by the light and picked her nicest silks. She had been looking forward to Halvor being attacked but with no luck.

"Why are we not doing anything Gulbrand!?" shouts a Beast as he slurred his words. "Tell me, have you lost your balls?" Another with his face planted on the table chimes in. "We are running out of food and letting them prepare what stupidity is this?"

"I say we raid those posh pricks down south and then attack Utopia."

"No, you slow idiot, why risk our forces with Zen? I say we just push into Utopia then deal with the southerners."

A sword is drawn and with a clash of steel, a riot quickly breaks, each shoving their plans to the next. In the end, Gulbrand had not moved from his throne, with hand on the cheek he watched as his men started to gut each other. The last straw came as Halvor tired of watching stepped out of the hall, with a crooked smile on his lips, clear enough for Gulbrand to see.

"Enough," Gulbrand said softly. " I did not come back to see my people my brothers and sisters fight like mindless animals. I came back because of other people's actions. But that doesn't matter anymore because I am the King. Me!"

Gulbrand staggard to his feet, stumbling forward. "Tell me, what does a King do, Elizabeth?"

"Leads?"

"No. He rules!" He roared. "Now, when I point you attack! Then we live in a renascence for the rest of our lives. Now stop with the bickering and the bullshit and enjoy your time before you have to fight for weeks or months or years on end. If no one has a problem with that lets drink..."

Outside, Halvor tried to warm himself sipping on the last of his ale, when he heard a thump right behind him and as he turned around, he saw an arrow firmly placed through a skull. "What is this?" he slurred.

"I believe it is what they call an assassin," Elizabeth said stepping out of the hallway. "I've had a few come for me in my time."

"You know what I mean. Why save me?" confused, Halvor asked. "If I died, your one opposition to joining vanishes."

"Call it a lady's intuition. It hasn't failed me yet."

The next day Gina shook Gulbrand awake from his dreams, sending him into a cold chill. Still groggy from the night before,

he stayed laying down slurring his words. "What!" he roared.
"Can't you see I'm nursing a hangover here?"

"Continue, but I think you might want to wake up for this,"
Ginna said. "Come in!" she shouted with a joyful look on her
face.

"I see five years did not change you," Gustav said." Tell me
Gulbrand, did you only come back just to party?" two other of
the white stags stood behind him watching Gulbrand struggle
to stand.

"Gustav, Frigg and Ingrid but where are the others?" Gulbrand
asked. "Where is The Troll? usually he would be swinging at me
for my crown by now."

"He stayed back at the border; you know how he is" Gustav
added as he walked over to lift his King up.

Gulbrand groaned. "I see. Well, I need to kill this hangover, so
come I will pour you some ale."

As they walked through the castle, Gulbrand told stories over
his travels for the past five years. Stories about: a land were Fire
roamed free, a land untouched by men. A land where sand
moved as if alive. Flushed and exhausted from walking he sat in
the nearest chair losing the smile on his face.

He laughed. "That fool will get himself killed one day..."

"Who Folke?" Gustav quickly chimed in, curious. "No. I've fought him before. The man might not be at your strength, but he is still The Troll."

"It's good to be positive," Gulbrand added as he tapped him on the shoulder. "But Folke has one glaring weakness. All the times he fights me I expose it but, he refuses to fix it."

Gustav, building in frustration started to grind his teeth. "I don't even understand why we are even talking about him and not the strategy against Pangea."

A smile lingered on Gulbrand's face. "Because he found someone he wants to fight right?"

"And? he will win."

"I hope so. But for now, we party for the reunion of brothers."

Logan

Some time passes the silence of the Beasts worries all including the Lions as they stand on the battlefield under the still grey sky. It was the night before their first battle, they did not know who would attack them, their weapons or their numbers. But this did not shake their spirits as they continued to drink and talk about the next day.

"I am starting to miss her," Pier says sipping on a cup of wine.

"Who?" Logan quickly asked.

"My fiancée you moron," Pier said. "How can you forget the woman who will soon be your sister-in-law."

"I apologise brother that I did not celebrate your political shame of a marriage."

Pier let out a small laugh. "This shame of marriage brought the richest family in all three countries onto the side of Zen. Father pushed for it because he knew it would help our country even more. Yes, I did not expect to be launched into another war, but I know once we take care of them our country's economy will be stronger than ever."

Logan looked saddened twirling the tip of his cup with his finger. "Brother, you are getting old. All your life you have taken care of the Lions now you want to sacrifice being happy with someone for the Lions. I just can't accept that."

Pier looked around to his soldiers warming to each fire, distracting their minds with coin or women or stories of old. They all knew tomorrow might be the last day of their lives, but they continue to think of the future and hear of the past.

Pier spoke one last time before retiring to his tent. "You do not have to worry about the responsibilities of a King. I have to think what is best for the future of our Lands far above what is be for me. That was what uncle did, that is why we are so powerful. Brother, I am the next King, and I will make the house Lion, powerful again. So powerful no one would ever be brave enough to challenge us like this. This is our last war. I promise."

"Now enjoy your night, tomorrow we battle together and win together." He adds walking away from Logan.

As the west dons its winter coats, the field crunches as a bed of snow had already settled. Lace winter ice laid on the tip of Pier's blade as he signalled for the first attack. "Show them the roar of the Lions!"

Screams warming the cold air around them echo throughout the battlefield as a rain of arrows appears through the fog hitting Velentin's army,

"I see its beginning. Shields!" Velentin shouts. "Ready for im-pact!" he screams again as the footsteps of the Lions roar louder. A thunderous slam begins the second battle of Bamier. The cold air and fear of the Beasts slowed strategy as all parties wanted to end this as quickly as they can. Some time passes and as the Rose army begin to gain ground an impact to their side shakes Velentin to his core, Logan had arrived with the Cavalry cutting through his army causing quick panic. The day ends with Velentin retreating but holding more men on the battlefield than the Lions. As the Lions take a breath of relief, a horn sounds and a second army comes from the fog fresh for battle. Pier smiles confusing those surrounding him.

Velentin had enough battles with the Lions to know of their mind games, he did not feel confusion or fear at Pier smiling in the middle of a battle but knew they had become more desperate.

"As agreed, the Rose army will cut their numbers even more," he says walking away. "This should give us enough time to move our armies into these lands, without them being able to fortify."

"I pity them". Pier said. " Even with such a large army all they will taste is defeat after defeat. Now raise your swords Lions and show them who the fuck we are!"

Apollo

Enough time had passed for the snow to settle, yet the Beasts had stayed silent. But as the horns sound at the gates of Utopia droves of Vassille soldiers march in. Lead in front by a man frail in size but carried beauty unseen before, he rode past residence of Utopia smiting them with his looks, his hair caressed by the wind curling it as he moved, his armour winged with the crest of the Vassille. To his right a man Larger in size with a face aged by war, greying in hair but a body that defied time.

"My son, welcome," Madas says with a glint in his eye as Hermies Steps off his steed. Madas quickly embraces him and caresses the back of the head of the veteran close by.

"My son and brother in arms standing together, I fear for them, truly." He says laughing.

Later that evening Madas' boisterous laugh could be heard throughout the halls as him and the Lord Commander reminisced on the past.

"Max, Max! Remember Cathryn, that girl would spread her legs for anyone!" Madas shouted. "Yes, if I remember, even you had a turn!"

"Brother keep your voice down or the woman will have my balls!" Maximilian snapped. "You know she married Augustus's boy, his name slips my mind though," he adds.

"You mean John? really? when did that happen?"

"It was during the war I think..."

"I don't remember, my age is showing!"

"Yes, now I remember," Maximilian says before quickly holding his tongue. Forcing Madas' laughter to slow. "Now I must know brother was this between your first or second wife?" he adds as he lets out a boisterous laugh.

"I believe it was at this time Apollo took grandpa's head" Hermies chimes in sipping on his soup.

Madas frowned, ruining his appetite. "My son, when do you think you will launch your attack."

"We leave in two days," He quickly responds before excusing himself from the table.

Deep in the wastelands of the Beasts, Apollo's men travelled sluggish, swaying left and right as the cold had wrapped around their bodies. Some hardly able to keep their eyes open and every so often a few would fall never to get up. They had made a name for themselves, butting heads with the beasts and at most times coming on top.

"It's like a game, we find a few on their own sometimes they're weak sometimes they put the fear of the Goddess in us," Apollo mumbles through his frozen beard. Before quickly slicing the air, causing one of the Beasts to fall through the fog. "Shield wall!" he shouts as they get ready for another battle.

The thud of the impact, as the Beasts quickly swam on them. The world around them grey and still with the red of blood gushing occasionally, as they desperately try to hold their ground. The Beasts, crushing hammers and axes against the shields of Apollo's men. Arrows hissing through the air waiting to poison an unlucky soul. There seemed thousands of them, but Apollo's men did not seem weak or weaver in fear, no sobbing snivelling messes. They were calm, holding the tide in place with their shields. "Attack!" Apollo shouts lowering the shields, their steel clapped together with the Beasts like the rumblings of thunder. Apollo looked around for only a moment seeing his men scatter too far from each other "Keep close!" he screamed. When, by chance, he saw Eros appear like a wasp, and take one down an enemy with ease, followed by an arrow from Jon.

He smiles, "They grow up so fast." He mumbles before pushing forward leading his men to quickly disperse of the Beasts.

As he lowers his Sword his eyes widened, his breaths became harsh, his hands started to tremble. The paralyzing feeling quickly spread through his body like a virus. All he could do was scan the area bewildered.

"Clean their pockets boys, these Beasts are making us rich!" Kaza screams as he steps well in front of his allies, all cheer keeping their morale up in this winter. Eros stood slowly joining in with the cheers and laughing along at his friend's antics.

Then in a flash of golden light Kaza's head shot past Eros. The moment though brief felt like a lifetime for all those watching as their ally's body slowly sink to the ground. Followed quickly by all so familiar laugh travelling through the fog as Folke slowly stepped out holding his hammer now freshly dipped in blood comfortably on his shoulder.

"The troll," Apollo said softly grinding his teeth. An explosion bursts through the ground as Sarrah launched herself forward screaming "Kaza!" in desperation. A rage shot into her, burning like fire, wrapping around her spine and deafening her, putting all focus on Folke. She screamed and cried intoxicated with emotion as she wore gloves of the earth beneath her feet, still charging forward.

This chill? Folke thinks as he uses Head of his harmer to block the punch, but her strength was far too great as he slowly watches his beloved harmer explode on impact. Folke surprised jumps back releasing his aura, dispersing of the fog in the area. This power of hers did not come free as she quickly realised. A sharp pain laced through her body, spots flashed in front of her eyes, and as she dropped to her knee, an ocean of sweat poured onto her. Raijin rushed past her swinging his sword in desperation.

"Electric boy!" Folke shouts tightening his fist. "I did miss you!" His fist brushed past Raijin's head at such speed, a small cut grew on Raijin's cheek as the boy quickly stepped back.

"Apollo, call for a retreat now!" Jon shouted as he shot covering arrows flying past Folke.

Apollo, silent this entire time watching on grits his teeth and points his sword behind him. "Regroup!" he Shouts, sending a bulk of mercenaries running away from The Troll. including Jon as he lifts the injured Sarrah running past the stunned Eros.

Raijin still standing there, got into a stance as the second round between Folke and him began. But unlike last time Raijin is quickly put into defence as he tries to survive the unnatural speed of Folke. Eros once again thinking he could take advantage throws his blade at Folke, who this time simply catches it crushing it in his left hand, then throwing a right punch barely avoiding Raijin.

"Hey, come on for real?" Asked Raijin surprised. "Since when could you crush blades with your hands?"

Eros quickly replied. "It's that aura thing."

Folke lets out a large amount of air from his chest, "Nice catch" he said. "If you are talking about will then yes, a bit hard to hold for a while but I thought this battle would be over by now."

With a sombre look, he gazed at the pieces that once belonged to his hammer. "Too bad, I liked that one."

Folke stretched his arms and cracked his neck never breaking eye contact. "Tell me what are your names."

"Raijin."

"Eros Senesto."

"Senesto, you say?" Folke gently said scanning Eros, with a cold gaze. "That name makes me itch; I don't like it. But Raijin I like that one. It's very northern, Unique for these parts. I won't forget it."

A sound of a horn grabs Folke's attention but as he turns back around, he sees the boys running away as quickly as they could. "How fun" Folke mumbles, when one of his men approaches quickly to his side laughing. "Look at them run!" He shouts before getting punched by Folke, getting knocked out instantly. "what's so funny? I consider them as equals. Now go catch them."

As Raijin and Eros run, they are slowly cut off by hordes of Beasts Leading them to a tight corner, where a spear comes inches from taking Raijin's life. When he looks up, he sees all his current allies standing there, trapped like rats.

"It's a game to them now," Apollo said, standing in the background behind everyone. When he could suddenly feel it as he slowly came to the realisation, a fear unlike any other, a fear of unavoidable death. He turned his head to see everyone, people who he had led for months cowering in fear. He drew his sword once again, calmly walking through them, and once in front, he looked down and with a sombre tone. "I'm sorry," he softly says. "But I cannot save you, all I can offer is a warrior's death."

"What?" confused a mercenary asked.

Apollo looked troubled. "We stand here we will die. we go out there we are probably going to die as well."

"So, there was no point in this?"

"It seems so, but in my eyes at least, you are no longer scum, slaves, or just mercenaries to me..."Apollo said. "You are brothers, sisters. Solders. But it comes with a catch." He said with a smile on his lips.

"What's the catch?"

"My solders do not cower in fear, the march forward to death, they rage against the world, the become berserkers fighting destiny itself." He said with a gentle tone. "So, my solders I have but one command... Rage! Rage against the world! Rage against

Humanity! Rage against destiny!" He charges forward into the fog screaming, "Rage!" in desperation.

Quickly followed by his soldiers as they rush behind him letting their Rage devour them this one time, as they fight against death itself. Bodies and swords alike fly through the fog, screams can be heard around all around, but the fog quickly disperses as Apollo and Folke battling to see who had the stronger will.

The sun passes and the moon stands on top of their heads still fighting, though sluggish and fatigued. Eros covered in the blood of his enemies steps back struggling to lift his hands, watching as men on their knees continue to swing their swords to the last breath, one of his enemies falls by his feet with an arrow placed at the back of his head.

"Pay attention!" Jon screams. "If you stop, you will die."

The sky, cleared, as the swords glimmered under the moonlight, Folke, laughing, dangling Apollo's body by his hand. Squeezing it by the second as it made a crunching noise hard to ignore even in the middle of battle. Folke's eyes lit up; all other emotions fleeted giggling like a small child as he saw Raijin calmly approach him.

"Raijin! here for another round?" Folke asks. "But I don't see any electricity. Are you by chance mocking me?"

Folke then scans the area with his one good eye. "Earth girl, the little sniper and Senesto's kid. Come let's end this before it gets boring!"

He throws Apollo out of the way and sprints to his prey like a hungry hyena laughing all the way. "Attack!" Raijin shouts as few of Apollo's soldiers barely a few dozen charges into a lone Folke desperate for a promised end if they could take him down. The troll unfazed brushes through them with his bare hands. Crushing the opponent then grabbing their weapon and slicing another in half. "What is he?" they scream in fear. Un-matched, Apollo's men started to waiver. Some even sobbing and snivelling at the presence of this monster. Until a stray punch reaches Sarrah who blocks it with both her arms.

"I do despise Earth Elementals the most, far too strong." He spoke. "But you are just a cub, untrained. I am sad I never met you at your strongest. Our fight would have been fun."

He goes to throw a punch with his other arm, only stopped by a sharp pain in his back. A stray blade had met his flesh once again, making a satisfying squish as the tip pocked through his Chest. "Die you irritant," Apollo says as he twists the blade with his good hand, whilst sinking it deeper with his shoulder. Then a sharp pain travels through the back of his leg as Raijin slashes it open forcing him to drop to his knee. As Folke struggles to breathe, Eros approaches with his last blade impaling him in the Neck.

Finally, the Troll stops as his power weakens, the pain that burned him so is quickly replaced by the cold numbness. He starts to fade away. Darkness, filled the edges of his vision, only hearing the comfort of his heartbeat. As seconds passed, he started to hear voices, voices from his younger days. He re-membered the day the Beasts were formed as his human heart-beat for the last time. "Adira," he mumbled, grabbing Eros' at-tention as Fokle's eye bursts wide open giving him a boost of strength enough to shake all of them off him, he pulls the blade from his neck, nearly collapsing as he does. One final scream escapes from his mouth sending waves of wind crushing into everyone, but as he tries to stand tall, the damage had been too much and he falls on his back, screaming with his fists close to his death.

"Finally," the hunched over Apollo says, when he suddenly drops to his knee, vomiting blood and panting, gasping for air. His sword pressed onto his body holding him up. With his vision failing he looked upon his ticket back, the corpse of Folke "The Troll" and smiled before passing out. Eros, however, stood tall with his friends, sweating through the cold air of winter. He wiped the blood on his face off to see more clearly, but with the black of the night all around all he could see was Folke a man who stood above most laying on the ground. Raijin and Jon fell on their backs, sitting up immediately with smiles on their faces.

"We killed the fucking troll," Jon says through his joyful grin. "I think I'm going to party for a few years to celebrate such a moment."

Sarrah however, felt nothing but pain, pushing her body beyond, because the need for revenge was gnawing at her soul. A single tear travelled down her cheek, as she stared at Folke. After some time, she turned away forcing a smile on her face as she went to embrace her friends. "We avenged Kaza. When we return and have these collars taken off the first drink is on me."

"I think I'm too young to drink." Eros chuckles as he sits down. "I'll have a glass of milk instead." Forcing those around him to start hysterically laughing.

"Well, you need to grow that's for sure!" shouts one of the surviving mercenaries as he hugs one of his brothers. As if friends all those who managed to live, continued to take quips at each other till the morning when Apollo work up. The astonishment of being alive failed in comparison to all the survivors once avoiding each other continued to joke holding their bellies in pain crying tears of joy. He stood using his blade to balance his body, telling one of the slaves to turn around.

"Witches, they say they were the goddess' mistake. Yet we use their talents so frequently..." He says in a foreign tongue with a broken smile planted on his face. Apollo studied the back of the collar and with a simple prick of his finger and a touch a click Heard around saw the collar, slide off the slave's neck. One by one he released them from their bind and the second the taste of freedom falls on Eros, Apollo is tackled to the ground by Sarrah, in tears she holds his head up and with blood gushing from his nose and mouth.

"I'm not your enemy," he said. "I took all the ones he did not want. I saved you."

Confused Eros cracks as he speaks up. "Saved us, you say."

Like a current, all his emotions build-up, as months of unbearable pain swims through his body, the rage, growing gathering everything with it and as he reaches the edge ready to be swallowed. He stopped looking at Apollo's glassy eyes. He grabbed a blade pushing Sarrah aside as he shoved the blade into Apollo's mouth. "Die you piece of shit!" He shouted and just before pushing the sword through Apollo's skull the main screamed.

"A spy!" Apollo screamed as clearly as he could.

"What?" a confused Sarrah asked as she gathered herself again.

"Eros let him speak," Raijin said with conviction. And as Eros obliged Apollo laughed taking huge breaths.

He looked Eros dead in the eyes. "There's a spy among us. No more than that I believe this particular spy is one of the White Knights."

The mention of this name put Eros into a rage as a dark aura started to form around him.

"Just kill him!" Jon said. "He will say anything to live!" Hearing this Eros gripped his blade harder.

Apollo opened his arms in surrender. "Think Eros, the attack on Utopia was a bit too perfect, the beasts not only knowing our location but our numbers and being able to mobilise that quick. Hell, even the random routs I've been leading everyone on, yet beasts have been able to find and ambush us over and over again."

Raijin surprised looked at his blade, "His right… that would explain why the beasts are so silent, but why do you think it's a white knight spy and not a beast spy."

"Halvor, invited the white knights to join them, people who don't believe in their gods and even killed some of the beasts. Yet now they fight as one, come on Raijin it doesn't take a genius to figure that out."

Eros stepped on Apollo's neck as he pointed his sword at Apollo's eye. "Sarrah, Jon what do you think?"

Jon took a second. "Kill him take Folke's head back and say Apollo died in battle. We already know of a spy, so we give that information to the King as well."

"Spare him, we need such a devil to fight with us. We become a clan, taking land and establishing ourselves. Then if he can oust the spy, we sell him to slave traders." Sarrah added as she grabbed Jon's shoulder.

"Not like this." Raijin said. "If I killed him, it'll be at best. But keeping him alive might not be wise, your call wimp."

Eros continued to take opinions from people around him, as he continued to gaze at Apollo. *'I should kill him for months he beat me half to death, gave me to those monsters, treated me like a dog. Forced me to fight, to kill.'* He thought. *'I should spare him, give him the same treatment. "The devil we need?" that is true his tactics will help us, and I could just kill him later on.'* He thought. It took what felt like a year for Eros to step back letting Apollo live.

The day goes by as Apollo sees himself limping deeper into Beast territory. No choice of his own, but he knew this was their best chance to live. Alone away from his meddling family.

Alexander

With a bed of polar-white snow tucked into the ground, the sight of Ava running every morning always fascinated Alex. He sat there watching as the days go by, watching as the people he once called rivals get stronger by the day. He had been begging for something, anything to happen. Since taming the beast, he had been cooped up in a grey world, filled with royalty and the rich.

"Alexander. Could you tell the class the Currency distribution system of The United Kingdoms of Pangea?"

Alex groaned, staring at the ceiling, uninterested. "It's printed by the treasury, distributed into each bank, and monitored by the district Chancellor, as it goes into circulation."

"Um...Perfect as usual Alexander" Master Tassos responds with a bitter taste in his mouth. After glancing at the clock, a hundred times over, he was finally released from his prison. One of the students sniggered as he walked past. He knew why. For one he had come into the statesmen class late and became the best student seemingly without trying. Most there hated him but knew not to fight as chances where he would win.

"Don't forget to have a lot of rest tonight," Master Tassos shouted. "Tomorrow, I will be teaching you Will control, so you need a lot of energy! to even learn it."

Alex travelled back to the domes, alone. He had found himself to be walking alone more often since the transfer. But he did not mind as he could take his time stopping by his horse Agtaris to ride it for hours on end. A fitting name he thought as he went through hell just to touch him. His mind travelled to home, wondering how his family was doing or if they had received his letters. At this time school would be starting, leaving her mother alone for most of the day. He wondered if she could handle the fields again or did he make her lazy. He wondered if Eros in all his short temper could handle another year learning about Pangea's greatness. He wondered about Fanisse, who she was asking her never-ending questions too. Alex feeling choked by these emotions quickly pinched his leg, painting on a smile as he jumped off Agtaris for the last time that night.

With the sun rising, the day went as usual for these cadets. Ava was running around trying to set her own record. AL'lioe was matching Basil in power. Kal Orrin and Kal Magus were taking turns trying to chat with the local girls. Amadeus was practising his bow with Icarus sat by him reading. Adonis was swinging his sword bragging about his skill to the guards. As usual, Alex Strood in late, unbothered.

He had heard this lesson would be the hardest he would face, as just a man he already stood at a disadvantage. The beginning was simple knowledge, common among the statesmen in training. The lesson dragged until one of the students frustrated shouted. "This is useless, when do we get to it!"

"You are not ready," quickly replied Tassos. "If you understood what I told you. You may have the decency to listen to what's between your skull about the dangers of trying to access Will without proper guidance."

"I'm already strong enough, I don't need guidance to let out some air." stupidly the student argued. Tassos, tired of his bravado frowned welcoming him to the front of the class to test his strength. "Ok boy, first focus on your core, find the fire that brews inside and release it from its cage as quick as you can. But be careful of it even the lightest wrong and it'll explode inside you, at best injuring you for a few weeks at worst instantly kill-ing you in seconds."

Alex's eyes rose, having a lesson finally grab his attention for the first time. The student unfazed smiled high fiving those near certain of his talents. Then as he concentrated, he quickly opened his eye releasing explosive energy, sending the teacher's hair flapping in the wind.

"Good," the teacher said with a sly smile on his face." Now when you wake up from this, I hope you can still move." He adds grasping the shoulder of the student, as he melted to the ground.

"He's one of the lucky ones, he's still alive, he will be able to train again. That's if his luck continues that is."

he points almost with pride. "Now, listen if you do not want to be a pile of mess on the floor or worse in the ground, do not re-lease to quickly or hold too long, find the boiling point and let it out then." As students rose to practice, the number of them quickly plummeted, few vomited an ocean of blood dying on the spot, some passed out, and others managed to barely grasp the power. Until Alex who took his time getting to his teacher, having a nervous feeling dragging his feet to the ground.

"Your turn Alexander," Tassos said grinding his teeth.

The day had begun to Dissolve itself bringing dusk along, with the lesson almost over, Alex still stood there with his eyes shut, desperately searching for his core.

"Enough boy," Tassos said with a joyful tone. "I see its true, not all men are born equal under her eyes. Some simply have not been blessed with her Will."

His ramble continued as he took joy in the small revenge of belittling Alex as much as he could. In a momentary lapse of judgement, Tassos reached out to Alex with all his confidence. A snap heard around Vassilles; Tassos immediately dropped to his knees screaming on top of his lungs.

"He broke my fucking wrist!" He shouted cowering in a mountain of pain. Then he felt it. The will of a man beloved by the goddess, warm and calming it hugged him like a blanket and kept him at peace, rocking him to sleep, as he passed out with a simple smile on his face. The next morning bandaged, with a trickle of sweat constant on his forehead, Tassos, rushed into the dean's office yelling and screaming.

"I refuse to teach him, he's rude and far too arrogant."

Dean Urion Vitallis chimed in this a joyful glint in his eye.

"Master Tassos, it's been a while, how are you?"

"Elder, the bastard brought in by Damien, broke my wrist!" shouts Tassos adamant about getting rid of Alexander. Urion lifted himself, balancing on a wooden stick as he walked closer to the teacher smiling, "Let me see," he said rubbing the teacher's hand.

He stared at it with great intent until he wet his lips frowning. "I think it's broken..."

"Yes. Yes, it is Elder Urion."

"Then you should rest and let it heal. If your nature it, it will become stronger the next time around."

He took a step back reaching for a cup of water, struggling to sip every last drop of it. He then sat back down still smiling, radiating an aura, found in a hot summer's day as a cool breeze brushes past you.

"The boy who did this, how was his Will?" Urion asked with a glint in his eye. "I mean when they found you, you looked happy."

Tassos groaned adding more veins to his failing hairline. "I don't know, at first it felt destructive, almost corrupt, but then it felt warm almost naturing."

Urion, happily stroked through the grey of his beard, smiling through what's left of his teeth. "Bring him here then. I wish to introduce myself."

"Come in you little monster!" Tassos shouted. Opening the door letting a sombre Alex in as he refused to look away from the ground.

"Young man, what's your name?" Urion asked.

"Alexander" he quickly replied with a soft tone.

"Edward? a southern name, how nice."

Alex smirked and shook his head. "No. It's Alexander sir."

"I'm sorry, you have to speak up. One's hearing at their sixties is just not what it used to be." He said digging through his ear.

"You are ninety, Elder!" Shouts Tassos frustrated.

"That old?" He asked surprised. "Maybe I should retire. What would a fossil like me be able to teach the youth anyway?"

Alex bowed. "You are very wise Elder; your wisdom is still needed."

Urion sat back baffled by these words, he looked around then gazed at Alex with a curious look. "Why do you think I'm wise? I'm sure we have never met each other. Yes, I don't know you. So why?"

"Because you are Urion Vitallis, one of the greatest minds in this world."

"And you are Alexander, a bastard who refuses to stop causing trouble. I can read that anywhere. But I have never met you. So, I don't know you. Master Tassos leave us." He says as he reaches for a board, with his joints creaking and his wrinkles stretching he pulls it out. Chess a game, Alex had never played but would always observe. "Would you like to learn?" Urion politely asked.

Alex quickly replied, "Is this not a waste of time?"

"Maybe. but when you get to my age you would have seen far too much pain. But grew wise enough to seek anything joyful. this brings me joy." Hours went by as Alex slowly learned the game, each time thinking he mastered it only to lose once again to Urion. Until finally in the cold night, Urion asked, "Why do you sacrifice the pawns so much?"

"Because they are weak, I use them to get my queen or Knight in position."

"Has that won you the game?"

"Not yet."

"Then learn their value. they may be a use to you."

A few games pass and as twilight is replaced by dawn the bright of the sunshine, blinds Alex for a second and as he focuses, he sees for the first time since they started playing an opportunity to win a smile break from his face, as tiredness and frustration fades, "Checkmate!" he shouts to the surprised look from the old man.

"I see, now I understand you better young Alex. Come back in a few days. We can play again if you, wish," he says as he releases a radiant smile, quickly followed by a small yawn as he gets up waving him goodbye. After some time, Alex had stopped going to class, preferring to converse and play chess with Urion. This continued till the small council's Ball.

As the night of the small council's ball began, the cadets nervous stood suits pressed with snow in their hair but pride emulating from them. Damien walked in front of them seeing every one of the cadets he brought with him with a subtle sense of pride.

"Sir!" shouts Alex. "Why is Ava not in a dress, she looks like a man right now and it's confusing me!" to the frustration of Ava as she stares at him, cursing him under her tongue.

"Attention!" Damien commands. "When we go to the hall, you will stay within the site of me. You will converse with the attendees. You will enjoy yourselves."

The march was simple, with Damien taking lead and the Cadets marching in rows of four, synchronised, perfect. When they arrived feet away from the entrance, they saw the visitors as they poured through the gates into the grand hall, doused in gold and silver shimmering off the moonlight. Everyone wore the most expensive silks, be it in sparkling dresses or crisp suits. The snow was light enough to add to the beauty. Everyone entered to wine, music and food but for those who stood above the rest, a loud greeting was announced on top of the stairway before they walked down.

Alex stood at the bottom watching as each major house that could attend be announced, each name bored him by the second. Convinced no one of power would arrive he started to let his eyes wander seeing what he expected, people who clearly hated each other smiling and conversing saving the stories for when they got back home. Nothing was natural, from the way they ate to the way they laughed, this however amused Alex as he continued to gaze until the announcer, confidently roared names that grabbed even his attention.

"Ladies and gentlemen please welcome, Lady Octavia 'The Kind' and 'The Iron Troll' Sergeant Major Titus Osemious Dragfier."

As they slowly walked down with large strides, letting everyone bask in their presence. When they reached the floor, eyes shifted all over as people start to quietly talk amongst themselves. But it was obvious how they were feeling towards the couple, as their teeth started to file down with their constant grinding.

A Nobel from the north approaches them eying them up and down. Before snorting at them. "You, the youngest of the Dragfiers use their name as if you achieved anything. Thinking you are above us."

"I do pity people who believe they have power," Titus said, in his brooding voice before lifting his finger to the heavens. Then in the same motion pointed it down Dropping the Nobel to his knees. Then quickly waves him off releasing him from his bond. Silencing the room.

Titus stood with a confident look. "Do not misunderstand me. I am better than you. All of you. You can try to prove your worth but don't bother. Even at my deathbed, you wouldn't be able to leave a scratch on me. How do I know all of this as fact?

My name, my clothes, my woman, my glowing hair, my rank, my control of the earth, your pathetic wills. You are garbage beneath my feet. Now I will let you bask at me as it's the closest you will ever get to glory."

"My son would have something to say about that!" shouts King Lieto Anemoi. "However, I'm sure he would be more than happy to challenge you for that spot at the top."

Alex among others looked frozen in time. His brain stuttering for a moment, the world around him going on pause as their reality catches up to them.

"Ladies and gentlemen, please welcome King of Cicano and the thirteen branches, Lieto Anemoi the third, and his wife 'the Archangel' Queen Sefora Di Anemoi."

All stood stunned; however, Alex's trance quickly broke as he saw Damien, the man he called master bending the Knee with conviction. Chaos was growing in the ball, everyone rushing forward to introduce themselves, to the Anemoi family and the Dragfiers. Kings of nations, Lords of houses all acted like children wishing for attention from these two great houses.

They entertained the audience for a short moment, but after Sefora walked past them with the grace of a swan, she looked moulded into her dress, as she approached Damien, who was still like a statue with his head down and knee to the ground.

"My Queen," He softly said. "Welcome to the Vassille isles. I hope the journey was easy."

"I vomited a few times, but it was ok."

Damien immediately looked at her with such a troubled stare. "Are you ill my queen? Alexander, fetch the queen a drink."

"Enough," She sang. "Alexander, don't fetch me anything. And you stand you are an Anemoi, but more importantly my nephew. So enough with the Queen speech."

She then quickly folded his arm around her own walking off with him talking about life. Alex still stunned, could hardly get words out. "Are you trying to catch a fly?" Ava asked as she approached looking at Alex as if he were a deer in the woods. Wanting to save face he suddenly brushed the imaginary dust off his jacket painting his signature smile on as he rolled his shoulders back down.

"She looks so much like my mother, one wouldn't blame me if I said she was her twin," Alex said still glancing at Sefora, admiring her beauty, feeling a sense of belonging and comfort.

"She's not," Ava said with a stern tone.

The thought of Alex being homesick troubled her. As it made her think of her home. Joyfully Alex added, "I mean she's perfect."

"I know what you mean," She agreed, "But if you need to talk about home come to talk to me. Sitting alone thinking about them constantly only makes time slow down."

"Her eyes, Her muscles, everything except those eyebrows." He added focusing on her more, "So bushy and erratic, I wonder if she controls them to do that."

"She doesn't, it's like they have a life of their own." A strange voice echoed. Snapping Alex's neck to the strange man. They were a few moments in Alexander's life when he felt fear. The time when he broke his mother's vase and she found out, the first day of camp, the day he had lost his siblings. But this was different, it was like his Adrenaline was trying to escape. His natural instincts screaming for him to run. Fast. Even at that moment, the thought of praying was as an option as he gazed on a man, scared not off his Will but the absence of it. It was unnatural.

Here stood a man, with a button-down flowery shirt, some beads on his neck, with some muscle and rugged hair, nothing special, but the only creature since the day of his birth he felt nothing from. The sweat from his brow starts to drip as his eyes seem close to exploding "What you doing?" Ava cautiously asked. Realising he was the only feeling this anomaly, he quickly cleared his throat, grabbing a cup of water close by, and Ava still confused approached the man crouched down.

From a simple look, she did not understand Alex's reaction, she upon scanning the man thought it was a homeless man who had found some nice silk and managed to sneak into this ball. "Ceaser, Kals, escort this man through the back," she quickly ordered.

"I see," The man spook. "Did I do something wrong young miss?"

"Sorry, sir but this is a private event. You need an invitation to be here." she quickly answered.

"I see. Why?"

"Because there are important people attending tonight." Bewildered the man scratched his head. "I think I'm important, at least to my dog. He's always jumping to me when he sees me."

Ava getting more annoyed grit her teeth. "I'm sorry sir but you have to leave. Please do not make this more difficult."

Calmly the man walked through the back, hunched over, whistling a soft tune. Before leaving his small beady eyes flicked to Alex and with a crooked smile waved before he disappeared from the venue.

"Your beads are far too loud, I tell you that all the time boy." Master Urion said as he started to make a cup of tea.

"Sorry master, but my cousin gave them to me. I can't throw them away." The man responded as he came out of the shadows.

"You look a mess," Urion groaned. "People would start to think you are homeless."

The man flustered quickly pointed to the tea marvelling at its texture. "Can I have some?" He asked.

"No."

"Fine if not for tea, then why have you dragged me all the way here Master?"

"Can I not miss an old friend?" he said as he began to take sips of his tea, blowing on it every once in a while, and on completion he spoke. "Have you met him yet. My new student Alexander."

"I think so. The look he gave though, left an interesting impression."

"He probably was confused or scared."

"Why?"

With a smile, only an old man could produce. "He couldn't sense your Will at all."

Concerned the man started to twirl his beads. "Only spawns of witches can do that though."

Urion gazed at him. "Not very smart are you. He is the son of a witch. His Will is powerful, to say the least. Thank god, goddess, G'al or whatever that he doesn't have an element."

"A witch's son... It's late and a party I'll let someone else have the glory of getting him." The man says as he jumps on a chair rocking tucking his legs in, rubbing the snow from his toes. "So, Master, want a game?"

Later in the evening, key members disappear from the hall unnoticed, as they sat in the back, smoking and drinking in small chatter.

"Fucking hell," Titus swore. "All this because of some shaved monkeys throwing their shit at us?! This Sigil means we are the most powerful empire. Why worry about The Animals or whatever?"

"Beasts... the Thousand Beasts," Damien softly replied. "Firstly, thank you for attending. Secondly, this is above them, this is about building strength for our beloved world. But you are right Titus, this is also about the beasts. No, about all the rampant clans plaguing the West from small to large."

"Clans are all over the world, they're insects which we seem to not be able to get rid of." quickly replied Sefora.

"Then my lovely wife, why don't they crawl all over our lands," Lieto added sipping on a glass of rare spirit. "The answer is simple, military police, for years I have been pushing this idea on the Grand meetings but now I realise, it's too grand for the world, so let's start with the west."

"You fail to mention how they get rid of some undesirable political faces as well oh great leader." Titus roared.

Damien needed only a glance. "I understand Titus, but with all due respect your family are a part of the Grand military and have no idea of the struggles in the Supreme Court system."

"Good luck putting laws outside our empire."

"We are not an Empire Titus; we have no Emperor." Sefora chimed in.

"Bounties," Damien told Titus. "Like in the old days, we put bounties on people, however, this time all would be welcome to collect not just the military police."

Titus groaned. "Ok. Then tell me where do we get this money if they capture them dead or alive."

Damien, formed a glint of joy in his eye as he sat down, playing with his cup of wine. "We will be fine with the smaller bounties, but for larger bounties, increase trade with the four great empires or the smaller nations that surround us. But I understand, that could take years, so in the meantime, I suggest entertainment for the masses, one we could charge and monitor."

Titus growing tired of the tedious conversation, took a long swallow of his wine, dropping the cup as he stood, and started to walk away. "Good luck, but right now I care more about gifting someone with my sperm than this theatre idea of yours. Now, where is my wife?!"

Logan

With the news of a clash between the Beasts and the Vassille armies spreading, People from Nero continued, as usual, praying to the goddess and praising their young men as they marched out to join the war efforts. In Pocasis a country that prides itself with slaves and trade. Could taste the gold from military upkeeps in Nero and their own houses. They could feel a renaissance approaching them.

However, in Zen a Country, constantly moving, with buildings being made, people screaming, tournaments and festivals constant, the part that determined the character of the Country. Now silent, with empty fields in the outskirts, to footsteps echoing throughout the cities. Nonetheless, the Lions' castle roared throughout the days and nights as Philip's parties started to grow in legend among the houses' Nobles. It was one of those yet again, promised to be special, the music was foreign but entrancing and the food bottomless.

A noble, with eyes already glazed from drinking too much, spoke up loud enough for the room to hear. "The problem is, they complain far too much. We are at war; sacrifices must be made. Am I wrong my brothers and sisters?"

"No!" shouts one quickly silenced by another.

"I completely agree but," He stopped lowering his voice.

"Never mind the prince has arrived with our future queen."

"That Mary, her beauty is almost unfair. I am jealous of Pier in that front." Enzo a Noble of house Couture chimed in with conviction, as Philip entered the room with his arms interlocked with the next Queen of Zen. He quickly tapped a shoulder of one of the guards before continuing forcing him to introduce them.

"Every time with this guy," whispered Lady Camille as she sipped on some fine wine.

The guard stood forward and with a loud voice begrudgingly introduced the new guests. "Lords and Ladies of the great houses that make up our powerful Kingdom please welcome our host for tonight, Prince Phillip St.Louis, third eldest of the Lions and Future Princess Mary Du Charrio of the great house Charrio." With eyes still on him and the music dimmed to almost silence the prince quickly jumped on one of the tables stretching his new suite. He stood with his arms wide open blinding some with his glimmering gold.

"My friends, welcome, tonight I thought because of the continuous success of my brothers in the front lines and our next Queen finally wanting to attend that I would provide you all with the best money could buy. With great help from our new trade partners please enjoy the food and wines that only I one of the Lions could offer."

After the speech, he quickly jumped off slicking his hair back as he approached women standing next to one of the Gungadads. "I expected your father, I'm sorry for not introducing you. But I see you were having fun anyway," Phillip said as he pointed to the women swarming around Archie. Though it was not surprising as his perfect skin could attract anyone to him.

"It's fine," Archie responded calmly. "I assure you, all our family including me care about is the money, not the fame."

"I see..."

Grown tired of the conversation, the prince took his leave conversing with as many powerful lords as he can. At the twilight of the night, he went to grab another cup of wine. As Phillip went to sip the cup of wine a hand quickly pulled him to the side.

"My prince I have agent news," said Obeh panting as he held his chest. "A letter from the district chancellor has arrived."

"Continue..."

"They have made a request for us to take up arms."

Still calm, Philip took another sip. "How did my father respond?"

Obeh scratched his neck flicking his eyes. "I have not told him, my prince. I fear if he knew his health would plummet further."

"Say what you will. Footman. Even though my father has grown closer to you since the departure of my brothers, you are not an advisor or someone who has the power to make such decisions. I am. I am the prince of this realm and as a Lion, I am insulted that you think of my father so weak." He groaned. Fearful Obeh quickly apologised. "But he is ill."

"But he is the King," Phillip whispered with a stern tone. "This is just part of his duty, a burden of power."

Obeh nodded as he escorted Phillip through the halls to an office, at the edge of the castle near the help's quoters, and as Phillip turned the rusty doorknob, he saw his father sitting in a dimly lit room reading old newspapers from the Country.

"Look at my people suffering, Deaths, starvation. How long? How long till Zen goes back to its greatness?" He asked with his eyes fixed on the newspaper. The King's eyes met with Phillips, both sunken for vastly different reasons.

"I'm sorry to disturb you father," He winced. "A letter came today."

"From?" King Christiano said softly.

"Pangea."

"Then read it, boy!" The king snapped. Though loud this did not surprise Phillip as he could clearly see the man was scared.

"It's mostly gibberish but, there are some parts that are very disturbing. Firstly, since the first battle between the armies of

Vassille and The Beasts was lost. Little casualties, though they have quickly woken up to the strength of The Beasts my lord."

"Let me guess," Obeh quickly chimed in from the background. "They requested our help."

Phillip stood confused, but before he could respond to Obeh's strange statement Christiano quickly interrupted.

"Requested," The King laughed. "As if we have a choice, they hold the trade road we have to assist them now."

It did not take a witch to predict the next words that came out of the king as Obeh silently sighed before the King could speak next. Christiano sniffled. "Force the people, they have to fight for their home, their King!"

Phillip frowned as it was too much for him to hear. "Why force father? we just need to give them a good enough reason for them to join."

"Yes, my prince, maybe showing them of the consequences of losing would be," Obeh said quickly interrupted by the king as his eyes grew brighter. He reached out to Phillip's shoulders.

"You are right both of you, first we will tell them what will happen if we don't help and much worse if the Beasts or the slavers won."

He then quickly turned his head coughing. "Obeh send word to recruiters, telling them those who joined the war efforts will be exempt from all taxes. Forever. Their families will be granted food for all time served. And after the war, they will be granted land."

This did not sit well with Obeh and Phillip as they could feel a disaster looming before them, they quickly argued trying to convince the king. But after a short while, a slap to the table silenced the room, "I am the King!" Christiano added. His face was red, as he struggled to breath. He then pointed his thinning finger sending the parties out of his small office.

As they walked out Phillip quickly leaned over to Obeh and with a stern tone asked him why he pretended not to know the contents in the letter.

"Because as you said I am a footman my lord," Obeh calmly replied as he put his hands to his back. "I am not a smart man. However, opening a letter directed to Royalty can never be seen as good."

Phillip still feeling the effects of the wine nodded, choosing not to carry this conversation further. "My brother, the man hoe Andrew, where is he hiding, this matter if for all the Lions to know."

"Lord Andrew is at one of the brothels in the inner-city sire."

"Brothel?" Phillip asked with a confused look plastered on his face. For he knew they were laws prohibiting such places and works inside the Zen kingdom. "I am not your friend," he said. "Your jokes do not make me laugh footman."

"It is no joke sir," Obeh said.

Phillip looking at Obeh as they quickly approached the party stopped. " Get me my armour, the King's guard. We will shut it down tonight!" He commands.

"What should I tell the king about this business?" Obeh asked moving away from the prince.

"The king does not need to know, he has enough on his plate." The hard frost was finally settling on the border between Zen and Nero, finished was the constant storms of snow and Pier could finally hear the emptiness of the fields.

"Did you hear," He asked warming his hands with his breath. "Vassille's armies have arrived..."

"I know" Logan quickly replied hiding in the warmth of his blanket. He stood up taking heavy steps forward, he tapped his boots together getting rid of the snow that laid on them. A frail smile came on his face. "At least after the war, you have a woman to return to."

"At least when we get back you can choose your wife," Pier quickly replied laughing. They gazed upon their men tired from constant battle, cold and unmotivated to continue. They did not blame them though, for days they would sit and wait and hold off waves of solders but after they would not feel any sense of relief or victory, just numbness as they carried those who did not survive to unmarked graves and wait alongside them for another attack.

Logan's squire would tend to his blisters and wounds at the end of every battle and Pier would disappear to his men sharing sacks of ale as he tried to raise their morale. Ezekiel, unlike the rest, had found interest in a particular and on this day holding himself for warmth walked towards a small group chatting amongst themselves. "I never thought it would be like this. War I mean"

Huffing and puffing one of the larger men chimed in. "First time? well with the princes too scared to move I suggest you get used to this."

Ezekiel shook from a gust of wind. "You are Gaston, right?" Amused Gaston smiled as he sharpened his blade with loose rock. "Yes. But how does such a frail man know of me, you are not a solder so I would have never seen you in battle."

"I hear stories, the unsung hero, Gaston the farmer."

"Well, I fight, eat, fuck. We are soldiers little man. I and my men have only each other and I will do anything to protect them. Even fight like the wild men from those stories."

Ezekiel smiled as he saw Logan take heavy steps towards him with a bewildered look on his face.

"Men, back information," Logan said.

His face had grown purple from the cold and was heading to a nearby tent to warm himself better. "Footman, what where you talking about?"

"I was praising them, my lord," Ezekiel said before quickly pointing at Gaston. "That one especially, I hear from the soldiers he is something well special."

Logan laughed, almost uncontrollably and upon wiping his eyes he smiled. "Special you say, tell me, footman, what would you know?" he asked. "All you do is stay with the women in the back and spread rummers. Even the craven square of mine is better than you, at least when he cries and shits himself it's at the frontlines alongside me. In battle."

Ezekiel looked at him for a moment before looking at the outskirts of the field, a once smooth land, had fire still burning, smoke filling the sky. For a moment, his face lit up. He looked back at his lord who was now starting to show battle scars prideful as ever still talking as if he were brave.

"Sometimes, not many but sometimes I dream about it," he said. "Fighting alongside you my lord, a hero whose name echoes throughout Zen and beyond. But what would a famous Prince need a frail footman like me for?"

This stunned Logan immediately planting a smile on his face he quickly took him under his wing bragging about stories of battle and in the end as night broke, he told Ezekiel that he would be fighting in the next battle. Ezekiel shook his head. "It'll be an honour, my Prince."

"Honour, you say that now but after maybe you and the women could have better stories to tell." Logan roared in laughter.

As the chatter died down, thinking it was time for sleep the alarm went. With boulders quickly crashed into the Lions. The smell of burning flesh quickly drenched Pier's nose as he started to shout, "Cavalry!" desperately. The sound of horses charging gave him hope as he quickly signalled his brother to flank once again. Without armour and the constant of battle clung onto him, his sanity was on the verge of demise.

Ezekiel however quickly moved forward meeting with Logan's squire, grabbing him by the collar. "Listen, young man, this is an ambush, pick up a weapon and be ready for the ground to move."

Although his prediction was correct it was far too late as Enemy soldiers, covered in the snow started to run towards the Lions, convinced of victory. Each of the Lions stood and fought none more viciously than Pier and Gaston as they swung wildly at anything that did not resemble and ally. The battle continued for hours, Ezekiel dragging the young squire who was blinded by tears out of the ways of the enemy. Logan, frozen in time, being defended by his men as he tried to crawl back to the reality, he was now in. Pier and Gaston at each end of the battlefield commanding those closest and fighting to the end and the end did come.

As the sun peaked through the clouds the enemy had stopped attacking. Again, a collective sigh of relief spread throughout as the Lions once again stood tall, half in numbers, toes falling from frost, minds being broken by the constant attacks and leaders unsure what to do next.

"My lord," said a Knight. "The battle is over."

Breaking his trance almost immediately, Pier dragged himself back to the tents hunched and in a rage past Ezekiel and the square. Ezekiel looked frustrated; the night of crying was too much for him to handle. "Are you even afraid of your own shadow?!" he asked. "Tell me, boy, I simply don't understand why you would become a square or why The Prince would let you be his squire. If you are so afraid of everything and build like a chicken, why are you here?"

The squire dropped to his knees his face caving in as he began to once again cry, dripping snort as he sobbed. The tears seemed to never end as he started telling his story. "My parents thought I was too feeble and didn't know what to do so they sold me on the slave market. But the slave trader thought I was so pathetic he gave me back. then... then the prince decided to take me, but the kingdom was getting rid of slaves, so he started calling me squire I think he thinks my name is Square. I should be celebrating my thirteenth birthday not getting shot at in a battlefield!"

Ezekiel took a short breath, holding in his laughter. "So, what's your name?"

"Olivier..."

"Nice to meet you kid." He added before walking off to Gaston, tired from battle resting in the snow.

Elizabeth

"Folke's death hit us all Gulbrand," Halvor said. "But look at what we managed to accomplish in that time. We won against the strongest empire in the world. All of us all the Leaders of the Beasts All Thousand Beasts stand as one once again. So, tell me, King, why are we not partying? why are we sat here ten members talking to your back?"

"Tell me Halvor if it where you would you not want us to cry for you. Avenge you?" Gulbrand said softly.

Halvor started tapping the table looking around to sombre faces once again. "Fine. Send one hundred maybe two hundred men to find these mercenaries, but the bulk of the leaders have to stay here that includes the stags. The men out there will collapse quickly without the right leadership."

"The Vassille are led by an idiot," Gulbrand said. "You will hold ground, I will take half the armies south to take Zen, whilst they are weak."

He turned around stone-faced twirling his finger on the table. "The stags will go avenge their fallen brother. They can have two hundred men to help."

Gjurd tired of listening chimed in. "I'm sorry. But my brother this is insanity if we split our forces, and the enemy comes back stronger, then what?"

"I agree," Elizabeth said. "If they smell weakness, they might push into us harder."

"They killed my friend," Gulbrand said softly still looking down. Halvor grit his teeth shaking with frustration. "That is still no reason to give up we are at an advantage, we can avenge Folke after, and we can take Zen after."

"No. I will take Zen now; I don't want to be attacked from behind and lose more of my family."

Halvor boiling with rage shouted, "Will you listen!"

Immediately Gulbrand smacked the table breaking it immediately. "They killed my friend!" he shouted to the immediate silence of the room. "I trust in you Halvor, you will win if attacked I know it. But this way we win in every angle cutting the wars down in time. Avenging our brother."

So, the night before the armies separated for what Gulbrand hoped was the last time they washed in the same water and those going into battle painted their faces stripping themselves off the wool putting light clothes with chainmail on. A thick silence spoke throughout the night till the morning as tens of thousands of soldiers began their weeks-long march towards the south. Hundreds headed east to avenge their brother. The rest stood battle-ready, bitter as they watched Gulbrand once again leave them as they head into battle.

As Halvor stood watching many of his solders move to the south in droves, he grits his blade, his face turning red and the sound of teeth being ground could be head from far away.

"I wish I could have seen the great Gulbrand in battle, but I don't think that would happen for a while," Elizabeth said. "I hope after our war is short though, I hate the cold."

"No one likes being cold, woman. It just keeps you moving faster than the sun." Halvor said softly. "Why did you stay?"

Elizabeth nodded, pondering on the question. "Victory over Zen or victory over Pangea, I know where I would like to be in the history books."

The thought of fighting alongside an enemy till recently still did not sit well with Halvor. It troubled him to see not only the full trust Gulbrand had given her but the peaceful nature she had shown throughout their entire time together. Even saving his life. "Tell me Elizabeth, do you agree with fighting with their rules. We line up we speak then we kill each other I find it idiotic."

"I do not know your ways, but I know that is their ways of battle," Elizabeth told him. "They are the gentlemen of war, the Vassilles I mean. They only ever fight honourable battles."

"They cling to the past..." Halvor frowned.

"You cling to the past."

Halvor groaned still griping his sword as hard as he can. " They existed before because they were the true gods, not this Goddess they pray too. You know they do not even sacrifice to her. Why must we fight their war? why not just ambush them and kill them all?"

"Why indeed," Elizabeth quickly answered. " When I ruled the White Knights, I would always take advice from my second. For he was in charge just as much as I was. Don't you agree?"

"He is the king," Halvor reminded her.

"He sits on the thrown that is true. Does that mean he is your leader though? I see him more of a ruler if you ask me. Five years he left then when he returned, he fought like them, talked like them, has yet to make a single sacrifice."

Halvor pondered on this for a moment before speaking up.

"Gather the men we attack at the break of dawn; we fight our way from now."

"Are you sure?" Elizabeth asked with a slight smile on her face.

"Yes," Halvor roared. "We are not with their goddess our ways are better and I will show not only them but Gulbrand as well." At the crack of dawn, a sweet silence is broken with Halvor's voice. "Icei! Skwroga! Igvrodwla!" chants Halvor as he leads his mean towards Hermes's camps.

"Lancer by my right at all times, Drominic lead the cavalry on foot, wait on my signal to attack. Al'Gadrood by my left at all times. Move out!" Commands Elizabeth as she moves away from Halvor's forces heading to flank. They slowly get in position, but lower in numbers the fear could be felt all around. Drominic lifts his hand breathing slowly. Then the horn is heard throughout the battlefield waking Hermes from his daily prayer. "Heathens," he softly said before bowing his head and continuing to pray.

On the Other side, Drominic shouts, "Loose!" giving the command for arrows to fly into the camp of the prince. "Again" he commands before seeing a flaming arrow from his Queen signalling a stop. Both sides attack the camp, climbing the slop and charging into half prepared solders, "Dismount!" shouted Elizabeth as her steel clashed with her foe.

A battle unlike any other began both armies stuck on either end of the slop, Maximilian taking full command screaming, "Hold!"

in desperation. He grabbed a soldier running to the front lines half armoured, "Boy where is the prince!" Maximilian screamed. "He's in the tent!" the solder quickly replied before being let go. Maximilian did not investigate though, simply sighed knowing what the prince was doing instead of leading his armies. An arrow zipped past his face forcing him to concentrate on the situation. On the left was Halvor swinging his dual axes cutting through the Vassille men without issues on the right was Lancer and Al'Gadrood taking turns hitting through Max's men. In front was a volley of unending arrows wiping out forces without any trouble.

"All forces, turtle!" he shouts before turning around pointing at three solders still putting on their armour less panicked than the rest, "You three, take the horses you are in command. flank the east with as many cavalries as you can get!" He turned back around.

"Give your hearts to the Goddess do not let heathens take an inch from you. Turtle!" he shouted again placing all his solders in rows of shields.

Halvor and his allies continued to crash into their shields but getting no inch forward. "This is giving them too much time to establish," he said. He then signalled a foreign sign.

"Far too soon to use this but I have no choice," he said softly. "All Berserkers to the front."

A command all those near loved to witness as they started banging the weapons together smiling cheek to cheek as they saw hundreds move to the font most being 'The Thousand Beasts'. "Signal the woman," He commands as he watches his strongest join him in the front lines. The push-in pinning the Vassilles in spot unable to help their allies as their screams rise. Max looks on as his men get tossed onto the air, "Open!" he commands with a sombre tone.

A man, a monster shook him to his core as he stared down a beast drowning in muscles with blood tattooed onto him. "Heathen," he said. "It's true what they say about you people, playing with blood magic."

He points his sword at Halvor challenging him to a duel and Halvor a man moulded by the old gods in his blind form moves forward for an attack. The fight is short and sweet, as the blood hard as steel immediately breaks Max's sword forcing him to jump back quickly going on the defence.

He quickly learns of the extent of this monster's power as a droplet of blood whizzes through him and as the sharp pain builds past his adrenalin he drops to his knee; he could feel it.

His hands trembled and eyes watered, with sweat trickling down his lips as he mumbled, "Surt Ignis Volos." As he gazed at the white abyss of this monster's eyes barely visible from the blanked of blood.

Then an explosion erupts giving Max a moment to look around, seeing his men behind him being pushed in by Elizabeth, the ones to his side drowning in arrows, and the ones in front being dragged to hell itself. "Retreat!" he shouts immediately strengthening his body with his will running towards the nearest steed barely avoiding the projectiles from Halvor.

Halvor desperate to eliminate the general screams for someone to catch him. Summoning Lancer whose speed is shown to be greater than Halvor runs past with a spear getting as close as possible before launching it grazing Maximilian but making him lose his grip on a steed and dropping to the ground. Blind to his surroundings Maximilian quickly stood limping to his prince's tent a shock to the back of his right leg forces him to drop forward into the tent, but as he opens his eyes, he sees only the absence of his prince. Bringing him a great relieve as he laughs.

The battle ended; Maximilian sits in the middle with what remained of his men tied up waiting for what they think will be a slow death. Halvor sits in the corner with a piercing look as the holes in his skin are burned shut.

"Good job out there," he says to a close-by Elizabeth. "You are good with your words, go find out where the prince is running off too."

Elizabeth nods unfolding her arms walking close by to Maximilian, a barrel is pulled up for her so she could relax and with her legs crossed and her arms linked she laughs.

"Look around, you are famous," she said with a slight smirk on her face. "See I do not believe in the old gods, but from what I know a great fighter is respected despite being an enemy or not. You, my friend proved to be a great commander and you survived attacks from that monster."

Maximilian proceeded to spit on the ground in front of Elizabeth. "Fuck your praise you heathens. I fought with my Goddess by my side as we speak, she leads our prince to safety, and he will come back. With mountains of her soldiers standing as one because now we know, your numbers in the other camps pale in comparison. We know how you fight now."

"Really? how do we fight then great commander." Elizabeth curiously asked.

"Like heathens, true heathens, together in a pile like dogs, attacking non-stop," Max said. "And like dogs, with no strategy." Grabbing onto consciousness as much as he could with his head swinging back and forward. His armour had been stripped so he did not feel the heavy burden of it. However, the strain of battle had forced the old man to recognise he was far past his prime.

Panting he smiled, "I know you are her enemy, defeating you will put me in her paradise no matter the wrongs I have done in my past. Defeating that monster even becoming one to do so would give me more joy than you could imagine, young lady." Elizabeth finished with the questions had already concluded Hermies would return with the full might of the Vassilles, maybe their last effort attack on the Beasts.

"Become a monster to defeat a monster," She repeated softly. "I understand that Commander, so why not put it to the test. Lancer dear, duel this man."

The noise stopped around them as The Beasts watched on, the man who had fought them twice now given an opportunity to show his skills against the sword of the woman outside their world.

"Accept commander. If you win you and the rest of your band can leave," Halvor announced with a cold look in his eyes. A blade still covered in blood was thrown at Maximilian 's feet and as he was released from his bondage, he stood holding the blade with both hands ready to kill Lancer.

The circle begins to form, as the music from the swords bashing on shields rage louder by each second. Maximilian grabs a shield from one of the Beasts before taking wide strides closer to the centre of the circle gritting his teeth as he takes deep breaths. The circle opens letting Lancer in with a bash of steel, playing the music for their final battle.

"A child," Maximilian said with a puzzled look. "I see you stay true to your name nonetheless," he adds as he looks upon lancer picking a spear as his weapon of choice.

"Woman, you send a boy to fight?" mockingly asked Halvor. "I would feel insulted if someone did that to me."

Elizabeth chimed in "Ignore them, Lancer. Show them the strength of the White Knights."

as the sound of the beasts roared louder raging the battle to begin, Max lunched forward trying to quickly close the back, swinging his sword but barely missing his target. Lancer though young had far more agility able to jump back like a startled cat fanning his spear to predict the distance. He took a few steps back closer to the crowd drowning the noise out with deep breaths, hands from the crowd started pushing him to get into the fight but he refused standing there with the tip of his spear stretched out towards Maximilian.

Seeing the hesitation Maximilian again launches himself forward staying close to the ground but only met with the tip of Lancer's spear as it barely misses Maximilian 's skull. "Close," Maximilian mockingly says before trying to jump in again only stopped only by sharp pain from his legs dropping him to his knee. Lancer seeing this, grips his spear with both hands, lunging it forward but in desperation, Maximilian hits the ground lifting the snow covering his body as the tip of the spear barely flies through. Max then lifts his shield above his head stopping a thunderous hammer from the spear that cracks the shield. Then a second hit breaking it. On his knees sweating, bleeding with no shield and hardly any strength left Maximilian laughs stopping Lancer's next attack.

Max looks up at the man who will send him to the goddess "Your eyes are empty," Max says. "Tell me, boy, before you send me to my maker I must know. Why do you fight?" The words ring in lancer's ear as he goes for the final strike hesitating for a moment but long enough for Max to strike. Leaving a small cut to the side of Lancer before dropping his sword passing out on his knees.

"Enough," Halvor says softly. "There is no glory in defeating a half-dead man, lift him up he will be our slave maybe one day he will be able to buy his freedom back." With the duel finished those remaining nursed their wounds, with ale or bandages. The snow left red-stained as piles of bodies were thrown into un-marked graves burned to the Grimm sight of Commander Max-imilian, as his rage grew stronger.

Elizabeth sat in one of the tents at the very back, biting into the leg of a hog, as Halvor walked in with a calm demeanour to his strides. "You want some food?" Elizabeth asked, never breaking eye contact with the meat. Halvor though starved and tired did not care for the food at this moment. "I'm more interested in that Isslander you have around you," he said grunting as he sat down next to Elizabeth.

"Well, I suggest you lose interest that boy is mine, and I will not let you take him if that's your plan."

"Take him?" Halvor asked chuckling. "No better I wish to train him. Today you proved to be by my side but if he doesn't get the training, he needs he will continue being bested by an old man like the commander."

Elizabeth sighed still trying to bite into the leathery meat of the hog. She looked at the enthusiastic Halvor and with a smirk asked why. Why he would put himself out for us no matter the reason.

Halvor continued to grin. "Call it a man's intuition, having you as an ally would be better, I think, and what's best to show my resolve than helping your meek boy."

"Well go ask him, he's no slave after all."

Halvor smiled as he dragged himself up and out of the tent.

Eros

"Heathens," A Knight said coldly, "we grant them the honour of fighting like true men, and yet they make cowardly moves towards you, my prince. Trust me the next time we meet with them none will survive."

"Calm yourself Knight, unfortunately, our roads are cut, so we will head east and gather the rest of our armies to attack, and the boy I sent west will do the same," Hermies commanded through the slits of his helmet.

His eyes were red from the tears he shed for someone he deemed closer than his father. Maximilian who had watched

him grow from the frail twin to the next King of the Vassille islands. Twice now he had watched the men in his life who had
granted him the most opportunity being taken from him. First,
his grandfather King Platottle Vassellet beheaded by his twin
Apollo and now his teacher and friend Commander Maximilian
thought to be killed in battle by the Heathens.
He travelled for days through the thick fog of winter, building
up the rage and salivating in the idea of killing the Heathens.
over in the east, deep in the lands of the Beasts, Eros opened
his eyes the bright field of his home. Emulating in the sun his
heart calm and eyes full of life as he looked around at the
golden wheat and birds singing to the sun.
"Mom..." he said softly gazing at her in the distance as she
picked on the wheat throwing it in the barrel. His brother not
too far in the background draining the blood from what seemed
to be a deer. His sister energetic as always, chasing the dog
down with her unending smile.
"Maybe I should help," Eros said with a smile inching onto his
face as he started to walk through the field. After a while he felt
it, the more distance he took the further his family were, he
started to breathe faster as he ran towards his family. A gust of

wind blinded him for a second and as he opened his eyes, he saw an empty field, with the grey sky to match.

"Mother!" he shouts, "Alex!" he shouts, "Fanisse!" he shouts to no response but the sound of a drip. He looks down and sees blood pouring from his hands, "Why didn't you protect me brother?" asks a frail voice and as he looks up, he sees a small rotting corpse standing by him. He can feel a cold sweat dripping through his clothes when he bolts up in a shed, covered in sweat under the cold moonlight, gripping the frozen hey as he tries to gather his senses.

Eros had begun to get used to these nightmares, each day the same dream, slightly different to trick his mind and each day being forced to wake up in the middle of the night covered in sweat. He wrapped himself in an old blanket and took a stroll outside but as with every night maybe to forget, the band of mercenaries he had been with would drown themselves in ale, even Jon and Sarrah had begun to join in more often. Eros left the area opting to go further up a small hill to watch the sunrise, not knowing how long it would take but not caring either way.

"Bit early to be moving around don't you think? Eros," Apollo says calmly. As he sat on the snow trying to keep hold of his ale through his shackled hands.

"The sun is about to come up." Apollo takes a sip. "Where did Raijin go? I swear I ent seen him for a couple of days."

"He left."

"I see," Quickly responded Apollo, "smart move, I guess. Could you not sleep because of the noise as well? Forgive them, I would do the same if I were in their position. Aimlessly moving across the Beasts' lands with no direction. Scared of their response to Folke's death. I mean you can't even go back to Utopia because you know, the spy and the fact you want to kill me." He blows onto the tips of his fingers, seeing they were turning purple trying to warm them up. "Well, I think you will be fine in the end."

"How dare you talk to me like we are friends," Eros said coldly. "Remember you are only here till you find the spy, or I decide your life is no longer worth it. Raijin left for his own choices which do not matter to me all that matters is the spy you promised. That for so long you have yet to find. Maybe I should just kill you and move on with my life."

Apollo smiled as he grasped his cup harder, "Very scary," he said. Before turning his head towards Eros, seeing him for what it seemed to be the first time. He sees this small frame wrapped in a thin brown blanket, his head barely picking through the top. His hair covering most of his face. A face still filled with fat of a child, though thinning. Eyes sharp like a hunter, a predator. "Sometimes I forget how young you are," Apollo mutters under his breath as he turns his head to the rising sun seeing the clouds quickly follow behind.

"A storm is coming," he says. "I wonder what sort of man you will become. One who perishes in the storm, one who weathers the storm or one who becomes the storm." He stands limping back to his camp, "I would have loved to see the man you will become" he adds chuckling under his breath. "Come, lets fight then."

On the outskirts, Astrid leads the veterans of the White stags, with one mission to avenge their fallen brother. Frigg and Ingrid followed closely, wanting to give the young shield maiden in training, leadership in this mission, of all the people Astrid was closest to Folke, she had seen him as a father when hers passed. And had more determination than anyone else to get revenge. Though finding it hard to calm down under pressure her voice steel peaked with authority.

"Stop," she said, " fresh tracks they're not far from here." Impressed though not that surprised Frigg spoke up. "The huntress, showing her ways. Ingrid when we go into battle you stay by our young leader, I will fight from the back with arrows."

"Not like you to hide from battle Frigg," Ingrid added tucking her hands though her leather armour.

"I'm not, but it will be quicker for me to fight from the back I can help all those who are losing," Frigg quickly responded.

"Don't forget my sister, they defeated Folke, it is very unwise to underestimate such warriors."

Astrid started walking forward with more determination in her eyes. More to the North stood Hermies as he finally arrived at one of his camps, "Soldiers stand!" commands the Knight that had been by his side throughout the journey.

"Knight, you have done an excellent duty bringing me here, when we win, you shall become the King's guard. Tell me what is your name?" Hermies asked softly.

"Ezio Ducas sire."

"Ducas, a great family. I'm glad to have personally met you, Sir Ezio Ducas."

Overwhelmed Ezio took off his helmet showing his orange hair and smiling through his freckles endlessly. "Thank you Sire, you will not be disappointed for giving me Sirdome!"

Hermies glanced at Ezio for a moment, then stepped off his steed, missing his beautiful armour but doused in robes. He moved forward into the camp, watching each man step out as they saw the prince, though frail in size, commanding respect from simply how he moved. He stood as far in the middle as he can and as his men began to flock to him, he raised his hand silencing everyone.

"The heathens, they attacked the camp, killing thousands, including my friend Commander Maximilian. This camp is one of four, ten thousand men stand here I will take this camp and the next to the east. I will take the glory of the Goddess with me, her will guarantee us the heathens die. We will pray for their souls and hope when they reach the gates of her home, they repent. Come, my solders Lift your swords! grit your teeth! make our brother's deaths not in vain!"

Finished with his speech he took a moment to grab his breath as cheers from the soldiers drowned all other noises. Further to the east, though without sunlight most knew it was midday as Eros stood opposite Apollo, their battle built up for months on end it seemed but finally they were ready to end each other. Apollo stood with his old body chainmail and leather, balancing his sword on his shoulder. He smiled through his growing beard when he looked at the meek Eros, wearing nothing but shorts and a shirt in this blistering cold.

"Dual knives, like an assassin," Apollo says as he digs his foot into the snow.

"Can I teach you something Eros!" he shouts, "Bloodlust comes from the core if you wish to win more and more of these duels that is a must to learn for the future."

"Enough!" Eros responds before charging into Apollo.

Jon sitting in the background chimes into the event, "Finally we can stop dragging this old fool with us. Right Sarrah?" he asked to no response from Sarrah as she chugs her Ale and walks away refusing to see her pup in this state.

"Your environment is your best friend, use everything Eros!" shouts Apollo as he kicks the snow blocking Eros' vision. Eros slashes through it quickly realising Apollo had moved.

"Next, your biggest strength your trump card," Apollo adds as he takes a few steps back. Blocking a Knife whizzing to him.

"Use your trump card scarcely unless your life is on the line of course. Revealing it too soon makes your opponent know you and how you fight much faster."

"Finally, the breath is absolving Will, only for a short time but enough to make you closest to the Goddess." He adds before launching to Eros slashing at him but barely missing his head. Eros smiles as he backs away from Apollo.

"You tried the same move with Folke and the smaller one, listen to your own advice old man."

"Old he says..." Apollo responds letting out heavy breaths. Before moving forward to another attack, he stops, lifting his sword closer to his skull, blocking a rouge arrow.

"You missed, " Ingrid announced. "Maybe I should be the one shooting arrows." Frigg glanced at Astrid to command. Which she quickly did pointing her blade towards the band of Stags, screaming for a charge.

"Shields!" "Shields!" Sarrah screamed as she jumped out, standing in the front lines. The sky had changed, blowing cold winds into the area. The white floor had already begun to be tainted by the blood of the White Stags and the misfits. Axes and swords were crashing into each other, each man fighting for their own life with no direction. Finally, from the top of the hill, the shield maidens appeared, painted in white and black, piercing eyes with their youngest Astrid pacing back and forward with an axe to her hand itching for battle. Her rage burned her so hot she took the leather from her body, dropping it to the ground before marching forward followed by her maidens. Like a wave, they drowned all those before them. and as they crashed into the main forces of the misfits, Sarrah screamed, "Loose!" in desperation.

Sending arrows hissing through the air reaching some of their targets. "Shields up!" shouts Astrid refusing to lose eye contact with Eros who paced in the background grabbing his dagger. "Old man, lead our army, I will kill their leader." Eros softly said as he tried to hide in the crowd.

"You head him, I'm in charge again," Apollo said twirling his sword. "Get in a formation you fools, close together!" He watched as they quickly listened to him as they started backing from the crashing push of the maidens, they felt pushed to the edge, quickly being trapped by their enemy. Encircled before the enemy stopped their advance. Like a snake, Eros appeared behind Astrid ready to sink his fangs in only for her to jump forward barely dodging the attack. both Frigg and Ingrid went for the kill stopped by Astrid as she raised her hand.

Without a single word, Eros knew what was happening and immediately launched his body forward clashing with Astrid, keeping light on his feet and dancing with her. The battle waged on as Eros and Astrid seemed about even but the misfits being picked off one by one from rest of the White stags. In the end,

Sarrah called a surrender, dropping her weapon along with many others. A panting Eros still stood strong. The battle-hungry Apollo refusing to let his weapon go.

"Imagine a day actually came when the great Apollo couldn't fight these unskilled apes..." He said under his tongue barely being able to stand from his fresh wounds. At the twilight of their battle, Astrid looked calm still holding her axe strong.

"Astrid?" Asked Ingrid, "why are you playing with that boy?" she said. Surprising Eros, thinking he was on equal ground with this young shieldmaiden. Just as quickly as he thought so reality struck, as Astrid's first offensive move knocked him unconscious. Seeing this Apollo dropped his blade raising his hands in surrender. With the ambush successful those remaining alive were tied up and brought to the middle conscious or otherwise.

Apollo

Flakes melted as they touched Eros' face, light snow was falling. The winds had grown heavier, as he opened his eyes. He slowly sat up looking around as he saw many of his companions tied to each other sombre from defeat.

"Are you ok?" Sarrah asked quietly. Eros nodded, rubbing the back of his head which had formed a small bump. He paused as footsteps grew closer to him.

"I didn't want to tie you up. You are just a child after all."
Eros looked up with a smile pained to his lips. "We look about the same age little girl," he said.

"Yet you fight like a baby. Remember little boy I only entertained you not to embarrass you."

"The storm has arrived." Apollo interrupted in the background staring into the heavens.

"Can you hear it Eros!" he shouted, " The footsteps of fate coming to take you to your destiny!" He smiled as he lifted himself up grabbing many of the Stags' attention.

"Rokkr!" he screamed with a sharp twist of his tongue. Quickly greeted by bash to the head by one of the Stags. A laugh grew throughout until a piercing arrow dug through one of them. The fog started to grow Heavier as the Stags finally turned around to see a field of soldiers standing in the background lead by a man with long blond hair. The winds stronger, the snow thicker and the fog growing, Astrid looked upon Eros smiling being swallowed by the fog.

"Next time we meet. Be stronger, little boy. I want my revenge to be against the ones who killed Folke not whatever it is I'm looking at." Just as quickly as her words flowed from her mouth, she disappeared into the fog alongside her shield maidens.

Hermies with hundreds close to him arrived at the camp slashing into the fog but hitting no one. Finally, as fate would have it Hermies on the back of his steed looked down at his brother.

"Apollo," he calmly says.

"You've grown little brother," Apollo responds. "I would have never imagined you in the front lines, let alone here in the territories of Heathens."

Hermies gazed down on him. "You look like shit."

"It has been an interesting few months, well years now years could say."

"Sir Ezio gives the order, we camp here tonight, give them food, clothes and send my brother to my tent we have much to catch up on." Hermies insisted.

So, the night began, meat spiting in the fire, soldiers drinking with their new companions, everyone calm and enjoying themselves. All but the misfits as each one had a lingering thought, that their lives were still on the line. It was no surprise for a long time they took the prince of the Vassille islands banished or not such a crime would not be ignored by Madas. They all glanced at each other throughout the night with fear in their eyes.

Apollo, on the other hand, was ripping into the leg of a hog freshly cooked and still hot on his lips. He did not care about it, looking past the burning sensation that flowed through his body from this meal even to the point of almost chocking. But saving himself with large gulps of wine. Each time he would gulp he felt the sweet taste that he had missed so much to the point of his eyes watering up.

"Pride of Vassille everyone," Hermies mockingly mentioned.

"I don't care, the food is good."

"I'm only joking brother," Hermies said softly. "Tell me what are you doing down here? if you returned to the Vassilles I would have helped you out."

"Help me?" Apollo responded as he cleared his throat. "Last time we saw each other you wanted to kill me; you know for taking that man's head."

Unable to control his emotions Hermies painted a hateful look on his face.

"There it is!" Apollo quickly responded. "That's the look I'm used to. The look that keeps me comfortable. You all hate me without knowing why."

"Why?" Hermies quickly responded. "Why you killed our grandfather!?" the shout shocks the maids and guards as no one had ever heard this side of Hermies.

"Leave," he commanded as everyone started to step out of the tent leaving only him and his brother alone. Hermies struggled to get his words together tapping on the table, opening his mouth every now and then but not saying anything.

"He betrayed our people Hermies, I saved everyone..."

"Betrayed, he wanted to save us from the clutches of Pangea." Hermies quickly responded. "Look where we are, in the lands of heathens in the cold not of our doing but because they told us to move. You betrayed everyone."

Apollo roared, "I saved everyone!"

"You saved no one but put us in the same position as slaves. Now we are stuck, but not for long, despite father's feelings you are family and I want a warrior like you by my side when the time comes."

Apollo bit into the bone of his meat, snickering throughout.

"To fight against these heathens?" he asked.

"To fight for our people's freedom," Hermies quickly responded.

Apollo stopped, looking up to his brother who sat dripping in confidence. He looked back down with a sombre look. "Twenty years I have been vilified and hated by everyone. I have been stripped of my name, honour, title, my home, everything. I saved everyone and that idea keeps me waking up each morning. You want to throw that away, brother?"

"I want you to come back home as Apollo Vassellet, I have the majority of our armies on my side, the aristocrats and the politicians. It's not like before, it's not like when grandfather did it. Everyone wants out. So please be on the right side of history this time."

"Alba insula..." softly responds Apollo.

"What?"

"It was the last mission before I came home to defend against the chosen people. Promise me you will use conflict as a last resort." Apollo responded with an optimistic tone.

"Of course, brother." Quickly responded Hermies.

Apollo thought for a moment. Then quickly nodded to Hermies' proposal. "I will help you. Not for anything but as an ageing man I would like to see if my choice just that one choice was the correct one."

Hermies filled with joy chugged his cup of wine smiling endlessly towards his brother. "Now on to other matters, that ebony child with you. Father is looking for another woman. Are you able to part with her?"

"No," Apollo replied. "She is no slave; I can't make decisions for her."

"It has been a long time," Hermies stated as he gazed upon Apollo as if he was a stranger. Because the Apollo he knew never would have vouched for a low born. "We will discuss it after the war is finished," calmly added Hermies.

"Why?"

"You are a smart man, Apollo. It's to keep father happy". Apollo snapped gripping the bone of his hog harder. "Why do you try to please that man so much? for the crown?"

Hermies growing tired of this conversation gulped his drink before taking few steps towards the exit of his tent, "As quick as he made me next in line, we are many almost 20 who could fight for the throne, I would like to keep him by my side till his death. So yes, that's why I please our father in anyway."

"Please a man who killed our mother..." Apollo added with a sombre tone.

"You know very well what happened brother," Hermies roared, growing in anger. "What you wish to kill our father next?"

"Just making conversation"

Hermies took strides out his tent refusing to continue this conversation with Apollo any further. Eros had already begun helping to bury corpses, when Sarrah walked near him from the shadows.

"What are you doing?" Sarrah said drinking the creamy nettle soup.

"Same as you but in a different way." Eros quickly answered flipping a corpse over.

"His not in the camp…" Sarrah said as her face turned sour.

"His not a corpse…" Eros responded as he grit his teeth.

"Maybe he just ran… wouldn't y-"

"Stop being childish," Eros said as he stood gripping his fist tighter by the second. "It makes sense now doesn't it…"

"Eros calm down, I can feel your anger from here, we need to think this rationally. Maybe talk to him he might have just became sick of this and left like Raijin." Sarrah pleaded as she tried to paint a smile.

"No," quickly responded Eros as he slowly turned his head.

"Raijin left to become stronger. Jon ran. Think why was he so adamant about killing Apollo? Where was he in the fight against the stags?"

 Sarrah unable to answer, simply slumped over. "What now?" With his eyes burning red Eros smiled. "Kill him in the worst possible way."

"No!" Sarrah shouted as she snapped Eros back to reality. "You're a kid when this war is over you will live a normal fucking life! I'll take care of Jon, ok?" she desperately asked. And in response Eros turned his head as he walked away from Sarrah. Eros disappeared into the camp. Large as a city, brighter than the sun, with the most important in the middle of it all getting blind drunk with drums and lutes drowning out the sounds of night. But the star of it all was its food, tables laid with delicacies, everything you could think off and things you would never have imagined. stretched out as far as the eye could see. However, with all the food and entertainment, the main event appeared as the prince covered in silk robes, approached the middle grabbing everyone's attention.

"As we speak a small band of solders has been sent east to gather the remainder of our men, their due to return any day now and when they do, we will strike the heathens down with the fierce power of the Goddess. The power of the goddess even brought my brother and me back together for the first time in years. signalling, she is ready to forgive 'The luck of Vassille' Apollo Vassellet."

However as if he predicted, whispers started to drown out the prince's voice. Until he raised his pail frail hand and with only a few words changing the masses' minds. "We will win against the heathen, then we will free ourselves from Pangea!" He shouts to a roar from the crowd who begin to chant his name raising their swords in the air in celebration. Apollo however stood in the background saying nothing instead sipping his mead and staring with a blank face into the grey sky.

"It looks like this isn't the time for us to fade into twilight." He mutters under his breath before the festival continued and the fire lit in the Vassille people exploded through the camp.

Alexander

In the state of half organized clutter, several stacks of paperwork, pens in a tin, floor to ceiling bookshelves with the books leaning against one another in different directions. Between this mess was Chancellor Damien Anemoi as he stirred blankly into space having but one thought of a few days before running in his mind.

In the last days of winter, Damien sat in his office as Ser Cleon Nikkos a young Royal guard barely graduated, holding a black sealed letter firmly in his grasp.

"Well, boy, don't just stand there read it" Damien commanded not showing and interest in what the letter say to begin with.

"With failed peaceful measures, as per arrival of this letter Vice admiral Theon Odysseus alongside Rear Admiral Julius Horatia and Staff sergeant Tiberius Romulus will shortly arrive with the fleet 'Aurum Neptunum' and on arrival will gather the assistance of District Chancellor Damien Anemoi in executing the classified command 'Project White'. Glory to the Goddess." Upon finishing the letter Cleon's face was filled with confusion his mind shouting many questions for him to ask.

But before opening his mouth Damien muttered words of apology as the young Royal guard numbed, collapsing forward onto the shoulder of the Chancellor with his eyes blank and his jaw flopping. Damien stayed looking stern whilst holding a blade, as it dug deeper into the young Royal Guard's chest. As Cleon's life faded Damien stepped aside and let the young Guard fall to the ground then with a big sigh, he lit a match burning the letter sent to him.

"How can you keep doing this brother?" asks an echoing voice that surrounded the room.

"It's my role as Chancellor to bring peace to the world under the law" quickly replied a distort Damien as he watched the letter burn too ashes. Damien then wiped his hands clean before fixing his hair and outfit, calmly stepping out of his office, "Go home!" He loudly commanded to the guards standing outside who in confusion slowly followed orders.

Damien kept moving in a calm pace with his face frozen in time looking emotionless. On arrival too his destination he quickly bagged into the Dean playing chess with Alexander, bowing his head then quickly commanding Alexander to exit the room.

"We were having fun Damien, why interrupt?" quickly asked Urion as he stroked his beard.

"Project White."

"That's sad..." Dean Urion muttered under his breath. He reached out with his frail fingers picking up a pawn from his desk then slowly looked up at Damien. "What will you have me do?"

"Put forward the curriculum, Educating our students on Gevana. They will enter battle with them within the year, so they need to have the mental knowledge of the enemy." Damien quickly commands with a broken tone in his voice.

"Educated you say. Lie you mean?" Dean Urion responds as he sat back with disgust growing on his face. "Fine Chancellor as the world commands I a simple old man can only follow as best as I can."

The conversation finished, Damien bowed one last time before exiting the room, however as he grasps ono the door, Urion stops him asking one more question. "Project White... Before the grand meeting?"

"At the end of summer during the meeting the matter will be brought up and as per usual majority will vote to execute the command. We are placed closest to the Island, and we will be able to execute the order within an hour of the announcement."

"Four I've witnessed." Urion expressed. "Now a fifth in my short lifetime, is Pangea that scared?"

Damien quickly hung his head in shame as he exited the room and walking past Alexander in silence.

"We will continue our game another time Alex..." calmly says Urion pasting an empty smile on his face. Unbothered Alexander quickly shrugged his shoulders returning to the barracks and conversing with his everyone from the old camp.

Ava quickly greeted him dragging him from everyone but still feeling the daggers being launched on their backs.

"Calm down little lady," Alex said, "Rumours will start to spread if you don't let go of my arm soon."

Ava sighed. "I'm sure no one would place you and me together you idiot."

"Stranger things happen in this world."

"Not that strange!"

Alexander grinned looking back as the barracks started to fade from his eyes. "So why drag me all the way here?" he asked with a mischievous smile and his eyes hiding behind his curly blond locks.

Ava quickly let go. "That night during the ball, you saw that hobo and it seemed like you saw death itself. Since then, you haven't returned to us, and I saw you the other day running your face looked troubled."

Alex let out a crooked smile. "You know Will, right?"

"Obviously..."

"He didn't have any."

"If so, then we all saw a ghost," Ava sarcastically replied. "He was probably hiding it, maybe that's how he sneaked passed even the guards no one could detect it."

"All living things have will, some can hide it but not completely it's still shows their core if you're close enough, that thing we saw didn't even have a core." Alex replied as he dragged his hair from his eyes.

"That's impossible," Ava said, "I'm telling you to live that long in these lands as a homeless man is to learn how to mask it." She jumped onto a ledge watching the clouds as she threw her arms back. "Is that what's been stuck in your mind?"

"No, it's that damn question that keeps being asked in homeroom," Alex squatted as he joined Ava in cloud watching. "What my goal is."

"Helping your family, right?" Ava asked.

"Ya, I guess." Alex quickly replied.

"That's nice, all we learn about is history, you know the 'sordes' it's so annoying we already know they're abominations, why can't we learn about philosophy or whatever they teach you to ask that question so much" Ava rambled as a vein on her forehead started to show more clearly by the moment.

As the night continued so did their conversation. The next day in homeroom, Alex, Tired from the night before sat in the back as per usual, watching the world go by through the window again pondering this worthless question. Once again after the bell he dragged himself towards the Dean's office but is stopped by Tassos.

"Tomorrow you must attend the physical mock exam." He commanded before letting Alex carry on with his day. As per usual as he entered the room a cup of tea and a game of chess was set ready for him.

"Tomorrow is a big day." The Dean softly said.

Alex snorted at the notion, "Bold words, but beating up rich snobs will be fun I guess."

"One day someone will cut that tongue of yours out" Urion quickly replied.

"Maybe but I'll enjoy it whilst I still have it" Alexander responded.

"However, you will not be beating up rich snobs Tomorrow, young Alex."

"Why?"

Urion calmly finished his tea, with Alex opposite him showing to be visibly frustrated. Finally, tired of the tediousness he tightens his fist, and in a tone, he thinks is most calm speaks. "Why can't I join in with other classes? Why must I stay in this room day in day out whilst others enjoy their youth?! Why must I still be punished?"

Urion smiled putting his tea down and moving one pawn forward on the chessboard. "You see Young Alex, each peace has a place on this table, much like each person has a place in this world unlike you they were not intended to change this world. Remember young Alex education though with bitter roots, natured, its fruits can be sweeter than honey itself."

Confused Alex stayed silent gazing upon Urion as if he were insane. "Bold words to think a humble solder can change the world." Alex says as he moves his knight forward.

"Humble he says," as Urion moves another pawn the far end of the table. "Balance. Will this humble solder escort this old man out for a walk?"

"What about the game?"

"Don't worry, the pieces tend not to move without command." Urion replied with a mischievous smile.

Even though he had grown frustrated some fresh air was needed for Alex to calm his growing thoughts. As they stepped outside the sun glimmered upon this strong young man and this hunched over elder as they slowly walked across a narrow path. Urion leaned over to Alex pointing as a small group of cadets as they ran in formation.

"Tell me young Alexander when you look at those future solders what is their most impotent virtue".

Alex with his hands behind his head seemed unbothered with the old man's riddles quickly answering "Courage."

"So, what happens when that one in front decides to leave his unit rushing into the enemy?"

Alex's interest being slowly attracted again quickly answered "He most probably dies."

"So, would that not be excess of courage that the young man used, would that not be stupidity?" Urion asks with his eyes wide open and a smile growing on his face. "But Young Alex tell me what would happen if that same solder in the middle of battle decided to run?"

"That's cowardness. Why are you telling me this we learned this in camp?" Alex quickly asks.

"Cowardness... I see, so if he wants to live and run, he is a coward, but if he rushes forward and dies, he is stupid, the middle of that would be perfect then. no?" Asked Urion who could no longer hold in his smile. "Balance, young Alex. You are a great fighter with a scary level of control of your 'Will', but that is all physical, without knowledge you are no better than a barbarian, that is my job to nature your mind as much as your body so it can find balance."

"If that's all you had to say, why bring me out here?" Alex askes more confused than frustrated at this point.

"I just wanted a walk. Is that illegal?" Urion joyfully responded. As their walk ended, they continued their games of chess into the night, and through the days Alex seemed more docile as he witnessed the world go by. Each day he would stick to his simple routine talking to the Dean for hours on end. Talking to his friends Deep into the night, training his swordsmanship and his Will control into the break of dawn, sleeping during the homeroom class and the cycle continued, until one day when his peaceful cycle was interrupted by an announcement to stand at attention whilst walking to his room.

As he stood saluting a short distance away solders in blue and white leather with red stripes, wearing sandals with shields boosting Pangea's symbol and short swords drawn close to their chest, "So that's the navy's uniform, thin..." Alex mumbles under his breath as the men their protecting slowly reveal themselves in the crowd of navy solders both wearing white and blue suites with Pangea's symbol on their chest calmly conversing with each other.

Logan

The early morning sunlight, soft and diffuse, gives way to the strong rays of the day, the ones that bring true warmth. Spring had arrived as a Nero solder's body flew across the land smashing onto the ground with his guts hanging out. The sky was shimmering. Red blood drizzled from the Lion's wounds. The Pocasis and Nero solders in desperation were crashing their swords and spears onto the shields of any who stood against them.

Arrows where hissing through the air, but one man cut through all forces against the enemy unfazed by the danger around him. His white Armor shinned brightly, as he blindly road on the back of his steed deep into the enemy forces. His brother held the front lines screaming "hold the line" shaking uncontrollably but hiding his fearful face behind his helmet. He, blind with fear rushed forward swinging wildly but being met with sharp blade that cut through his helmet leaving him on his back. Before a finishing blow could strike him, Gaston lunged himself into the enemy, immediately striking him down.

At the edges of the battlefield Velentin and Marie sat on the back of their steeds watching on as the lions though low in number held their ground. "You promised this war wouldn't reach spring." Marie stated. Velentin gazed upon this frail, famous and fair skinned woman, as she spoke to him in such a tone.

"The lion's pride gives them this much resilience," Alec spoke from the background.

"The lion's swords have grown smaller in number though," quickly replied Velentin. "A few more days and they will surrender; they are less than a thousand with no more forces joining them."

Marie clearly frustrated shouted. "Yet our men are the ones falling so quickly!"

"Calm down, clearly the other houses of Zen have given up on the lions, hence no reinforcements, three days and if they don't surrender, I will personally pay back every penny lost in this war." Velentin proudly declared.

"Sire!" Shouted a squire as he road towards Velentin. "The Beasts are coming!"

With these few words, adrenaline flooded each of the leader's systems. Velentin held his chest as if his heart were about to explode. "How many" he disparately asked.

"Thousands, I could not see the end." the Squire exclaimed.

"So Halvor has finally made his move, as the Lions predicted." Marie said.

"An army so large, how long until they reach is?" Alec calmly asked.

"A week or two at most." Quickly answered the squire.

"Squire! this is a direct order send every bird out to both king-doms, anyone who can fight, must assemble here with-in the week. Towns guard. Royal Knights. Trader's gold coin army. The eunuchs' forces. Peasants with pitch forks it doesn't matter. The beasts are coming we need them." Velentin commanded with a nod of agreement from the rest of the leaders.

"What of Hugo?" Asked Alec.

The fear still growing Velentin spoke once again. "He likes bat-tle draw him from the front lines, draw everyone from the frontlines. Give these lions a cease fire for now. We can't afford to lose any more men before the beasts arrive."

Marie, roared. "We are winning, let's just end this war now!"

"We can't," Velentin sighed. "You are young, so I don't expect you to know the power of the Beasts, years before Halvor be-came their leader one more stood on top of the mountain Gulbrand and during the great war this monster was known as a natural disaster, wherever he went that area disappeared. His shear influence, fear and power stood the test of time, it's been fifteen years since the peace agreement and twenty since the Beasts started their domination of the west. Yet they still stand tall. They say when the Beasts come find a god and pray."

Velentin still in shock held his blade tighter, "Halvor is simply trying to replicated his old king's power, making him dangerous, First challenging the world, and defeating them many times, now coming in full force towards us."

Marie said calmly, "Fine I agree with the plan, its already in motion, but what do you mean replicate his old king's power."

"Before he became Gulbrand King of beasts, many knew him as the third pillar, Gulbrand the Plague. Now it seems Halvor wants the infamous title." Valentin added, "during the great war he became the third pillar and a few years back with E's control of the north becoming the fourth pillar, the underworld was in balance his exit left that powerful spot open. Now how much do you think the next king wants that spot?"

"Perfect time to strike as well, with the World still weakened from the chosen ones and all" Alec said mockingly.

Within a few days Zen, Nero and Pocasis's greatest houses stood before each other, signing a ceasefire vowing to fight alongside against the impending arrival of the Beasts. For the first time in history these long enemies aimed their swords at this natural disaster approaching them.

"Logan St'Louis and the Crown cub Pier St'Louis. Are you certain of your Reinforcements are coming?" Lord Velentin asked him.

"We needed to hold the frontlines only for three more days before our allies arrived," Pier quickly replied. "Within a few hours the first of our allies will arrive, ten thousand solders from four of the major Zen houses, alongside twenty thousand Peasant armed forces."

"Such numbers, I wonder what your father promised Zen's people for them to take arms so quickly," Father Alec interrupted.

Lady Marie grinned. "The all-seeing Velentin did not see this coming indeed." As they all sniggered, she started heading back to her steed finished with the conversation.

Lord Velentin was the only one who did not smile. "They are still pups Lady Marie, even if they were about to outnumber us. Wars are not won by men. Be sure to remember that."

By end of the week, the sky turned black, as a tsunami of arrows flew into the Allied forces' camps. Beginning, the attack from the Beasts. Few days is all it took for Gulbrand to bring

Tens of thousands of soldiers to their knees in desperation as their forces where being Slaughtered.

Night and day the fight continued. This endlessness was beginning to show on the crowned Prince, with his eyes darkened and his body becoming frail from tiredness.

"My prince, Logan will arrive shortly from the rear with the remainder of our troops. Hugo and Marie are still in battle. Velentin's forces are almost gone. Father Alec and the eunuchs have dwindled to such small numbers they have collapsed into Marie's forces. The lions though holding out are less than half their numbers as we speak."

All hope looked lost as Ezekiel read out this news until a young solder ran into the prince's holding a newspaper with a glimmering smile on his face.

"Speak!" a confused Pier commanded.

The young knight obliged reading out the article. Simple words of victory rung clear towards Pier, the Vassilles had counter attacked against the beasts and gained a major victory. A victory that leads to the capture of the King Beasts' Halvor.

"Gulbrand, please," Gingi pleaded. "We have to save him. Much like Folke he is like a brother to us all, I don't want another of our family dying when we can help it."

"The fool did not listen again," Gulbrand spoke in a sombre tone slouched in his chair rubbing his temple. "I told him to hold the ground, I told him not to make unnecessary movements. How did he respond? Within days he attacks their camp and brags with his letters of an easy victory, not for one second did he think they would notice the lack of numbers. Tell me Gingi if you are a leader facing an enemy with more troops than you would you not wait for them to attack? would you not wait for reinforcements before attacking?"

Though calm the pressure from each of his words started to choke the life of those close by. With difficulty Gingi finally spoke "He is a fool who should have listened to your word, but he is your brother thus you must help him."

After a short silence gazing on some still Ale, Gulbrand finally spoke, "We cannot abandon our post, when the war is so close to being won."

A startled Gingi with passion in her eyes shouted at the top of her voice, "If you don't help everyone will abandon you! they will come for the uncaring King's head!"

"Then let them come, as long as we win this war. I am not blind or stupid, one man's life does not outweigh all of ours, we win this we take Nero and Pocasis. We have the west, we have trade, we have a kingdom. If we return to help Halvor we will save his life, but Pangea will send more of its forces, the winners of these lands will assist the world against us, and we will all perish."

"That is all fantasy," Gingi told her king. "Only thing that is bound to happen is the beasts killing you."

"I have not lived a simple life. I was born in battle, lived through bloodshed but I refuse to die the same. I am growing old, and before death comes for me, I would like a family, a son, and something for him to look forward to." Gulbrand said softly, refusing to give eye contact to Gingi.

However, Gingi looked down on Gulbrand, saddened by the man she once knew as the western pillar, a man she fought side by side during the days where the Beasts where nothing, a man she saw as the true follower of the old Gods. The man before her, the man who had returned after years was so different. So weak.

Gingi quickly rushed from Gulbrand's side, pulling a horse and quickly riding North a motion of events that did not go unnoticed, as beasts around the camp talked amongst one another, Gulbrand straddled from his tent, marching forward with an apple in his hand and leaning on a pole staring at Gingi as she slowly disappeared from his site.

"Sir?" a Beast questions, "Youve seen the paper, what will you have us do?"

Gulbrand bit into his apple, "Take arms, win against these weaklings."

"What of Halvor my King?"

"What of him? he made his choice when he didn't listen to me. Now all of you remember it was not Halvor who brought the Beasts their glory. It was me, Halvor was only warming my seat! Now let's kill these fools who believe in fake gods. Let's make the beasts even more powerful!"

As per usual his speech would bring a glorious roar from his people but this time, it felt empty though sound came from them, they all looked disheartened at the situation. As the news spread, the world reacted, in Vassell Isles, having tea with the Vice Admiral and the rear admiral, Damien saw the news that brought joy to his face. "In these times you found something funny Damien?" asked Theon Odysseus through his thick white beard.

"The leader of these Heathens has been captured. it's only a matter of time before the Beasts fall. Why not move with our plan?" Damien asked with curiosity in his eyes.

"The bounties?" The younger more dashing rear Admiral Julius Horatia chimed in. "You are betting your name on a proven to fail idea. If it fails, you will be nothing Damien."

"But if it works," Damien insisted. "We will eradicate clans in the west forever."

"I'm old, this mission will be my last before retirement, at least I can see some good being done in this world." The vice admiral took a swig of wine and glanced at a hopeful Damien across the table. "Move it forward boy if you fail you still have the contributions of this mission. Second outing, right? At least with this some of the sins you are about to commit will be omitted."

"Sins? sir forgive my disobedience, but Project White is the glory of the goddess being done!" Shouts the frustrated rear Admiral.

"I forgot, we have a child with us Damien, I'm sorry boy," the now heavily drunk vice admiral admitted. "I will watch my tongue." he added as he struggled to get himself up from his chair.

In the south as they marched towards the front lines Logan finally handed the newspaper, raised his hands in the air shouting "Zah bless!" He looked around at the confused faces of his countrymen. "What is it sire?" Fearfully asked Oliver.

"Halvor has fallen! the beasts are falling!" roared Logan once more. As he sat, he let his arms flop as the weight of the world suddenly dripped from him. He took a heavy breath as steam rose from his mouth, "Lets show them the power of the lions!" he roared once more with his head to the sky. The thought of going home had finally slipped into his mind a thought he had tried to bury during these months of war and constant battle. The golden lion sure of his victory against not only the beasts but all his enemies rode faster to the front, "My prince please stay with the guards." Shouted a young guard catching up to him. "The beasts still hold power despite Halvor falling." Logan let out a boisterous laugh. "Power, he says, listen young knight, the beasts follow their king to hell if they could. watch as we reach the camp not one beast will be left in the lands; they will all turn towards whoever captured their king!" The young knight silence by the lion's confidence slowly backed off allowing him to ride as quick as he wished towards the frontlines. The day went on as Logan finally arrived with the final twenty thousand solders all bearing the Sigil of the lions. House Louis' private army an army that was to be the last line of defence for Zen now in the front lines aiding blood sworn enemies against the disaster that is the Beasts.

And at the sight of the prince in white armour forced them all to their knees, whilst Logan chuckled to the side amused by the dedication.

"Here are the real lions," Logan said. "What are your orders crowned prince?"

"Halvor's capture will disrupt the beasts, we attack at dawn." Pier quickly replied with a smile on his face.

"My prince many who kneel before you are nobleman that make up house Louis," Ezekiel whispered. "They have never seen or been in battle. Look at them all noble now but the second an arrow comes flying they will run, the men in the camps now are soldiers, who them and their fathers before, have fought for the name of the Lions relentlessly. Calling these the 'real lions' in front of them would be an unwise move my prince."

"Enough!" The prince roared. "I employed you because of the friendship you have in the camp. But I'm sick of the talk, of the war, of horrible food. Tomorrow as I said we charge at the beasts and end them once and for all!"

"What of the Goliath Gjurd, he has been sighted many times?"

"He will fall by my sword!" declared Logan.

"What about the rumours of Gulbrand's return and being here?"

"Rumours? are you a woman speaking of rumours?" Pier through his tiredness started to show frustration.

"Enough, peasant!" he warned, pointing. "You have helped me greatly during these last months don't make me cut your tongue out because you won't stop interrupting. Tomorrow, we attack."

Logan ready to be the hero again he personally led the Lions through the village, taking each step slowly, hearing the drums of his heart, breathing slow deep breaths. You are the Hero, he told himself trying to keep calm encase an enemy showed himself. The lions followed suite checking every inch of the village but like ghosts the Beasts had disappeared. Pier, being told the news as he stirred deeply into the horizon.

"Pulling all those forces from our defences seemed silly, doesn't it, Ezekiel?" He asked to no response.

"Lions do not apologies, even if they act a fool." He adds with a sly smile to his face.

"The leaders of Nero and Pocasis are in the camps as we speak, correct?" Ezekiel quickly asked.

"yes"

"So, they refused to help our push towards the beasts?"

"It seems so."

"Ten good men, and your permission my lord and I shall end the bloodshed."

Pier cleared his throat, letting out a forced laughter. "You do make me laugh Ezekiel, but you are a footman with some brains nothing close to an assassin as you're suggesting. Even if you were one, they're highly protected individuals, even now, they do not trust anyone to come close to their camp, what will you do to get past their guard? how powerful could you and your ten men be to stop people we the lions have failed to tame for hundred years?"

Ezekiel amused under the sun's rays with his hands behind his back proudly declared, "it's the perfect gamble sir if I and some men die nothing will change for you for the lions, eventually as they have shown they will attack you again. If I succeed the last of the great houses that hold Nero and Pocasis will be crippled, leaving only the lions standing at the top for a thousand years. Imagine accomplishing what even your forefathers could not?"

"I'm sure you have the men ready; you are cunning Ezekiel but not that smart, fine you have till tomorrow to accomplish this impossible task. Gather your men and leave."

"Yes, my lord." He bowed as he straddled a horse back to camp calm as if he had already accomplished his goal. The nightfall brought a welcome coldness to the land after the warm bronze sunlight was swallowed by the horizon. Now protected and hidden in its velvety blackness, Ezekiel along with Gaston and his allies stood just outside the camp as it breamed with life.

"We found it Ezekiel," Roland announced.

Ezekiel quickly rose. " Then let's complete our mission."

"Yes boss," Roland, Gaston and the rest of the men quickly responded as they started to move forward. As the guards of Nero and Pocasis stood watch, they saw the familiar trees and rocks take ominous forms but thought nothing of it as eyes tend to play tricks in the night.

In one of the tents deep within the camp the leaders of Nero and Pocasis sat in there, drinking the night away.

"What if they win?" asked Marie, "then they will spread the news that we did not help them in this time of need."

"If those pups won, they would be shouting from the heavens as we speak." Velentin quickly said.

"His right, the lions are one to boast a little too loud," Father Alec reminded everyone in the tent as he raised his glass of wine in the air to toast.

Hugo shouted from the heavens already drunk from the wine, "His not lying they're probably licking their wounds as we speak. Tonight, we drink, tomorrow we defeat the Beasts and the lions in one combined attack!"

"Well, do you mind if we join?" asked a hooded Ezekiel as he entered the tent followed closely by his ten allies.

"What is the meaning of this?!" Velentin's voice cracked as he shouted at those present before him.

Ezekiel took his time as he paced forward. Scanned all those sitting before him, took a sip of wine from Alec's glass and sat on the chair beside Marie. "Such powerful people before me, strong, wise and hold so much power over their kingdoms. Whilst I have ten men who some have never seen or tasted wine in their lives. A long time ago I figured out something, I'm weak in all aspects except one. I know how to play this game called life. And in this game the only way to get what you want is power, I want some of that as well."

"Power?" Hugo asked, "I'll give you land armies, gold whatever you think will give you enough power. Ok?"

"Yes! me too, me and Hugo are from Pocasis we hold enough power to gift you some." Marie quickly added with a crooked smile.

"Then I would lose the game of life," Ezekiel quickly added.

"My friend," Alec interrupted, "No my lord, you will win. You seem like a smart man, and you climbed the ranks to stand by the side of those egotistical assholes. Come to Nero and you and your entire family will live comfortably for the rest of time I swear on mine and my future generations' lives of this. I swear on the Goddess herself."

"The Lions send their gratitude for all the efforts Nero and Pocasis have put into fighting the Beasts." as Ezekiel said this, he waved his hand signalling his men to slaughter the four leaders sitting beside him. With blood splashing and the sound of blades piercing skin cutting through the air, Ezekiel finished the glass of wine with a blank cold look on his face. At the break of dawn sunlight shined on the golden plates of twenty thousand men as they stood ready on top of a hilltop. When along with several of his men Ezekiel approached from the bottom of the hill four bags painted in red, being held by the group as they got closer to Pier.

"My lord, why the army?" asked Ezekiel as he kneeled before Pier. The warm light bounced off the pale Prince as he looked down at the bags placed in front of him.

"Logan, you take the Calvary and draw their defences. The rest march with me! We finish this today!"

"Ezekiel you and your men will stand by my side in this attack!" Pier added to the command. Logan nodded and put his hand in the air to signal the Calvary quickly moving forward. Ezekiel stepped onto a saddle, Gaston and others followed suit. Panic was spread throughout the base as they found their leaders beheaded, one guard looked out to see an army, thousands riding at the back of horses in full Armor, nearby thousands more marching towards their camp. In line formation, eyes unblinking as they approached like monsters coming for their meal. A lord young with small land desperate to survive took leadership ordering the few thousand in the camp to take arms and ready to defend. However, this was worthless as within hours a war that had lasted for hundred years finally ended with the combined surrender of the remain forces of Nero and Pocasis' most powerful houses.

Elizabeth

At the barracks of the Beasts as many lay in wait Maximilian sat near a post showing Lancer how to best deliver fatal strikes in a packed battlefield.

"Keep your hands further apart," he said. "You need to be able to switch between stances to defend yourself. Never rely on your Will, its finite and should only be used in bursts. Now pivot as you deliver a strike, get all your weight behind the spear but always remember to have one hand lose to change between stances easier."

Drominic dashed the butt of his cigarette sniggering in the process. "Look at that, he might be able to beat you up now old man."

Al'Gadrood turned his head slowly with his arms folded. The gaze of his eyes struck like a dagger. "We are supposed to be guarding our Queen remember. Be more focused."

"Why do you think his helping the little monster?" Drominic quickly interrupted.

"His happy," Al'Gadrood observed to Drominic. "He is also an instructor in his lands outside the command of the armies, so with the news that he will be freed in exchange for Halvor this was his instinctual response." Al'Gadrood said proudly as if he had analysed everything about the man before him with a simple look.

Drominic laughed. "You might be right old man. But I'm still surprised that Halvor known second to Gulbrand was captured so easily, but you old men always overestimate how strong you are after all."

"Did your insect like brain make you forget that we are the same age?" Al'Gadrood snapped holding his favoured sword.

"Always with that old dusty sword, with women, funerals anything do you ever put it down, well I guess old people like being protective over such things," Drominic mocked. "Also! you can be senile at any age, so in my mind you are closer to Halvor's age than mine!"

Filled with anger Al'Gadrood quickly grabbed Drominic by the collar of his shirt shouting, "I'm not old you rotting twig!" and Drominic doing the same action shouted back "I'm not skinny! you fat fossil!"

Only for Elizabeth to push them out of the way, with a glint in her eye only the commander could fully understand he marched forward with his hands cuffed. The queen, he thought "Shall we?" he said with a smile on his face. Beside them hundreds of white knights and beasts stood armoured and ready for her command. For a people that followed the old gods and only bowed to those stronger than them, even the strongest of the beasts standing there could not say a word. Soon the marched out into the plains, lands that was bare and dry, vast and flat. Land that stretched out into the Horizon.

"A trade on no man's land, how poetic" said Maximilian as Elizabeth commanded the army of the beasts to stop.

"He is every talkative today," Drominic added as he sat with his arms hanging of the edge of his steed.

Al'Gadrood smirked, "He is free today."

Drominic scratched his head. "What's your orders lizzie?" he said. "It's a beautiful day, me and the boy can accompany him to the exchange."

"As you will, take five men with you as well, you never know with Goddess believers, they could just as quickly kill the commander in her name if they wished." Elizabeth said calmly.

She could feel the ground start to move, and looked up to see the great Vassille army, larger than anything she's faced. "So, what we fought before was truly just one section of their army." She muttered under her tongue as she saw spears that's touched the sky in endless rows and few men in front perched upon dressed steeds.

In a serious tone Drominic spoke, "So that is the legendary Vassille army of Pangea. In the middle none other than Hermes himself I bet."

Maximilian quickly responded, "Yes, though today we are civil, be ready heathens for Vassille will show their glory once more!" Armed with his lance and a simple shield, doused in white armour with the helmet closed, Lancer rode forward, "They're moving," he said. So, the march across no man's land began and after only a few minutes Maximilian and Halvor stood opposite each other, with one healing from his injuries and Halvor still showing fresh cuts from his battle. "I'm honoured, I see so many white knights to greet me today." Halvor said with a smile on his face.

Drominic stoic in the background did not give Halvor a glance as his eyes were fixated on Apollo standing close to him. "The luck of the Vassilles, now that's an honour." He said calmly.

"Drominic! You know this false believer?" Halvor interrupted.

"No, but I've seen him, during the war, we faced each other once, well faced is a compliment, they had me pinned down in the village of grass, four times I shot this man, yet here he is sitting on the back of a steed unbothered."

Apollo smiled, "I remember that I thought I was dead but-"

"But that monster, Ivan, arrived and Cecile with the band of white knights turned our game of cat and mouse into a mass scale battle." Drominic quickly interrupted.

Halvor exploded in laughter, "I've not heard the name Ivan in a long time, he was always entertaining!"

"Drominic, we need to go" Lancer said in the background.

"The exchange is complete send the Commander off to his people and we shall leave."

Drominic smiled. The tall man found it amusing being ordered by lancer. He waved his long thin hands commanding the release of the Commander and they took Halvor back into their hands turning their backs towards the Vassilles. "Next time we meet, Luck of the Vassilles I won't miss." He proclaimed and he rode away.

As they were riding away Halvor once again smiled whistling Lancer over, "Boy you have a fan in their camp."

Lancer paid no attention to this statement quickly changing the subject towards his training. Their conversation was thorough Halvor telling him as much information on controlling his will as he could till, they reached the camp past the masses of tents, as the beasts alongside the White Knights slowly followed Halvor heading towards Elizabeth.

"You seem hurt King of Beasts." Elizabeth said mockingly. Halvor smiled as he nodded his head. "Let us talk, we need all the leaders of this army ready for the Vassilles' attack."

"Yes sir."

As he was having his wounds dressed, drinking enough Ale to kill a horse, his smile was never ending. "You saw their numbers right Lancer... Drominic." He says as he chokes on his drink.

"Pangea is taking The Beasts seriously." Drominic added and as he sat back with his head looking at the sealing.

"They outnumber us and now they have their commander with them, what shall we do my queen." Al'Gadrood added with a stern tone.

Eric one of the heads of the thousand Beasts took his time sipping on his Ale. He looked around seeing all these new faces and whispered a joke under his tongue. "Outside this tent are two hundred of the thousand Beast leaders, why is some unknown new people sitting on the same table as I or you Halvor." he said lightly, "More so, the apparent Queen sits there as if she rules us? Have the Beasts fallen so -"?

"Eric," Halvor interrupted, "every decision she has made has led me to being free, the attack on Vassille forced capture on their commander and my attack on their eastern barracks though stupid forced capture on me. Because she intervened making sure the commander lived, the false believers kept me alive, and now we know their full strength."

"Each move was to make sure the King of Beasts stayed alive." said Elizabeth with a sly smirk.

A silence fell in the room, ten set in there looking around in their eyes the simple words Elizabeth said where blasphemy, they found it hard to speak until with a serious tone Eric opened his mouth. "You stay quiet Halvor, correct the woman. Gulbrand is our king."

"When he feels like being a king, he did leave us and who stepped up." Oddmund a fat man and one of the Thousand leaders spoke up from the background, forcing the room to erupt with some siding with Gulbrand and others siding with Halvor.

"Enough!" Halvor shouted. "He will come, and he will kill me. I defied his direct order but here me out. Why should we listen to someone who left us in our time of need, who forced us into battle with the World, who acts, talks and fights like them?"

Eric again looked around the room with a concerned look on his face. "Then fight him for the crown, that is our way Halvor."

"He is stronger than me," his voice cracked as Halvor said that "one vs one Gulbrand will win. But I ask you believers of the Old Gods why should we give this imposter the same treatment, he does not believe in our gods so why should we let him hide behind that?"

He sat forward with his hands interlocked, "For years we let this man ran wild with his ideas and when they started to fail, with The Beasts falling into myth, he left. Then when we had grown in size and power, he came back acting like he could do whatever he wanted. Again, he ran wild and look at us now facing the World's Wrath, fighting within each other, Folke is dead because of his ideas. I plan to fight him for the crown, alone if I must but I can no longer sit back and watch Gulbrand crash The Beasts once more."

"The White Knights stand with him," Elizabeth spoke, "From my short time, one man has fought for his people whilst the other has thrown his weight around."

"Me and my men stand with him," Oddmund spoke. "I've known these men from the beginning, Gulbrand is far too reckless and the short time Halvor had ruled, I only saw The Old Gods shine on us."

"I and my men will stand by Gilbert and," Eric shouted!

"Ganging up on him is the way of the Goddess believers it's against our code! I will not sit here and listen to blasphemy!" he shouted once more as he quickly exited the tent. Quickly followed by the majority of the Thousand beasts who sat listening to this.

"There you are Halvor all those who will fight to protect our ways will stand by Gulbrand, all those who see you as the true King and Gulbrand a reckless man will stand by you. What off the Vassilles. Surely with the Beasts going into imminent battle, they will take this moment to strike will they not." Ake another member of The Thousand Beasts spoke proudly.

"We leave the camp tonight, those with me will travel with me, those against will head towards Gulbrand, and I will send a letter for us to meet in the mountains due west. We will settle everything using our ways. We will issue a challenge of Holmgang towards Gulbrand, winner will rule loser will leave these lands and our people forever." Simple words but enough to shut the mouths of anyone who were sceptical of this decision. All but

Elizabeth as she pointed out the name Holmgang confused by its nature.

"It's another way of settling disputes in our people, without the need for solo combat. If enough people on each side differ in values, they will all battle for the idea of their side, the leader of the losing forces with die or be banished." Oddmund added with a sombre look on his face.

Like ghosts they disappeared into the night, leaving no trace of their existence, some went with Halvor, some went to join Gulbrand and most found this opportunity to quietly disappear from the ranks of the Beasts. Then if the gods where weeping, the sky started to rain uncontrollably, as days later Halvor marched into the mountains on a cold morning stopping only feet away from Gulbrand and his allies.

Gulbrand looked around only to see the lack of numbers on both sides, "Even the stags did not show," he muttered under his breath before drawing his sword, pointing it towards Halvor. And in turn Halvor held his great axe with no armour and warpaint all over his body pacing back and forth muttering under his tongue. Thus, with their allies beside them two of the Greatest in the west erupted in battle deep in the mountains. The winner to be able to proclaim himself as King of the

Beasts. As stories of this monstrous battle where told, many only knew of their struggle between each other lasting three days and three nights. On the final night both would lose as a third party, the White Knights who had pulled most of their men away from this battle hiding it under honour for their culture, made their move crashing into both sides. By the break of Dawn only one party stood.

No movement, no wind, no arrows. The battle was over as Elizabeth marched into the middle of the mass bodies of Beasts that had fought to the bitter end.

In the middle of this, laid Halvor with endless arrows and swords peaking from his body, still breathing the man laid on his back, dead in Most's eyes with a pool of his blood drowning him.

"I don't see Gulbrand here," Elizabeth said softly.

"He was taken away... but his wounds... are too deep..." Halvor responded as best he could.

"Give me...Sword..." he added as he struggled to role himself over.

 Elizabeth obliged handing the weapon over to him and lancer stepped forward with his spear in hand. "Lancer... you are strong... extraordinarily strong...I wish... I could... have taught... more."

"Thank you for teaching me the ways of Will, I will never forget everything you did for me Halvor!" Lancer shouted to the surprise of Elizabeth.

As Halvor raised his sword above his head Lancer launched forward, the spear pierced through the tattoo of The Beasts, stopping Halvor in his tracks. The world silenced by one attack, Gulbrand gone, Halvor dead, many throwing the banner of the beasts away, an era that lasted twenty years on a cold Easter morning, the legendary Thousand Beasts where no more.

Eros

"It's been months brother, maybe the rumours are true," Apollo said standing on the edge of a hill facing another clan's barracks.

Hermes stood still, watching another of his enemy about to fall to his army. "A few years from now we will free ourselves from Pangea. Until then we need to follow their orders and I have not been told to return. I agree with you brother maybe the rumours of Halvor's deaths and the collapse of the Beasts are true but in the past month these heathens have started growing with their own banners all over us. Parasites like them need to be taken down early before they become a plague."

"I understand and I see you are still adamant with this plan. If you fail that will be the end of our people." Apollo concerned quickly responded.

"If we tried to vote out, the people that are scared for petty loses like trade or danger of clansmen will surely rather stay as slaves." Hermes said calmly.

Apollo smiled. "I already pledged to you but don't think I won't question your conviction whenever I can."

"I know, I will remember that brother."

Over in the field, a captain starts marching forward signalling an attack. "Oi, which one is the leader?" Eros calmly said with a cold look in his eye. The Solder he spoke to looked surprised as he could feel the bloodlust in this child. "The one with the thick black fur over his shoulders" the solder stuttered.

"Levy in front with shields high protect the ladders!" shouted the captain as solders begun to move in for the attack. "Lose!" shouted the enemy leader as he started bombarding the Vassilles with arrows. And as they marched in unison, the captain at the corner of his eye saw Eros run past with a small dagger attached to his hand and an axe tied to his back. As per usual his small body allowed him to slip past everyone not being noticed till he jumped onto the edge of the wooden wall piercing it with his dagger and quickly untying his axe and using it to climb the barrack's walls.

Watching from afar Hermes could not help but laugh, "These days my favourite moments is watching that child move so recklessly."

"He moves as if death means nothing," Apollo muttered.

"Your entire crew we found you with Apollo. They will do well under our army well, all but the girl, she has other duties when we are dismissed from these horrible lands."

"I told you before brother she is no slave, you cannot do that."

"I am the crowned prince I can do what I wish."

They continued watching as Eros scaled the walls finally reaching the top and quickly taking care of one of the archers. "A child?" asked one of the soldiers. As Eros cut through each of them like butter using his small stature to his advantage and aiming for the legs before slitting their throats. "Four left" he muttered under his breath. Before cutting them down one by one, "An amateur, kill him!" the leader said referring to the stiff movement from Eros but to no end as again he slices through the last two standing before him. Finally, he launches wildly towards the leader who in turn thinks it'll be an easy kill seeing all the openings swings wide towards Eros but as their eyes meet, the man freezes for a split second but long enough for Eros to plant his dagger into the leader's neck. "Close" he mutters before a rouge arrow gets launched into his arm forcing him to fall off the edge of the barracks' wall.

"Ouch, did you see that brother!" Hermes shouts in excitement. "My eyes are old, but I think he just pulled that arrow out and used it to break his fall... impressive." Apollo quickly responded. They continued chatting till the Vassilles signalled the occupation of the Barracks with the raising of Pangea's flag. As night fell, the moonlight splashed down its glow onto the camp and as they rested, they knew another campaign would be within a few days.

"You have become so reckless my little pup," Sarrah said softly as she bandaged Eros's wound.

Eros looked at her coldly. "I'll be more careful from now on..."

"That's fine, I wish I was fighting with you is all." Sarrah quickly replied. "Hermes does not believe women should fight though."

"You are the best of all of us, he is just stupid, seems their family are all the same. Has Apollo said anything about Jon's location?"

"No, seems he turned into a ghost." Sarrah responded with a cold stare. "But remember if we found him, I'm the one who gets to kill him."

"I know, first we need that fool's help. Afterall, he did figure out it was Jon months before any of us could."

Sarrah laughed. "I remember you almost cut his head off for even saying it. But the more he explained it the higher toll it took on us."

"Leading to Raijin leaving." Eros responded as he flinched from his wound.

"Tell me about your homeland again," Eros said quickly changing the subject with a smile sneaking onto his face. "I always love hearing of it."

"To the animals, to our relatives, everything is linked in our lands. Some call it primitive but we like the simple life, all of us move with the earth, when the government at the time fell to the Rebellion and succeeded from Pangea at first everyone was scared but years later, we are still the peaceful nation we have always known. We have archaeologists that are hundreds of years ahead of anyone else I thought I'd become one when I grew up."

Eros continued to listen not fully understanding everything she was saying but could only smile at how passionately she described her people and her lands. In another world in another life, her choice to come to Utopia would have granted her the experience she always wanted.

"Boy!" a solder shouts from the distance. "The Crown Prince wishes to speak with you."

With their time cut shot Sarrah grabs Eros by the hand caressing it like mother would but feeling the roughness left by wilding a blade. "Eros it's just me and you now, we still have each other, ok?" simple words but enough to put a childlike smile on his face. As he enters the prince's tent, for the first time Eros sees the elusive prince up-close "you look like a thin woman..." quickly says to the slight chuckle from the prince.

"My brother got all the manliness. I was left with this."

"You should keep the armour on, its more intimidating."

"I'll keep that in mind. But enough of that, I brought you here for praise and an opportunity." The prince says enthusiastically.

Eros still looking defensive stayed near the exit to the tent.

"What opportunity?"

"I'll speak quick, when we return, I want you to join my army officially. Obviously, we can't let a child be a soldier in our lands so until you turn sixteen you will learn and stay in my castle. Do not worry I have a son no older than you I'm sure you will get along. How old are you twelve, thirteen?"

"Nine. At the start of spring."

"I see, well don't you worry your life will just get a lot better what do you say?" Hermes quickly asked.

"I can't my brother will still be in the cadets; near the south I plan on going to him after this is finished."

Hermes did not honour that with a reply. The only thing he could offer was leave from his tent for Eros. He quickly called in a guard, "Find me his brother, I need his location, if we have to ill bring the brother with me. I cannot lose such a competent warrior."

"You know it's amazing how quickly you kill but that cute face will fade, so you need to find a way to quickly kill whilst using what the goddess gave you." Apollo said from the shadows as he started walking near Eros.

Eros paid no attention to him. Continuing to walk but as Apollo goes to throw a punch Eros quickly dodges snapping his eyes towards Apollo, for Apollo to only laugh.

"I see, through your eyes... I mean you can use that but eventually that will make you blind. Not to mention that doesn't work on someone with stronger Will than you". Apollo said. "One night, let me show you how to use your power just tonight, in a way you can train on your own."

"Why?"

"As an apology for you know everything really." Apollo scratched his sculp. "And I have news on Jon."

After a few minutes of silence Eros finally spoke, "Fine," he said softly. "One night."

As they sat around a campfire Eros invited Sarrah to join in, but only witnessed Apollo scratching his head as he tried hard to put using Will into words. "Well, you've felt my Will and since its stronger than yours it felt like you were being crashed correct. Well now Eros has awakened his, and he is using it through his eyes as bursts. Now in order to get its full strength one has to use it through their core. Now best way I can describe it when facing an opponent, scream through your core, the louder you scream, the easier it will be to dominate them down to their instinct."

Tired of his worthless lesson Eros chimed in. "Thank you for the lesson now about Jon?"

"Impatient as always, Sarrah teach him please." Apollo sighed. "From my sources Jon is with the White Knights in the south." Sarrah pondered for a minute. "How do you plan on getting us close enough?"

"It'll take a while, but I guarantee at some point Jon will die." Apollo said with conviction. "For now, drink and enjoy yourselves." As he said that the kids stood fading into the camp.

"Why you smiling brother." Hermes interrupts as he sees his brother eating along at a camp site.

Apollo continued to smile, standing and stretching his bones. "Eros let his Will out."

"You felt it?" Hermes asked, "Is it stronger than yours?"

"No. But I pity whoever makes him angry. His Will is so attached to his rage that he doesn't even notice the potential it has yet." Apollo quickly replied. "But brother, when was your idea supposed to take place?"

"Trying to talk me out of it again I see. Well two years from now, why?"

"No reason." Apollo said. "I wish I could have seen him grow, a Will attached to Rage, it's almost biblical."

"You will, he will be joining our military after all." Hermes quickly replied. Only for Apollo to respond to him with a smile as he feels the sun rise behind him.

"Come on... I think it's about time for us to fade into the twilight."

"Wh-?" before he could finish his sentence, he felt blood flowing from his mouth as his head flew from his body. It felt warm, and as his body jolted from his heart to his toes, the blades of the grass beneath his feet moved pointing towards the sun waiting to be fed by its rays. His eyes wondered around for a moment as each person's expression widened. He moved his lips, but no words could come out. He blinked once pushing the tears from his eyes as he saw his men grab their weapons, he blinked again seeing them start to rush towards him. In one final blink as his head landed on the ground, he saw the empty expression on his brother's face as blades crossed around his neck.

"What the fuck?" Eros said softly as everyone around him rushed towards Apollo, tripping over campfires and each other, within seconds thousands are sent into panic.

Apollo

Maximilian sat watching the young soldiers rough housing and trying to show which one of them is stronger. "You lot are so hopeless; be happy the prince likes you lot or you would be on the streets by now" he said as he started to laugh.

"Shut up old man, you should be at home waiting for death at this point," quickly responds one of the soldiers.

Maximilian laughed louder, "me? Look at your hand's boy their so soft, you should be cooking for real men not fighting!"

Through the laughter, a group of soldiers came rushing towards Maximilian with a distort look on their faces. Immediately as he saw them Maximilian thrust his sword into the ground lifting himself up and rushing back with them.

At the scene of the crime with panic from everyone a soldier sees Sarrah and Eros, "Capture the children as well!" shouts the soldier, quickly snapping Apollo back into reality.

"Me? I'm not involved in this!" quickly responded Eros as he tried and failed to fight of the soldiers, who in turn quickly overwhelmed both of the children holding them down in place.

"Leave them, his was my choi-" a punch from a frantic soldier quickly flew onto Apollo's face before finishing his sentence.

As the camp fell into panic gathering to the prince, Maximilian, in the crowd quickly pushed everyone out of way until he saw Hermes' body on its side and his head feet away.

"My prince..." he softly said as he collapsed to his knees, quickly drowning in pain. He held his heart struggling to catch his breath, and the screams of everyone around him quickly silenced.

"Why, my Goddess, why?" he asked, he begged staring blankly into the skies before quickly snapping his head towards Apollo growing in anger.

"You, blight of the Vassilles! on his knees!" he shouted breaking his voice throughout.

With the soldiers close to Apollo quickly attacking him, mobbing onto him, until Maximilian stops them. "Raise his head!" he shouted, as Apollo now bloody barely conscious, had his head raised high. Within moments, for the second time in his life Apollo was in chains. He quickly looked around to quickly see the children's faces also locked down in chains.

Feeling the looseness of his jaw, sure that it had been quickly broken. He tried his best to slur a few words out, "They... are... not... involved."

"First the King, then your own twin. You shared a womb!"
There could be no denying the rage felt from Maximilian.
"They were near you, moments later... my prince." he adds as
he struggles to finish the simple sentence.

As Maximilian sat down with leg raised balancing his arm, and
his eyes pacing through each of the people in chains. He coldly
ordered everyone to leave the area. Though for a few seconds
they could not simply follow such an order they felt a cold chill
in the back of their necks and quickly understood. This was
coming from the Commander, though old they knew at any
moment he could snap taking few of them to the grave before
he died.

So, with everyone watching from the background they felt the
sun above their heads, the sky cloudless and dry. The thick
moist air covered the camp, and with each movement of ones'
shadow one could hear a worm dig through the ground beneath
their feet.

"Why do something so reckless?" Eros asked. "If I live, I'll be
sure to kill you Apollo."

"They should not... be involved Maximilian." Apollo struggled
to say to the silent response from the old Commander.

Finally, as the sun begun to set, Maximilian opened his mouth with a simple "Why?"

"He... wouldn't stop."

"I should have let you perish that day, both me and your father, we knew you from birth and wanted to protect you, but as I look at you now, I see you are as the Goddess described. Amon, shall rain hell onto her people, hiding as one of us." Maximilian said with a cold gaze. "It makes sense, you sided with our enemies, hidden behind Her name."

As nightfall came, Maximilian finally stood, waved his hand, for the surrounding soldiers, and within hours they carried their prince, wrapped his body and started traveling towards Utopia, with the prisoners being dragged near the rear by chains. The journey was filled with silence, no man spoke as they mourned the death of their beloved prince. Through the forest and into the vision of Utopia, the soldiers had won against the Beasts but lost the prince in the process.

"They're on their way back?" A civilian spoke into the crowd.

"Then it's true the Beasts have fallen! Utopia was avenged!" shouted another as streets filled with cheer to the returning Heroes and chants of the army reached even the ears of King

Madas Vassellet himself. With a smile quickly mounted on his face he moved towards the main gate at great speed.

With the gates being swung open, Maximilian rode in leading the army with a blank face, everyone who was cheering at their loudest, slowly stopped, feeling the gloom pressure coming from the Vassille army. Then as Madas Vassellet ran through the crowds to greet his son. The mood of the people swirled in currents beneath their faces. Each lowering their head as more of the army flooded in. Finally pushing the ocean of people aside, King Madas Vassellet stood face to face to his friend. Maximilian dropped to one knee and bowed his head in helpless sorrow. "Forgive me my King, I failed to protect the crowned prince." With these few words the King slowly turned around dragging his feet towards his home and vanished into its halls for several days and nights.

Within these days word had quickly spread throughout Utopia and beyond. At the Vassille isles, all military operations were put on hold as the country begun to mourn. "Why should we care, we are just visitors on this land not the archbishop's subjects." Asked one of the Royal Guards as he helped load the Pos-one Trireme St' Maria, prepping for the upcoming journey.

"Because we are guests and thus, we must respect them in these times," quickly responded one of the legionnaires, as he helped in the background.

Damien wrinkled his brow. "The bill passed, and the meeting concluded Oder 'Project White' must be executed immediately."

"Then why are you uneasy Damien?" quickly asked Rear Admiral Julius Horatia.

"The letter from Commander Maximilian, their request came at an annoying time, we have to be ready within a week, schedule a meeting with the trade union in Nero about the coliseum and Launch bounties into the west. It's a lot for a simple district Chancellor, maybe State Chancellor Lisa will take some of these duties of me."

Julius Horatia could hardly hold his joy as he begun to laugh, "You sound like a woman!" he screamed through his tears of joy as he continued to mock Damien.

In the Land of Gevana, the homeland of Sarrah through the clouds of dust, and the man-made mountains stood the palace of the former king. As the current elected leader an ebony man with scars across his arms barely covered by the lose robe stood by the window reading the newspaper and just as quickly as he read the title, he threw it to the side in anger. His second, a fair skinned man, in a white robe walked in "Anubis, you are the Leader remember, try to control your anger whatever it is." "Net, I'm sorry, that did seem childish, but it seems Hermes fell in battle. This would make the coalition, much harder without the Vassille isles." quickly answered Anubis as he walked back to his chair.

Net walked towards the table grabbing a glass of water and sipping it. But as he approached closer to Anubis, the Elected Leader grew curious of the strange sound coming from Net. "What is that ringing sound?" he asked.

Net stopped still smiling, raised his wrist to his ear, "Affirmative," he calmly said before dropping his smile. "Leader of Gevana, I'm sorry to say the rebel group 'the royalists' have made an attempt on your life and succeeded. Mr Nobody sends his regards."

"Net?" a confused Anubis asked before a loud bang, loud enough to break the glass behind him panted the walls with half his skull as he fell backwards still in his chair.

In Country of Zen, as the country prepared for the wedding between the crown prince Pier and Maria, Logan bagged in as his brother was being dressed in his wedding clothes. "Brother, you have to talk to father, the people are starting to talk against the crown. Not to mention, those bastards the Beasts killed The Vassille prince in the last moments, this could be the fire they need to rebuild and attack!"

"My father made many foolish promises to allow us victory, I agree. However, I have taken over a lot of his political baggage as he seems more ill by the day. With you by my side, Commander of the Lions. I'm sure we will win anything." Pier calmly said whilst looking in the mirror one last time smiling back at his brother as he started to take steps towards the exit of his room. "Today, Zen and our vassal Pocasis watch as the Lions only grow stronger."

Far south of the west nearing the great ocean, in a small village, filled with what seemed bandits and clansmen. Inside one of the few standing buildings large enough to be where the village people came together sat Drominic as he bit into a chicken's leg smiling throughout reading the newspaper. "Someone grab me a messenger bird we need to alert Lizzy, seems we won't have to hide for two years after all, the Vassilles are surely to pull their armies from the west, I think it's time to establish the new Pillar."

Finally, in Utopia deep in its dungeons chained to the wall Apollo turned his head slowly towards the small crack of light from the ceiling, **one day they will understand,** he thought as if he could feel the many whispers about him and his brother. He hears a small creek from the cell's gate, with a masked man carrying tools, and the sight of those sends a chill down his spine as he grits his teeth preparing for another day of relentless torture. But after a few minutes he opens his eyes yet again to see the torturer seeming to struggle. And through the muzzle of his mask, he lets out a muffled chuckle "You must... be... new, not... used to this?" he asked mockingly.

Before his eyes froze robbing them of any warmth. For a moment he looked like he had passed onto the afterlife, his skin pale and clammy, as his hands shook bloody and raw onto the chains, and every few minutes his voice would return to him only for a short time, screeching to the point blood would pour out of his mouth. Sharp pain lanced through his head, and he could feel his bones start to ache.

Blood was oozing out of numerous wounds, but a vast amount was coming from between his legs as they begun to numb.

"I was sure you would die, Apollo." The hooded figure said as he wiped the blood from his face. "I'm surprised I stopped the bleeding in time. I'll let you rest for today, tomorrow we continue with the normal torture... though your father surely is a cruel man. Take what's important to him, like he has to me, take his manhood. He said so casually. "

Apollo slumped his head over unable to so much as hold his eyes open for long periods of time. But as he started to fade, he could hear faint laughter, only seeing their burned feet he knew who was laughing at him. **Goddess**, he prayed, ***I promise to atone for everything, please give me the chance.***

Alexander

There are many variations that when combined make up the fighting force for Pangea, from legionnaires to Royal Knights, to Templers. However, throughout history when the combined forces moved, no one refeed to them as such they simple called them Galient forces. Thus, over the horizon of the sea, the grand fleet carrying twenty thousand soldiers, sailed towards the terrorist island of Gevana as reports of the assassination of the ruling power, and the occupation of several clans, ravishing the land grew. The grand fleet made their way to bring back order to their former nation.

"Absolute victory!" Shouted Staff sergeant Tiberius Romulus to the resounding roar of army stationed on St' Nina alongside her Triremes, as they travelled to the island due south.

"Make this a simple one," sighed Rear Admiral Julius Horatia siting on a chair waiting for his drink at the bowsprit of the St' Pinta. Heading due East towards the Island.

"This better be over soon," said acting Captain of the Royal Guard Tassos, as he emptied his bowls from stress in the toilet of St' Gallega heading due west towards the Island.

"Si vis pacem, para bellum" Western Second Sector District Chancellor Damien Anemoi whispers as he looks over the bowsprit of St' Maria, seeing the smaller Triremes surround it as the site of the island due south begun to show more clearly.

Alexander, boasting in chainmail armour with his helmet to his side overhead the saying from Damien quickly asking him what it was.

To a small chuckle as a response. "Not something you would understand, don't be distracted you are a Statesman today; thus, you will protect and lead your own unit on the battlefield." he adds before an Icanix flew onto his arm carrying the message that simply said ten minutes.

"So that's the legendary message bird, it looks as though it's on fire..." Alexander added, to the simple amusement of Damien before the District Chancellor raised his hand to prepare the ballista's. Within moments the thunderous blasts echo everywhere as white balls the size of small carts were launched into the air, towards Gevana. With his hands behind his back, Damien watched as the White balls eclipse around the Island, only for his face to sink, as some begin to explode in the air.

"Man, why did they have to go and do that?" The Rear admiral asked, sipping on some tea. "Navi, move St' Pinta forward and prepper to engage!"

The shipwright nodded, immediately sending messages for the rest of the fleet to move towards the target. The fear could be felt from him as he knew, this simple attack was about to turn into a full-scale battle. In moments large amount of Water elementals, used their power to boost the speed of each of these Mammoth-like vessels, whilst the bulk of the front line rowed their Triremes close by to keep up.

Damien, chuckled. "Become part of the court Alexander, you won't have to endanger your life as much."

"It's the duty of everyone to defend the flag." Alexander said as he put his helmet on holding onto the edge of the ship ready for any more attacks from Gevana as they quickly approached the island. But for a moment as he focuses towards Gevana, his attention is quickly grabbed, "Damien!" he shouts as he feels a shock that cuts through his body. Damien feeling the mass aura coming from beneath them, quickly orders the ship to stop but before he could get his words out, as if they hit a giant iceberg the ship made a sudden stop causing all those standing to fly into the edges or simple fall off the edge.

"What in the goddess' name is that?" Damien filled with confusion and fear asked as he got himself up looking at a creature large enough to block out the sun itself. Before he could be completely in shock of the beast that stood before him, he quickly bit into his hand breaking the skin and breaking the trance that he had been launched into.

"How unsightly, a simple anomaly and an Anemoi can fall like this?" He muttered as he broke into a smile. "Prepper for battle! Ballista's! Archers! Loose at will!" he shouted at the top of his lungs. Immediately gathering everyone still on the ship back to their senses.

Each stood picking up bows and some arming the ballista and as the Galients prepared to counterattack the monster, it vanished. Surprising everyone including Damien and Alexander as they scanned each area around them to not find a single trace of that monster or its Will. Remembering the Plaza, Alexander's fear grew as for the second time in his life he could not feel another creature's Will. Necks suddenly snapped as they looked up at the head of the ship, gazing upon a robed man, as he gazed back pulling his hood down to reveal long spikes where his hair should be, and its ruby eyes almost glassy shinned as it looked down on Damien.

It opened its mouth, "He was not suited to fight you Chancellor Damien Anemoi." It said as it raised its arms with palms wide open, it took a large breath expending its forearms and releasing a large amount of air through its hands directly at Damien. And as it impacts the blasts expands outwards.

"Cleaver, Chancellor Damien Anemoi, however that is reckless for a seasoned fighter," it said as he referred to the pealing flesh on Damien's right arm which seemed to take most of the impact of that attack before redirecting it.

Damien took a quick look around as his soldiers armed and ready to fight only waited for his order to attack. "Kill him..." He ordered as large numbers of soldiers charged forward into the strange man leaving only a few of the trainee soldiers as Alexander's hand stayed in the air ordering them to holt.

For a short moment, his disobedience for the attack order seemed rushed and cowardly, but he quickly felt reassured as the man before them again raised his hand. "60," he muttered before launching another blast directly at the soldiers.

"Not this time!" Damien shouted as he swatted the air, launching a counter towards the man's attack forcing it to explode when the two attacks impacted causing a blinding cloud of air. Alexander's eyes widened in surprise and Damien rushed forward dispelling the air only to once again see the man had disappeared. "Again?" he shouted.

Before they could rest, Damien scanned around to see that the ship was damaged quickly confirmed by the ship's shipwright as he informed the chancellor that St' Maria was too damaged to move.

"Fine, all climb onto the available sailboats and head towards the shore. Alexander make sure those in the lower decks makes it to land that's a direct order!" Commanded Damien as he jumped onto the first sailboat going into combat before anybody else.

After a while Alex alongside some familiar faces including Ava boarded their own sailboats close to one another as the last of St' Maria's Galients started to move towards the shore.

"You are doing well, Alex." Ava said as she grabbed his shoulder.

Poised at the front of one of sailboats, focusing on shore Alex spoke, "The battle is yet to begin."

Ava quickly replied. "But now we know they have several Anomalies, our goal when we land is to all move towards that hill. Secondary mission is to protect the Kal brothers, as they're our strongest elementals and we need them ready to fight these creatures."

With the drums beginning, the small unit row forward to reach land, till the hear the shout "Shields!" from a distance quickly raising them, before odd arrows fall from the heavens landing on the boats killing some but leaving all those who stood on Alex's sailboat. "Row!" Alex shouts as their boat continues moving forward.

"They have the advantage in every way why not attack us in the sea?" asked a frightened recruit as he struggled to row the boat. Ava looked at Alex who looked desperate, barking orders had his eyes locked on land ignoring the question of the recruit.

"Did you not pay attention, they are primary Earth elementals, water is their biggest weakness." She added as she grits her teeth looking at her feet.

A horn echoing a distinct sound clearly one from St'Pinta due east, brings warmth to them as the signal at least one ship has touched land. "We lost our track; we are closer to east than North waypoint now." Alex muttered as their sailboat drew near to land, seeing everyone already engaged in combat. He took off his belt and drew his blade, for the first time. In that moment Ava finally saw him as a soldier as he looked like a proper Statesman, with chainmail, as long as robes covering the leather beneath and clothe with Pangea's Sigel visible from miles away. "Land is there, stick together no matter wh-" Before he could finish his sentence, an arrow pierced the side of his helmet knocking him off the boat, "Shit! Move forward ill grab him!" Ava commanded as she took off her metal chest plate, jumping into the sea quickly grabbing a dazed Alex. Not long after Ava dragged Alex onto the beach, which had quickly been turned into a battlefield, Alex on his hands and knees took his helmet off trying to grab his breath and as he looked up at a concerned Ava, he quickly pushed himself up unsheathing her sword and lunging it into an enemy that was rushing into her. "Thank you..."

"Call it even, let's find our group" Alexander said as he held his hand trying to calm himself down. Looking down at the man whose life he just took.

"Enough!" Ava said as she grabbed his shoulders. "You can ask for forgiveness after, right now we need to survive."

To the west of them, fighting seemed to slow, as the enemy showed visible signs of fear, while Damien Anemoi wearing formal military suite instead of his armour, marched forward with a blade in one hand and rage in his eyes.

"Kneel before the crown..." Damien said softly as he launched forward, seeming to glide on the ground effortlessly cutting through the men that stood before him. As he cut through them, blinking his bleak grey eyes, hunting for his next target, each slice accurate and lethal. Suddenly he stopped, jumping several paces back, narrowly avoiding the descent of one of the anomalies. His eyes widened as each second another appeared and another after that. Finally, four stood as they quickly went into formation. Each standing in perfect distance protecting the First anomaly Damien saw.

"Chancellor Damien Anemoi, I will be your opponent." Roared a hooded figure in front as he slowly lifted his hand from his robe. Damien, in response signalled any of those not in combat to focus on the hooded figures standing before him.

At A distance Alex and Ava approached the destination, to meet the rest of their comrades, they saw a figure, hidden in the shadows sat, peacefully watching over the battle. As they carefully approached the figure it finally spoke.

"Lovely day isn't it" he said with a soft voice.

Alexander tightly holding his blade, "Who are you?"

The man smirked, "That's rude young man, one who is holding a blade should introduce themselves first it calms the other down faster."

Alex now still, few feet away lowered his weapon to the surprise of Ava, even more so when he let it go and started walking towards the man, "Alexander Senesto, First of his name, Statesman in training."

"Senesto? It's a pleasure to meet you Alexander, you may call me Lael if you wish," the man spoke again in a calm tone. And as Alex finally reached him, he could see not a man in a chair but one in a wheelchair, frail, looking malnourished, but with long unkept silver hair and eyes that resembled a ruby. Alexander laughed as he scratched his head.

Lael sighed, "We didn't all go extinct, if that's what you're wondering."

"What happened to you?"

"A lot," Lael responded, as he let out a slight cough. "Enough about me, what brings you here Alexander and not fighting with your people?"

Ava quickly started approaching Alex and as she caught up, she saw, the strange man's eyes immediately drawing her sword and pointing it at his neck. To the sheer surprise of Alex who told her to sheath her weapon immediately.

Ava glared at Alex grinning in confusion. "What do you mean?" she asked pointing her finger to the battlefield. "This man has the same eyes as the anomaly, yet even crippled and frail he sits here unfazed, watching all of this, this man is not normal. He might be one of those anomalies."

"That's very true young lady, I am allied with said man, well, I did tell them this was not our battle, but they convinced me it was." The man said gripping his hand with his smile slowly fading. "Tell me Alexander do you agree with this, look beneath you, people from this land are fighting not each other but the world. Why do you think?"

Alex obliged and looked over the hill, watching more clearly as people with primitive armour and weapons desperately fought a losing battle. "They deal with the underworld, turned Gevana into a terrorist nation, they know if they do not fight, they will be jailed and re-educated or worst case executed, so this is their one chance to escape with their lives." He quickly answered with conviction.

Lael felt a pinch of rage but quickly calmed himself, "As master would have said, I suppose from your perspective you are right. But tell me Alexander, when the people here lose or surrender which will happen soon what do you think will happen."

"Easy, we bring order back to the land."

"Order? To Archaeologists who have learned so much? I don't believe the fleet is sent to bring peace young Alexander." Lael quickly responded. "You see Alexander your Goddess gave you the right to protect whom she loves, at least that's what your people say. I hope you soon realise that you slay for no more than semantics and greed, blind to the truth that was never hidden. You step on this land with your lies and get angry when the lamb changes into a lion."

Before the conversation could continue a voice appeared from behind them, "Lael looks like you made some friends." He said as he took long strides towards the group. "Well, I think it's about time we go, they took the south and East, North is about to fall as well only these few are left fighting."

Lael, once again coughed into his hand and as he pulled away a slight drop of blood, lingered. "How disappointing, what of Justice?"

"That? Damien fell as you said he would."

Simple words that shot through both Alex and Ava, the wind tugged at their hair as it blew it out of their eyes, showing a confused expression. "You are lying," Alex quickly said with Ava nodding.

"Well, it's true, but damn was he a fighter, shouting he is an Anemoi, he even awakened which was surprising, I thought Justice would lose at one point," the man said with joy on his face failing his arms around in excitement.

"I see, and you came for this man. I'm guessing he is important to you?" Ava said before swinging her sword towards the neck of Lael, but as quickly as she swung, she found herself in the position of the strange man and the man in her position. And the man proceeded to grab the shoulder of Lael, "I don't believe we will ever meet again Alexander however I wish you good health" he said as both the man and Lael disappear into thin air.

"Another anomaly, one who is larger than giants, one who can blast air from his hands and one who can vanish into thin air," Alex said before heading down the mountain in a hurry, quickly followed by Ava.

As they ran the vision of heroes and battlefields that read about the land where legends are made seemed anything but. With now simply a graveyard for the unburied as many of the Gevana corpses laid. Alex on the other hand ignored all that stood before him running towards his teacher blind to the world that was around him. Finally arrived at a group of soldiers unable to move Damien as he took his final breaths, he looked at Alex, "I'm... Sorry..." he said before shutting his eyes one last time. Word quickly arrived at the different posts of the island as soldiers enraged of Damien's death demanded retribution.

Logan

Through the hallways of the Royal castle, hundreds of noble men and women continued the extended party with the music loud as thunder making one's skin tingle. Still celebrating the wedding of the war hero Pier St'Louis, the light from the sun spilled across the floor, echoing the shimmer from the rubies, gold and diamonds that decorated the beautiful cattle. Watching the throne for what seemed to be the thousandth time with a glass of wine on hand and a sombre look on his face. Phillip St'Louis hated the idea of being ruled by his brother and one could tell by a simple look.

The chair was carved in the finest of oak, dressed in rare jewels and decorations. Though it looked impressive Phillip could only laugh as he gazed upon it.

"To think, that single chair has withstood everything," Elizabeth said as she slowly approached Phillip from the shadows. Phillip quickly took a look and be it the alcohol or fate he was immediately bewitched. As Elizabeth approached with the sun's rays billowing around her dress, her pail skin and red hair complimented the dress which had the calmness and complexion of the ocean. "What do you mean?" Phillip asked trying to get his composure to return to him.

Elizabeth smiled as she held her hands behind her back, "from the Junche dynasty to the Saber dynasty all the way to two hundred years ago when House Lion won the war for the throne, creating this land called Zen. This chair has managed to survive all that."

"Even before we were royalty, we protected this throne because we are the Lions!" Phillip roared in pride as he looked back at the throne. "Like Pocasis Nero, will once again be under the lion's name one day!"

Elizabeth could understand Phillip's ambition as she has heard stories from her mother a time when the three kingdoms where one. Though her dream simpler to rule Zen, the idea of joining these three giants together once more floated around.

"Your grace I'm sure one day that will happen," Elizabeth responded calmly.

"Grace?" Phillip said with slight anger in his voice griping his glass harder as he looked down to the floor. "That means nothing to me Sorde! I'm basically a bastard in the eyes of my siblings."

Elizabeth nodded. "You held the country together, through your father's illness and your brothers' campaigns on the border. Some would say you are the true people's Prince not Pier."

"Pier is a glory hog; people celebrate him so easily. Not knowing I'm the one who came up with the tax system, I'm the one who has calmed the masses after my father left them to starve to death and everyone just sits there praising the fat slob that is Logan and that glory hog that is Pier!"

"That's why I said the people's prince," Elizabeth said as she bowed her head. "I hope this is not out of tone, but with the nobles living so lavish, the people need someone like you, someone who they can rely on to voice their grievances. My prince you are known in my small land as the voice of the voiceless so do not worry too much the people know who is the real hero of Zen."

With Phillip's curiosity raised he calmed down and turned his head, "What province do you live under my Lady? I'm sorry how rude of me what did you say your name was?"

Elizabeth raised her head with a beaming smile on her face, "Lady Elizabeth my lord, I alongside the Gungadad family rule over the small land on the borders of Zen, its filled with sordes but when you give such people a will to live, they fight like no other."

"Or dear," Murmured Phillip. "Last time sordes banded together they almost destroyed the world, but they seem to have good morals. So, a new house then? Did the Last lord fall?"

"Yes, my lord during the war, large numbers of his men fell with him, the land was sold to me and gave me the strength to protect Zen's borders." Elizabeth said. "You should visit, the population of sordes might intimidate you at first however, we do love you, my Prince."

With a slight smile, the couple continue their conversation laughing and enjoying each other's company. But in the great hall as interesting as the room was, as pleasant the four walls around it where, as bright its jewels shined. You would have been surprised that all eyes were not on the hall or the king who sat in the background but plastered on the crowned prince, as the king watched him with envy drinking glass after glass of wine. He continued watching when he finally saw the poultry prince Logan, making a fool of himself in the corner of his eye. With a simple move of his wrist, the prince stopped his enjoyment and quickly approached the King.

"The great golden Lion," King Christiano mocked. "To think that is how people will remember you now Logan."

"Well, I have much more to achieve, after today we march towards the northern borders. Even The crowned Princess will join us in strengthening the Lions' new power."

King Christiano handed his glass away as he started to let out a small cough. "Nonsense, you need to establish your power, not be your brother's lap dog. And fight these endless battles."

"The beasts still stand; I will crush them before they become the force they were."

"That could last your natural life you fool."

"Then let it be, people will tell stories of my great conquests!" King Christiano smiled. "No look at your brother loved by nobles and the poor." He leaned close, lowering his voice. "He will be remembered not you not me not any of the Lions, those House leaders are even call him Pier the great, imagine. So, Logan, I will advise you again, build power and step from your brother's growing shadow before it consumes you."

"Your words have envy written all over them," Logan said with hate in his voice. "I am the Golden Lion Father! I will not be consumed as you say."

In the outskirts of the kingdom, far from the castles and high-ranking nobility, where people survived by the little food they received from the farmland. A hooded man approached Gaston as he ploughed his fields.

"There's no rest for the poor I see," the man said as he lowered his hood.

"Ezekiel! sorry I mean My lord," Gaston said. Leaning on his hoe as he relaxed waiting for Ezekiel to come closer. "You look well, I mean who wouldn't from such a glorious promotion.

The boys and I were talking about you not too long ago and how you managed to trick those fools into giving you the tittle of lord!"

Ezekiel smiled looking around as the side of the Kingdom the Lions would rather disappear. Well, calling it part of the kingdom was like comparing horse shit to royal cuisine. There were no roads, crumbling buildings in the far distance and the people just outside Gaston's property looked malnourished and fatigued. And as he looked down at what he thought was a bountiful field, was mostly covered in weeds, all this was not the result of drought, bandits or clansmen, but simply the max taxes from the crown. Ezekiel quickly understood how Pier had brought the country out of despair so quickly, those in the middle and top ate whilst the weak peasants who barely held onto their life were demanded more and more of.

"I thought the King promised at least to the ones that fought to stop taxes."

"Him and the Crowned prince, fulfilled that promise, however they took from everyone around us, so we helped, and the prince had the balls to send a thank you letter instead of actually helping." Gaston quickly replied, "What brings you here, you are far too clean to be around dirt like this."

"Conscription," Ezekiel said. "A new law, by the prince and the King, all men able body have to join the military for the next campaign."

Gaston visibly angry rested his hoe on his shoulder, "No, if we leave again our lands will be nothing the next time we return." Ezekiel with a straight face made it very clear to Gaston if he did not fight, they will make an example of him and his family. Forcing the already enraged man to throw his hoe in the air and quickly clench his fist looking down, "Fuck the crown to the depths of hell." he mutters to the slight smile from Ezekiel.

"Look at those ants, Gaston!" Ezekiel shouted as he stood pointing at the ground still with a slight smile still on his face. "They are small, yet they are so powerful, even their stronger enemies fall to them".

"What are you talking about?"

"Nonsense I think, but it makes me wonder if these ants banded together, they could accomplish so much, why not us the simple folk!?" Again, Ezekiel shouted.

"Well, that's just me talking nonsense, now shall you invite me to your home, I'm thirsty and traveling so far does bring some hunger."

Simply brushing Ezekiel's words beforehand Gaston quickly invited him in, with a queer look in his eye as if he were trying not to ponder on the simple words from his friend. They quickly retired indoors and just as quickly began to be loud and boisterous as they drank the only commodity Gaston had, Ale that was left over from the war.

Eros

The mansion loomed behind the iron gates, high upon the hill looking over Utopia, even as Eros wiped the walls clean, he could tell how new it was. The white of the stone walls glistened in the spring sun. The Vassille King's home away from home had been completed, twenty times the size of ordinary houses with staff ranging anywhere from people trying to make a living to slaves. Every room had to be cleaned, on a daily basis, all apart from the basement. Eros had walked past it again and again throughout the time he spent here but what the other slaves and help say is it is forbidden even to the queen and the young princess herself. Many thought of the reason but many knew it was where the King tortured Apollo. It was odd no one knew what happened in that room as it was locked in the day, and slightly open in the evening as if inviting you in.

"Hi, my name is Gaia what's yours?"

Shocked Eros turned around to see a young girl, who looked around his age, but soon after the curiosity faded, and he started to move away. However, each step he took he could feel the presence of Gaia following him like a lost puppy.

Eros finally stopped. "Eros ok, my name is Eros!"

Taken back for a moment Gaia quickly composed herself. "Nice to meet you," she said cheerfully. "I see you around here a lot, but you don't have one of them black collars, so do you live close by?"

Eros amused pointed far outwards towards the stables, indicating he lived with the ones with the collars. "The old man does not believe in enslaving children, and the way he does it is by not putting a collar on me, how kind."

"So, you belong to father... That's sad."

"Father? You must be the princess. What do you want?"

"Hangout maybe, like I hear you are good at fighting, so am I, so like we can fight a little and such."

Eros scrunched his face in distain. "No!"

"Now that's no way to talk to your master," Queen Hestia Vassellet calmly said. "Go get your play swords my darling and teach this child the Verselet's way of fighting."

Soon after Gaia returned with a butler holding two wooden blades, small enough for a child her size to use. "She amazing you know," Queen Hestia warned as she sat back under the sun, watching the match between these two.

The difference in strength alone was almost comical, with Gaia holding the blade with both hands, in fighting position and her feet firmly planted onto the ground. Her stance alone showed that she was used to this. However, it was clear that it was a simple hobby, Eros smiled thinking of all the ways he could take her down, her form from the outside looked near enough perfect If this was a sport. ***In battle these ones die first*** he reminisced, as he calmly lifted his blade with his right hand, holding so light that a gust of wind could blow it away. He had no stance or poise, and his eyes could barely pay attention.

"Begin!" the Butler shouted as Gaia lunged towards Eros and on impact, launched a fury of attacked from left to right high to low, all being easily blocked by Eros. Until his attention was stolen by the Queen for only a simple second but long enough for him to move his blade away from him allowing Gaia to knock him to the ground.

"You are strong, let's do this again tomorrow!" Gaia joyfully said as she got escorted away.

"I've heard stories of you, your speed and suicidal fighting." Queen Hestia said approaching Eros as he sat up. "Well, you made the right choice of letting her win, so as a reward you shall do that every day now."

"Fine. But I have a request." Eros said begrudgingly.

"Speak," the Queen quickly responded.

"Sarrah, where is she?"

"The girl you came with, well I wouldn't know."

As soon as the queen answered she carried on with her day sending Eros to continue his work, through to the end of day into the night and as he was about to retire for the day, he hears a distance voice coming from the basement's door. Eros still with childish curiosity quickly looked around before opening the door and quickly walking down the unlit stares. As he reached the bottom, he saw wines and cobwebs feeling disappointment he quickly turned around and as he was about to climb the stair once again, he hears a shout, "Already?!" from the same voice more clearly and deeper down the almost hidden hallway to the side. Testing his luck, he walked down the hallway, all concrete and no personality. Dimly lit with one or two fires in its long stretch. When he reached the end all that stood before him was a wooden door, smooth to the touch. Curious he twisted the nob pushing the door open.

"Sarrah?" the slight voice from Eros reached a naked Madas as the king was panting with a wooden club painted in blood firmly in his hand.

"Who are you?" Madas asked as he tried to catch his breath.

"The child that came with her, well you see your King is in an unsightly manor, I apologise now leave and I will forget you were here. Ok little boy?"

Eros tilted his head, seeing the disfigured body behind Madas. "I don't understand."

Madas clicked his tongue pointing the club towards Eros. "Boy I don't want to hurt you now leave! This is your last warning!" Eros lifted his hand folding it into a fist, smacking his teeth together to the point one cracked. Red. Everything, he could see was red. His vision blurred as all the muscles in his body shook. His mind blitzed through images of everything he has endured to this point. He could feel it crawling through his veins and seeping from his body. A black aura begun to consume him; the wind begun being dragged towards him. It was when the room started shaking Madas finally lowered his club, feeling as though a ghost's hand was caressing his heart.

"What...is... that..." Madas whispered as Eros's body drained of all colour leaving only blackness from it. Whatever it was it couldn't be human and as it looked up showing white voids where its eyes would be, it tilted its head once more and immediately erupting. Like water currents it downed the room, sending Madas from being paralyzed in fear to screaming in pain. And as he desperately ran towards the room's exit, he continued to let out screams, "Water! Help!" he shouted as he ran. Being slowly followed by Eros.

Finally, the King escaped for a moment reaching the top of the basement and as he took a look into the hallway now filling with Guards a hand sank into his face feeling each agonising second of Eros's flame engulfed hand. The guards paralyzed in fear stood there, as they gazed at what they thought was a demon killing their King. "Amon," the king muttered before he stopped struggling having his entire skull slowly cave in and crumble from the fire.

Eros then stood with his clothes mostly smouldered off, his hair redder and his eyes dead. He looked around to the clear fear emulating from the guards, stepped over the king's body and immediately ran into the guards, who quickly moved from his path. "Get him!" a single guard in the distance shouts. The chase began breaking through to the morning, as Commander Maximilian raised his banner leading every soldier in one objective to capture or kill Eros. Within hours posters went up with a staggering reward for the capture.

"The sky is beautiful," Eros said as he sat watching the clouds go by trying to gather his breath. When an old man sees him hiding in the corners.

The old man calmly approached standing next to Eros as he himself looked up at the sky to gaze on the clouds. "You look tired." he said with a warm smile on his face.

"It's been a long day."

"Your clothes are in pieces boy. You look like you fought a bear."

"You'll do well to continue with your day, old man," Eros said with a cold look.

The old man glanced back anxiously. "Come, let me give you some food and warm clothes, at least give you a chance." He looked fairly honest, Eros thought before gathering himself, and following the old man to a small house where he was quickly greeted by what seemed to be the old man's wife.

It seemed normal, with a simple meal of soup and bread, a change into their grandchild's old clothes, and even a fairly normal sleep into the night. Until few of the guards burst into the room Eros slept only to find nothing. "You said he was here old man!" one of them shouted as they held the old man by the collar.

Again, morning broke, adding to another day of Eros's evasion as he hid in the shadows close enough to the southern wall watching as soldiers stood watch. "They can't keep the city locked forever," he muttered as he bit into an apple ready to move the second those gates opened. When as the sun shined on top of his head a soldier came running, though he could not understand what was happening he quickly figured it out as gates started to open. With the site of the gates opening and a stable close by, he took his chances Evading everyone staying in the shadows until he reached the stables jumping onto a steed and rushing past the entrance. Charging as fast as he could as he could as more and more fields surrounded him. However, a slight sound of a hissing arrow flying past his head took away the growing feeling of hope and as he took a glance, he saw endless horse archers chasing him down.

Arrow after arrow flew past, for a person who had never road a horse before one would think he had an unmatched talent for it. However now it was angering the horse archers, who could not land a hit on Eros despite their best efforts. "Looks like I lost them…" Eros muttered as the sun hit its highest point. Minute after minute Eros could see his horse struggle to move and as he smiled petting its head, he jumped of immediately running towards the distant forest. Again, hope rose with the forest getting closer and closer. But just as quickly as that thought came, he felt a wet drip his back, and as he lifted his left arm, he could see the shaft of an arrow peaking from under his armpit. Then as his heartbeat faster he pulled a knife from his boot and staggered as fast as he could into the forest.

He continued running still looking forward another arrow cut the flesh from the side of his head as it flew past, making the right side of his vision blurred. Again, he continued running, taking heavy breaths as his arms dangled and finally, he entered the forest.

"Hold!" The captain shouted stopping all the soldiers.

"Captain, his right there it's easy for us to kill him!" a soldier quickly responded.

"That's the forest, an army struggles to get through it what can a child do," the captain insisted. "Amon's spawn is dead! Be it in a few minutes or a few hours, let us celebrate!" he added as he ordered the unit to turn their steeds around.

Heavily breathing barely able to see Eros dragged his feet, deeper into the forest with no direction but filled with fear and anger. Each step he took he could remember, the first time his mother made rice and beef stew and how he instantly fell in love with it. The first time he sparred with his brother, and how strong he was. The first time he watched the clouds with his sister and how she would always hold his hand. The first time Fargo wondered into their lives and how they fell in love with him.

In the dead of night, Eros muttered "I'm tired…". This night had a special kind of blackness, one where it only wanted to hold the stars and help them shine brighter, as an exhausted Eros, now on his knees looked up for the final time. When a howl in the distance, made him grasp his small blade, which surprised him, **why? I can finally meet them** He thought as he lunged forward killing the wolf in front of him. **Why, am I still moving?** He thought as he dodged attacked from other wolves, killing another in the process. **Why not?** He thought a final time as he continued to fight the waves of wolves coming for him, "Why do they get to live!" he shouted into the heavens feeling tears roll down his cheek. The fury of attacks continued throughout the night with fire bursting from Eros's hands as he screamed in pain.

Tears from years of torture burst from his eyes, as he screamed and fought his way till dawn, where the mood of the forest changed as birds sang to the shine of the sunlight. Two men came running through the forest both holding weapons with light armour on them. "See brother I told you I saw a light last night" one said enthusiastically.

"This is more than just a light brother there must be ten or twenty wolves here." The other quickly responded in shock as he walked past corpses of the wild animals.

"Appius look at this," the younger looking one said as he pointed at Eros's still body, perched up on the edge of a tree painted with blood.

"I can see, Aulus but, is he dead?"

"I think so..." quickly replied Appius.

"Go check then."

"No."

"Why not?" asked Appius.

"Look around," Aulus pointed. "Dead wolves leading to a dead child, clearly the work of a witch."

"Now why would a witch care about us?"

Aulus looked anxiously. "Who knows maybe the selling of people, we might have sold one of her children or something."

"Shut up," Appius said as he carefully approached Eros and as he snapped a twig under his foot. Eros's eyes popped open bloodshot with dried blood cracking from his cheek.

"I'm... going... to kill them... all," Smiling, Eros said softly as he raised his arm pointing his broken blade towards Appius.

"Every last one!"

"Get him!" a fearful Aulus said. As Appius jumped forward placing cuffs on Eros with a cain attached to the end. And after half a day's walk, they made it out of the forest, to the far east, where one of the beaches laid.

"Goddess save me another one," A man glancing at a map with fancy clothes spoke. "Do you two imbeciles want me to go mad?!"

"Wait here" the two brothers said in unison as they ran towards the well-dressed man.

Eros had never seen a beach before he marvelled at the gentle hue of gold as it stretched alongside the water. And as he tried to take a step forward, his body could not hold, and he collapsed forward. Taking short uneven breaths as he tried lifting himself up.

"What fresh hell did you crawl out off?"

Eros looked up to see someone who barely looked older than him with ragged clothes and black unkept hair.

"Don't try fake dying, they make sure you know," the boy spoke once again with a blank look on his face and scratching his hair.

"Water," Eros croaked.

"Wine," Ulfr quickly answered as he pointed the bottle towards Eros, who in turn staggered to his feet dragging himself forward and gulping in such force most came back up.

"Eros," he said. "Just Eros."

"Ulfr, just Ulfr."

Elizabeth

"Ale."

"Ale?"

"Yes, and some cherry pie."

"You look young to be asking for alcohol sir." The barmaid said as she held empty cups returning to the back. "Well, whatever you have to pay upfront though."

"How much."

"Twelve Cuni."

The boy lifts his hand pointing at the wall of posters. "His going to pay." Instantly silencing the bar, with the loud music fading, the crunching of food stopped, and boisterous conversations stopped mid sentences.

"Shh, do you know who that is?"

"I believe its black bone Ron, wanted for a thousand Cuni dead or alive, I don't usually go for small fries, but I've run out of money it seems."

In the background a man stood striding across the bar dragging a thick black club alongside him with a wide smile pasted on his face. "Boss, this child is being awfully chatty what shall I do with him?"

"You must be the second in command of the Black bones, you don't even have a poster yet so sorry if I can't remember your name."

"Wild eye Victor," the man quickly responded as he gripped his club with both hands ready to swing. "How old are you anyways boy!?"

"Fifteen and it's not boy its Raijin. One of you better write the name down because one day I'm going to be the greatest swordsman in the world." Raijin smiled as he lifted his hat up.

"Miss, I'll take your silence as you accepting the trade, with Ron's head I'll be able to have forty-two pies and ale!"

The barmaid confused quickly responded, "Your math is way off..."

"Victor kill the little Milo," Ron said in the background before his face dropped in shock seeing Victor's arm fly across the bar. As victor's screams sang through the bar, Raijin danced to the tune, as he cut down each one of Ron's men, leading to the man filled with fright running outside the bar, instantly tripping and turning around to see the blood dripping from Raijin's blade. "Congratulations Ron, you get to be the lucky guy to spread my name, if you want to live that is."

"Wait!" Ron shouted scrambling to show his shoulder band. "See that Sigel, I'm one of the White Knights, you can't touch me this is their land you won't walk out of this town alive!"

"I know this is their town, but damn you have to give it to Lizzy, expansion is her speciality, ruling over Zen, Nero and Pocasis in what a little under two years and she is already expanding into the wastelands. Doesn't waste any time, does she?" Raijin said as he looked around at the banners of the White Knights plastered everywhere around him. Immediately after he lunged the blade into Ron's band.

"Lizzie plays ball with Pangea; she won't protect you." he said with a cold smirk on his face, as the rest of Ron's men came crawling out of the corners.

She was of a sleek nature many came to realise. As she strode across the castle of Zen, in difficult times at the beginning of her rule she was the leader that was needed. Within a year of her regent, she made Nero and Pocasis bend the knee. The people loved her and when they rose against the Lions only one person deserved the crown, Elizabeth St'Louis queen of the White Knight kingdom wife of the people's Prince Phillip 'the Kind'. Her climb to the top was felt throughout the world, a woman with many tittles, many achievements above all else, the Sordes regarded her as a shadow that walked into the light and found herself more legend that woman. Thus, with floods of them bending the knee to her, her influence became unmatched in the west.

"Good afternoon my Queen," Chief financial adviser Lachlan Gungadad quickly announced as Queen Elizabeth entered.

"The northern merchants did you justice, you look absolutely poured in that dress."

"That's enough Lachlan." Chief Drill sergeant Al'Gadrood commanded.

"Shall we proceed with the meeting my queen," Head commander of the five armies Ser Lancer calmly said with his hands folded.

"I hope this has to do with the Lords and ladies of the Kingdom, and how the request for lower taxation has yet to be met my Queen." Voice of Noble houses Ser Corentin Etienne spoke out with slight tone in his voice.

"What off food and education for the people?" Voice of the people Lady Delphine St.Louis proudly asked. "As a St.Louis who grew up in the outskirts of the lands I do love what our queen has done so far, however there is still a lot to do."

"The Goddess did not create the world in a day my lady these things take time," Voice of Church Father Gael responded as he put his hands together.

"I do not respond kindly to a Eunice' respo-" Lady Delphine St'Louis lashed out quickly stopped by The Master of Law-and-order Lady Oceane.

"The queen is waiting to speak."

"Thank you, Lady Oceane. Lords and ladies of the White Knight kingdom, Firstly I would like to apologise, the right hand of Crown will not be joining us as he has other matters to handle. Secondly, I would like all reports from all parts of the land passed to my advisors after meeting. Finally, I brought you all here as I would like to proceed with the expansion onto the wastelands and your opinions on it."

Over in the automatous zone, a small plot of land, two thirds of the size of Utopia that set closest to the city of Thieves. The automatous zone a city that never sleeps, some might not call it a city at all. At this land with no King people from all over the world many came visited and made it their home. This field of Mable stretching to the horizon and back.

At the centre, a place which has found peace in the west, where people who talked differently, looked different, dressed different all came together to watch the West's own Gladiatorial games. Annual Games supported by Pangea and the White Knight Kingdom, where merchants could smell the money and placed their homes in this area. Building a new type of power in the west only seen deep in the empires of Rodinia and Precambria called the Lanasta. Owners of gladiator schools, and mass slave traders, the Lanasta.

Near the coliseum, one of the brothels that arose there, Drominic stumbled out still drunk from the night before and as he sits on the corner looking worse for wear in his tunic, jacket and stockings that looked tailored from the finest black fabrics.

"This is not a fine look for your Rank 'Bishop'," said Lady Charlotte Al'Jacques with her head held high followed closely by Knights.

"Wine?" Drominic asked.

"No," coldly responded Lady Charlotte as she gripped her sheathed sword. "You need to report to your post Sir 'Bishop' Drominic!"

"Man, can't you give me a break. You're also one of the five leaders, right? So, you know it's hard," Drominic responded as he held his cheek and crossed his legs, "Well, I don't blame you. You must feel big being what ten or whatever and leading one of the big armies. I mean daddy had a lot to do with that but whatever."

"My father fought hard for his rank, and I fought twice as hard to be called the third leader Lady 'Knight' Charlotte Al'Jacques. So, I ask of you second leader Sir 'Bishop' Drominic to respect my rank and to recognise us as equals!"

"Man, I said I just wanted a cushy job why did lizzie have to put me alongside this prone." Drominic said as he stood striding away. "Fine, fine, little miss I need to go talk to Lizzie to make us swap posts I've grown fond of this place."

Eros

Eros set foot on the beach, his eyes moving from sand to stone. He dug his toes into the gentle hue of gold. With his eyes closed and his head tilted towards the sky he felt as if he was being hugged by the summer sunshine.

"You look peaceful over there, Brother!" Shouted Ulfr scratching a slight scruff of hair on his chin.

"Afterall It's been five years since I've been here," Eros muttered as he looked into the distance.

"He does... Eros get too work!" shouted Aulus as he bit into a squid annoying his brother who with the other crewmates, walked onto the sand helping to unload the ship of its goods.

"Let him enjoy it," Captain Peter Williams said softly. "He alongside a few of these lads will be sold off to the Lanastas tomorrow, probably won't live much longer so a little freedom would be the humane thing to do."

"Or this is your cheap way of repaying all of the insane things this kid accomplished in the sea?" Aulus responded to the sly smile of Peter.

Through night and day, Peter's band of bandits, pirates and slaves marched into the automatous zone, laying rest on its borders, and breaking their fast on a hog and some fruits. "There he is," Peter said before approaching, a man in fine robes, surrounded by large group of Legionnaires, though similar looking to Pangea's forces, their leather was dull, and on their chest a strange coat of arms stood.

"Even slave traders have their own army in this land now?" Peter said in excitement. "Surely the Goddess would commend this practice?"

"Evening ser Peter, correct?"

"Correct, my friend what shall I call you?"

"Tittles are long, I am part of the unofficial slave trade Union, you may call me Ser Adrian Aegeus".

"A Pangean slave trader, how strange." Peter responded with slight smirk on his face looking at the sun symbol hanging from his neck with a bit of string.

"Please ser Peter, I have a lot of work, which one of those lads would you like to sell?" Adrian said smiling.

"Ulfr, Minato, Thutmose, Eros come forward!" Peter commanded as the group of boys begrudgingly moved forward. Adrian could not help but notice, the vast differences each one of these boys possessed, from Height to the colour of their skin. Though with a deceiving almost inviting appearance, the opinion of peter quickly changed. From the names of these boys Adrian knew this man was a world traveller, trading people like its rice. And by the short glance in the background, he could tell this man was making his crew richer than their wildest dreams. Adrian quickly held up a number nearly double the asking price knowing disrespecting a man like this will not only cause bloodshed but keeping him on your side will grant you more territories to trade. With a simple nod, the day passed the crew returned to their ships, and the boys where chained, washed, put in fresh shirts and shorts, removed of their hair from head to toe, and fed bread and some water, left in a small cell.

Ulfr glanced at the moon from the small window just above their heads. "We should rest, tomorrow these pricks will be selling us to the highest bid." He was fairly come, as he spoke, almost disregarding the sad fact of their current situation.

"From slave to gladiator, I guess we got promoted...I blame Eros for that one," Minato said anxiously as he scratched his collar.

At this moment Thutmose started to reminisce. "Speaking off remember when the fool, jumped into the mouth of Sub-Kraken..."

"Then Ulfr, the fool jump right after him screaming for Eros to comeback as if he was his father!" Minato said smiling.

"The second I was in the air I thought I was going to die," Ulfr laughed as he responded.

"Since that day you two would not stop fighting, through hurricanes, retreats, battles on the sea, you name it they were there fighting each other." Minato added starting to laugh.

"We agree on something don't we brother?" Ulfr said lovingly.

Eros, trying to focus on his workout snapped. "I agree you should shut up."

"You want to make me you muscle brain!"

"Come on then you chicken leg freak!"

"Now, now boys, like Ulfr said we need some rest tonight, tomorrow is going to be long day." Thutmose chimed in calming the situation.

Inside the small cell, the boys caught the morning light, as they slowly work up, used to sleeping on hard floors this process was simple for them at this point. And as a guard came rushing to wake them up, his heart filled with disappointment as the boys simply stirred, then the guard ordered them to be escorted out of their cells.

As the boys approached the Auction house, they were surprised at its architecture. The sculptures Infront drew the eye, they were set at the entrance amid the water of the fountains and perfectly trimmed hedges. Instead of a roof common around the world, it had gold domed hands attached to each other reaching for the clouds. The hallway in the front was open, with mostly detailed pillars, painted in white. It was so massive when the boys walked through, they were not surprised at the village of slaves bounded there to take care of it. As they stood behind the thin layer of sheet, the event eventually begun.

"So, another year another group of fighters, I hope this group is less miserable than the last one. Fucking hell, I almost went bankrupt on the amount of loses my school felt." Lanasta Lovita Jovian spoke siting calmly near the front with his wife's hand firmly wrapped around his.

"Well, that's an easy fix then, Lovita... No elderly men this time and we should be fine." Lady Marcella quickly responded. Lanasta Lovita Jovian sat back. "With the loud one we got cheep the other day, we only need what four at most and we can rebuild our school to its glory."

As the goods finished being bet on, the hallway went silent, the sheet was removed revealing fifteen men and boys standing in rows with the smallest Infront. No one moved as they desperately anticipated for the Auctioneer to arrive. And so, after a few minutes' Ser Adrian Aegeus approached the stage.

"Let us begin, we will start with the younglings' number one at eight hundred Cuni."

"One thousand," Shouted Lanista Estienne of house Amis. Lanasta Gosse from the trader guild stood, "Two thousand!"

"Do you not wish to be involved love?" asked his wife Lady Marcella.

"Too young, I want to compete in the games not wait years for them to grow." quickly responded Lanasta Lovita Jovian as the room started to get much louder. The bets continued until Minato stood forward, the awe of an eastern man standing before them with such a physic made everyone in the room ecstatic.

"One hundred thousand Cuni!" Shouted Lanasta Lovita Jovian to the surprise of everyone including his wife.

"That's a lot for one person don't you think darling!"

"His from the east as you can see, he might even be one of them Yin sect people." Lanasta Lovita whispered. "If he is, hundred thousand is worth it, if his not look at him, he looks stronger than everyone there and his young so he will only get stronger."

"One hundred and one thousand Cuni," Lanista Gosse said to the obvious distain of Lanista Lovita. Unable to match the amount, Gosse managed to secure Minato. Due to this humiliation Lanasta Lovita quickly snatched four gladiators with the hundred thousand Cuni.

"What are you looking at Lady Charlotte?" asked one of her Knights escorting her back to her post for the day.

"Nothing, just one of the slaves had this look..."

"Look my lady?"

"Yes, just reminded me of the first time I met Lancer is all. Let's move!" she quickly commanded calmly marching through-out the streets.

As the sun set on another day, over in the northern outskirts of the Autonomous Zone, a squeaky "Their back!" was heard being shouted by a kid on the roof of a villa dousing the Jovian family crest, the child energetic as ever quickly scaled down the roof, grabbing the attention of many of the Jovian gladiators as they begin to laugh and cheer.

"Young master!" shouts a timid slave girl as she grabbed onto her dress. "Please your mother has told you a million times about climbing!"

"You worry too much, let's go meet mother and father!" the child shouted sprinting out of the gates, into the farm fields of the Jovian family. Past the crowd of slaves, working and flying into the hands of his mother.

Lady Marcella quickly embraced her son, putting on a warm smile in the process. As they stop the carriages, the family quickly converse to each other about their day, Celsus the young boy bragging about the small adventure he had to the silent distain of Marcella. And Ulfr watching the convo through the small window to his left.

"Look at that beauty! Do you think she could be my wife?" Ulfr asked with a bright smile on his face.

A scarred man peaked from the shadows. "You might as well give up on women young blood, where we are going, you will never touch a woman again."

"But won't we become famous?" Ulfr quickly responded. "I mean from the Precambrian Empire I saw a few gladiators; they were treated like gods!"

"I keep telling you Ulfr, that was for show, you've been a slave for years, I'm guessing it's that but with fighting." Eros responded attempting to scratch the back of his head but struggling because of the cuffs.

Ulfr's eyes filled with tears. "So, I'm going to die a virgin?"

"I mean I'm sure there's a lovely man waiting for you in there," said Flavius a narrow eyed ebony man, lacking muscle but looking more confident than anyone there. "I'm sure the big guy over there might be interested."

"I'm not that desperate yet, and the name is Gallus young blood," the man roared as he stuck his chest out.

"Looks like we are moving," Eros said as he rubbed his head on the back wall trying to reach the itch.

The following journey was short, as they arrived at the villa, the click of the locks on the carriage, alerted the new slaves, as their calm dementor changed, knowing at that moment their lives would include a lot more death they all stretched themselves as if preparing of what was to come. "Move out!" shouted one of Lovita's men, as he marched out each one of the new slaves in single file lines. Until they all stood facing the balcony where Lovita stood.

"Look around you!" Lovita shouted. "All these men before you are better than you, stronger than you, have been immortalised in history and are men not simply slaves! All men are not born equal, some are faster, some are smarter, some are born with one leg, some with poor vision, some are born with the power to manipulate the elements. Some are born to fight; some are born to die, and some are born to rule! Though you cannot change everything about yourself, you can be stronger, and can be immortalised in history. Fight in glory under the name of Jovian!"

"Look at him, scars across his chest, and even on his face, damn how did they catch this little animal." a man with long dreads spoke. "Look another scary one to his left, is that his father, they both have a lot of scars after-"

"Cyril...Enough." roared Kilian, as he sat with his cheeks balanced on his fist.

"No," Eros answered to the surprise of everyone. "I will fight, because I have yet to meet my brother, not for your useless glory." It was strange to hear a slave talk back to his master so comfortably. Swimming in bewilderedness, Lovita did not know how to respond to this situation, until his Doctares Zachariah stepped forward with his left hand raised high and a whip on his right.

"This child just insulted all of us, as if fighting for the glory of house Jovian is not more than enough reason. Who will shut his mouth!" Doctares Zachariah spoke proudly, as the sunset glimmered through his one good eye. Kilian stood and walked forward being handed two blades from the house slaves. As he walked to the outside his frame was even more visible. Taller than most men, with large muscles and hair like that of Cyril.

He threw the blade to Eros's feet. As a guard unlocked the chains on his wrists.

Eros immediately released the full force of his Will, knocking the guard out and stunning Kilian for only a second but long enough for Eros's blade to be mere inches from his chest. In quick thinking Kilian jumped backwards losing his balance putting Eros in high spirits lunged forward but quickly tucking his head in dodging the stray kick from Kilian and as he sees the man's back inches from his blade, Eros then grasps the blade as hard as he could launching it forward but only to feel the side Kilian's right foot firmly pressed under his chin launching him into the air. Gladiators are commonly referred to in the world as the Kings of close combat and Eros felt this skill for the first time in his life, dazzling him until he hit the floor with his back.

"Come down, Eros..." Ulfr whispered. Before walking forward, and past Kilian confusing not only Kilian but everyone standing there to a stop. As Ulfr approached Celsus's personal slave, dropping on one knee and loudly shouting "Please, please marry me!"

"You don't even know my name!" the slave responded.

"Names will come at our wedding day, don't let me die a virgin!"

"Enough!" Shouted Doctares Zachariah.

Ulfr slightly turned his head in disgust. "Creepy old man... we are in the middle of something here!"

"We are in the middle of nothing!" quickly responded the slave girl.

Now with a slight smile on his face, Lovita lifted his left hand in the air. "Enough, Guards take the disrespectful boy and tie him next to the other one. Doctares, show these new recruits where they will be sleeping from now on."

Alexander

"Looks like we have a customer!" announced Basil, "He looks rich as well. AL'lioe, Adonis get the boss I think Mr deep pockets over there is about to make us enjoy the next few weeks." He stood up ankle deep in the fields with his sharp brown eyes not looking away from the target once.

Ten? No twenty men Basil thought as he gripped his sheathed blade. He looked almost happy, not for the possible fight but the upgrade from his leather armour.

In the hectares of the thick grass, with one tree solitary on the empty field, past the men sleeping under the sun, or conversing among each other laid a napping blond hair man, tall with small muscles a thin white shirt and some brown trousers.

"Alex wake up," Ava calmly ordered. She marched down towards the napping Alex, in haste almost as if her iron armour weight nothing. With the heat being unnaturally warm, it was odd to see someone move with that much iron and leather on their body, without so much as breaking a single sweat.

"Yes, lady Ava?" Alex responded sarcastically as he slowly opened his eyes.

Ava unimpressed quickly pointed at the merchant in the distance surrounded by well armoured guards. "That man wishes to talk to you."

"They look annoying fine... fine let's go talk to them."

"I'll join, I can't trust you not to do something stupid."

"Come on Ava, I am the strategist remember, stupid doesn't exist in my mind."

"Whatever." Ava said as they approached the merchant. "Afternoon sir, I am Ava Dansu, the right hand of the 'Phalanx of Basilisk' and the man to my left is the leader Alexander 'the Basilisk'."

"Ser Tumas..." the unimpressed merchant said, "the man Alexander is described as someone so terrifying; he could kill with a single look. Yet, I'm looking at a frail man, who is more suited to be queen Elizabeth's Concubinatus. Is this one of your fool-ish jo-?"

"Please forgive this fool ser Alexander!" quickly interrupted Ser Tumas as he took off his helmet bowing his head in fear.

In that moment almost uncharacteristic Ava let out a small chuckle. "As he gets older, he does look more feminine I thought that was just me who noticed."

Alex looked curious at the statement scratching his head at the idea. "It would be an easy life I guess, but that's not my way, well then Mr merchant, what do you want?"

Ser Tumas quickly raised his voice. "Ser... Alexander... Please hold in your Will..." he said struggling to let his words out, even struggling to stand.

"Sorry, sorry, now then merchant... what do you want?"

Ser Leonard cleared his throat finally able to speak. "It's Ser Leonard, member of the trade guild, I'm sorry for the disre-spect, however I hope we can look past this."

"Did Alex ask for your name?" quickly replied Ava now holding the tip of her blade's handle looking displeased.

"No, my Lady, he did not. it's simple the rumoured club that the saint Adira Senesto was holding at her death, I believe we found it."

"Man, word spreads quick, where is it?"

Now composed Ser Leonard quickly negotiated. "First, I want someone dead, you do that you get the information you want. You can take his cargo, gold anything. Kill Lachlan Gungadad". Alex scrunched his brows as he folded his arms. "Lachlan... Head of the trade guild and the queen's chief financial advisor. Then you Sir must be Leonard Gael. Information would not be enough; make it a fair payment and I'll bring you, his head."

Ser Leonard feeling slight frustration, glanced coldly at Alex. "You think you have the advantage here. Don't make me laugh, your hundred idiots will not compare to my twenty trained Knights!" shouted Ser Leonard before a rock spear flew through his head sending him flying into the ground lifeless. Kal Orrin, in the background almost too far to see without one focusing raised his hand. "Sorry, I was aiming for my brother then he dodged it."

"Oi you idiots the spear almost hit us be more careful!" Shouted Ava as she marched towards the brothers. When she got far enough each one of the knights dropped to their knees holding their necks struggling to breathe. Leading to Alexander calmly walking past Ser Tumas, drawing one of the knights' swords and marching to the one furthest in the back pointing it in the eye slits of his armour.

"One hundred thousand Cuni now, and another hundred thousand with the information after. Ser Thibault Gael." Alexander commands to the single nod from Thibault Gael.

With negotiations complete, the band of mercenaries watched the knights of Gael quickly leave the area and once they left their site, they immediately begun to drink and relax again. All except, Ava, Stavros and alexander who were packing their bags to move out to their mission. "Why him as well," Ava asked.

"He is our muscle; in case we have to fight a lot of people."

"This is supposed to be a coved mission, the muscle head over here is the opposite of that."

"Don't worry so much Ava, we won't ruin the mission right Stavros."

Stavros took a few steps back before slashing the air with his hands. "You won't even see me unless someone try's it on little Alex."

Alex laughed as the conversation continued. And at the break of dawn, with Basil left in charge of the camp the small group on horseback marched out, with Stavros holding the rear with his massive frame poorly hidden under the brown robe. Ava, also in a robe, reading the map, to make sure they do not get lost. A small child barely able to ride his horse focusing heavily on not falling and Alex poised in the front with his hood down whistling the day away.

"Calm yourself Marcus," Ava spoke. "If you hold on too tight the horse will not listen to you."

"Ay," Marcus responded. "But my Lady, it's as if ToTo won't listen to me, it's like she's scared of something."

"You must be new boy, that's because ToTo, has never seen that monster Infront of us." Stavros quickly replied.

"Ser Alexander?"

"No, the beast his riding Agtaris. A mythical beast, the Arki. Not only did he tame that monster, but he has managed to hold on to it till this point." Stavros laughed, holding his belly. "Oi little Alex! Your idiot horse is scaring the boy's steed."

"Arki, not a horse but sorry Marcus, you just have to bear with it." Alex quickly responded.

"Ok, well I have been wondering Ser Alexander, why risk having an enemy like the White Knights? To try and kill such an important figure of theirs." Marcus curious as ever asked.

Ava chimed in from the background. "We are technically already an enemy of theirs. But if the information is correct, that would simply put us one step closer to creating the perfect kingdom. One far away from the monsters of Pangea."

"Monsters... then you believe the rumours about the Gevana incident." Marcus quickly responded to a deafening silence.

With no response they continued marching towards Pocasis.

And as Marcus started to change his questions the joyful atmosphere once again returned to the group.

Logan

Logan was showing Oliver how to best swing a sword when Ezekiel approached from afar. "Plant your feet boy!" Logan roared. "If you lose your balance in battle you will die. Now swing the sword with all your weight!"

Ezekiel clapped impressed by Oliver's progression. "You might be ready for the great war, young squire. Sir, may I have a word."

Logan quickly turned marching away with Ezekiel, the stress seemed to have gotten to him as he looked heavier in his golden armour, looking almost trapped by the iron. Though with darkened eyes, with his health for the worse, all those in their camp still saluted their King as he walked past. "What is it Ezekiel," Logan said with an oddly familiar demeanour as he walked. One that resembled Pier.

"My lord!" Shouted Ser Vauquelin Josee saluting Logan as he entered, a massive red tent. "Ser Ezekiel..."

As they entered only Ser Vauquelin followed, in the silver iron armour with his family crest in the middle, he looked ready for battle at any moment. Not even taking off his helmet, people would joke at the amount of fear the young Lord held. However, Throughout the last two years he had fought hard in the front lines earning Logan's respect in the process.

As Logan sat, he waved for Ezekiel to speak, above all else, above the fact the man was regarded a glutton by all accounts, he was the man Zen needed in these times. A flowed man with powerful ambitions, is what gave him respect in the end. It's what made Ezekiel bow before conversing with him.

"My king, we found people who would be willing to join your fight." Ezekiel stated with hesitation. "The band of the Hound wishes to fight under you, my lord."

Logan winced at the notion. One of the new clans that came about because the beasts fell, though others minded their own lands or had a code to follow, these men used the idea of the old god to rape, pillage, plunder everything in their path. No one not even other clans felt calm when they were around.

"However, that can't happen, we are desperate for men but..."

"But would it not be better to kill them off my King," Ezekiel interrupted to the slight smirk of Logan.

"Continue."

"Bring them here, say the King accepts your offer and well take care of them." Ezekiel spoke with great confidence.

"No!" Logan roared at the top of his lungs. "We are lions Ezekiel, we do not fight like cowards, we face our enemy and kill them!"

"My lord ple-"

"No."

"My lord, we do not have enough man to just fi-"

"I said no Ser Ezekiel."

Logan stood from his chair stepping forward with his chest out and a beaming smile, "What is my name Ezekiel."

"King Logan St'Louis 'The golden Lion'" Ezekiel quickly responded begrudgingly lowering his head.

"Then this King, will lead his men and kill the band of the hound..." Logan calmly proclaimed. "Ser Vauquelin Josee, raise the banners we march at dawn!"

As the two were about to exit the tent, Logan in a calm voice asked simply "How about the other mission ser Ezekiel..."

"I'm sorry my lord we have yet to find the murderers of Pier 'The great'." Ezekiel responded with his hands on his chest. "However, there is a rumour of a small mercenary group that currently holds his armour."

"Ok... first we claim the hound then we go retrieve my brother's armour."

Chief Halfdan leader of the Band of the hound sat around the campsite reading the latest news from around the world, snickering as he chugged on some Ale. "These new bloods, to attack one of Pangia's Laboratories how brave." he said as he took a glance at the new batch of slaves ready to be sold. "To escape that's even braver, I wish to meet this Lael one day, our battle would be grand!"

A scout in leather armour came running through, sweating and looking frightened he quickly spoke. "There's hundreds maybe a thousand men!" He spoke. "They had banners my lord, yellow with the red lion!"

"The Lions, I guess they did not accept our request," Chief Halfdan said.

"But to come towards us?" The right hand Frode asked. "Either their stupid or think themselves so strong whilst thinking us so weak!" He said this as he drew his axe, a large frame man, waiting for his larger leader to stand and declare war. Within seconds Chief Halfdan stood, dwarfing all those near him, "Height second to 'The goliath' Gjurd," one whispered as the chief grabbed his great Axe marching past all his men with a smile planted on his face.

"To arms, the true gods shall guide us to another victory!"

As the Lions and hounds stood across each other, "Lions! To victory!" shouted King Logan St'Louis on horseback as he led the charge towards the hounds.

"The True gods watch us!" Shouted Chief Halfdan as he ran towards the Lions gripping his great Axe with both hands. There was no strategy, or formations, the winner was simply who would stand after the clash and as the day went by, both sides' takin heavy casualties. At the end with a strike through Halfdan chest, Gaston, took the victory for the Lions.

Ezekiel gasping for air sat at the edge of the battlefield spoke. "Did we even win?"

"We are standing, and they have fallen," Gaston quickly answered as he cleaned his blade.

"How did he swing that thing with such little effort?" Ezekiel asked wearily. "He was human as well, I know monsters like this exist, but even they would have trouble with that axe, it didn't even make sense. I've never seen such a top-heavy weapon used like that."

"It looks like the King wishes to keep it," Gaston expressed as he pointed at the few soldiers in the distance loading the Axe. "I wonder if he wishes to use it."

Logan roared as he approached, "What are you fools talking about?"

"My king," Gaston quickly saluted. "We were wondering if you wished to use the strange Axe."

"A heathen's blade, no..." Logan quickly answered. "The only blade that can handle my might, would be the King Slayer, the blade passed down from one Lion to another, it holds the strength of all the past leaders, now why would I give up such a power for a badly made Axe. No, it'll be a test to the next champion of the Lions. If he can hold and use such a weapon, then he shall be my next champion."

As he spoke Oliver quickly approached with the King slayer wrapped around his hands, making Ezekiel reminisce on the story of the Celestial blade 'God slayer' a sword last held by Scar. But before he could get lost in his thoughts, the loud Logan, proudly bragged of his leadership towards Ezekiel almost mocking him for doubting Logan's victory. Slightly annoying the Advisor but nowhere enough to anger him.

Elizabeth

"My Queen, Ser 'Bishop' Drominic has arrived," One of the Knights announced to Elizabeth, as she was de thawing the roses in the castle's garden. Though she would usually hate being interrupted during her small windows of leisure, the idea of seeing her friend got her excited, quickly ordering the guard to bring him through.

As Drominic walked in the first thing he noticed was her smile, with mud on her fingers, dirty clothes, and her hair tied back, she could not look more at peace if she tried. Even with all the titles, she was still just human, and this simple idea made a smile creep up on Drominic.

"You look happy to interrupt your Queen," Elizabeth jokingly said. "What brings one of the White Knights' leaders all the way to the capital? Not even to send an emissary, or messenger bird, must be of importance."

Drominic quickly returned to his usual demeanour, slouching and dragging his eyes. "Why did you give me this role?"

"Bishop? Because you didn't want to be hand of the crown."

"Ever thought why Liz? I wanted less work so I can enjoy my old life." Drominic calmly said as Elizabeth took him by the wing, quickly going for a walk throughout the castle. As they passed each worker and guard, they all saluted or bowed to the Queen, not moving until she had walked past. "I tend to forget how powerful you've become Liz," Drominic whispered as he turning his head watching each personal doing the same thing. A mischievous smile crept on his face again. "I don't think your husband will be pleased with another man on your arm."

"The people's prince is too preoccupied with the people," Elizabeth coldly said. "It does not matter though, as he has done his duty." She added holding her belly.

Drominic's smile dropped, replacing it with a forced smirk, "Congratulations, now your legacy will be secure, however I came to wi-"

"For a Transfer, to the autonomous zone I'm guessing."

"Yes"

"No."

"Why not!"

Elizabeth let go of Drominic's arm as they approached the Castle's training grounds, seeing Lancer taking on several opponents, with a single wooden sword. "There are three people in this world I trust more than anything, you, Al'Gadrood and Lancer. And with the remnants of the nobles and loyalists that rejected me having the crown standing with the fool Logan or hiding in Pocasis I need someone I trust to crush any rise up from them in Pocasis."

"I understand. Speaking of Logan, if reports are right, he fought a sizable clan and won," Drominic said grimly. "If he is gathering so much power, everyone who is silent right now will rise."

Amused Elizabeth responded. "The fool lost hundreds of soldiers, even if he came for us, they would follow him for a battle at most and once we crush them no one will ever follow him again. He himself attacking is not the problem. It's the idea of him that makes me unable to take you away from your post."

Drominic sighed. "Monitoring so much has to get to you, how are you doing Liz?"

"I could use some sleep old friend, otherwise I'm fine."

"Come then let's go get a drink, then." Drominic grinned as he stretched his collar.

Elizabeth shrugged. "I can't Drominic, I have much to do, and you should be wearing your uniform instead of those street clothes, you are a representation of the White Knights, always remember that lazy fool." She said slowly approaching Lancer.

"Will do Liz, then I'll talk to you later, a bottle is calling for me."

"Champion of the White Knights, the Gladiator King, Beast slayer, the undefeated Lancer!" Elizabeth roars proudly. "So many accolades for someone so young, enough for him to retire knowing statues will be built for him and songs will be sung throughout time."

"My queen, I disagree." Lancer says as he bows.

"Disagree?" Elizabeth sarcastically responded waving her hands around. "You are a man who many fear and respect, so why do you insist on fighting in these primitive games?" she asked in a calmer tone folding her arms like a disapproving mother. "You could marry, have land, anything you wish could be yours in a second, yet for the fourth year you wish to step into a cage with those animals?"

Lancer raised his head with determination leaking from him.

"As long as you stand as Queen, I will stand as the best fighter you have, no one not even an elemental will ever stand before me."

Elizabeth snorted. "Bold words little man. But is this really what you want to fight forever, when you have the option to let others do all that for you."

"Do you want to keep this crown?"

"..."

"Then I need to show my strength."

Elizabeth sighed taking a step back and watching Lancer as he continued his endless training regiment, jumping from body exercises to swinging a wooden pole in all directions, pretending there was opponents standing before him.

"My queen, we have summarised the quoter report..." ser Yoan St'Timeo softly spoke as he approached the queen holding a stack of papers. The advisor's presence always annoyed Elizabeth as he had never brought any good news.

"Speak,"

"We are quickly going into national debt; you might have to call for Ser Lachlan Gungadad to move forward with the trade deal regardless of how much profits they will get." Yoan said calmly. Elizabeth sighed once more scrunching her eyebrows. "Fine, send a messenger bird to Lachlan, also Yoan whilst you are at it keep a close eye on the Provence of Therouzen it seems people there are being louder than usual. I'm not surprised it was one of the highly Loyalist parts of Zen."

"As you command," Ser Yoan St'Timeo's voice dropped as he spoke. "I will place men from my house at the border and send scouts into the Provence until your next order."

Eros

The sun licked their sunburned faces, coiling around their limbs, Raijin tried to lick his dry lips to no result. The muggy heat pressed in on them, to the point his body could not swear to give him some relief. Raijin turned his head to see Eros, looking unbothered as he yawned.

"How are you able to withstand this heat?" Raijin calmly asked. "Just looking at your body you must have adjusted to pain, I guess."

"Fire Elementals tend to thrive in this weather," Eros muttered. He lifted his head feeling the heat breathe onto his face. And as he looked around his surroundings even the horses that tended to the fields were hiding in the shade refusing their master's orders to step outside.

"A sordes hu," Raijin stated, as a smirk creeped up on his face. "I head sordes can't control their emotions, so I'm guessing you let your anger get the better off you that's why you ended up in such a place."

"After you left, we continued with Apollo, his theory on Jon was correct. Then his brother captured us, I killed the Vassille King, ended up on a ship for a few years then sold here. you?" Raijin tried to free his wrist from the chains to no luck, and in the end pointing awkwardly to the sky, "Because I was heading to the top and they got scared of me. So, they sent a town of soldiers to capture me. Lucky for them they brought elites from the White Knights otherwise I would have killed everyone there."

"I remember now, you wanted to be the greatest swordsman when we were younger…"

"Still on that journey misfit." Raijin smirked. "Did Sarrah come with you?"

"She died."

"So dead sister, mother friends. That could be annoying." Raijin said as he glanced back at the sky. "Betrayed, enslaved damn you've had an interesting life."

Eros looked at Raijin, seeing the toned body he had formed over the past few years. "It's not our time to fade into the twilight."

"What?"

"I can help you escape."

Raijin smirked as his eyes turned blue. In a second Raijin opened his palms letting out an arrow of electricity sharp enough to break Eros's right wrist chains. Then Eros quickly blew up the chain on this left wrist, slightly scorching his arm. "Is that how awakened sordes uses their Element," Raijin asked, "Seems aggressive, I guess the fear of them is justified." He added as he closed his eyes braising for Eros to blow up his chains. The sting from his arms made him grit his teeth, the burning sensation forced his eyes to open to the sight of guards running towards them.

"Don't slow me down now little pup!" Raijin screamed as he started running towards the guards coating his body in a stream of electricity as he started to pick up speed.

"Hey, you sto-" screamed one of the guards before getting hit at full force by Raijin knocking him out instantly. As the guard fell Raijin quickly unsheathed the sword, turning around about to strike when Eros like a beast pounced out grabbing the second guard's skull with both hands and releasing his fire blowing up the guard's skull instantly killing him.

"I didn't slow you down did I," Eros quickly responded.

Raijin scratched his head glancing his eyes to his left. "Such a destructive ability. Look over there, little pup, reinforcements."

"What... What are those idiots doing?" Flavius screeched as he grabbed onto the gate looking downhill at them.

Ulfr put his hand on Flavius's shoulder. "That's just Eros, the man is a mad dog, you know since I've known him his escaped nine times, survived mortal wounds and won against ungodly beings, and yet look at him still standing and fighting."

"So, are you going to join in?"

"No,"

"Why not?"

"Timing, some big players are about to fight, if I join in now, we all die."

As Ulfr finished his sentence the gates started to open, Cyril holding two gut knives stepped out, "Make it quick," Lanista Lovita calmly ordered. Leading to a sadistic smile from Cyril as he stretched out his arms.

At the other side, Eros noticed the appearance of Cyril slowly approaching behind ten Guards, he held his left out arm with his palm open, firmly grabbed onto his left wrist with his other hand and planted his feet. "I won't be able to use my left arm for a while, think you can handle the other guards?" He quickly asked.

"Aye," an amused Raijin answered. "Surely you forgot who I was, the next strongest swordsman cannot lose to fodder."

Eros smiled as he released an aggressive amount of Will, shocking Raijin into a fighting stance. Leaving a slight smirk on Ulfr's face, forcing Flavius to drop to his knee, stunning Lovita to almost unconsciousness only to be held up by the Doctares and waking a beast. But most impotently Grabbing Cyril's attention as the mad man launched himself towards Eros. ***To think after all these years, I'm still using his technics*** Eros thinks as he watches Cyril approach, ***I'm so pathetic***, he once again thinks as all the air around him vanished with a blinding light expanding and engulfing Cyril.

"Come on now... that's too... bright."

"Shut up about that's bright who do you think you a-" Lanista Lovita stopped mid-sentence as he quickly activated his slave crest. Forcing every single slave and Gladiator's collars to glow. The being lifted his head in confusion, looking around at all the terrified faces, as all attention was firmly on him. "Calm down Lovita, the little boy just caught my attention." The being slowly said. "Look." he added as he pointed his toe towards Cyril's corpse.

"One hit..." muttered Lovita as his fear-stricken face turned looking at Cyril, with what's left of his body burning.

"Kill them!" Shouted the Doctares as the ten guards quickly launched forward for an attack. "Lightning user ei," the being said as Raijin made quick work of the ten Guards.

The being took a few steps into the light reviling his enormous body. At least seven feet, with a deep scar on his forehead. With bits of his unkept red hair waving past his cold yellow eyes. His bare feet peaking from old brown trousers. And lastly his metal straight jacket which held his arms in place.

"What is this presu-"

The being silences Raijin glaring at him. Eros and Raijin glanced at each other before dashing forward, their weapons poised to strike. But the warrior was ready, his years of experience honed into instinctive reflexes. With fluid motion, he dodged the swinging blade of the sword, his feet moving with surprising agility. Using his bound striking with precision and force. Each blow found its mark, driving back his assailants and buying him precious moments to assess the situation.

Eros and Raijin, taken aback by the unexpected ferocity of the warrior's defence, faltered for a moment, their confidence wavering. But they quickly regained their composure, pressing forward with renewed determination. Eros swung his axe in a wide arc aiming for the warrior's head. But the seasoned fighter anticipated the attack, ducking beneath the deadly blade and delivering a powerful kick to Eros' midsection, sending him stumbling backwards.

Meanwhile Raijin closed in, his blade flashing before him. But the warrior was ready, his feet a blur of motion as he danced around the strikes searching for an opening. With a burst of strength, the aged warrior surged forward, delivering a devastating kick to Raijin's chest, sending him crashing to the ground.

"I don't like that look in your eyes, too much hope..." he said before setting his foot ablaze slowing striding forward.

Raijin grunted. Grabbing his sword and going into a stance, before coating his entire body in a string of lightning. **Red hair pointed tips on its ears, yellow eyes. So that's a true sordes;** he thinks **fine old man I'm finally using it just like you wanted.**

"Thunderclap ai, let's see if its strong enough to cut me..." the man muttered before Lovita raised his hand.

"Edward! Raijin! Enough" Lovita shouted as the seal on his hand became brighter quickly incapacitating everyone wearing the collar including Edward and Raijin as both though standing had a vivid expression of pure anguish. Though Edward's smile never left his face the sight of Raijin dropping to his knee as he grabbed his collar was enough for him to turn around, taking heavy steps back into the compound. Finally, Lovita's seal stopped shinning and a collective gasp as every slave and gladiator grabbed their breaths again.

Later in the same day, as events calmed down the slave guild started marching towards the villa to talk about the incident, Lady Marcella sat behind an oak table in a dim lit room watching her husband pace back and forth. "We can't have them killed" she muttered.

"I know that I'd lose so much money," Lanista Lovita said. "I have an idea, but you won't like it."

"What?"

"The pits," Lovita quickly responded with a cold look on his face.

Lady Marcella frowned. "That's a risk, what if he dies in the first round?"

With his voice heavy and blunt filled with confidence. "He killed Cyril in one hit, and the other one took out ten guards in seconds. Come on my lady." He said as he pushed the table to the side grabbing her cheeks with both his hands and spreading her legs with his. "They won't die, one will be earning us money in the pits, the other will be the next champion!"

"This husband of mine," Lady Marcella said softly, "two sordes bound to eventually fight each other. A lightning swordsman on the rise, these are stories in fairy tales."

Lovita lifted lady Macella's dress as she quickly lifted his robes. "What about the union they're on their way," she said as he entered her.

"Fuck the union, the sordes will be gone by the time they arrive anyway." he quickly responded.

Alexander

Standing at the peak on one of the biggest buildings in the city, Alex is slowly approached by Ava and Stavros both in hooded robes as they watch over the district of Thinis, a densely populated area that sat on the borders Pocasis quickly gathering a reputation of being the trade capital of the White Knight Kingdom. It showered, with simple turn you could see massive eye-catching buildings and pyramids that housed the richest of the Kingdom. On the other side you would see mass shanties of people who came here hoping for a better life but never succeeding.

"I hate this place," Ava muttered as she watched on. "In my land these types of places were a horror story you told your kids. Places where the rich flaunt their wealth over the poor. And the poor just beg for scraps."

Alex put on a slight smirk. "From bread to people, everything has a price here, no wonder the chief financial advisor lives here."

"Enough," roared Stavros. "The kid is taking care of the steads. when shall we move out Alex?!".

"You see that white villa in the distance, that's our friend's lovely home, so Ava with me, Stavros you keep in the background and be ready to attack if things go wrong."

Both nodded before all three jumped off the roof of this building disappearing into the smog that surrounded the city. Alex marched through crowds of people stopping only once and flicking a gold coin to a beggar. "Softy," Ava muttered with a slight smile on her face.

"Looks like she's finally falling for me," Alex quickly mocked. "Come let's get a drink."

"We are on a mission Alex."

Alex quickly begged with a crooked smile on his face. "It's only a drink, we might not ever come back I would like to see if their Alcohol is any good."

"Fine," Ava responded with a stern tone. "Just one."

As the two had their quick drink in the bar that looked like it was on its last legs. Alex stopped, "Do you regret it?" he asked.

"Regret what?"

"Leaving your home, the military, everything..."

Ava looked up with a big smile. "No, their actions turned us into monsters. And with you I see a world where we could be free from armies and wars."

Alex sighed. "That's good, but I have to admit something."

"Don't ruin the moment."

"Sorry I have to," Alex quickly responded as he slightly tapped the table. "We seem to have company, right miss?"

"Alexander 'the Basilisk' I assume," A girl said in the background as she came closer sitting beside Ava. "This must be the right-hand Ava."

Alex shook his head. "Such a young girl, sneaking around. It's dangerous you know."

"Such a cute man, acting the assassin is dangerous you know."

Ava glared at the girl. "Watch it..."

"Calm down Ava," Alex calmly said. "What's your name little girl since you already know ours."

"Rose..."

"Beautiful name, and those people who are being a bit too silent right now?"

"Eyes of Argus."

"We need to leave," Ava muttered. "If she's telling the truth that means Dafrak is here."

Alex and Ava slowly stood up, with Alex tossing a few coins onto the table as they calmly stepped out of the bar, taking a deep breath before disappearing into the crowd. "Ooo that was scary," Alex mocked to the glare from Ava.

"I counted Thirty." Ava said with less confidence. "But the little girl Infront of us she would have been trouble."

"Na we would have won," Alex lied knowing the fight would have gone either way in that moment.

As dusk approached Ava Alex and Stavros stood closest to the villa without drawing attention, when on the top floor a window opened, allowing a bird to fly out off. "Ava!" Alex commanded as Ava jumped a few feet into the air quickly killing the bird and grabbing the note attached to it.

"Looks like he's replying to a summon from the Queen." Ava said whilst landing back down.

Alex smiled as he put on his wooden animal mask and turned back to Stavros giving him a nod. Stavros planted his feet breaking the floor below him, Alex then placed the sole of his right foot onto Stavros's left hand and Ava placed her left foot onto Stavros's left hand quickly launching them both forward as if they were as light as arrows into the windows of the Villa.

"What was that!" Lachlan Gungadad shouted.

"We believe they're assassins sir, please stay inside the room!" the captain of the guard quickly responded shoving Lachlan back into his study.

"My family better be protected!" Lachlan warned them. "One scratch on my children's heads and ill have your head captain." With each ticking moment the sounds of battle carried on, Lachlan continued sitting anxiously in his chair as he suddenly sees his doorknob turn and as it creaked open a masked Alex stepped into the room closing it behind him and slowly removing his mask. Alex grabbed the nearest chair siting opposite Lachlan and the cold gaze he gave clutched at Lachlan's heart. Poised with his head up, "Evening Ser Lachlan Gungadad my name is Alexander," he said with a blank look on his face.

"If you kill me, you and everyone you love is as good as dead," Lachlan cautioned. "The full force of the white knights will be on you."

Alex scratched the back of his head. "I know, but only you know whose attacking you, if I don't kill you then I believe Dafrak will have a problem with my actions. And at the moment that's not a wise opponent."

"I can guarantee your safety."

He smiled. "Ok you have my attention, but can you bring me one thing."

"Anything."

"A club size of a sword maybe smaller, saint Adira Senesto was holding it on her death, any clue where it might be?" Alexander said as he sat back on his chair looking at the ceiling.

Lachlan looked amused. "Whatever that is ill personally find it for you. Saint Adira what a joke making that filthy witch into a saint what was Pangea thinking."

Alex's eyebrow twitched at that comment but kept his cool. "You have a deal then Ser Lachlan. But how do I know your just saying what I want to hear."

"Are you a betting man Mr Alexander?" Lachlan responded in a calmer tone. "You just have to trust me."

"Fair enough, you know this reminds me of a quick story."

"I'll have to hear of this story anoth-"

"30..."

"What?"

Alex sat forward. "So anyways here I was standing above a defeated Pier, you know what he says on his knees. 'I can guarantee your safety.' Like damn is that some sort of amazing coincidence or is it part of the manual for people who think they have power?"

Lachlan cleared his throat. "What are you trying to s-"

"0..."

"What..." A confused Lachlan asked one more time before he felt a cold steel quickly drive through his chest.

"You know Ser Lachlan you should have not called my mother filthy," Alex said as he drove the blade deeper. "And you should have not lied to me that easily, maybe I would have considered your lovely deal." As he finished his sentence a large explosion is heard from a distance prompting him to exit the door.

Elizabeth

News of Lachlan's death spread quickly throughout the west and beyond. Near the Vassille islands in a country that morphed with the water with streets filled with boats and white marble glistening on nearly every building. At the centre stood a church the size of three houses, and inside sat an aging man as he smiled at the statue of the Goddess. "District Chancellor, what's with that look?" he said calmly.

"It's the man that has recently been heavily involved with us; he was killed three nights ago." said District Chancellor Ser Marcius Jullian Ceaser, a spitting image of his younger brother Amadeus, down to the thin figure and dark eyes.

Chancellor Octavius Nero sighed. "That is a tragedy, that sort of crumbles our plans to take this little empire of theirs. Fine I guess it's about time I visit the Autonomous zone, as someone who signed off on it it's my duty to see how the project is going."

"What about the terrorists sir?"

Frustrated Chancellor Octavius Nero jumped up stretching his arms through his Kimono. "Why do you ask me so much? Damien would have just handled that, so handle that."

District Chancellor saluted. "Yes sir, I have already put forward names for the Jullian task force, names including my brother Amadeus Jullian Ceaser and Ser Tassos sir. We just need the western Chancellor's approval, and we can Eliminate the terror-ists."

Damien why did you leave me with this doll, Octavius thought as he walked past the saluting District chancellor with a katana hanging from his aging shoulders. "Sure, make sure the mission is successful."

In the Autonomous zone, during the toast from the biggest in the trade union as they praised Ser Thibault Gael for becoming the new head of the Union, Ser Tumas approached him and quickly whispered in his ear. "We found it," he said leaving a bright smile on Ser Thibault Gael's face.

"To risk the wrath of Elizabeth over a fucking club," Thibault Gael muttered. "We need to keep him close, that idiot will be great soldier for us."

"Not only that, Elizabeth's hold on the west's financial world is about to crumble without Lachlan, we should act quick," said Ser Tumas.

"I've already made the move my friend," Thibault Gael whis-pered. "Without that irritation gate keeping Pocasis those shan-ties are about to become out new empire."

West of the Autonomous zone in King Logan's occupied area, in a simple tent Ezekiel sat playing chess opposite Gaston. "Be ready to move when I tell you "He says to a concerned Gaston. "This might be a bad move; the King doesn't like these types of tactics."

Ezekiel smiled. "As we speak everyone who knows the significance of Lachlan's death are moving. Some maybe already be moving into his territories; some will have to change plans in how they approach the next move. Whilst we sit here and occasionally fight some useless clans for what glory? Gold? I won't need much from you my friend I just need your protection we will be gone for a few weeks at most, the King might not even notice that we left."

"Getting the loyalists and hiding lords on our side..." said Gaston still concerned.

"We have a small window; without Lachlan the queen would be too busy to care about the movements of small creatures like us. And yes, it's not upfront like how Logan would like but this is life not a story, you want to convince someone to risk their life for you that much it'll take more than you boasting your strength."

"Well, you haven't failed us yet Ezekiel, when do we leave?"

"Tonight."

In Zen's castle Elizabeth sat in the back of a room filled with piles of paper, as all her standing personal Advisors scrambled together to find a solution to Lachlan's death. However, she was not as panicked if anything she looked eerily silent. Pacing her eyes back and forth with her fingers interlocked. Obeh, a low standing advisor to the crown only here from the request of the prince slowly approached the Queen, immediately bowing and avoiding eye contact as the Queen glanced at him.

"Unless you have a solution for this mess, I suggest you return to work." Elizabeth said.

Obeh cleared his throat as he glanced over at the Queen seeing she was angry but trying her hardest to hide it. "My Queen, everyone who has seen an opening in the Kingdom has already taken moves, I mean you might have noticed many of the people who came alongside Lachlan have already left the court. I suggest you switch the way you function if you stay peaceful too long people will take advantage of you."

Elizabeth closed her eyes as she sighed, she knew the importance of Lachlan, she now knew his death gave two people unmatched power in the guild. She knew without his foothold of the finances holding onto land and armies this huge would now be a problem. She realised that only after his death she had lost a true friend one who shielded her throughout these years.

"What is your name?"

"Obeh my Queen."

"Obeh, tomorrow my convoy will attend Ser Lachlan Gungadad's funeral you will report all suggestions and matters to the prince he is the Crown's hand after all and will take over leadership till I return." Queen Elizabeth said as she quick stood exiting the room. "For the rest of my Advisors have a solution by my return."

The journey went by with no problems, all bowing at the Queen's convoy as she passed through. And on arrival as the queen along with Lancer to her right, Al'Gadrood and Drominic to her left twenty of her guards stood Infront of the funeral. Everyone's heads where down. All but the Gungadad family who were collapsed on the knees crying. The silence dwelled as the Undertakers lowered the casket, with each second Elizabeth remembered all the times she had with Lachlan the drinks, the jokes. With one of the Undertakers taking quick glances at the Queen she took deep breaths to stop herself from crying Infront of her people.

"Vive les Lions!" Shouted one of the Undertakers as he let his rope go pulling a dagger from his boot and charging at the Queen before being quickly cut down by Al'Gadrood as Lancer launched his body Infront of Elizabeth.

"Guards protect the Queen!" Lancer roared. As half her guards quickly circled her whilst the other half moved out to secure the surrounding area.

Drominic quickly ordered all the Undertakers to not move, before turning his head to see Elizabeth's face. He quickly took her under his wing shielding her from the public with his jacket.

She looks tired, Drominic thought. "Above all else you are still a woman," he whispered to her. "I tend to forget since I hardly ever see you crack, I bet a lot of these people think you are an unmatched god of wisdom. Don't worry yourself to much Elizabeth, take a few days rest the prince can lead without you for the time being without fucking it up. I think."

By the upcoming days, all the undertakers where imprisoned, with one being found guilty of conspiracy. All this taking place under the prince's order as the Queen hid in her garden tending to her flowers.

A figure spoke hidden in the shadows. "My Queen, we have found the members of the Loyalists in the court."

"Good keep an eye on them, don't make a move without me." Elizabeth Calmly said with her usual calculated tone returned to her.

Obeh alongside all the Queen's Available Advisors approached her in her garden with infectious smiles on their faces. "We found a favourable solution to the impending financial problem my Queen."

"Speak."

"Slaves, re implementing the slave union in our main borders will allow for so much including free labour."

Elizabeth smiled. "Not possible, people do not favour such things."

"Simple, instead of outwrite buying slaves, we make criminals serve their time not behind bars but helping the economy. Allowing production of products to multiply." Obeh roared in joy.

"Interesting... come tell me more about this plan of yours over some wine."

Logan

On a road looking towards the vast wastelands, the Lions had placed their camp there. The army had begun to visibly shrink, those who stood by Logan's side begun to look lazier by the day. And on one of the camp sites Damon and Fini sat with one stirring a pot of stew and the other keeping the flames alive.

Damon pointed his finger. Grabbing the attention of a man with an unkept hair and beard, and dirty long robes. "Old man, you asked what makes us free right? Well, me and my sister have been fighting since we were kids, having each other's backs. With our years of experience that would make us true warriors, thus making us truly free right?"

"Right, that's why Ser Ezekiel keeps us as his personal guard, I'm the shield and my little brother is the sword."

Damon looked up at his sister in amazement. "Our relationship is the envy of the Lions. Right Big sis."

Fini looked down at her brother and proudly stated. "Obviously, it's like we have the same mind. So old man what do you think, do we pass your test?"

The old man stopped looking at the clouds, glancing slowly at the Ale that was next to the siblings. "Who knows." he said before slowly pulling his body up and pouring a cup. "I always hated this taste." he quietly stated before sitting back down.

"You don't know anything old man," Damon said. "Just sit there and get drunk it's all you are good at."

"You two, where is your Lord!" roared Ser Vauquelin Josee, with King Logan St'Louis approaching not far behind him. The siblings instantly stood saluting King Logan as he got closer. "We don't know my Lords" they both said stiff as a board.

"Why are you not wearing armour?" Logan asked analysing, their casual shirts and trousers. "What if an enemy attacks, then what will you do?"

"If the enemy managed to get past your scouts... probably die." The old man quickly answered still set sipping on his Ale.

"Who are you and why have you not shown your King the respect he deserves?" Ser Vauquelin asked glaring at the old man.

"An old man... I think."

Ser Vauquelin slightly frustrated held the tip of his sword. "A jester I see, show your respect or I will cut you down!"

"Calm down Ser Vauquelin, we are here for these two," King Logan Roared as he raised his finger calling over some knights. "Get rid of this old man."

"Logan St'Louis, King of the Lions. May I ask you a question. Why are you scared?" The old man asked.

"Scared? Foolish old man I am the man who has taken the heads of many Beasts. What would I be scared off?"

"I don't know but, you seem unable to make actual movements towards Queen Elizabeth. I hear her friend recently died should you not attack now when she is weak?"

Logan pointed at the cross hanging from the old man's neck. "Listen here you have never set foot on the battlefield, war takes time to build up too, and when I strike at the White Knight, I want to make sure they can't get up after."

The old man looked down taking a sip from his Ale. "Maybe I'm wrong then. I hope you have enough gold when you decide to attack."

Logan looked down, with a stern tone he commanded his men, "Leave us" with them following command by taking Fini and Damon away with Ser Vauquelin Josee leading the small group towards the King's tent.

"Do you believe in the Goddess King Logan?" The old man asked.

"That is not the Lions way..." Logan quickly answered. "Now tell me, how do you know of our finances."

"What do you believe in King Logan?" The old man asked again.

Frustrated Logan pulled out his sword pointing the tip at the old man. "I am the King I will ask the questions!"

"Sorry, sorry, it seems I overstepped. I do not know of your finances but, the food your men were eating, looked spoiled. Their armour looks damaged. This Ale tastes worse than usual. Which made me think, why would the King wait so long to attack the Queen to the point where his money is depleting so much."

Logan sighed lowering his sword. "We do not believe in the Goddess or any other god, the Lions do not bow to anyone or anything."

"So much pride, I think I understand why you are scared." The old man softly said. "It's not dying, its losing and having that pride dented. You have a lot to live up too after all, who would want to take over after the White Lion."

"Pier, he was so well known." Logan sombrely said as he sheathed his blade.

"Because he was willing to risk his pride. No matter how shinny your armour is, you will always be in his shadow if you are not willing to risk your own pride." The old man freely spoke.

Logan laughed, "Who are you?"

"An old man..."

"What is your name old man."

"I have none, if you wish you could give me one King Logan."

Logan started to walk away tired of the conversation. "Bern, since you where brave enough to talk to a king that way."

Logan soon after strode into his tent, dismissing everyone but Ser Vauquelin. He looked at the Lord and smiled. "Prepper the soldiers a week from today we attack Pocasis." He commanded to the surprise of Ser Vauquelin.

"What of Ser Ezekiel my King?" quickly asked Ser Vauquelin.

"He will return, he is a trusted man Afterall, now go do your duty for your king young Lord."

Eros

"In a few days, the season begins, so prepper yourselves and serve house Jovian. Those who are new will be officially accepted into our house. That is all continue your training!" Lanista Lovita Jovian announced on his poach before retreating inside. "Slave girl!" he shouted.

"I tell you this every time Its Ella," Lady Marcella said as she walked past her husband, in fine silk clothes. "I've already told her to look after the young prince, now, shall we?"

"We shall, pity about them pirate ships, we could have got a few new slaves," Lovita says catching up to Lady Marcella.

"Apparently they annoyed him... so he sank them."

Ulfr whilst practicing with a wooden sword glanced at the couple as they got escorted into town. With the events that's recently happened he could only imagine what they were up to. Each person highly affected looked sombre as they sat opposite each other, Raijin gazing upon a sleeping Edward. Thutmose trying his best to be closer to Kilian who looked enraged without his friend here. And the Doctares covered in lash marks for failing to control the gladiators.

"Vitus, right?" asked Ulfr as he lazily exchanged attacks with his sparring partner. "What's this season Lovita was talking about?" The bald Gladiator smiled. "Simple, gladiators from all over the Zone, compete to see who the champion is. First the race to see who even qualifies to fight."

"Ok, what happens if you lose, are you out of the competition?"

"Those you do not make the cut of point are killed on the spot."

Ulfr jumped back surprised. "That's over the top though." he said.

As the day ended Ulfr was the first to head back to the cells ready to sleep. This trend continued for the next few days with many including Lovita noticing, writing him off as one of the people who were going to die. Until the day of the race. Hundreds of gladiators stood in rows surrounded by everyone from the poor to the nobles. And as the bell went the gladiators moved like clueless animals not knowing where they were heading but the point of a finger.

How many hours has it been? Raijin thought as the sun rose from the east, he looked around to not see anyone behind, and only few shadows Infront, ***the new ones are behind, but every gladiator is so far ahead.*** He once again thought as his burning lungs squeezed gasping for air. "What have I been doing for five years," he muttered with his legs feeling numb and unsteady as the seconds go by.

As Raijin's eyes melted into his skin he started to catch up to a figure. "That symbol, why are you here?"

"Why not..."

"I see..." Raijin smiled as he let his arms flop. "Back then, when our master was training everyone, I couldn't reach them. Apollo's Will scared me, and when I felt Folke's power, I understood I had a long way to go. Even Edward a drunk who could only use his legs made me use my full power. The pup got so strong, yet I just stood still."

"Talent is a curse Afterall..."

Confused Raijin quickly asked. "What do you mean?"

"You were always talented, so you never trained, but look now all those who struggled have caught up and some have overtaken you."

Raijin taken back rubbed his eyes and when he opened them again the figure had disappeared. The race continued onto the last day with the sun beaming on top of his head Ulfr with his eyes at the back of his head limping forward he bumped into Thutmose falling on his back gasping for air before sitting up in confusion.

"Looks like you made it right on time..." Thutmose said.

"What's...Happening...." Ulfr quickly responded barely able to get his words out.

"I don't know some old man is Infront and a few people who walk near him just fall to the ground."

Ulfr scratched his head and started pushing people out of the way. "Sorry but dying isn't an option yet."

"Finally, someone coming through," Chancellor Octavius Nero spoke as he sat up on his chair. "Don't disappoint me now."

As he said this Ulfr took a few steps forward and the closer he got the more he could feel his entire being crushed, like a hand was pushing him into the ground. "What your name then?" Octavius Nero asked whilst Ulfr slowly passed by him.

"Ulfr..."

"What a powerful Will Ulfr." Octavius stated. "Why push yourself so much?"

"I'm... not...Allowed...to...die..."

Octavius Nero laughed while the pressure around him disappeared. "You are my new favourite!" he announced walking past the rest of the racers with a huge smile on his face.

"Who are you?" shouted Ulfr from affair with a sombre look on his face.

All he had to do was open his mouth and say his name and everyone froze, akin to seeing the grim reaper himself. Thutmose inched closer to a shocked Ulfr, making show not to alert death whilst he was striding away from them.

"That's one of the strongest swordsmen?" Thutmose asked in confusion.

"If that's true, we should start thanking whoever is looking after us..." Ulfr replied.

When they returned to the starting line, Ulfr could not help but notice half the gladiators where nowhere to be seen. But quickly noted in his mind three of the gladiators Kilian, Raijin and

Gallus where being praised by Lovita for coming first second and third. "He looks pissed," Ulfr said glancing at Raijin. "Probably because he came third," Yamato whispered to Ulfr's surprise.

"So, you made it here as well!"

"I came fourth, only because of that man."

Ulfr grinned. "Octavius, Ya he had his fun with us I guess."

"So that was Octavius..." Yamato muttered biting the nail from his finger. "Well, whatever. I haven't seen Eros yet is he in the back?"

"He tried to escape again, revealed he was a sordes and got taken somewhere."

Yamato was quiet but firm. "That fool, well he won't die like usual. The idiot doesn't know how to die."

"that's true, I hope..." Ulfr said as he started walking away towards Lovita's call. "Don't die ok, there's hope this time."

Confused Yamato simple waved at him as all the remaining gladiators that belonged to Lovita, quickly lined up as he stood smug as ever.

Somewhere deep in the Autonomous Zone, in a dark, empty cold hallway, being dragged by chains Eros walked through with a glare in his eyes, so piercing the guard dragging him could feel it at the back of his neck. "Welcome!" a voice echoed.

"You are famous here!" another screamed from the shadows. "You challenged the king and lived!" Another screeched as he shook the bars of his cell. "I can't wait to cut you up!" Soon after the guard pulled Eros and pushed him into a cell quickly locking it and with his voice returned demanded Eros's hands. Which he calmly did not breaking eye contact with the guard. "We can live peacefully, or I can kill you all," Eros calmly said as the cuffs fell from his wrists. He stretched his left wrist still feeling the effects of his attack and as several people came closer a dim smile could be seen by the guard as within a blink of an eye, he witnessed a man's eyes be gauged out and flashing lights leading to the soul crushing screams of the people in the same cell as Eros.

Alexander

A stream of light irritated Alex as he tried his best to sleep in the carriage provided by Ser Thibault Gael. He lifted his head and sat up, letting his legs dangle from the back of the Carriage, all he could see was a stream of villagers following behind looking content. And as he glanced left to right, he could see his men and the Trade Union's soldiers riding side by side. Alex looked up joyful at his next destination, quickly noticed by one of his closest men, Kal Magus. "You look happy."

"I'm visiting home for the first time in years."

"We should arrive by midday," Kal Magus said.

Alex smiled back at Kal Magus. "Good, then after I get what I want and say my goodbyes, we leave this accursed land."

"If what we read is true, word will get out," Kal Magus said with a stern tone. "That means we will be hunted down the second Pangea finds out what that club actually is."

Alex rolled back into the back of the carriage, grabbing his sabre, "It took us five years to figure out that a staff the Gevana people where researching was encased inside the Club my mother was holding. I'm sure It'll take them just as long. Now brother give me a lift to my steed." He said as he hoped at the back of Kal Magus's horse.

"Amadeus knew as much as we did, don't you think he's been trying to figure it out as well?" Kal Magus asked as he tapped on his horse making it speed up.

"That's why we need to disappear the second we find it," Alex said as the two approached his horse followed behind by his men. "Whatever this is, they wanted it so hidden they destroyed an entire island of people. Our friend Icarus died the second he spoke of what we read. Even if it takes ten more years." Alex added as he jumped onto his steed ordering the Phalanx of Basilisk to charge into an approaching horde of bandits.

"We will get their precious treasure and take it with us to our dream land!" Alex shouted as he begun to stand on the back of his speeding steed. "A land with no war, armies or death a real Utopia now Phalanx of Basilisk show them our power!"

With the sudden shock of watching a man stand on the back of a speeding steed whilst arrows flew past his head, the bandits before even engaging crumbled in fear ignoring their leader and charging forward blindly. The fight was quick and simple the union's soldiers could only watch on as this group of mercenaries showed their battle prowess. Their movement, their attacks, their organisation, one would not be surprised if this group less than hundred warriors where secret Galients. Within the hour of the attack Alex raised his sabre indicating the end of the battle.

"Round as many as you can up!" Commanded Captain Jean Luc of the trade Union.

"That's not fair," Alex jokingly muttered as he jumped off his steed. "They already lost why capture them as well?"

Captain Jean Luc walked past Alex with his thick steel armour smiling. "You are a good leader, Alexander; however, you clearly are green when it comes to war. Did you not notice they all attacked at once, organised, yet they don't seem to be a clan or anything of the sort?"

"No," Alex sang. "I just thought they saw the many people and the amount of loot they could get if they won. I mean wouldn't you do the same Captain." Though this was the first time Captain Jean had seen Alex. What he had been told about a carefree person who could switch moods just as quickly as he could draw his sword was vividly true from what he witnessed.

Jean quiet but firm asked. "Why do you switch moods so easily Alexander? You are so 'carefree' at most times yet when you were attacking, I could feel why they called you the Basilisk."

"That's your answer right there, in battle I have to take care of my crew but outside of battle I can just be myself."

The man didn't even wear armour Captain Jean thought bowing to Alex and quickly moving towards the captured bandits to interrogate them. *Is it a testament to his power?* He pondered once more with a stern look painted on his face.

The trip continued without any more incidents, finally at the gates of Utopia, as the horde of people entered into the market area, a spot that was built to accommodate the trade union but stop anyone from entering the walls to Utopia without permission. Alex paused at the first gate looking at the massive wall hiding the city over the horizon and did not miss a step as he noticed frontline legionnaires surrounding the market and the small village that had spawned in the area.

"Pangea, they look scared with this much," he muttered as he smiled. "Captain where is it then?"

"It's on its way."

"Ok, Ava will receive it for me, I have somewhere to be."

"Don't cause any problems, these guys are itching for someone to try." Captain Jean stated.

"Yes sir, I understand," Alex waved as he walked outside the gate into the fields.

While he walked through the fields quickly grabbing the attention of farmers close by, he could feel the thick grass dancing on his feet. He could hear the birds singing, he could see people working hard to harvest their food. "Beautiful," a comment flowed in the air as Alex glanced to see a woman holding a brush scanning him up and down.

"I'm not sure," a child quickly responded. "He looks sad..."

Alex stopped having his attention grabbed calmly stood towards the mother and child. "How much?" he asked. "For a drawing how much?"

"Free…" A man seeming to be the father answered. "We don't get to see someone who looks like you often, so this one time we will do one for you for free."

"How kind, however we have to do it at a different time I have somewhere to be." Alex quickly answered with a sombre tone.

"Our boy Adam has a special talent, as long as we have your permission, he can start painting you and we will send you a copy at some point." The man said.

"Just ask someone from the trade guild where we are, and we will send you the address." said Alex with a playful tone in his voice before waving the small family goodbye.

Soon after as Alex saw it, he took his time walking towards the old house. He let his hands flow through the overgrown grass walking unusually slow almost robotic, as if his brain were struggling to tell which foot to move. Finally, he stopped "I'm home," he muttered gazing upon where he grew up, only holding back tears as he dug his hand onto his thigh.

"Sorry sir but you have to exit!" shouted what seemed to be a guard as she ran towards Alex.

"I can't," Alex interrupted, "you see I made myself a promise that I would come here again. So, I'm sorry Lady but could you let me have this one for a little while?"

The lady looked at Alex and all she could see was his smiling face with sagging eyes. "Five minutes..."

The warm sunshine hugged Alex as he walked past the house towards a tree, that stood right behind. "You hated apples as well..." he muttered when he saw two crosses one for his mother and the other for his sister.

"Excuse me!" he shouted to get the attention of the guard standing at a distance.

"What?"

"There's one missing..."

The guard looked puzzled for a second quickly approaching Alex. "You must have known them in the past to even say that." she said.

"I'm an old friend of the boy Eros, the name is Adam..." Alex said.

"Well Adam I am Flavia one of the guards of Saint Adira's home, the reason his name is not on here is because he was found out to be Amon's spawn." Flavia stated. "Thus, his name was stripped, never to be spoken off to not risk the Wrath of

Goddess Sen." She added as she quickly put her hands together in prayer bowing her head as her short brown hair danced in the slight gust of air.

"He was? Shame..." Alex spoke. "What happened to him then?"

"He was struck down for his crimes."

Alex hearing this did not react as for the last five years he had grieved his family's death and this statement though making him sad only confirmed even his stubborn brother could not escape this fate. But after hearing this he bowed to the guard and thanked her for letting him see Adira's resting place quickly moving away from the house, after a short walk back to Utopia between the farm of the painter and his old home he looked up from the ground to see a familiar face drenched in sweat as he approached.

"You look good kid..." Khan said as his eyes started to fill with tears.

"How have you been Uncle..." Alex responded with a sombre look in his eyes. "You look well." he added as he pointed to Khan's stomach.

Khan came closer, but when he stood right Infront of Alex his emotions drowning him, forcing him on his knees. "I'm sorry, I'm so sorry. I could protect any of them, please forgive me..."

"You didn't have the strength to do any of that," Alex quickly responded. "There is nothing to forgive, this was not your fault Khan."

As Khan looked up, he could only see Alex's smile, a smile so tremendous and sweet he could feel some of the guilt being lifted from him.

"So how did you know I was here, I'm sure Ava wouldn't reveal my position that easily?" Alex asked.

"I didn't," Khan said as he opened his bag pulling out an orange club slightly bigger than a dagger. "Something just made me think you might be here." Still on his knees he then lifted the club with both his hands. Presenting it to Alex, and as Alex reached out to grab it everything that had happened in the past five years, the countless battles, the desertion of the army. The glimpse of truth that set everything in motion came rushing back as he firmly grasped it.

Elizabeth

On the outskirts overlooking the village of Marsell-Yvoire one of the many villages that stood as the frontlines for the White Knight Kingdom, a peaceful land that with few farms and fewer soldiers on a hill overlooking the calm road that many of the trades Union would die before losing. A group of children playing around stopped as a young blond child stepped forward seeing figures in the background approaching. "Abel... get Abram..." the child said with fear in his eyes.

In Zen, Elizabeth barged into the throne room to see Prince Phillip sitting on the throne with a young maid on his lap. With a single look she quickly hurried off leaving the Prince and the Queen gazing at each other on opposite ends.

"Perhaps I should not be surprised Husband of mine," Elizabeth said coldly. "You are the Hand of the crown my Husband, thus I advise you to stop with these childish games, Logan attacked one of our villages and that action has caused problems that have come to my attention."

"Dear wife maybe a few more days off will do you well," Phillip mocked as he crossed his legs.

"This is no time for jokes."

With his hand on his cheek Phillip continued mocking. "Fine, let me be blunt queen, what does it matter that a peasant village that you made as a buffer fell?"

"Two reasons, one I only found out today days after the attack." Elizabeth replied. "Two this attack has given a lot of the people on our lands a reason to rebel."

"Peasants?"

"Nobles…"

"So, my brother finally made his move, I hope he doesn't resent me for siding with thee, I was bewitched Afterall," Phillip frowned.

"Bewitched? You are entertaining." Elizabeth replied as she took a few steps forward. "Phillip, do you know why you are still here? Why you have so much power?"

"Because you need a Lion to not turn Zen on you…" Phillip quickly replied.

"Yes, however that was at the start, your one role was to keep your nobles in check, one word of Logan's movements and they turn on me, they destroy my crops, they ravage my cities."

"Then kill them," Phillip said. "A few nobles scaring the great Queen of the White Knights?"

"They fled already."

"Then prepper for war."

"King and Rook's banners have been raised."

"Then what's the problem?" Phillip asked.

Elizabeth sighed. "The hand of the crown failed in so many ways. Even preparing for war. Tell me my husband why have so many titles when you can't handle the responsibility?"

"I ask you father of our future child to step down from your duties, for a while." she added Gently.

Phillip leaned forward. "You see this Sigel, my name my influence I have the power that you fear. Don't overstep yourself my dear wife."

Elizabeth smirked, simply lifting her finger and a dozen of the White Knights came barging into the throne room pointing their spears directly at the prince. "Kill him." she commanded as they quickly lunged forward to the fear of Phillip as crawled into the throne. "Stop," she calmly commanded and the Knights responded in kind stopping in their tracks with the tips of their spear's inches from the prince. "Step back," she again commanded as the Knights moved.

"Do not overstep your importance my husband. Now go to your hoes, I need to rule my lands."

As Prince Phillip quickly exited the throne room with his head lowered Obeh entered announcing his presence. "My queen, the province Therouzen along with many other villages have risen up. Many houses are flocking towards Logan and his forces are becoming a dangerous number."

"What off Rook and King?"

"Ser 'King' Andre Constantin is quickly silencing the uprisings in Zen he will be at the borders within a few days, Lady 'Rook' Hannah Florine Gisele will start marching her army towards the border of Pocasis." Quickly answered Obeh.

Elizabeth looking tired approached the throne gently sliding her fingers on it. She sighed at the thought of being launched into another war. "Put out an order for the standing army to siege Therouzen and order their surrender."

"As you command my queen," Obeh bowed as he exited, quickly followed by the remaining guards. Her legs felt heavy she was no machine after all, as she fell siting on the floor with a constant tiredness sinking deeper into her. With her moment of weakness over she stood dusting her silk dress as she elegantly left the throne room. As the days went by it was becoming more vivid that the past was about to repeat itself, more people mostly in the upper class flocked towards Logan or began rebelling inside the Kingdom's borders.

Yoan St'Timeo having given Therouzen enough time to consider the surrender knew their time for a decision was up. And as the brave Knight settled onto his steed accompanied but a dozen of his trusted men, they approached the Provence's walls greeted by the ones who had taken control of the area.

"The queen ordered your surrender; I even gave you days to come to your senses, Will you peacefully, do it?" Ser Yoan St'Timeo asked.

Ser Edgard Frederic the Earl that ruled the Provence Therouzen looked around, seeing his forces outnumbered, his people scared. He sighed, "What will happen to me?"

Ser Yoan looked at the old man feeling sorrow, "No blood has been shed, so you will live, however your title might be lost."

"I see," Ser Edgard said in a sombre tone. "Then we surrender."

In a moment of bliss Ser Yoan felt relief closing his eyes for a second but feeling his body drip onto the ground, as a sharp pain charged from his face down to his toes. "The captain has been struck!" shouted a knight as another solder hopped of his steed getting closer to Ser Yoan, bleeding out as an arrow from Therouzen's militia managed to strike him.

"Vive Les Lions!" shouted Ser Edgard as the Provence's people screamed in joy.

Word of Ser Yoan quickly made it to Queen Elizabeth so in a move of emotion she launched all the notes on her table, with visible rage plastered on her face. "Order 'King' to move to the Provence."

Lancer standing next to Obeh witnessed this, with Obeh simple asking what he would have 'King' do. two word shocked even Lancer who had known Elizabeth most of his life. "My Queen is that necessary?" quickly asked Lancer.

"It's the only way. Therouzen will never stop, for years now they have always been loyal to the Lions. They have been pushing against us on all fronts, I can't convince them, but I fear if I ignore them once more, it'll cause more problems than it's worth."

"My queen, this may backfire." Obeh warned trying to calm the queen down. "A more subtle way might be the answer to a lot of these problems; however, this will put an image of you that you might never recover from."

"I am the Queen! You will execute the orders I give, ok?" Elizabeth shouted however when the words left her mouth, she quickly composed herself. "I apologise, I understand your concern Obeh however this is the best way. I promise you."

Obeh studied the queen for a second. "I shall send the order to 'king' for a scorched earth."

Logan

"It's another victory my lord," Ser Jeremy Pierre stated as he struck his sword into a dying White Knight.

"It's funny," Logan giggled as he sheathed his sword. "This is the power of our enemies how disappointing."

"My lord, Ezekiel has returned," Oliver said as he quickly approached with Ezekiel by his side.

Ezekiel frowned, seeing the graveyard of the unburied. Their corpses piled on top of each other with the banners of the White Knights being burned around them. "My King," Ezekiel bowed with Gaston doing the same.

Logan stuck his chest out. "My advisor you see, your paranoia, schemes or anything was not needed. This is the second line of White Knights quickly disposed of. My people are flocking to me, our numbers grow by the second. Do you know why? because they follow the Hero King Logan, not the shady Pier."

"My spies say 'King' is moving towards Therouzen..." Ezekiel quickly spoke. He did not want to anger the King anymore and thought changing the subject was for the best. He forced a smile through the strings of white hair growing on his stubble. "What would you have me do my King?"

"Spies?" King Logan asked with distain as he handed his sword to Oliver. "I do not hate you Ezekiel, but your ways are unnoble, I wish you would change them."

"Just stick by my side, try to not disappear anymore and I am not angry Ezekiel you are a friend, so you get a pass this time. However, I do know all these evil deeds you tend to make are for the greater good to help me secure the Crown." At that moment Logan took Ezekiel under his wing, hugging him closer to the steel of his armour, he marched forward through the corpses to his steed, laughing and talking to Ezekiel. At the end of their short journey seeing Bern sipping on some Aye sitting next to his horse he quickly introduced the two before climbing onto his steed.

"I promise my King, I will dethrone the White Knights." Ezekiel proclaimed to the joy of Logan as he rode to the frontline with hundreds of his solders following close by.

"You know," Bern mumbled. "He might be stupid, but he is very charismatic. He might even win this war of his." He did not seem confident in his words but still smiled through the lie.

"At least I wish he would, the story is set, a King pushed out of his kingdom by a foreign power comes back and frees his supressed people. It almost writes itself don't you think Ezekiel?"

"I hope so, however I believe he underestimates the White Knights Greatly." Ezekiel said calmly. "If 'King's banner has been raised what about the rest of the five armies. What if the

'Beast slayer' is joining this war? Too many unknown variables to be acting so carelessly. I only wish my King would see that."

"Beast Slayer? That child Lancer?"

"Yes, the leader of the five armies."

"You believe in the story that he slayed Gulbrand?"

"And Halvor." Confidently Ezekiel answered to the surprise of Bern. "Surely you have seen him or heard of his battles in the Arena, he has the skills to accomplish such feats."

The road did not rise, and the road did not sink, but the march carried on as night fell and dawn broke. All those in the last stretch either joined Logan's growing army or surrendered to his presence. It was unstoppable the buffer villages for the White Knight Kingdom had failed and Logan was getting all the closer to the Northern Border of Pocasis.

In Zen just to the south of Therouzen's gates a sea of Calvary heavily armoured had arrived. In the front, stood a Knight with a white fur cape, silver armour with beautiful red pattens on it and a bright red and gold sword on his left hand with a matching shield on his right hand. He lifted his sword as it absolved the light from the sun. Turning everything around him into darkness as the sky became engulfed with burning arrows and boulders flying towards Therouzen. The man then pointed his blade towards Therouzen signalling the mass Calvary to charge at full speed towards the gates.

"Lock the gate!" shouted the soldier of Therouzen. "Lose!" another on top of the wall shouted as they tried to return fire, to no avail, only seeing the sea of Calvary part ways giving an opening for carriages carrying ladders on a clear path to the walls. The Calvary stopped feet away from the walls raising their shields as the climbed off their horses. "To the walls!" shouted Lord Lambert as he took control of Therouzen's soldiers. A smart move he thought as they quickly pushed the ladders down for his head to snap to the gate as it begun to break. ***Battering ram?*** Lord Lambert thought and before he could get the word out for his man to secure the gate it bashed open. Within hours the scream of the people could still be head as 'King' continued his destructive attack on the Provence. Destroying buildings, killing everyone from woman to child, salting the earth behind him to make sure nothing could grow. It was relentless, nothing similar could be described. The pleading the begging the crying could not stop this rampage.

As the streets continued to be painted in red, the man with the fur cape marched through with only few of his guards present by him. "Ser Andre Constantin, Edgard Frederic is hiding in the town hall what shall we do wi- " before the Guard could finish his sentence a civilian screamed "Fuck you all!" as he grabbed a dead soldier's sword rushing towards Andre only for the imposing figure to lift his weapon in the air slicing the civilian down in half with one strike. Sending chills to all nearby.

In a brooding deep voice Andre spoke. "Elizabeth ordered a scorched Earth, that means no survivors, meaning even the foolish Edgard Frederic. Kill him!" He ordered to the salute of his soldiers.

In the wash of the new light, sunlight shines on Logan's army as the king himself sits inside his tent listening to Ezekiel give his report. His anger slowly growing, burning inside him looking for a way out. Each word coming from Ezekiel's mouth made him tense up more. His eyes turning red as he clenched his fist, "Enough..." he muttered. Standing from his chair quickly ordering Ezekiel to ready the army.

"My king, they will be expecting your retaliation to this you will be walking into a trap." Ezekiel warned.

"Then they will feel a Lion's bite!" Logan roared slowly stepping to the front of the tent.

"Please," Ezekiel said, "This is a mistake." Logan's body vanished from Ezekiel's eyes and as they day went by there was no joy, there was no talking everyone had this cold look in their eyes. Armed and angry they quickly marched out with Logan in the front. The golden Lion would avenge their people they thought. The golden Lion will kill Elizabeth they said. Over the hill as the sun stood above them, they met 'Rook' in that moment they knew, this would be the only battle between these two armies.

"That is her correct?" Logan asked on top of his steed with Ezekiel to his left, Oliver and Ser Vauquelin on his right.

"Tall masculine, spiky blond her, a metal bra. That is correct my King that is Lady 'Rook' Hannah Florine Gisele the bastard child of a Beast and a Zen noble." Ezekiel quickly responded.

"She looks strong..." Oliver quivered.

"She is," Ser Vauquelin quickly responded.

Logan groaned as he watched her walk forward alone. "Looks like she wishes for a challenge, did she forget beyond the muscles she is still a woman?" He said as he charged forward drawing his sword in the process.

Hannah raised her hands with a spear in one and an axe in the other. The ground begun to shake as her soldiers slammed their feet to it. Banging their shield with their swords, as if playing music for her battle.

"She began running..." Ser Vauquelin commented.

"Oliver, you said you had a knack for the bow, right?" Ezekiel asked.

"Better than the sword..." Oliver quickly answered.

Ezekiel then ordered one of the archers to hand their bow to Oliver, "Then aim and lose when ready ok."

Confused as he had never seen Oliver even hold a bow, Ser Vauquelin quickly asked. "What are you attempting Ezekiel?"

"Trust me." Ezekiel quickly responded as Logan held his shield to his chest pointing the tip of his sword towards Hannah as they charged closer to each other.

Lady 'Rook' Hannah Florine Gisele Moments from impact smiled as she threw her spear hitting Logan's horse in the chest forcing Logan to fly forward off the steed towards Lady Hannah, only stopping her axe with the edge of his shield has he fell past her. He quickly stood still grasping his sword with slight shock in his eyes.

"You are sharp woman." Logan muttered.

"Hannah thinks you are as well Ser Logan," she spoke proudly.

As Logan took few steps towards her with his defences up making sure not to be surprised by her again.

With just a small axe and no shield Logan knew he had the advantage, inching closer to her with his sword close to his body until she swung wildly opening her body for attack. Which as veteran Logan took pleasure in exposing by lunging his sword towards her heart only for his arm to be pushed by a gust of wind a snap loud enough for Logan to hear echoed around him. And with a large upward swing of the axe cutting through his helmet and ripping apart his cheek, his eye and his forehead. Sending the King flying and landing onto his back as he desperately started to catch his breath. As the blood started gushing, only the slight blue of his eye reflected of the sun as Lady Hannah calmly approached Logan ready to finish him off. When she looked up to see his army rushing forward and on instinct swinging her axe and cutting an arrow that would have made its mark had it reached her.

"That's... not fair..." Logan cried.

Lady Hannah laughed as she glanced at logan's army quickly approaching, "Did you forget Ser Logan, this is war." She said as she turned to her Enemies charging headfirst into them. By days end Logan work up on the back of a carriage there was no words, but he could tell he had lost to what extent he did not know yet. As he watched the clouds cover the sun, he pulled the bandage from his eye, and felt tears flow down his cheek. Thinking of his past, thinking of Pier. Every girl wanted Pier. Every man wanted to be Pier. He was the next air. He was the strategist. He was Pier the great, and Logan was Pier's brother. A man stuck in an infinite shadow he could never escape and in this defeat, these memories came flooding in, while he continued looking at the sky. He reached his hand out to the ghost of Pier. Past Pier's arm and firmly placed it on his neck. ***I am just as good as you... Right?*** He thought before a bump in the road shook him back to reality back to the endless clouds in the sky, back to the pain he felt throughout his body.

Eros

Grey light streams through the pits as prisoners stretch their arms through the holes of their cells to feel natural light even for a moment. "Did you hear, Logan lost against Elizabeth..." A man in chainmail and leather's soft voice echoed through the hallways grabbing the attention of Eros as he stopped his push ups. Eros stood edging towards the small hole to his cell to hear more clearly, only stopped by the only other prisoner in his cell. "One name stopped this wild animal from excessing how interesting."

"Shut up," Eros expressed.

Ake looked down at his food grabbing a large handful of the mush. "You will die you know, no matter how powerful you think you are, without the power of Fire the King will kill you... If you make it that far that is."

"Your ways don't work for me, I listened, yet nothing changed I would rather train my body," Eros quickly replied. "You should focus on your next match you don't want to lose anymore limbs do you."

"My leg you mean... You are right but maybe you should keep trying, the old gods did not give you some special power. The power is as much as you as breathing."

"Since when did Beasts speak like wise men?" Eros mocked.

"Since the words thousand beast fell into legend."

"One word and those beasts will be more than legend." Eros quickly responded.

"I forgot, you needed me for your plan to work even got on your hands and knees after showing your strength." Ake rubbed his stump. "Join the beasts, become King, Launch an army against Elizabeth. So simple its almost laughable."

"Theres more to the plan than that. But anyways I pulled a lot of favours to meet you," Eros roared.

"You bet on being sent here to have a chance to meet me. You were lucky and now you want to do what Halvor couldn't. What Gulbrand couldn't?" Aka said as he glared at Eros. "Do you think the Beasts as jokes?"

"No… Though history will never admit it, the beasts fell to Elizabeth not the Vassilles." Eros said as he started shadow boxing. "My plan is to simply have enough power to avenge the beasts and my family."

"If you live long enough, get in contact with the Stag's leader. She might agree to your foolishness, but I won't risk my people's lives to rescue a crippled old man."

As they continued their conversation, a herd of footsteps grew louder, and guards came towards Eros's cell. Still feeling the pain from the last time, they entered his cell, this time they came armed and ready for war. "Old man you are next! Feral thing, you are after!" A guard screamed far from Eros's cell. As Ake struggled to stand, stretching his bones, he looked up to see Eros pacing back and forward, and his eyes fixed on the cell's gate.

Ake was quiet but firm. "Stand down Eros, you will need your energy."

Though the words where simple Eros rolled his eyes moving himself to the back of the cell, amusing Ake as he sniggered. Slowly making his way to the gate. "Trust in this old man Eros, your fire is you, do not treat it as something special."

And so, as Ake left, Eros sat with his knee balancing his arm, watching the tip of his fingers, after a few minutes without change he could feel the walls vibrate, and the hallways get louder, though there was no way to see it this was the sound of battle that he heard only a few times since he arrived. The audience above played this music with their feet when they were happy. **The old man is entertaining them,** Eros thought with a bright smile on his face.

However, as the stream of light escaped Eros's eyes grew heavy, trying his best to keep them open to welcome the old man. The sands of sleep grew too heavy only waking up as some light clashed with his eyes and sleep as the hallways grew more silent. In time Eros understood, Ake was never coming back. *I hope to see you again one day old man, your stories kept my head clear for a time,* Eros thought as he crossed his legs holding his right hand out focussing his fire towards the centre of his palm. A loud bang from a guard disturbed Eros as he lifted his head splashing sweat across the walls.

"It's your turn, Sorde!" Shouted the guard as Eros's gate swung open with only tips from Halberds peeking through into his cell. With a cold gaze and a smile coming from Eros the guards sighed knowing he would not come in peace.

As Eros's body came flying through crashing into the dirt below him, he turned his head covered in blood, to see the guards quickly close the gate. "Nice entrance." a figure in the shadows said as he watched through the iron bars that made up this ceiling.

"Does he not care that they will kill him?" A pale, lanky man standing across eros muttered. "Goodbye you ape!" He shouted as he aimed his arrow directly at Eros, letting it lose only for Eros to quickly roll to his left.

"Again! Another of these Apes dodged my arrow!" Shouted the man. "Listen here Ape, I Adelino will grant you quick death now stand there and except your fate!" Again, Adelino launched another arrow at Eros, this time however grabbed it breaking it with one hand without severing his gaze at Adelino.

"What an adorable little ape! You show some potential however this will be it for you!" Adelino said as veins grew on his neck sucking in all the air he could before letting lose a powerful shot. But it soared past Eros barely missing him and piercing the wall behind creating a crater.

Clearly frustrated Adelino grabbed the remaining ten arrows placing them tip first into the ground and going on his knee.

"First that old man now you, do you apes enjoy annoying me?"

"Old man?" Eros asked as he edged towards the stack of weapons.

"Grab whatever you want, you will die either way." Adelino stated. "However yes, the old man I fought a few days ago made it this far as well, the crowd was getting exited well until I showed them the difference between a civilized man and an ape."

"You died to this weakling old man?" Eros muttered in disappointment.

"What?"

Eros laughed as he grabbed a dulled rusty sword. "I'm just surprised the Oldman died to a weakling who can barely imbed his Will."

Surprised Adelino's voice dropped as his eyes narrowed. "Only someone who has fought a skilled Will user would say that. Who are you ape?"

"Eros, the Fire elemental who challenged this place's King."

Adelino bowed his head for a moment quickly lifting it with his eyes sharper, loading an arrow to his bow. At that moment Eros knew the time for talk was over, and as their eyes met Eros charged forward, with Adelino letting lose arrow after arrow barely missing Eros by a hair's length. The crowd noticing begun their song. Building up the music as each arrow flew, as each moment passed. Finally, tired of being kept at distance Eros spread his fingers launching explosive fire into the ground covering his surroundings with a cloud of sand. Adelino smiled as his eyes started scanning the area and when he saw a shadow to his left, he focused his arrow infusing it with his Will and launching it at the shadow. Only for Eros to jump out from the middle at full speed grabbing an arrow placed on the ground lunging at Adelino "Fuck..." Adelino muttered as the arrow struck his neck sending the crowd into frenzy. Moments of joy ended.

Days few by as Eros fought tooth and nail. The suicidal movements confused his enemies, whilst his brilliant battle strategies amused the crow. day after day fight after fight, the myth of Eros grew past the underground into the streets and finally reaching the ears of Ulfr.

"That's my brother for you," Ulfr said proudly.

Raijin smiled as he swung his wooden sword harder. "I won't fall behind him; the future greatest swordsman cannot be second to a fire Elemental!" he shouted filled with enthusiasm.

First, he kills my friend and now his name is spoke louder than mine? Kilian thought as he gulped down his drink. "Doctares get me a sparring partner!" he shouted as he quickly stood. The mood was high in Lovita's house all looked inspired by Eros one way or another all but Edward as he sat in the shadows scanning everyone. "That idiot, doesn't he know having hope will get you killed..." he said under his tongue as he tried to pick up his drink with is foot.

"A moment!" the Doctares spoke as he unwrapped a lengthy scroll. Eager with the announcement Lovita stepped out to his poach to hear who his gladiators would be fighting in the games. "My love, it's time to see who my gladiators will be fighting." Lovita said with a bright smile and shaking in excitement.

"A week from today the fourth annual games will officially begin. The first match will be Ulfr taking on house Gozzo's Widukind. Second will be Raijin taking on Lanista Gosse's Minato. Clovis! Taking on house Amis's Basile Bastien. finally, our new second, Gallus will take on... the Champion of the White

Knights Lancer..." As Doctares' announcement finished Lovita's face filled with despair, thinking, why his gladiator had to face that monster so soon. Ulfr however could care less about that announcement but was more focused on the second fight, his friend Minato taking on an old ally of his brother Raijin. And so, he quickly marched towards Raijin, with his head hung low.

"He is strong, very strong. If you go in underestimating him, you will die quickly."

Raijin glanced at Ulfr surprised at this warning. "I'm guessing it's the guy you spoke to after the race. You seemed friendly with him."

"We were on the same ship."

"Then you survived alongside him is he another one of your brothers?"

"Only Eros is my brother. But Minato is more than a simple Gladiator."

"How so?"

"He was to enter the Rookie Hundred before he got captured."

Raijin smiled as he rubbed his head. "Then it'll be an interesting fight. They don't just recruit anyone." He leaned close and lowered his voice. "I guess I'm about to make one of the pillars my enemy."

"Odd words," Ulfr said Grimly before his eyes caught the attention of Ella quickly dashing towards her with his hand to his chest, he proclaimed his love once again as loud as he could to the laughter of the gladiators.

"Maybe when you win, she will finally respond to your gentleman ways Ulfr!" Gallus roared as he stuck his chest out. "Hope she does not fall for the Champion of the arena!"

Ulfr laughed. "Who?"

"Me!" Gallus roared once more sticking his finger to the air. "Once I defeat this Lancer of course."

"Most would be weary to face a champion."

Gallus kept his smile wide. "Most are not me. Once I defeat this champion, I will demand Lovita bring Eros back. The boy reminds me too much of my own."

"Brennus, right?"

"Correct. Unfortunately for death my life is already forfeited to my son. That is why I will win."

Ulfr let out a slight smirk. "I understand those words more than you will ever know old man, now Raijin looks like he needs a sparring partner."

With wild witch hunts for traitors sending fears in the White Knight Kingdom a picture is painted of the Queen and how much power she really held. News of Therouzen finally forced Octavius to make his move to meet the Queen. Alexander even felt a cold chill knowing that he had already wronged such a ruthless enemy.

Thus, time flew by, with the west silent, trying their best not to anger the awakened beast and as the crowd flood into the grand Arena of the Autonomous Zone, Ulfr whistled through the cage's gate gazing upon each inch of sand in this new playground of his. Then as Lovita approached, he raised his hand saying a small chant and releasing Ulfr of his collar for the first time since he was bought. "That always feels good boss." Ulfr mocked bare chest with only a leather loin cloth to his name. As he took a few steps out into the Arena, he threw his sword into the air and immediately held his ears shocked by how loud the crowd was. Then he took another few step into the sand, marvelling at it as he stretched his toes into it before spreading his arms and letting out the loudest yawn he could. Before quickly laying on his back, closing his eyes and relaxing under the sun. "What is he doing?" Lovita said as he approached his chair at the top of the staircase.

"Who knows, but these are great seats darling you can see the entire arena." his wife quickly said as she sat with only two seats from the front.

"The idiot Gosse gave them to me," Lanista Lovita said as he melted into his chair. "Something about being scared of Elizabeth." as he finished his sentence, a line of White Knights led by 'Knight' Lady Charlotte Al'Jacques marched through the stands surrounding Lanista Lovita and his wife quietly taking their sits as Queen Elizabeth herself covered in jewellery and a white dress made from the finest of silk with laces hanging of its ends, approached from the right and Octavius in a simple Kimono and wooden sandals approached from the left. Lovita finally set up feeling sweat drip from his back as these two entities calmly sat Infront of him. The silence was short-lived however as Octavius grinned. "Even in such an economic state the Queen looks so... rich...."

"The boy sleeping does not look battle ready," Elizabeth said, reaching her hand out for a glass of wine. "You wished for a meeting I granted you one Chancellor. Your time will end when this battle ends."

"How cold, Gungadad did not describe you like this, Queen." Octavius replied swiftly to a stern glance from Elizabeth.

"Fine, I'll be direct," Octavius Added, "Though Pangea and the White Knights had a good relationship our main trade has fallen through with Gungadad's death. Which in another life we could have worked out but your massacre of your people and your involvement with sordes leaves me in a difficult position."

"The world will challenge me next?"

Octavius smiled. "The world cannot be involved in another conflict so soon... Not after our little incident anyway. I'm here to inform you, no warn you as an old friend. Be careful of your actions or we will be forced to act."

The idea of Octavius warning Elizabeth amused her, as she took a large gulp of her wine. "You fear me."

"I'm alone, you stand with an army, I don't believe I'm the one afraid." Octavius quickly responded and as Elizabeth snapped her head towards him house Gozzo's Widukind entered the arena holding a sword and shield slowly approaching the sleeping Ulfr.

"At least the boy will die without ever knowing it." Octavius laughed.

"Won't," Elizabeth corrected as she turned her head back around. "Years as a chancellor and you still underestimate people so easily..."

When the crowd got louder Ulfr's eyes struggled to open, he slowly turned his body around to see Widukind inching to him. Being the first time, he saw the Gladiator all he could do was marvel before jumping up stretching his limbs. "So many muscles, so big you are scary man." Ulfr added before dashing away from Widukind who in response chased after Ulfr at full speed quickly catching up to him and swinging his sword barely missing the slippery Ulfr who rolled forward grabbing his own sword and immediately planting his feet to the ground preparing for an attack.

"Impressive, the little boy managed to survive the first moments, but look at the size difference, unless the boy is an elemental this will be a simple fight." Octavius responded as he clapped.

Widukind sighed at Ulfr holding a stance. Placing his sword and shield into the ground planting his left foot forward raising a boulder from the ground and smacking it, launching it directly at Ulfr.

"I'm sorry young man, I need to reserve my energy so please quickly fall!" He shouted, only to be surprised as Ulfr effortlessly dodged the boulder. "Fine then!" he added as he grabbed his sword and shield causing a small creator beneath him as he lunged forward.

He got faster... Ulfr thought as he stood firm watching Widukind inch closer to him at inhuman speed.

"Good see if you can handle this!" Widukind screamed as he braised his swing, with his veins growing on his arm he put all the power into the swing, only for Ulfr to turn around and run once more. "You are boring..." Widukind sighed as he took strides towards Ulfr. As he did this the once energetic crowd begun to boo, throwing all they could towards Ulfr, who at this point stopped running and was firmly pointing his sword towards Widukind with a slight grin on his face.

"So many muscles would tire a man out," Elizabeth spoke to the surprise of a disgruntled Lovita and an unfocused Octavius. "That was his plan, I don't think the big Gladiator can even notice over his own anger."

Widukind smiled as he advanced, and Ulfr responded in Kind. For the first time the duel begun, as Widukind blocked each of Ulfr's swings and Ulfr dodged Widukind's responses. Finally, as Widukind made a wide swing his miss led to a wide opening giving the opportunity for Ulfr to strike which he quickly took. Only for his momentum to be stopped as Widukind tightened his rock moulded hand onto Ulfr's sword. "You let go of your shield..." Ulfr muttered as Widukind snapped his sword in half causing the crowd to cheer as loud as they could.

"Ok..." Ulfr stepped back raising his hands in the air and forcing a smile on his face. "It's my lose, so I surrender..." He said once more to the slight laughter of Widukind who made a steady approach towards him. As he stood towering over Ulfr he raised his sword straight to the clouds putting all the power into his arm and swung it down wards. Hitting the tip of his sword into the ground as his face turned pale. With Ulfr taking a few steps back glancing at Lovita with a sinister smile on his face.

"All that for one attack..." Octavius muttered. "What a crazy individual."

"Who is that child?" Elizabeth asked stunned.

Lovita stood from his chair with a growing smile on his face, watching Widukind plant his face into the ground with his hand touching the tip of a knife now firmly placed into his heart.

"This clown... Amazing!" Lovita announced as Ulfr bowed ending the fight in a surprising fashion.

"Sleight of hand, hiding bloodlust." Raijin commented as Ulfr approached him. "You're fighting style is like Eros, more refined. I didn't even know you had a knife."

The other gladiators where all celebrating Ulfr's win when the crowd begun to raw, as Minato took stage in thick white trousers and a strange sabre in his right hand. "Xian pants and a Dao..." Ulfr said. "Such an accommodation, they must like h-."

"The strongest of all the Gladiators under Lanista Gosse!" A man shouted as he entered behind Minato. "From the Eastern Empire Pannotia. Minato!" Hearing the words from this strange man the crowd exploded, forcing even Octavius to stay in his seat as grew curious at the fight at hand.

A White Knight approached Elizabeth's ear and whispered. "We found Gungadad's killer." to which she smiled ordering her Knights to start moving.

"Leaving so soon queen?" Octavius asked with a mocking tone. Elizabeth looked down at the chancellor as she stood. "I told you, your time with me was during that entertaining fight. Now our business is over."

"See we could talk more, I might have something that would benefit the Queen," Octavius said with a sly smile. "Something that would solve your money issues."

"How kind of you Chancellor, however I do not make deals with people that threaten me. I kill them. So, it'll be wise of you Chancellor to stop pushing your luck, you have made yourself clear that you have no ambition to continue our friendship instead you wish to challenge me in your own sly words that is."

"I'm sorry it sounded so," Octavius insisted. "I shall bid you goodbye then Queen, I don't believe we will ever meet again." He added as the Queen left with her Knights all but Lady Charlotte Al'Jacques who sat silently behind Lovita, taking quick glances at Octavius's sheathed sword.

In the arena, Raijin entered with his sword resting on his shoulder, dressed like Ulfr, all looked confused as he continued his large strides towards Minato. Noticing Minato took a stance ready to fight as Raijin calmly approached swinging his shoulders with a large smile on his face. **What's he doing?** Ulfr thought as Raijin finally stopped feet away from his opponent. Raijin took a large breath, sharpening his eyes before swinging his sword as hard as he can for Minato to block it with all his might. Minato smiled, before Raijin took another swing only to be blocked. And another one after that to the same result. This continued, as Minato felt Raijin getting faster after with each swing.

"Wasting energy what a fool." Lady Charlotte Al'Jacques commented with a smug look on her face. "Look at that Minato boy, calm collected parrying all his attacks waiting for a moment to strike."

"His getting faster little lady…" Octavius commented as his hand shivered a little.

Finally seeing the Opportunity, Minato swung his sword, only for Raijin to vanish before his eyes. His eyes glanced down to see, as electricity begun to wrap around Raijin. In one moment, Minato could see a dozen swords fly at him one after another he tried to parry but as the wounds got deeper, and more frequent it stopped. For Raijin to stand turn around and swat the blood from his sword gazing at Octavius and then pointed his sword at him as Minato fell onto his back.

"The first one a crazy strategist, the second brave enough to challenge me. You have an interesting group Lanista."

Laying on the floor with the sun beaming down his face, Minato took heavy breaths as he thought back to his past. In his entire life, him or his late father had won a single match. His small family of him and his father travelled across Naite-Iru-Machi getting any work they could. And whilst Minato would work in the fields or beg his father would challenge any Dogos in the area. The name Takauji Hibiki had become famous for all the wrong reasons. Dogos started welcoming the man knowing on this day they had a practice dummy some would even pay him for his extended stay. On the day of the raid, Takauji had challenged another Dogo's sensei and like usual the fight begun as normal, with each blocking attacks and entertaining the masses, Minato was part of the crowd on this day watching as his father stood on the same level as a Dogo Sensei.

"I give up." Takauji said as he started to pant, causing laughter throughout the Dogo and anger inside Minato. He had seen this pathetic display from his laughing stoke of a father but would always grit his teeth holding his anger in.

"I am Minato 'the undefeated'" he said as he snapped back to reality watching the clear skies with the crowd cheering behind him.

"Strong…" Charlotte said as a bloody Minato stood taking his fighting stance. Both Minato and Raijin glared at each other before quickly advancing towards each other.

Minato took the first strike however Raijin quickly dodged as he swung his sword towards Minato, "Unbalanced!" Minato shouted as he used all his body weight to lift the sword straight up forcing Raijin to stumble back. Confused Raijin grabbed his face, *what was that? Death?* He pondered as he took short breaths before bracing himself blocking Minato's second strike. *His slow, and easy to strike but my body feels heavy around him, what is he?* Raijin thought as he parried Minato's sword and slashing across the man's chest.

"Third form…" Minato said before vanishing from Raijin's gaze and appeared inches from the man's neck unable to block Raijin dodged most of the attack leaving a small cut on his neck. *Fast but weaker on his strikes this time,* Raijin thought as he glanced back at Minato with a smile on his face.

"Forth form…" Minato said as he cut Raijin's head off. Raijin quickly snapped back into reality as he held his neck jumping backwards before a strike pierced through his chest. Again, he snapped back using his sword to block Minato's attack. *I understand now* Raijin thought as he took a stance.

"A true swordsman's ultimate move, a Will that shows his opponent dearth…" Raijin said as he focused his lightning, circulating it across his body. "You won't be able to do anything now, you are too weak to reach my level. First thing you did was make sure my strikes avoided your internals. Second was use Will to make your attacks heavier, then you broke your will

focusing it on your feet making you faster. Finally, you used your strongest move to scare me. Anything else you Worth-"
Before he could finish his sentence blood gushed from his chest silencing not only him but the audience as well.

"I thought you figured me out you insignificant shit." Minato said as he stood behind Raijin swatting the blood from his sword whilst Raijin collapsed from the deep wound. "Fifth form… flash." Minato added as he glanced at the sky.

"Disappointing…" Octavius said as he stood walking away from the surprised audience around him. As the day went on, news of the fights travelled down to the pits as Eros tried his hardest to focus a flame to flow out of his palm a familiar voice grabbed his attention.

"Eros, remember what I taught you about earth elementals how in a way they use invisible hands to throw rocks?" Ake said with a cheerful smile.

"Another one," Eros muttered disgruntled, his head turned to sees a copy of himself and the first person he ever killed. "This place is getting crowded…"

Ake laughed. "Come on kid, focus, control the fire as it flows out, don't just push it out."

"Or you could go to sleep, lack of sleep is bad for you. You can't be a Galient if you lose your mind so soon!" Eros's copy said proudly.

"Why do you get too live?" the man spoke with a sombre tone.

"Focus!"

"Sleep!"

"Die!"

Three words that kept echoing, in his cell until he heard another prisoner scream of Lancer's destructive victory. "He cut his head clean off!" the prisoner screamed in joy as all others joined in the conversation Eros in silence let out a menacing chuckle.

"Lancer..." he muttered as strings of fire flowed from his hand Until finally erupting circling around his folding fist.

"Yes, he did it!" Ake screamed as he started dancing with the younger Eros.

"White Knights!" Eros screamed as a dark aura leaked from his cell startling the surrounding prisoners as they edged away from their gates.

Logan

A light drizzle started falling. Logan could feel it on his face as he stepped out of his tent, he immediately grabbed some leftover Ale quickly drinking it before walking past a concerned Ezekiel. The Golden Lion, the great King many people to viewed him as many things, but above all else he was a man. A man who had carried so much responsibility it finally crushed him. His weaknesses being shown to the world was his biggest fear and now with a camp of a little over fifty people, it had confirmed his fears to be just.

"Everyone needs somebody to be a child with..." Bern spoke as he reached out his mug of Ale which Logan grabbed enthusiastically, sitting next to the old man and sharing the drink with him.

"Do you know what a true warrior is Logan?" Bern asked. Logan shrugged his shoulders looking back down at the ground. He had an idea, and knew if he spoke the words, they would be truth.

"I don't think it was Pier, if that was on your mind." Bern chuckled as he watched Damon and Fini challenging each other to their now infamous daily duels.

"Then I don't know, maybe the Beasts were true warriors. Maybe Milo is." Logan added as he clutched the mug harder. With the skies Gray, the world felt aimless for Logan, who had failed in his one mission, so much so most who followed him with conviction left, formed their own clans and fought the queen to the bitter end. 'The Lionic wars' they called them, which Logan could find some humour in as all they did was fall to the sword of the White Knights. Never making ground, only making the Queen look stronger. "At least her bank is hurting," Logan muttered as he chuckled.

"Where is Oliver?" Logan added as he glanced around.

Bern scanned around ending up pointing in the far distance, "it seems he is shooting some arrows..."

"He really took a liking to that. That's good, when I leave, he will have something to push him forward."

"Leave?"

Logan smiled. "Yes, I think I'll open up a shop in a small village." He said hesitantly as he tried to paste a smile on his face. Noticing this Bern huddled himself into his robes feeling a gust of wind approaching.

Bern spoke with a light and joking tone. "Will you hire me? I promise to be as useless as I have been." This comment forced a giggle on Logan as he nodded his head.

"I had hopped you would find the answer," Bern said as glanced at the skies. Before answering Logan looked at the old man sat next to him. His face dominated by sadness and worn from years of seeing the worst in people. He saw him struggle to hold the mug of Ale.

Logan looked down his injured arm and lightly dragged his fingers across the bandages covering his eye. "You saw what happened to me, but somehow you look worse old man. What's your story?" Logan asked.

"Same as everyone who lives to my age, just one mistake after the other and somehow I get to be the one who lived."

"A warrior then?"

"No, a fool with a fictional ambition. However, my mistakes have led me to the decision to never take another life. Even though with these hands it'll be almost impossible." Bern chuckled as Logan held his mug still allowing the old man to take a big swig.

"Is it insane to still want the crown?"

Bern shook his head. "No."

"Then how can I do it..."

"Well start small, get people who you trust and listen to Ezekiel, his methods maybe questionable but I sense he is a great assert."

Logan glanced at Ezekiel approaching him. "I had hoped to not turn into my brother. But for the crown I might have too..."

"You're looking well," Ezekiel mocked. "My King, I have some urgent news."

"Speak."

"They found who killed Gungadad, some merchant, high up in the trade union. I believe his name was Tumas. However, I doubt a bunch of merchants could pull of such an assassination, I believe they hired a mercenary group. If we found who they hired we could recruit them, enemy of my enemy Afterall." Ezekiel added with an enthusiastic smile on his face.

Before Logan could respond he glanced back at Bern before letting out a sigh. "Then find them, and we will organise a meeting."

"The Golden Lion shines once more," Ezekiel observed. "I will put all the recourses we have remaining to find these people. First will be the trade union I'm sure more than Tumas would have an idea of what happened."

Elizabeth

As water splashed Tumas's face, he saw the cold gaze of the Queen looking down at him. He knew in that moment no amount of begging could free him from this situation. And a stream of tears flowed from his face as he hung his head surrendering to the Queen.

"Don't be scared," Elizabeth commented in a chilling tone as she removed the gag around his mouth. "Once we are done here, I will free you, to go do whatever it is you do best Ser Tumas. So, calm yourself and answer my questions truthfully. Do we understand each other?"

"Yes."

"Good, first I must thank you. Your actions got rid of a few rodents in my Kingdom." Elizabeth said. "So first question my friend, why did you have Gungadad murdered?"

Tumas shook for a second before speaking. "So, Ser Thibault Gael could take over the Trade Union. I swear on the Goddess herself we never meant to anger you. We thought Gungadad's death would be nothing to such a powerful person."

"If you truly thought so, you would have not hired a third-party Ser Tumas." Elizabeth said as she pulled a chair closer to relax herself. "Fine, you did a stupid thing for such a simple reason. So, who killed Gungadad?"

"Just some nobody mercenaries."

Elizabeth wedged her boot onto Tumas's groin slowly adding pressure. "Who killed my friend?"

Tumas started to screech. "Basilisk!" He shouted taking heavy breaths.

"The eye of Basilisk or something like, their leader is some arrogant blond kid. They keep in the wastelands and don't really interact with many people." He added. "But do not worry, I knew this would happen, so I've been hiring people to take care of them. For you, my Queen!"

"Good, I think we are done here then." Elizabeth replied as she called for one of the guards to bring a key to free Tumas of his chains. "You know Ser Tumas I have a lot of enemies. From Logan to people wanting revenge. So, I am glad you did not become and enemy. Frankly, it gets tiresome watching your own back so consistently."

"Of course, my Queen!" Tumas screamed with joy, as the guard uncuffed his hands and feet.

"However. You killed my friend." Elizabeth stated before the guard handed her his sword. In response Tumas latched onto the wall behind him before the blade cut through his skin and pierced his heart.

"I thought... you said..."

Elizabeth looked up at Tumas with a sharp glare. "I lied."

As the body slid down to the ground and Tumas's life faded from his eyes Elizabeth pulled the sword out as blood splashed on her makeup. She did not look happy or content but had a stern look on her face as she handed the sword back to the guard. ***I will not make my mother's dream fail*** she thought as she walked away from the cells.

As she walked up the stairs, she saw two of her maids, waiting for her return with a carriage. "The prince would like to have a word with you, my Queen." One of them said with a stern tone to the surprise of Elizabeth.

"I suppose," Elizabeth said with a hint of doubt, she entered the carriage and as it started moving Prince Phillip finally spoke. "Your war is all but over, the economy is getting worse by the day, give me back my power so I can help you fix our King-dom."

"Assertive, I can respect that," Elizabeth responded. "However, my husband I don't believe you want this responsibility. You al-ready have freedom and all the power you could want why take the weight as well." She added as she wiped the blood stains from her face. Revealing the dark patches under her eyes which Philip quickly noticed.

"I am a Lion, the Sigel over the throne is a Lion. I have to be responsible." Philip blurted out with more passion in his voice than before.

"Fine, I have a personal issue to take care of so, congratulations you are reinstated."

"Good," Philip said with a sigh of relief, as he begun to laugh. "What happened to us Liz?"

"I don't know, power I guess." Elizabeth responded with a sombre tone.

Philip yawned. "Remember the days before all this, when we would sneak around, making sure Pier or Father never found us."

Elizabeth interrupted with a short laugh, as she reminded the prince that his playboy ways where already well known in Zen. "Yes, however this was different it wasn't a short fling. I mean we fought against Pocasis and Nero together. When Pier died, we held the country together against my family. Even the people put us on the throne. Our meeting changed me; I don't think I ever thanked you."

Elizabeth sighed. "Yes, well maybe we could return to the days when it was me and you against the world."

"Maybe. But when is the baby due?"

"On the next full moon."

"When the games end? That means Lancer will miss his nephew's birth." Philip said.

"He will... I have told him many times to stop these dangerous games." Elizabeth said.

Philip stretched his arms pasting on a large smile. "Even though I've been a questionable husband. I will still stand by your side on that day." Simple words but enough to leave a smile on Elizabeth's face.

Alexander

"A modern-day classic, the terrorist group that call themselves Justice, led by Lael invaded the Hippocrates Centre almost capturing the Great Dr Machinima Lepius. Stopped only by the task force led by get this Ser Tassos and Ser Amadeus Jullian Ceaser. Our boy is famous Ava!" Alex screamed as he read the newspaper.

"Do you really think now is the time to care about other people Alex?" Ava asked. "A few days ago, Elizabeth put your poster up, so now you have a bounty from Pangea and the White Knight Kingdom. So please be serious Alexander!"

"I will," Alex responded. "But you must read this insanity, it goes on to say though the task force failed to kill the terrorists, and even Ser Amadeus got injured they managed to make the terrorists flee and kept Dr Machinima safe. You don't understand I think I'm feeling the pride of a father right now."

"Yes, I understand, so what shall we do now leader?" Ava said grimly as Alex sat up scratching the back of his head.

Marcus came rushing whilst Alex himself kept pondering about the best action to take. Thinking of even leaving the west finding a new base away from everything. It wasn't surprising however he lacked enough funds to safely take his people with him through Pangean waters and beyond.

"Boss, a letter came for you, some guy named Ezekiel wants to meet you."

Alex lifted his eyebrow. "You opened a letter directed at me. Come here." He said pouncing on Marcus, siting on him as he read the rest of the letter.

"At the games' finally, seat thirty-two b. Looks like Ezekiel expected me to come."

"If you are going, we are all coming." Ava demanded. "We don't know who this is or why he wants to meet, give the word and we will get enough tickets for everyone."

Alex yawned. "Do what you wish, you are the second remember. I'm just the pretty face darling. We have just under a month so good luck."

In the cells of Lovita's Villa Raijin laid on his back watching the ceiling as he counted each crack for what seemed to be the millionth time. He scratched his bandages knowing he had to clean them soon. The thought of the fight flew back as he looked at his hand, "There's no welts or blisters…" He said starting to clench his fist.

"Not joining us again?" Ulfr said as he sneaked out from the shadows, startling Raijin.

With his bright Ember eyes Raijin glanced at Ulfr. "Your hair looks terrible…"

"I know, I need to maintain it more for Ella, right?" Ulfr said as he scratched his head, smiling through his freshly shaved face.

"Can't even show off with a beard with that one, she doesn't seem to like it."

"You are finally talking to her?"

"Well, I talk she mostly just smiles, beautiful if you ask me" Ulfr said as he stretched his arms showing discomfort from a hard day's work, but all Raijin could notice where the blisters on his hands.

"You should be training; the tournament is still going on." Raijin said as he turned his head.

"I lost my last fight though." Ulfr said as he shrugged.

"Sorry to hear that, was the opponent strong?" Raijin asked.

"Crazy strong, scared as hell though you did a number on Minato." Ulfr quickly answered to the shudder of Raijin. "Don't worry he won't win on the count they pulled him out of the tournament not long after."

"Why?"

"Injuries, his Lanasta lost a lot of money doing so but there's always next year I guess." Ulfr said as he took a sit.

Raijin turned around confused at the state of Ulfr. "Did you give up?"

"Yup."

"Why…"

"To strong, I would rather make Lovita angry than end up in your state."

Raijin laughed. "I guess so."

"Everyone loses at some point Raijin; you just need to get back up and continue." Ulfr said as he sighed.

"Not Milo…"

"That monster can't be classed as a person I refuse." Ulfr laughed. "So, will you give up after you lose?"

Raijin grit his teeth wanting to say yes before lifting his fist forward. Letting out a pool of tears he screamed at the top of his voice. "Never!"

"What an unbreakable soul…" Ulfr muttered before letting out a sly smile.

The world seemed peaceful once again, With the first leaf falling from a tree, crowds from all over the west gathered to watch the final bout.

House Jovian's camp of gladiators stood in the Arena's hallways ready to watch their brother enter the final match.

 Raijin smirked looking through the arena hallway's locked gates. "This could have been you."

"Fuck," Ulfr swore flailing his arms, the tone of his voice was so sarcastic, the rest of the gladiators standing behind them could not help but chuckle. But before they could continue, the glimmer of light from his white war paintings grabbed the attention of the gladiators. As Killian walked past them with bloodlust seeping through his skin. He stood near the gate waiting for it to open, tapping both his scimitars against it eager to get into the fight. The announcer saw leaving a small smirk on his aging face.

"Ladies and gentlemen let the final battle take place. We have a hell of a match today, the second time they meet in battle!" The announcer shouted. "Representing House Jovian hailing from the Lost continent, the 'Sand Snake" Killian!" with simple words the crowd's raw nearly shook the heavens, forcing Lady Charlotte to close her ears, and grabbing the attention of Alex sitting on the opposite end.

"Well, he's popular," Alex said mockingly.

"He is the favoured winner, a man who controls sand, in an arena filled with sand against a simple human he could not ask for a better situation." Ezekiel quickly responded as he sat next to Alex.

On the other side Drominic took large strides towards Lady Charlotte, making himself comfortable as he sat down with his arms wide open. "Don't be mad little girl, the Queen told me to come here encase someone tries something against our lovely stoic Prince."

"I didn't ask."

"Sorry," Drominic mocked. "I see someone is still not happy about me, being free and all that." Charlotte glared at Drominic until the announcer cleared his throat.

The Announcer took a deep breath. "His opponent, the three-time Champion. The Beast slayer, The strongest In the West ladies and gentlemen the White Knight Kingdom's General. Lancer!" A bit of animal skin over some wooden cylinder appeared as the thunder roaring of the drums shook the earth

Lancer made his entrance. From the tip of his White hair to the soles of his boots all anyone could see was a monster. A monster who had deemed his opponent worthy enough to dawn his White armour.

"He looks pretty don't you think Ezekiel?" Alex laughingly said. "I'm sure you don't care about this," Ezekiel told him. "So, I will be as direct to you as I can, would you Eye of Basilisk like to join Logan in his campaign against the White Knights."

"Right into the wall!" Alex shouted as Lancer's body crashed being compressed by a pile of sand.

"First hit goes to..." Drominic mocked.

"Something so small won't even leave a scratch." Charlotte said. Ezekiel paused for a second. "Two Million Cuni after the mission is finished." The number so large Alex could not help but laugh.

"Almost as high as my bounty," Alex responded with a sly smile on his face. Before again his attention was grabbed this time by Lancer's speed as the White Knight himself blitzed towards Killian closing the distance in a matter of seconds. Lancer Jumper as he got within feet of Killian and swung his spear down only for it to be absolved by a wall of sand. And as a reply to this Lancer let out his Will destroying the sand wall and slashing Killian across the chest. However, Killian not wanting to fall controlled the sand with his feet launching it to the side of Lancer and sending the White Knight flying towards the side of the Arena. These two, thought to themselves that the opponent standing opposite was strong. This was the first time since their first match that either person thought this.

"So, the real match begins," Ezekiel quietly comments as both Lancer and Killian slowly approach each other.

"Well Basilisk, what is your answer to my offer?"

"Sounds amazing, which is immediately concerning. How do you expect me to trust your word?" Alex quickly asked.

"After the match I will hand you three hundred thousand Cuni in treasure. "He told Alex. "Then you will receive the rest after we win the war and if we lose, you keep your three hundred thousand and are free to retreat."

"You mock me..."

"Why is that?"

"Because you know the Queen wants my head, so you know we need each other to survive her wrath. I like the money touch though, makes me see you in a different light Ezekiel."

"Yet, I am still unable to figure you out Alexander," Ezekiel commented as the crowd once again roared reacting to the all-out brawl that had engulfed the arena. With sand swords and spears Flailing around everyone knew whoever let up would lose the match. Finally, as Lancer used all his strength into the final swing of his Spear, Killian blocked it breaking the spear in half.

Killian instead of celebrating smirked as he saw Lancer's Legendary Iron Spear land behind the White Knight himself. "Then the next attack wins..." Killian muttered as he took his stance. The two ran at each other clashing one final time and as lancer took a few steps away from Killian's back he fell to his knee panting. Whilst Killian's head rolled off his body.

"Curse of the ordinary," Alex muttered in a sombre tone as Ezekiel glanced at him. With the crowd chanting, Lancer slumped back through his side of the tunnels. As soon as he disappeared from the crowd, he collapsed into the wall, holding himself up with his spear trying to stop his legs from shaking.

"You over did it again young master," Ser Noham Pascal told him as he tilted his glasses back in place. "I could hear your bones rattling from the second you entered the tunnel. Also, some of that blood surely is yours."

"I'm fine, my leg just won't stop throbbing is all."

Ser Noham handed Lancer a vial filled with strange liquid. "To stop the pain, long enough for the Beast slayer to make it to the carriages."

"You are too kind, 'Pawn'."

"Thank you. However, my mission is complete, and I shall return to Lumina."

"Still keeping an eye on him... I do apologise you got stuck with such a job." Lancer said as he gulped the drink.

"It's peaceful, so I can't complain." Ser Noham Pascal quickly replied.

Lancer smiled as he stumbled past Ser Noham. "It's always good to see you." As he walked past Ser Noham smiled.

"She will be arriving at Zen soon." A simple comment from Ser Noham, but enough to fluster Lancer as his pace begun to quicken waving Ser Noham off.

"My Lorde," A Knight commanded holding a sealed scroll. "For you."

Lancer studied it for a moment and upon seeing the stamp he frowned. "I wonder what Jon could want."

In the stands as everyone continued to make their way out of the arena, Drominic finally stood glancing across and locking eyes with Alex only for a moment but long enough for him to warn Lady Charlotte.

Lady charlotte smirked. "The great Drominic scared of a child." she mocked.

"Keep an eye on that one," Drominic said grimly. "There's something off about his Aura."

"Yes, ser Drominic I'll keep an eye on some weak looking child if it puts you at ease." Lady Charlotte mocked. "You go back to the outposts and drink yourself to sleep like usual."

As Alex and Ezekiel seeped into the crowds, trying not to attract attention he quickly ordered his group to disperse, saying his goodbyes to Ezekiel as he grabbed a chair outside a nearby bar. His smirk made it even more obvious for Lady Charlotte as she sighed calmly approaching him. He kicked a chair out for her frustrating her even more.

"Frowning like that hides your beauty too much."

"Should you be saying that to a sixteen-year-old?"

"Are you not an adult all of a sudden?" Alex quickly replied.

"How did you notice me?" Lady Charlotte asked.

Alex laughed. "When the old man glared at me, I knew one of you will be following me. So, what does a Knight of the White Knights want with little old Adam."

"Adam?" Charlotte lifted her eyebrow. "Nothing I guess you just have a similar resemblance to the man we are looking for. You know Alexander." she added pointing at the poster to the wall by her side.

Before Alex responded he noticed more White Knights in the surrounding area, quickly dropping his smile and lifting his hands out waiting to be arrested. "I don't wish for trouble; you can arrest me if you find me suspicious." He announced. "However, once I'm cleared of all wrong doings would you mind grabbing some food with me?"

"No."

"Ouch such a quick response, I guess I'm no match for you."

"Enough," Lady Charlotte demanded as she stood. "Go home Adam, we made a mistake."

"May the Goddess bless you and I hope we meet again in better circumstances, miss?" Alex replied with a faint smile.

"You may call me lady Charlotte."

"'The Knight'?" Alex asked as he dusted himself off. He was thrown back for a moment with how young a leader of the White Knights was but also understood she needed to be strong to have so much authority as he waved goodbye disappearing into the crowds once again.

With the tournament over, the west filled with people returning to the homes and in Zen's castle an Aura seeped through the oak door as Phillip felt it sending shivers down his spine. He peaked through the door to see the Queen's face closed in grimace, with her skin pale and clammy. Her hands sinking deeper into the bed, her eyes screaming for someone to kill her. Phillip could see the pain she was in but was bewildered by the silence echoing from the Queen. For what seemed to be an eternity, the loud crying finally started, not from the Queen, but from the bright-eyed prince as he held tightly onto the midwife. Seeing this Elizabeth laid back with her eyes feeling heavy and a smile calmly rested on her face. "He's beautiful..." she muttered as Phillip burst into the room Elizabeth smiled at him, but he returned with a stern look.

"You shouldn't have underestimated me..." Philip said as he ordered a dozen guards to rush into the room holding the midwife's hostage as he grabbed his son. "What did you say if we had a son. That's right his name shall be Alfred."

"What... Do you think you're do-"

"Take her!" Phillip ordered as the guards grabbed Elizabeth from her bed dragging her out of the room. She looked around as her feet dragged on the floor, piles of bodies from Knights to her staff laid there.

"Al'Gadrood..." she muttered to Phillip's laughter.

"In order to win this game, I needed to keep some of you alive how else would I keep Lancer away, that ogre will be your new cellmate." He quickly replied as he strode across the castle's hallway holding his son. Elizabeth continued to be dragged into the castle's dungeons Phillip reached the throne room kicking it open and quickly ordering his soldiers to rip down the White Knights' Sigel.

"Vive Les Lions!" he screamed as he approached the throne.

Elizabeth

The slim shaft of light penetrated through the walls. Waking Elizabeth from her nightmarish slumber. She gazed at it wishing it where a little bigger, she could feel her life draining by each second, despite Phillip's efforts of keeping her alive. Some old bread and some water, whenever time for her meal came, she felt oddly happy to see another person as days would quickly pass with her having short conversations with her neighbour beyond the wall.

Is this how I will die? She wondered, if so, what a pathetic way she thought. *Damn them, Damn them all*. She thought.

Mother I'm sorry I made a mistake; I trusted too much and fell on my own sword. She continued to ponder as she reminisced on her past. She closed her eyes and saw herself, a younger version full of hope with bright blue eyes engulfed in wonder.

"Faster!" Esther screamed as she lunged at a young Elizabeth slashing across her chest. The sound the wooden swords clashing woke Drominic in shock.

"Dodge!" she commanded as she struck her wooden blade down with full force, blowing the curly red hair from her eyes. "Good," she grinned stretching the left scar from her cheek. Before being rocked by the waves below her forcing her to turn her cheek gazing at the shipwright. "Control this better boy!" She wiped the sweat off her face onto her tank top before approaching Drominic sticking the blade onto his chest and with a big smile laughed. "You are dead now."

Drominic looked unbothered. "Damn I guess I can finally retire." he mocked. "What about the little princess is her training done for the day fearsome White Fang?"

Esther stepped forward onto opening the door onto the cabins. "No, you take over. The next Queen of Zen can't be satisfied with such a short lesson. Right Elizabeth!"

"Yes…" Elizabeth made a face.

"Good. Now I have important matters to handle, Drominic call the young doctor to help me with something."

"No problem he will be over soon as," Drominic said as Esther stumbled away. "Now princess Lizzie, instead of training how about we go fishing instead?" he said as Al'Gadrood approached him with a sombre face.

"She's getting better…" Al'Gadrood muttered as he walked past Drominic.

"That's a lie…" Drominic quickly replied to silence as Al'Gadrood walked into the cabins and Drominic picked up Elizabeth to go fishing.

As the sun finally set, the ship docked, as quickly as they could the mercenaries armoured themselves and Esther took charge leading her men forward with Elizabeth by her side.

"We travelled for weeks Esther, are you going to tell us why we are here?" Drominic asked.

"I told you to help an old friend." Esther quickly replied. Though Drominic could tell it was a lie he rolled his eyes and continued marching with her. Night finally broke into dawn as the mercenaries looked drained from moving without a single break. Elizabeth was sleeping in Al'Gadrood's arms when a loud Order from Esther to be ready for battle woke her up to the site of mutilated bodies lying across their path. With a pile of them not too far from their site carefully placed. But even with such a horrible site before them all including Elizabeth saw a toddler sitting on top of this pile of bodies watching the sun rise. Suddenly a loud bang woke Elizabeth from her dream as she once again realised, she was still inside a cell.

"Are you ok Elizabeth?" Al'Gadrood's groggy voice seeped through the walls.

"Forgive me, I just slipped of for a moment," Elizabeth said. "I was thinking about the day we met Is- Lancer."

"That mission. What a mess that was."

"A mess?"

"Don't you remember it was the first time your mother started those insane chases across the world."

Elizabeth looked up to the ceiling. "She was a driven woman."

"Driven... that's one word to describe her. I'd say crazy was closer." Al'Gadrood mocked.

"She is the reason we made it so far, she was a great mother and leader." Elizabeth sconed. "We should save our energy, for the moment we can escape."

Al'Gadrood let out a slight cough. "Elizabeth, from the second you were born your mother only wanted to mould you in her image. Because she was dying."

"Enough!" Elizabeth screamed. "She had me because she needed me and trained me for the harshness of this world. What more could you want from a mother?"

"Love?"

Elizabeth grasped onto her blood-stained dress. "You have become sentimental in your old age. Well enough of that we need a plan for escape."

"Maybe," Al'Gadrood quickly answered. "I've been counting the meals, once every three days our fourth should arrive tomorrow or the day after, meaning Lancer will be at the closest point. I say we escape then."

"Good so far, but we'll still be in the castle."

"You are a warrior Queen remember? We fight our way out and remember our pact." Al'Gadrood enthusiastically answered.

Elizabeth smiled as she touched the wall to her side. "Always face the enemy."

"Die in honour, never beg."

"For we are the band of White Knights!" Elizabeth said proudly.

"Fighting through a castle, screaming the pact your mother forced us into, Ga'Al's humour is unmatched." Al'Gadrood added.

Elizabeth pushed the back of her head against the wall trying to hold in her tears. "It's not fair!" she screamed. "I might never see my boy grow!" she added as finally her eyes filled with tears. As time passed, a guard kicked Elizabeth awake "Time for food!" he commanded as he threw a sack of water on the floor and some bread, Elizabeth played her role perfectly ripping into the bread like a wild animal and gulping the water as quick as she could. The site amused the guard as he started to snicker letting his guard down long enough for Elizabeth to grab his sword and lunge it into him putting all her weight into the attack. She rolled forward and as she struggled to stand, she saw the guard struggle to breathe and in response she approached the guard pulling the sword out and stubbing him repeatedly until Al'Gadrood's groggy voice broke her trance.

She approached the cell, to see her old friend heavily injured covered in dry blood, his leg purple with a small cloth wrapped around it. "Ga'Al would welcome you with his arms wide open. However, my old friend this is not the time for you to die."

"I promise to bury that irritation Drominic first before I go to his domain." Al'Gadrood said as he reached out his hand. "Let's get out of here!" he added pulling himself up with the help of Elizabeth.

At the end of the dungeon's hallway a guard sat sleeping by the stairs until a sudden pain in his chest work him from his slumber. As he saw one last time a red-haired crazed woman and a blood wrenched man standing before him before he closed his eyes.

"Two, why is there only two guards in the castle's dungeons?" Elizabeth asked as Al'Gadrood grabbed the dead guard's sword. "Phillip might think it's not worth having many people here." Al'Gadrood answered as they approached the top of the staircase. Unlocking the last door into the castle. "Or not..." he added as he saw a dozen guards run towards them from the opposite end.

"Elizabeth! I will be all but useless after this, so you will need to take point guard, ok?" Al'Gadrood asked before strengthening his body and launching rock spikes from the wall beside them into some of the guards and lunging into the rest, making quick work of them.

"Fool..." Elizabeth stated as she put Al'Gadrood's arm over her shoulders. "Something is not right even those guards look un-prepared for an escape. I have a proposition why don't we hea-"

"Lancer is coming!" shouted a guard as he ran towards the main gates.

"Mystery solved." Al'Gadrood said. "If lancer is pushing forward Phillip is either in the frontlines or..."

"Throne room." Elizabeth responded. "Not even in the city yet and there is this much panic, I think we might have created an unstoppable army."

As they made their way to the throne room, taking out any strugglers heading for the main gates. At the borders of Zen, the first of Phillip's allies fell. As Lancer pulled his spear from an enemy soldier Charlotte approached him quickly saluting before a glare from Lancer's eye sent shivers down her spine.

"Sir, 'King has risen his banners inside the golden city and Rook has already taken lead pushing her soldiers deeper into Zen." She communicated.

Lancer pointed his spear forward. "We don't stop till the enemy falls!" he shouted as he started to march forward. Without the King guard, Lady Charlotte and Drominic followed Lancer.

Drominic and his archers flooding the skies with arrows and the planting the ground with bodies. Whilst Charlotte with a simple kick to the ground sent soldiers flying into the air before falling to their death and with her strengthening blitzing through a squad of enemies as if they were paper. The White Knights on this day showed their true strength decimating anyone who stood in their way.

As news of the dominance spread back to the castle, Elizabeth and Al'Gadrood finally made it into the throne room and when they opened the wide gold trimmed oak doors Elizabeth halted her friend entering alone. "Golden lions, protectors of the Kingdom, kings of Zen," Phillip spoke sat on the throne holding Alfred tight in his arms.

"Not the White Knights, the Golden Lions!" he added as his eyes filled with tears.

Elizabeth frowned. "Give me my child," she said as her voice sharpened.

"Everyone said you will be trouble and after Apollo's death I saw it, I saw your true intentions, like a cockroach you just wanted to sneak your way into our lands and spoil them!" Phillip said with spite. "But I was stupid enough to side by you because I thought you really loved me!"

Elizabeth seemed puzzled as she approached Phillip dragging her sword. "The only true thing I did was love you. Despite your faults I always loved you. I loved the way your mind worked, your stupid jokes how even as the world rejected you, you stayed optimistic. You fought against your destiny; what woman wouldn't love that."

"I'm sorry," Phillip apologised as he cracked a smile. "You can't love. A monster can't know love. I know you best Elizabeth and as you get closer to me, to kill the father of your child. I can truthfully say you are no more than a puppet. For your glorious mother."

Elizabeth lowered her eyes for a moment as she stood feet away from Phillip. "I will not let you trample on her... on my dream." Phillip noticed that, quickly wiping his tears. "Do you think we could have ever had a normal life?"

"No," Elizabeth answered. "Our relationship was built on my lie for that I apologize. But every now and then either the cold nights under the moonlight or when we would just take walk together. I thought it was enough."

"We could change our names; we could even be farmers if you want." Phillip laughed.

"In another life maybe."

"But too much has happened right..." Phillip said.

"Far too much..."

Phillip leaned forward as he placed Alfred on the floor below him sitting with his back to the chair. "Promise me one thing. Don't turn our son into you..."

Elizabeth ignored that as she drove her sword into Phillip's chest. Watching him struggle as blood started to flood the throne with even some spilling on Alfred. It was only the beginning though as all three countries that made up the White Knight Kingdom begun to feel the bloodshed, under the queen's orders the five armies raided and destroyed houses. Anyone who did not stand by her side during Phillip's attempt to take over was deemed an enemy.

"House Yanis, this is our stop. "Announced Lady Charlotte. "Draw your swords Knights, our order is simple anyone who bears the name Yanis or stands under their Sigel dies today." She said as she raised her sword with a sombre look on her face. As her army burst through the gates of the small village that bordered Pocasis and Nero. The war cry quickly faded as they found the village streets empty. With only Ser Philibert Yanis sat in the middle with his bare chest out and his eyes closed.

"Kill me but spare my people!" he screamed as Charlotte froze on the back of her horse. Tangi however did not seem fazed jumping of his horse approaching ser Philibert and quickly decapitating him with a strong swing of his sword.

Lady Charlotte shook her head. "May the goddess rest your soul..." she muttered before turning her steed around preparing to march out.

"Mrs 'Knight!'" Tangi shouted as he took his helm off showing his croaked smile through his uneven red beard. "Anyone who bears the name Yanis or stands under their Sigel dies remember..."

Lady Charlotte quickly glanced at Tangi. "Ser Philibert Yanis is dead, I'm sure the queen will be pleased with just that."

Tangi was not pleased with that answer quickly pointing his sword at Charlotte. "We failed to protect the chosen people's savour in her time of need, I refuse to disappoint her again!"

"Sheath your sword no-"

"No! Soldiers raid this village and kill everyone!" Tangi commanded.

"Tangi, enough one more word and-"

"What? The Iron Lady will kill me?" Tangi mocked. "There are around three thousand soldiers around here. Unless you are a secret wordbreaker, I doubt you have much chance of escape. So, what will it be Lady Charlotte finish the mission or become the mission?"

Charlotte gazed at Tangi; her face filled with anger unable to respond she sighed simple placing her helmet over her face and grasping the saddle of the horse.

Tangi grunted. "Like I said boys, lets finish our saviour's command, kill everyone!" he screamed as the soldiers begun to raid the houses pulling mothers from children. Killing all men immediately. Bursting through the church killing the priests and Fathers even if they begged for their lives. Charlotte heard all of this from the centre of the village, the screams the cries all she could do was sit unable to stop it. This scene was the same everywhere the next coming month was horror as heads of nobles were planted throughout the Kingdom, and a road of crucified soldiers reached to the farthest ends of the Kingdom.

Sometime after the purging, Elizabeth was having a light breakfast some eggs and soup sat at the end of a pine table that stretched throughout the dining room. When Charlotte burst in furious from the mission, she quickly bent the knee. "My Queen may I have a moment of your time?" she asked with a stern tone.

Elizabeth looked at her and had a quick smile. "Be quick its almost feeding time for Alfred."

"I'll be brief I wish to duel with one of my subordinates."

"That is entirely your choice 'Knight' do as you wish," Elizabeth said continuing to smile.

Charlotte glanced up anxiously. "Another thing my Queen, I found the last mission to be against a knight's honour..." She could not stop her eyes from twitching or her fingers from moving as she said this. She expected everything from Elizabeth from the Queen ignoring this comment to feeling her full wrath, until one of the midwives came in with Alfred showing a glowing smile from the Queen as she held her arms out for her child.

"Had it not been for Jon I wouldn't be seeing him today." Elizabeth said as she continued to smile. "A simple Architect now but he still acted as the best spy I have and saved us; I wish I could reward him more."

Alfred quickly latched on to Elizabeth's breast amusing the Queen, as she started to stroke his head. "He will be my little piggy soon with how much he eats." Charlotte could not understand this behaviour from the Queen, she felt bewildered by this new side of her until Elizabeth's stern tone returned. "War is not like in fantasy books, there is no evil guy who must be stopped. War is simple kill your enemies before they can become your enemies or be responsible for thousands of deaths in battle."

Elizabeth stood proud as ever, slowly approaching Charlotte with Alfred still cupped in her arms. "If you can't manage it say now 'knight' and I will strip you of your command and place you in a safe environment where if it's by Ga'Al's Will you won't ever see battle."

Charlotte did not move or say a word.

"Good," Elizabeth said. "Now your duel, I wish to see it we will make it an event and invite the biggest names. I wish to hold a council meeting soon so some entertainment after would be more than welcome."

Charlotte nodded her head. "Yes, my queen, I am ready whenever you deem it."

"I expect nothing less, 'Knight' now go back to your post, and I shall send you the details as soon as everything is set, my powerful soldier."

"Yes, my Queen," Charlotte said with a sombre tone paying her respects and quickly leaving the dining room.

Eros

The roars from the crowd could be heard all over the pits as Eros once again stood tall over his opponent with his fist still burning. As usual the guards carefully approached him trying their best to not provoke him. Unlike at the beginning Eros looked tired unable to fight the guards of and simple walked alongside them.

"Congratulations you little monster," Vibius a guard who had been around Eros for nearly a year spoke. "You get a month off; do you want any special meals some ladies maybe?"

"Why?"

"Because your funeral is coming up, "Vibius mocked as he took of his helmet showing his sunken eyes and balding head.

Eros glanced at the guards whispering behind him. "Unfortunate, this one made me a lot of money, but all good things must come to an end."

"They're talking about you," Vibius whispered back to Eros as they continued walking through the hallways to the applause of the other prisoners.

"Is it execution?" Eros Asked with a stern tone.

Vibius scratched the bit of hair on his chin. "Something like that, you get to fight the King. But don't worry he usually kills his opponents quick, so you won't feel much pain. But you made me and the boys so much money betting on you let us fulfil your last rights."

"Then I'm about to make you a rich man, because I will win." Everyone surrounding laughed as they started to mock Eros, the King vs the beast they mocked and begun acting out how the match will go with Eros quickly dying. They continued even forcing a smile on Eros.

"He's human after all!" they screamed before Eros entered his cell and as Vibius locked it his eyes met with a piercing glare from Eros.

"Scary..." Vibius said as he quickly looked down walking away from the cells.

"Exciting time right now," Ake said as he peered from the shadows.

"Your early today..." Eros said as he slumped over humming his mother's lullaby as he tried to get some sleep.

"Because you are scared, so you need us," his younger self appeared from the far-right hand corner.

Eros glanced around before rolling over to his back. "Where's the third one, the one who tells me to kill myself a few hundred times?"

"I don't know..." Ake said puzzled at the situation. As time went by Eros fell asleep only for a short while before he workup in a cold sweat. The same dream he has had for years, it changes slightly each time but always ends the same him seeing the people he loved die one by one. Each time he would wake up he clenched his chest and sighed. And so, his routine started again, he would dash between the walls and the door until his legs numbed. Then he would do push ups until His arms numbed. Finally, he would cross his legs sitting opposite the door holding his arms out and engulfing them with fire, each time lasting a second longer until his stamina ran out and he passed out. Wake up in cold sweat eat the food left for him and so the same routine.

In House Jovian, things were different Edward would wake up each day around noon and sipped on some left-over wine and ate some food before watching the new ace Raijin train directly under the Doctares. He would analyse each move and laugh whenever a mistake was about to happen then a maid would bring him his daily bottle of wine and he would drink that till he passed out.

Ulfr hearing the rumours looked at the passed-out Edward.

"The king doesn't look that powerful..."

"He used to be different... Full of life." Doctares said as he slashed at Raijin.

"Then what happened?"

"His been in chains far too long, the only reason he hasn't gave up entirely is because of the wine. He says he likes it." Doctares answered as he parried a sudden attack from Raijin.

As the sun rose and sank, a knock-on Eros' cell as the guard announced ten minutes. Eros calmly opened his eyes "The king sits on the high throne..." he muttered.

Ake laughed as he knew what Eros meant. Before glancing round the cell to see that he was the only one remaining.

"They all left why are you still here?"

"What do you mean?" Ake asked.

"I mean..." Eros snapped his head to see no one standing there.

"Encase this really is the end..." Ake said as his hand reached out to Eros's shoulder. "Go out like a true beast... But if you pull off a miracle... promise me one thing Eros." he said as his voice changed to the younger version of Eros.

"Stop being so hard on yourself and get some sleep."

Eros stood tying his hair back as he glared at the mirror next to him. "I have to live…" He muttered clenching his fists and taking heavy breaths. "I have to kill him…" He said punching the wall by the mirror still gazing into the void as it gazed back. "I have to keep moving… Until my enemies are dead. Every Last One."

"Creepy…" Vibius muttered as he watched on from outside the cell.

"Time!" The guard shouted as he opened Eros's cell. Eros took a large sigh before stepping out either way he knew this would be the last time he would step out and walk these hallways. The guards mocked "Dead man walking," they said as the other prisoners hummed funeral music, until Eros stepped on the sand feeling it crawl through his toes.

All he could hear was one voice, Vibius. "I bet on you, so don't lose." this simple sentence put a smile on Eros's face as he stood near his gate hearing it close. He started to stretch as opposite him the gate flung open. The roars from the crowd exploded as Edward stumbled out looking drunk as usual, still in his steal straight jacket. And as the gate behind Edward shut, an odd silence fell in the Arena and neither man moved. ***He looks out of it,*** Eros thought as a crooked smile edged onto his face. Eros not one to waste an opportunity launched forward coating his right hand in fire and throwing a right hook onto Edward's face sending the man flying across the Arena. A smile fell on

Eros as he felt relieved before Edward's knee crashed into his face sending Eros flying cross the arena.

"That hurt you idiot..." Edward slurred his words as he tried to shake himself sober. The crowd like sheep cheered on as they watched the exchange. Each betting among themselves the seconds the fight would last not who would win. As they were betting a smoke screen of sand went in the air and they all knew this as Eros's signature move. Edward on the other hand looked unbothered whilst his eyes snapped directly at Eros bursting from the sand smoke to the shock of Eros who immediately retreated. ***His eyes followed me perfectly...*** Eros thought sighing.

 With the thick dust disappearing, the glare in his eye sparked Edward's interest.

"Fine then." Eros said coldly when he started to walk forward. "To the death." Edward responded in kind. As they got within reach Eros immediately engulfed his hands in fire then he started to throw a fury of punches, but all dodged without effort. Then threw a faint forcing Edward to dodge into Eros's left hand and barely duck under that into Eros's right knee, making the King stumble sideways forcing him to flip kicking Eros in the face with his heal forcing them both to fall to their side. Before jumping back up Eros noticed Edward's feet had been set ablaze, so he responded in kind by setting his hands ablaze. The crowd looked puzzled as minutes had passed making this the longest match the King has had. "Come on King you drunk shit!" shouted a member of the audience.

"Stop playing around, my wife will start to wonder where I am!" Another screamed as Edward laughed quickly hoping up, with a different aura to him. He hoped once before blitzing towards Eros and before Eros could react Edward kicked him across the arena. When Eros Landed, he glanced up to see a ball of fire heading towards him barely dodging it. His face told the entire story, as Eros felt absolute fear engulf him.

"Come on... Stand... Ablaze, throw some fire balls at me.... something..." Edward said with now his entire body engulfed in fire while he took strides towards Eros. **Why am I so excited?** Edward thought before stopping in his tracks and making the fire disappear. "Maybe it's because you're the first Fire Elemental I've seen in a long time..." he added as his eyes wondered before snaping back where Eros was only to then feel some pressure on his chest. He looked down to see a clearly frightened Eros press his hand against the steal straight jacket. "Funny kid even I can't break this, it's not any normal steal you kn-" he stopped talking as he flew into a wall with a puzzled look on his face.

"Ha!" Edward screamed from inside the wall silencing the crowd in fear. "You can break steal overflowing with those witches' fucking seals on them?" He added as he stepped out of the wall with his fire pulsating in and out of him. His arms looked how you would think, with skin hanging onto the bone darkened by lack of sunlight and him barely able to move them.

"Your arms... your chest..." Eros said in sorrow.

"Ding, you found my weakness, two years like that does that to you." Edward said as the audience stood shocked. "Can I ask kid... why are you fighting so hard I mean look at your arm?" he said glancing at Eros's burned right arm.

"I'll be honest that's the most I've ever released; I think I broke my arm." Eros laughed as he pointed up with his left hand. "I'm going there."

Edward glanced up before looked back at Eros. "Why? You will still be in chains just with some sunlight."

"Because up there is a chance to escape."

"Stupid... you are stuck here forever..." Edward said with a stern tone as he coated his body in fire. "Come ill at least give you true freedom!"

"You talk too much old man, let's just see who stands in the end." Eros responded as he coated his hands in fire walking towards Edward.

The curtain to this battle was about to come to an end, everyone knew whoever withstood the next attacks wins. As they stood across from each other Eros took the first swing knocking the air from Edward and in turn Edward put all the effort he could into a kick, knocking Eros to his back before Eros stood tall once more. In a development that left the spectators speechless with those admiring Eros's endurance and others surprised by Edward's control of fire bending it to his will to best suit the next attack.

The fight seemed to last an eternity, with Edward clearly having the upper hand without a single scratch on him and Eros covered from head to toe in his own blood and yet Eros refused to stay down standing after each blow. Until each end of the arena had some of Eros's blood covering it, "the gladiator Eros... what a monster..." Edward said with a smile on his face as he watched Eros put his fist up in a pool of his own blood.

"His still standing..." the crowd said in shock, as Edward got rid of his fire once again approaching Eros for one final hit.

"Kill him, Edward!" shouted a spectator, as Edward lunged forward, to meet a devastating right hook from Eros as it swung Edward's head into the air. ***Blood?*** Edward thought as for the first time in the match Eros had drawn Edward's blood. Edward glanced down at Eros before falling onto his back, closing his eyes. ***Seriously... How long have you been unconscious?*** Edward thought as Eros stood tall with his hand still in the air. "I quit!" Edward said.

As the silence grew and with no movement in the arena, "And new!" shouted an audience member.

"And the winner... the new King... Eros dark King? Eros?" Another stumbled on his words trying to announce the new champion of the pits.

"Beast King Eros!" another screamed quickly joined by the crowd as the audience finally came back to life.

After the hardships for the battle news of his victory quickly made it back to Lovita who jumped for joy at Edward's defeat but immediately sat sound with a long gaze as he realised the money he would lose from this event. "Why couldn't he just die?" Lovita whispered as his maid looked confused at the comment.

"It doesn't have to end like that you know," Lady Marcella calmly replied.

"My best gladiators are dead, now that Sordes is no longer a king. We are losing money every minute, the debt collectors are on our ass, and you say it doesn't have to end like this?"

Lady Marcella could see the grey hairs growing on her husband from the stress she smirked before approaching him. "Raijin will be the next champion and now you have a fan favourite as the new king. Someone who is easier to control than Edward."

"Then what do I do?"

"Simple, lets host a fight a single fight. Between the Beast king and the Beast Slayer." Lady Marcella confidently answered.

"Would anyone care that much for such a match?"

Lady Marcella frowned as she saw doubt on Lovita's face.

"Elizabeth will get sixty percent of profits and we get forty percent. Solving our issues in more ways than one, firstly weakening Lancer during his fight, secondly solving our financial issues till the next tournament and finally prepping our new star Raijin to be the next champion."

"She has been under a lot lately I'm sure she would be up for showing off her strength again." she added.

Lovita's eyes shined brightly. "Why stop there then my queen, why not add a few interesting people to the mix, make it something she won't resist."

"Like?"

Lovita set up proudly. "Invite the trade union, the Yang sect even the Vassilles, if any of those names show up our lives would be set forever."

Lady Marcella rolled her eyes. "It's a stretch but what do we have to lose."

On the next moon, Eros took off his last bandage as dozens of guards including an ecstatic Vibius came to escort him back to Lovita's Villa. Lovita watched from his poach from what seemed hours until the glimpse of Eros in the distance put a smile on his face, Ulfr ran to the gate to greet his brother, Raijin stopped training for a moment.

"Four weeks fighting for his life, I'm glad you look so good, Sorde." Lovita said from the distance.

"You look terrible..." Ulfr said as he stood face to face with his brother for the first time in a year.

Eros smiled, as he stretched his shoulder. "I'm home brother."

"Welcome home," Ulfr laughed as he hugged Eros glancing at the skies as a bird dropped a sealed note by his feet.

Alexander

"Begin!" Damon and Fini dashed towards Ava as Oliver shot arrows from the distance, immediately she deflected the arrows before sliding under the arm of Fini and pointing her sword on Damon's neck. "Enough..." Logan said as he scrunched his eyebrows in disappointment.

"She seems like a frail lady, but strong very strong." Bern said in the background before everyone was set free to continue their day.

"That's why she's my second." Alex mocked as he stood up.

"Like I said if you can defeat her then I'll listen to your orders King Logan."

Logan quickly scorned. "Insolent fo-"

"Enough..." Ezekiel interrupted seeing how the situation could escalate further.

Alex sighed rubbing the back of his head. "You're right that's enough, I need to be somewhere anyway."

"Where?" Ava asked as she sheathed her sword tightening her belt around her leather trousers.

"A village near here, I head they have the best dumplings." Alex answered as he started to walk away strapping a sack of gold coins by his waist, quickly being tailed by Ava before Lilou a servant girl who recently joined grabbed Ava by the arm.

"Let's have a girl's day out instead of following Alexander..." Lilou calmly said before Ava reluctantly nodded.

"Oliver, you said you needed a new bow, you go as well!" Logan quickly ordered before returning to his tent.

As they arrived at the lively village, in the middle of the street Oliver stopped as he had a distant look on his face. **Wait... I'm alone here... Around so many people,** he pondered before quickly looking around and shedding a small tear. "I can escape!" he shouted before dashing forward as fast as he can, "I'm free from that fat idiot and his creepy friend! I'm free from these dumb wars!" he screamed in joy before colliding with a heavy built man.

"You... Come with me..." The heavy built man said as he picked up Oliver holding him like luggage. Not long after he found himself standing Infront of a tavern with a blank look on his face, unsurprised of the circumstances.

"Did you hear, the White Knights are hosting some event," A girl said as she walked into the tavern with her friend. Oliver glanced down holding a stack of leaflets before dashing them on the floor in a fit of rage and starting to walk away.

Another voice spoke. "Move kid!" a man screamed and as Oliver turned around, he saw a group of men dressed similar with tattoos surrounding their bodies. "Do you know who we are, we are the Poison Toad gang, you better act more respectful" the man added as he stuck his chest out.

"Leave my leaflet boy alone!" screamed the heavy-set man as he exited out of his tavern. Soon after a fist was thrown and a brawl broke out with Oliver stuck in the middle, before men wearing the Sigel of the White Knights came rushing in. Stopping the conflict in a second.

Later at the station, Oliver sat watching the leader of this militia reading a newspaper. "Is it good?" Oliver asked with a frail voice.

"Well, good is a stretch. Apparently, a new anomaly has been found in the Olorun mountains, and other than that just new bounty posters." The man said as he handed the posters too Oliver. Although at first, he didn't look that interested he continued glancing at the posters till he saw three, the first for Ava worth thirteen million Cuni. The second for Basil worth six million Cuni with an odd alive only on his poster and the last for Alexander Senesto worth twenty-eight million Cuni.

"The Basilisk clan or something, I heard they're in the west. Don't know what they did but Pangea wants them desperately." The mad said before sighing. "Go on kid get out of here." He added as Oliver quickly took his leave.

Over in the heart of the village, Ava and Lilou stood in front of a massage parlour with Lilou filled with joy and Ava bewildered. "This village is growing fast, soon it'll will be named a city or even a Provence. I understand why we are here so we can figure out how the structure of the White Knight Kingdom works." Ava said proudly.

"No..." Lilou quickly responded. "We are here to relax, and not think about war or battle or being stronger."

Inside the Parlour chaos quickly broke out as several maids held down Ava trying to massage her and apply makeup, with her fighting at every moment. "Hold her down!" one screamed as she tried her best to apply nail polish. With laughter and crying echoing from the building time flew and as they started to walk out Lilou quickly complimented Ava.

Ava's eyes filled with rage responded. "I don't see the point of this unless we are going undercover."

"It's just a nice thing to do for yourself you know," Lilou said joyfully. "Not everything has to involve a mission. Sometimes a girl just wants to feel pretty, for herself. Now don't you feel pretty?"

Ava was quiet but firm. "It's ok I guess, where to now?"

"How about some food?"

"Fine..."

As they sat outside around an oak table, they slowly ate the ball of fruits whilst talking with each other. Even though it was mostly Lilou asking Ava of her simple childhood in her parents' manor or her father she wanted to make so proud. "Wow," she said. "So, you left to follow Alexander because of something great?"

"Something so great the world would kill us for even talking about it."

"What is it?"

"We don't know, but we are getting closer to knowing." Ava said.

"Then I hope you find it, then I can join you in your perfect Kingdom." Lilou said as she stood seeing Oliver approaching from afar. "Something so powerful it would challenge even a wordbreaker. Now that's true power."

"Lilou!" Oliver screamed as he arrived. "Can I speak to you in private?"

"Give us a moment my beautiful lady," Lilou said as she smiled walking away with Oliver.

Alex was near the edge of the village whistling away with his hands in his pockets glancing at all sides as he took the sights in. When he saw a girl crying on her own, holding onto her dress, he scratched his head before striding towards her quickly going to her level and asking what was wrong.

"I can't find my mum!" the girl screamed before Alex smiled reaching his hand out.

"Then let's go look for her," he sang with a cheerful tone making the young girl laugh a little. As they continued to walk side by side Alex saw a pregnant lady struggling with some boxes and like the gentleman, he is quickly rushed towards her giving her a hand with the little girl doing her part by carrying a small toy for the pregnant lady.

"Hey pretty mister, do you like this lady?" the little girl asked flustering Alex as he picked her up and left in a rush.

Finally, as they reach her home, the little girl rushed towards her mother who looked to be in trouble with one of the guards stationed at the village. "You are short again third time this month!" the guard scorned.

"It's because taxes are rising almost every day, how can people like me keep up!" the lady shouted back till her daughter ran and hugged her calming her down.

Alex scanned the guard up and down. "Full armour, white cape beautiful short blond hair, I like the look Mrs guard."

"The dirty trousers and loose shirt do nothing for you, blondie."

"I guess not, I need to go shopping don't I." Alex said. "The name's Adam, what seems to be the problem and how can I help?"

"These tyrants keep raising the taxes where am I supposed to get one thousand Cuni from on this short notice?" The pregnant lady scorned again.

Alex grabs a sack of gold by his waist tossing it at the guard's feet. "That's just a few gold coins, keep the change it will help you out a lot." seeing this the lady and the guard looked confused before the little girl quickly thanked Alex as he started to walk away into the outskirts of the village finding himself in front of a lone tree and quickly laying down.

"Our body will be used by the earth, feeding the grass that will one day feed another deer it like us has a duty to use all of the animal without leaving a single piece." Alex muttered with a blank face. "That's the last thing I ever said to you right? Man, if I could go back, I would have told you all how much I loved you instead. Happy birthday Eros..."

"Alex!" screamed Ava quickly grabbing Alex's attention as he glanced at them with slanted eyes and a croaked smile. "Did you see the newspaper our bounties went up again!" she added.

Eros

"He will die if he fights." Raijin said.

"Do you believe in the Goddess?" Ulfr asked as they both watched Eros struggle to practice his sword swings under the light of the moon. Constantly grasping at his chest and rubbing his eyes.

"No, never imagined you as the religious type..."

"I'm not but if she exists then Eros will need her in a few weeks."

The two refused to rest that night and instead helped Eros as best they could, laughing with him training with him teaching him their own special moves. Then on one fateful night a few days before the fight, Eros glanced into the darkness of night and saw Ake, who had a sombre smile on his face, but before Eros could react a slash from Raijin's blade barely missed him.

"Are you insane?" Raijin shouted. "Don't lose focus in the middle of a fight training or not I could have hurt you badly then!" Eros stretched his back before going into a stance continuing their training. And in the break of dawn Raijin begun his personal education as Ulfr came in swinging his sword. "Do you think he's ready?" Ulfr softly asked glancing at Eros on his back sleeping in the middle of the grounds.

"Edward did a number on him, his injuries will take a while to heal, however he is an elemental. If he goes in hard from the beginning, he has a chance." Raijin calmly explained as he parried Ulfr's sword.

Lovita came onto the grounds with four guards quickly ordering them to pick the passed-out Eros from the floor. It was simple, with only a day left till the battle they wanted their sheep to look its best before the slaughter. A sold-out event, When Lovita read the people attending, he simply started to sweat in joy. Finding it hard to put his feelings into words and for weeks his mood had been so amazing he would let the gladiators and slaves freely interact and let them out at all times of the day. Who could blame his mood though with names like Kenzou Nobuyuki third monk of the Yang sect, the vanguard Ryo Noboru of the Yang sect, Members of the Valeria family, the universal paper and the trade union all attending. All Lovita said to make this true was say one name, sprinkle some evidence in and the world paid attention.

"Make sure he is good and ready by tomorrow!" Lovita commanded. "Give him everything his heart desires, women food whatever he wants give him it!"

Lady Marcella looked at her husband with disappointment.

"You will make a lot of money tomorrow; however, a lot of people will be pissed off."

"Why?" Lovita quickly asked confused.

"Because 'E' is not attending is he...."

"Who cares," Lovita said. "We have everyone from the Queen herself to members of the fucking Yang sect."

"I suppose..." she sighed. "I will be with Celsus tomorrow, I already promised."

"You baby that boy to much love; he will never be a strong man like his father."

"You leave him out of this if he wants to be a mama's boy for the rest of his life then I'll gladly accept it." Marcella quickly answered before going to the bedroom.

Eros was fed, bathed, his brand sharpened for all to see the next day. And even though he laid on a soft bed with fresh air blowing through the windows, his nightmares still lingered cutting his night short as he opened his eyes stirring blankly at the red patterned ceiling. When dawn broke with a knock on his door, he knew the time had come. The day was bright, the Colosseum was Loud Eros could hear them from the end of the hallway. He took a large breath before kicking his sandals off and bashing his shield against his sword. Lovita spared no expense with a leather chest plate consisting of metal strips reflecting the light coming from the end of the hallway. And decorative leather skirt attached to the chest plate like the armour of the Pangean Legionary.

"Should we have cut his hair?" Lovita asked desperately from the stands. "It's so long it might hinder him."

Doctares smirked. "He is the one who refused, who cares anyway, if he dies you are still a rich man sire."

"That's true maybe I -"

Before finishing the announcer screamed down the megaphone.

"Ladies and gentlemen from all over the globe. Kings, Queens, legends. Introducing the Beast King Eros!" as he said this Eros stepped out to a respectable response. But mostly grabbing the eyes of four ladies sat near the back-left side of the Colosseum.

"Sis?" Asked Ingrid glancing towards the Arena towering over her sisters. "That's the man who dares take your title."

"Let's watch the fake king fight shall we..." Astrid quickly responded as she cracked her knuckles.

Frigg looked to her left to a visibly angry Astrid pushing the string of hair from her sister's eye. Before being captured by Eros's calm movement of his sword as he it glides in the air.

"Interesting... a swordsman... Lightning or wind I can't tell yet." she muttered.

"The beast king... wonder how this man defeated Edward..." Kenzou Nobuyuki said as he locked his arms inside his robe.

"An amateur swordsman at best, Edward probably gave up knowing him." Ryo Noboru quickly responded as he pulled his straw hat down. "The wild Dog, one of the strongest Fire Elementals would leave more than a burn on someone's arm." he added pointing at Eros.

Another voice broke in from behind the Yang sect' members.

"Look at the next pillar, sat with her generals like a majestic goddess." Octavius scorned as he dug the snort from his nose.

"Chancellor, it's been a while." Ryo Noboru said. "I thought you retired."

"Me? I didn't hear anything." Octavius responded. "I'll retire the day one of you two old farts defeat me."

"Elementals do believe they're gods do they not Brother?" Kenzou mocked.

Ryo glanced over with a smile. "Ignore him he does not know what true power really is."

"Up next." the announcer interrupted. "The leader of the five armies, the beast slayer, the undefeated Champion of the Arena Ladies and gentlemen put your hands together for Lancer!" As Lancer appeared from his side of the Arena, the roars where as loud as ever, though it did take everyone who had never attended the fights back.

"Such Will..." Ryo muttered.

Kenzou sat up filled with interest. "What a monster, I wonder what sort of Elemental he is."

"Try just human," Octavius laughed. To the surprise of all those surrounding him.

"Insane Aura, however, what's with his outfit." Ingrid commented. "Tight white and black long sleeve, plate armour pants and boots with a robe around his waist?"

"The designer must have been drunk when making that..." Frigg laughed. Though the crowd was loud, and everyone had their own opinions Eros surprisingly took a sit with his eyes closed. And as he opened them Lancer held his spear tighter glancing at Eros's eyes all he could see was stillness. There was no fear, ambition, hope just a hunger so powerful for a moment Lancer felt as though if he kept looking, he would be eaten. Eros himself could no longer hear anything. But could feel his blood rush throughout his body. Each time he took a breath he could feel it getting hotter. His teeth viciously grinding at each other. His fingers twitching uncontrollable.

The crowd fell silent watching. Astrid found herself at the edge of her seat entranced by the amount of bloodlust flowing from Eros. Lancer composed himself planting his feet to the ground refusing to be intimidated by Eros.

"Lancer." Eros said coldly. "Die!" he added before jumping up and dashing towards Lancer setting his arms on fire and slashing at Lancer barely missing him.

"Did lancer... just.... retreat." Elizabeth said in shock.

"An awakened Sorde..." Octavius muttered with his eyes bulging from his skull. Lancer looked at Eros trying his best to calm himself down. **What sort of Will is that it's like I'm being eaten** Lancer thought before courting himself in his Will. **My queen is watching I cannot make the White Knights look** *weak!* He thought before lunging with his spear forcing Eros into the defence. Eros Refusing to be a punching bag used all his strength to bash Lancer's spear out of the way spreading his fire to the tip of his sword as he swung it down at lancer screaming at the top of his voice. However, as a veteran Lancer easily dodged this changing the direction of his spear thrusting it towards Eros's head. In response Eros let his shield go grabbing his sword with both hands launching the strike upwards. Lancer once again retreated to gather himself and as he touched his cheek, he felt a rage engulf him as he wiped the small blood from his face and advancing forward no longer feeling threatened by Eros but angered by his own weakness. Eros seeing this plastered a disturbed smile on his face as his bloodlust leaked uncontrollably responding to Lancer's advance in kind. Lancer started whistling as he thrust his spear forward breaking Eros's skin in an instant. Again, he lunged his spear barely missing Eros the second time. "What's wrong?" Lancer said with pale gaze. "You had so much confidence before, you cockroach."

"A human this fast. The west has hided some monsters." Ryo said excitedly.

Octavius no longer able to enjoy the match couldn't take his eyes off Eros and Kenzou noticed. "What's wrong old man, you look like you've seen a ghost."

"You don't see it do you. That thing if we don't kill him today, he will become a problem."

"Calm down old man, he probably won't make it out of this fight look at him that Lancer boy is purposely missing the vitals. Cutting him slowly." Ryo responded watching the match quickly turn into a one-sided slaughter.

Eros covered in his own blood started laughing before dropping his sword, "I knew I'd need to put my life on the table to win." he said as he set his arms on fire sprinting towards Lancer and throwing a massive swing comically missing the man. Lancer looked even more annoyed prepared to launch an attack before an explosion dropped him on his back. "Remember the name of the child whose life you destroyed!" he screamed before throwing his entire body into a punch which lancer barely blocks with his spear breaking it in half forcing Lancer to roll away.

"I don't even know who you are." Lancer scorned as he stood up. Blitzing towards Eros and drowning him in a fury of kicks and punches. *No matter how fast I am this man, is simply*

on a different level Eros said as he tried his best to block the attacks barely being able to block a tenth of them and taking heavy hits every other second.

"If I wronged you in the past, I hope you understand it was nothing personal." Lancer calmly said as he punted Eros away. Eros however refusing to stay down stood with an empty smile on his face. "I've always wondered on that day what were you thinking when you attacked Utopia. Thanks to that I lost everything, forced to fight just to live. You remember right?"

"Utopia..." Lancer said. "Like I said that was nothing personal. However, if you want, I will apologise on behalf of the White Knights."

Eros stood stunned at the lack of empathy coming from Lancer. "You psychopaths that killed thousands of innocent people. If the end goal was just, you simply didn't care. I understand you now."

"You turned my world into a living hell, yet just looking at you. You couldn't care less." Eros added.

"Like I said would an apology be satisf-"

"I'm going to kill you. I don't care how long it takes." Eros said as red fire started to materialise around his arms. "I'm going to kill... every... last... one of you!"

A man hidden in a brown clock smiled. "Well said." he said before placing his left hand onto the colosseum wall and freezing it spreading the ice as far as the eye could see.

Ryo, Octavius, Kenzou and the rest of the yang sect quickly noticed dispensing from their seats into the fighting ground as they watched half the arena freeze. "Damn...looks like a monster came along..." Ryo said stretching his arms preparing to fight.

"'Knight make sure Lancer gets back the rest protect the Queen with your life!" Andre screamed as he stood opening a path for Elizabeth to leave the Arena. As the White Knights begun to exit, followed closely by the trade Union and the Valeria family the ice exploded and as Eros saw this, he looked beyond seeing a way out. And when adrenaline shot through his body, he ran into the shattering ice grabbing Octavius's attention when he tried to follow quickly blocked by large boulders of ice landing near him.

"Fine then," Octavius said as he started seeming floating higher. "I'll just catch you my way Amon's spawn."

Eros filled with pure adrenaline kept running as fast as he could past all the people stood in shock. ***Just keep going!*** Eros thought feeling his bones crunch. And his legs get heavier by the second. He took a left and kept going, then a sharp right, then kept running straight until he suddenly stopped as he saw Octavius sat Infront of him.

"Fast, but not fast enough," Octavius said before he slowly stood. Eros in response set his arms on fire ready to fight again. This however angered Octavius who let out a monstrous amount of bloodlust. So powerful Eros felt a fear so intense his fire burned out and his legs could not stop shaking. "You want to fight me Amon's spawn. Fine let's fight!" Octavius said before taking a single step forward and in response Eros ran the opposite way as fast as he could to no avail as Octavius quickly blitzed Infront of him.

"Fine," Eros said as he took a stance. "If I have to fight you for freedom so, be it."

Octavius found this amusing as he swatted his hand instantly cutting Eros in several places. And before Eros could react, he felt his neck being crashed as Octavius forced him on his back with the heal of his foot. Octavius then unsheathed his sword pointing it at Eros's eye. "I'm going to kill you now..." he coldly said before thrusting it forward. Only being stopped by a distant voice inches away from Eros's eye.

"Excuse me Chancellor.... But I can't let you kill this one." the hooded man spoke feet away from Octavius. "Could you get off him now?"

"You... well He won't even feel it look at him, his eyes are closed probably unconscious trying to get some air." Octavius responded as he again lifted his sword before thrusting it downwards being immediately stopped by a flood of ice as it covered the entire area.

However, Octavius stood at the opposite end barely able to block the attack. He stretched his bones before scratching his head. "I'm too old to be fighting a world breaker." he said as he sheathed his sword walking away.

Elizabeth

In a moment, Elizabeth watched as the coliseum she built from the ground up crumble, as she watched thousands panic below her. Ignoring the plead from her Knights to exit the area. Watching Octavius fly into the air and disappear from her sight. She shook her head knowing this was only the beginning. An attack in this area broke her deal with Pangea, Gungadad's promise that led to Pangea forgetting Elizabeth's past. Elizabeth cracked a smile. "This was the work of Pangea. This is their warning as Chancellor Octavius said."

Ser Andre studied his Queen for a moment. "Then Pangea will feel the wrath of the chosen people!"

"Then be ready, we are alone now 'Crimson Lion' surrounded by many enemies." Elizabeth said. "Five years I will create the perfect Utopia, so my son can have a simple life as King."

"Point my Queen and whoever is in our way, the White Knights will end them." Andre said as he bowed unsheathing his sword and escorting the Queen out of the Coliseum.

As Charlotte stood waiting by the exit waiting with lancer for the Queen's arrival, she noticed him gazing at the clouds with a sombre look in his eyes. "What did you two talk about, I mean everyone heard the last part, but he must have said something else to put you in this mood."

"Not really. Too me his just an angry kid."

"Then if you would look less depressed boss." Charlotte mocked.

"The old gods, the goddess, Ga'Al one of them must be real. Because people like you exist."

"What's that supposed to mean?"

Lancer glanced at her with a cold gaze. "I am of nothing. Born with nothing, expect to die at every turn. Yet day after day year after year I have shown I am more than what this world intended. But each time I show it people who can fly, bend the earth, set their arms ablaze... Simply makes me realise that I'm still just human in an unfair world that one of your gods must have created."

"I hate that." Charlotte quickly responded. "I did not make it to this point because I am blessed, I worked for everything I have."

"Worked? Your father mentioned that from birth you had perfect connection with the earth. Most Elementals don't become one until their toddlers. Your god blessed you it's that simple."

"I wonder what you two might be talking about." Elizabeth interrupted.

Charlotte studied Lancer for a moment. "Nothing my Queen, Ser Lancer, shall we?" Lancer simply nodded as the White Knights begun to enter their carriages making sure the Queen was safely in before moving, Until the Queen stopped Charlotte.

"This is your station 'Knight' defend it." Elizabeth told her before ordering her Knights to move. Charlotte simply bowed. Knowing she needed to be successful in defending the Autonomous zone encase more terrorists attacked. In a moment she grabbed a city guard who was escorting people out of the

Coliseum and ordered him to sound the horn to raise the flag of her army.

"But lady 'knight'" the guard stuttered. "The flag has already been raised and your army is gathering at the south end station as we speak." This confused Charlotte for a moment as only the Queen Lancer and her could raise her army. A moment that quickly disappeared as she grabbed the nearest horse quickly riding the south end station. Hastily riding towards it a sudden earthquake forced her to lose control of the horse momentarily. **another attack?** She pondered. **is this justice?** But as she felt a cold breeze she looked up to her left and the scene was quite unbelievable. Her mind stunted as it was unable to comprehend or process what her eyes where witnessing.

"This is a joke, right?" Raijin asked as he stirred blankly. Charlotte gathered her thoughts to look down from her horse to see Raijin looking up at what seemed to be a sudden mountain of ice reaching the heavens. "You boy... get out of here..." she said as Raijin in excitement sprinted towards the ice mountain that had just appeared. In a hurry Charlotte ignored him wiping her horse to move forward.

Tangi blew air into his hands as he felt the cold wind, he quickly pulled out the map of the city and pointed. "Two units move to secure here," he said. "The rest move with me, if we are dealing with 'Justice' they will be a few hundred, so we just need to push them into an open area." His fingers kept moving across the map as the man in charge with commanders listening intently. Whilst Charlotte sat on the back of her steed watching coldly. When Tangi noticed he sighed before forcing a smile and saluting his general, clumsily followed by the commanders that surrounded Tangi.

"We are ready at your command Lady 'Knight'" Tangi said.

"You take command Tangi, you already prepared everything." Charlotte watched as her soldiers quickly moved out, the sound of horses pelting the ground went through her. As her attention laid elsewhere while she gazed into the outskirts. For a second, she couldn't hear the panic, the horses just marvelled at the beauty of the sun setting.

Logan

The attack on the autonomous zone left a bad taste in everyone's mouth, In the country of Tarragon, a land known for its wheat and temples. Colonel Liviana Julia marched throughout the streets eventually reaching barging into the hospital room where Amadeus had been nursing his wounds from the previous battle with justice.

"A scar across the face... it suits you."

"The long grey hair suits you as well Colonel, how can I help you?"

"Talking to a superior so casually, you are unlike your brother Amadeus." she added before sitting across Amadeus glancing at Octavius's report. "'Justice' is heading towards the city of Pangea. You will also be heading to the city of Pangea to intercept. You will capture their leader alive ok."

"We need a win that badly."

"Read the report and you tell me." She said as she handed Octavius's report with a stern look on her face.

In the White Knight Kingdom's sister city, Elizabeth scorned as she read the newspaper. "They pushed the blame to 'Justice' what a surprise. Pangeans the snakes of the world."

"My Queen, Dafrak is waiting..." A Knight said.

Elizabeth glanced at him and started walking through the streets to Dafrak's bar. Each time she would visit this man she knew he would try his best to irritate the Queen. Or belittle her in any way. However, this time she was greeted by a young lady in her teens, drawing on a scroll as she leaned on an oak table. "It's nice to see you again aunty. Dafrak is not here but he assumed you will be making a stop here first. The price is the same as last time. You need raw materials, right?" She asked still paying very little attention to Elizabeth.

"No," Elizabeth said softly. "I'm going into a large recruitment drive. I need to borrow some coin."

Rose looked concerned but a quick study of Elizabeth she already knew how to respond. "I will send the request to Dafrak. How will your war affect these simple people my Queen?"

Elizabeth quickly turned to the door, letting the light shine on her pale dress. "One of my army's leaders is in Charge of this territory. I trust him to make the perfect deal with Dafrak. I expect the coin within the month."

"As you wish," Rose responded softly before returning to her drawings. Watching the Queen exit with such grace made her feel bitter, for reasons she could not explain. But the feeling quickly left her as she glanced towards the balcony of the bar. "She's gone." she added.

"Good," Ulfr said as he stepped out of the shadows in simple cloths but better than the rags he'd been wearing for years. "Can't let her catch me can we."

Rose laughed. "You are too paranoid."

"It's what you think dear sister, but that woman is my brother's enemy. And we caused hundreds of slaves to escape. I know she looks tame, but she is smart, and would figure out I was one of those slaves."

"You don't even have to collar anymore how would she know?"

"Like how she figured out who killed Gungadad... well mostly figured out."

"That was different it became too obvious in the end."

Ulfr shrugged his shoulders. "I guess. I would rather be careful around her non the less."

On the outskirts of the west, Logan's camp was once again briming with life. As the Golden lion himself plopped down on a bench watching several Nobles from his Kingdom argue amongst themselves. "We should kick out the mercenaries they have no loyalty and will betray us when more coin is offered." Geoffrey the fifth of House Anjor spoke proudly.

"Truly? We would lose thousands of men because of your para-noia!" Ser Rupen de Foix of House Fox spoke. His demeanour and lack of respect showed his age as he stood as tall as his el-ders.

Isabella O'Alencon of house Alencon laughed as she watched her peers argue. "Why let this last, Golden Lion. We have thou-sands of men, a common goal and now the Queen has been weakened on the world stage and knowing Pangea they will make their move to get rid of her soon enough. Tell me Golden Lion what are we waiting for?"

Logan's eyes kept lingering towards Alex in the distance, the news he had received from Ezekiel did not sit well with him. Not only that his bounty being so great made Logan ponder if Alex is too dangerous to keep around. "His influence brought us to this point... I suppose." Logan muttered to the confusion of the Lords and Ladies standing around him.

"Boy!" Logan shouted to Oliver. "Bring me a map." Soon after Oliver came rushing with the map of the west at its current point.

"We attack Dafrak's lands." Logan added moving his finger towards the autonomous zone. "And we take the zone."

"Are you well Logan?" Lord Gabriel from the trade Union asked mockingly. "We don't have enough man to fight in two fronts."

"What was it two, three hundred man. Alexander?" Logan asked.

Alex frowned as his attention was captured by Logan. "Something like that."

"Good that's your mission Kill 'Knight'."

"I'm no assassin."

"And I'm not strategist. So, your point?" Logan quickly responded. "But you are right you are no assassin. So, attack her as a soldier. You have a great armour to protect you do you not?"

Ava grumbled as she grabbed her sword. "So, a suicide mission. You are right Logan; you are no strategist."

"We move at the same time. One month from today." Logan concluded as he folded his map quickly rising from his bench and turning his back on Alexander. Which Alex laughed off walking away from the area.

Eros

Slowly and reluctantly Eros opened his eyes to the sight of a hole in the tent. He blinked, to wet his eyes as the sunlight shot through the small hole. His muscles felt weak, but for the first time in years he felt at peace. Even wondering if this what death felt like. He wanted this moment to last forever but as his senses came to him, he could hear the loud music coming from outside his tent. He could feel the ground shake maybe they were dancing maybe they were fighting. Finally, he let out a sigh as he could smell the cow being roasted, he felt some saliva drip down his face as the hunger pushed him to stand up. "Look at me." Eros muttered. "Hunched over with bandages all over me, how pathetic." he added as he took a step outside.

As twilight draped its soft hues over the horizon, the crackling campfire leapt and danced in tandem with the gathering rhythms of a native drumbeat. The air carried the scent of pine and earth, and the shadows flickered on the faces of a diverse assembly of people adorned in vibrant, ceremonial regalia. The pulsating heartbeat of drums resonated through the clearing, inviting Eros to gather around the flickering flames.

"Holly shit he's awake," Ingrid said as she dropped a bucket of soup. "Holly, shit he lived!" she added as she grabbed the attention of all those around the camp site. Eros glanced around, there were no more than thirty. Most looked like beggars but their builds made it obvious they were gladiators. Some looked familiar to Eros, but he couldn't explain why.

"Need a drink?" a voice spoke. It was strangely familiar but took Eros some time to place it. "Raijin." He said as his face lit up turning to his old friend. "If you're here then I must be in Amon's realm." he added with a soft laughter.

"You are alive and… alive." Raijin said as he studied Eros.

"Drink, Edward said he wanted to talk to you when you work up. Also, I think you pissed off the beast King, somehow."

Eros Lifted his arm up for the Mug, but Raijin could notice it twitching. "What's wrong, you look like you've seen a sick puppy."

"Ingrid, would you mind?" Raijin asked as he handed the mug to Ingrid. Which she simple shrugged her shoulders, grabbing the mug and shoving it in Eros's face.

Eros tried to swallow but could not grasp what the taste was.

"It's thick..." he said as some dripped from his mouth.

"It's some old gods remedy, we've been making a new one each day encase you work up."

"Speaking off, how are we here?"

Raijin sat down inviting Eros to join him, which Eros struggled to do. "Long version or the short version?"

"Long, takes me a while to get back up it seems."

"When your fight started, Ulfr's collar fell off, I looked up and some hooded people where just standing there, few seconds later Ulfr had killed the nearest guard took his sword fought his way to the Lady of the house. Took the son hostage, freed us all and left, he didn't even blink or say goodbye. Anyways not long after I find myself running to you since I knew you'd be too stubborn to take the opportunity. Then a mountain of ice appeared. The thousand beasts appeared in the streets. Then I saw you unconscious in the arms of the big lady Ingrid over there and now we are all here."

Eros frowned. "Thousand beasts? Why would they save me? Some sort of honourable revenge? Will they try to duel me when I'm fully healed?"

"No," Ingrid responded. "We came for our brother, Ake but only found these gladiators including Edward."

"He died." Eros said.

"We know."

"I didn't kill him."

"We know," Ingrid responded. "Those animals say you were friends with him."

Eros nodded his head. "We were. So why am I alive right now?"

"We were told to keep you alive, beast king." Astrid said with a bitter tone.

"Don't be cryptic who do I ow my life and freedom?"

Astrid cut some meet from the roasted cow. "We don't know, some guy from the revolutionary army sent him. You must have some very powerful friends. Something that powerful for such a weak person it annoys me."

Eros stretched his arm still feeling as though he was being stabbed. "If you want a duel for what I've done in the past please wait till I'm healed."

Ingrid marched up to Eros. "Have some respect, sis is the one who kept your body wa-"

"Enough!" Astrid shouted. "Edward wanted to see you when you work up hurry up to him!" she added shooing Eros away.

Edward saw Eros limp from afar. "Good you can walk!" he shouted striding towards Eros.

"You look like shit!"

"I feel just as bad"

"You are still this weak…" Edward sighed.

"I know…"

"Be conscious of that I doubt you will survive a second time if you overestimate yourself or underestimate the enemy…" Edward exhaled before looking up at the sky. "Since You got your ass handed to you kid, I'm going to teach you a little something."

Eros glanced at him. "Teach me what?"

"Controlling your fire. But I'm leaving tomorrow so you know what, ill teach you one thing that'll help out."

"Why?"

"Because I don't like being in debt. Even though this doesn't resolve it fully, it'll have to do for now." Edward said as he swept his foot across the grass. Eros studied him for a second and did the same. This begun a slow dance of two snakes intertwining ending with Edward releasing a stream of fire into the air through his fist and Eros perfectly mirroring It. "There you go you just learned the first dance of fire. Welcome." Edward muttered as Eros fell onto the ground with his muscles locking up. "You should be fine soon enough but keep practicing that and add your own personality into it. When you can move come down to have some food."

With the birds starting to pick on him Eros could finally move, he slowly gathered himself before heading down to the camp. It was as loud as it was in the day's eve, maybe even louder, and a fire cracked in the middle of the campsite, stretching the shadows in the surrounding area. People were eating dancing fighting, living. Even Eros cracked a smile as he ate some ribs. Participants moved in a circle, their footsteps creating a soft drumming on the natural floor of pine needles and soft earth. The fire, more a useful necessity than a mystical beacon, cast an amber glow upon the weathered faces of those who had weathered the harsh realities of the wilderness. The flickering flames painted their expressions with shadows, revealing a collective history etched in lines and scars.

The dancers wore garments practical for survival: leather, fur and woven textiles that told the story of resourcefulness and resilience. The dance wasn't an otherworldly display but a reflection of the daily struggles and triumphs of those who had made a home in the unforgiving wild. The dance was a celebration of unity, a shared acknowledgment of the challenges faced, and victories won.

"Go join them," Raijin said as he bit down on some meat.

"I can't dance..."

"Ask Astrid, she looks like she knows how too."

"Last time I got that close to her she knocked me out with an axe handle." Eros said.

"Suit yourself." Raijin said as he continued to eat. "I have to ask though are all you so... Fire elementals like this. Your healing is close to that of water Elementals."

"If you mean Edward, his arms where much worse, the fact he could move them answers your question." Eros said as he sat next to Raijin. "But I have a question, why did you not escape with Ulfr?"

"I told you to help your stubborn self."

"But why?"

"Because we are friends Eros, it's what friends do."

Astrid noticed Eros's empty gaze and immediately ran up to tease him. "Are you two going to kiss or something?"

Eros looked at his hand, then glanced at Raijin and Astrid. "I'm going to destroy the White Knights. Will you help me?"

"That's sudden." Astrid quickly responded.

Raijin smiled. "As long as there's strong swordsman for me to defeat, I don't see why not."

"Well, she's the reason our clan is in this state, so I don't see why not." Astrid reluctantly said.

Eros pointed north, "first I have to go somewhere."

"Now?" Astrid asked.

"Now." Raijin responded. "His home is near here, right?" Eros simply nodded, as he stood.

"Then ill accompany him," Astrid said as she shot Infront of Eros. "Raijin meet us near the forest entrance. In two days."

"Why you?" Raijin said with bitterness.

Astrid just gave him a blank stare. "Because look at him. Can you give him the right medicine? Help change his bandages. I thought not. Now then shall we Beast king."

The journey before them was simple, but as they got closer to their destination Astrid noticed Eros's demeanour change. He stopped slouching, his eyes looked shaper, and he was gripping the strap of his horse so tight, you could hear it slowly rip. They arrived at the farms, with the birds waking up, and the farm life starting their day. From afar the farmers feared Eros as his outfit and expression looked to cause trouble. Astrid quickly noticed but decided to ignore it as she kept trying to answer the few questions in her head.

Why is he so special? she wondered. Everything that has involved Eros, has only left her bewildered. Fokle's obsession with killing him. Ake befriending someone outside the thousand beasts. **Damn, even a monster that dwarfs Gulbrand wanted this boy protected. Why?**

A guard in chainmail and leather quickly pointed his sword at the approaching duo calling for all troops surrounding Adira's resting place. Hearing this Flavia stopped playing cards arming herself and stepping out to see Eros dismount from his horse. Hunched over with thick hide, and sunken eyes the boy looked injured adding confidence to Flavia. "You two, no one is allowed here but true believers, leave or be struck down by my men!" She said, as Eros ignored her slowly moving forward.

"Fine, Galients ready to fight!"

One quickly rushed forward and as he was about to swing his sword Eros looked through him, stunning him in place. Astrid laughed as she followed Eros.

"Kill hi-" Flavia commanded.

Eros quickly interrupted in a chilling tone. "Move..." One simple word froze all the guards in place, even Flavia herself as she felt death slowly caressing her neck.

Eros raised his hand, stopping Astrid from following, which at first annoyed her, but as she could feel Eros' Will leaking, she knew disobeying him would lead to a fight between the two.

As Eros vanished to the back of the house, Flavia dropped to the floor taking heavy breaths. "You girl... What was that monster... your boss?"

"Boss? I will only bow to someone stronger than me, if anything you should still be afraid since I'm much stronger than that big scary monster."

As Eros arrived Infront of his mother and sister's grave he immediately grabbed his shaking hand. "Well..." he sighed before quickly rubbing his eyes. "They built you a statue... Looks nice..." he said before slapping himself. "Sorry, I look pathetic right..." he added as his eyes filled with tears.

"I'm sorry," Eros said as he took a step back with tears dripping from his face. "I'll kill them all, everyone... I hope that's enough for lying, for getting Fanisse in that situation, I hope you can forgive me then. In the end I never found out what a Hero was... you were a great mom; she was a great sister... We will never meet again... if the gods exist, I don't think they would welcome me..." Eros quickly whipped his eyes as he turned back walking through the back door of his old house. He glided his hand across the walls, with memories flooding back until he saw a painting of him as a baby. Alexander as a joyful child, his mother and his father embracing themselves in the background. He pulled some of his hair forward before glancing at the table. It was longer than expected with Astrid starting to worry, and Flavia finally gained her composure as she grits her teeth screaming the Pangean code of honour "We are the heroes the front lines! The Goddess will shield us from all heathens!" she said as she gripped her sword ready to attack.

"Old Gods..." Astrid muttered. "You took long enough Eros?" Eros was quiet. "No, it's because I saw a painting, it distracted me for a moment."

"Eros?" Flavia asked as she turned her head.

"Who was the painting off?" Astrid quickly asked.

"My father, Ivan."

"What?" Flavia asked again as she lowered her sword. "Amon's spawn Eros is Ivan's child? As in Ivan the wordbreaker... Ivan the ghost of Pangea?"

"So many names..."

Astrid was thrown back for a moment. "So, the Water Elemental that saved you, came from your father?"

Eros gave her a sorrowful look. "I doubt it... Ivan abandoned us years ago, right after my sister was born."

"Ok..." Astrid said softly still shocked by Eros's revelation. "Now where are you going?" she added as Eros walked past her mounting his steed.

"South."

"South?"

"Yes."

"I can't just let you walk away," Flavia said. "Lady, that thing needs to die before it becomes a monster like his father."

Eros glanced at Flavia one more time before turning his horse around. "If you follow me, I'll kill you all." As they began riding down the road, Astrid noticed the guards disappear from her sight before her horse is suddenly stopped.

"Eros..."

"Bart..."

Eros couldn't look at Beltramino in the eyes as his old ally stood Infront of his steed. He kept his hands on the strap fighting with himself to ride off or talk to Beltramino.

"I knew you were alive..." Beltramino said as he shed a tear. Eros looked around, still trying to avoid Beltramino. "I killed him for Sarrah, I know you liked her. Don't worry ill kill them all, the White Knights, Justice. Ill avenge us."

"No Eros," Beltramino said with a sombre tone. "I don't want revenge, I have a family now a wife, Kid. I have a life I believe that's what they would want for us."

Eros saw the child in the background gazing at him. "Is that him?"

"Yes... Adam come say hi to... to an old friend of your dads." Adam came running still gazing deeply at Eros. He stopped as he saw Astrid in the background making faces at him, but his attention quickly turned to Eros before running back into the house. "That's new..." Beltramino said as his son's actions puzzled him only for Adam to run out with his painting showing it to Eros.

"You look like him!" Adam shouted as Eros's face dropped.

"That's an amazing painting, looks a little like that Basilisk kid." Astrid said forcing Eros to laugh uncontrollably holding his chest as he could feel pain in each laughter.

"The world seemed so big, is it fate?" Eros said as he started to calm down.

Confused Adam asked if he knew the man. To Eros simply nodding and asking for the painting, promising he would hand it over to the right person.

Alexander

"Alex? Are you ok?" Ava asked as Alex's face sunk into the newspaper.

"You haven't read it have you?" Kal Orrin asked.

Kal Magus sat back watching the sky. "She clearly didn't you idiot."

"Who are you calling an idiot!"

"You ugly fool!"

"We have the same face," Kal Orrin responded as he swung at his brother.

News had spread to all four corners of the world of a battle that would remain in history till the end of time. The day started with news flying throughout Pangea, of a battleship charging straight for the City of Pangea Quickly bypassing islands and the calm belt with near perfect precision. Reaching the shores of the City's Last defence, General Marcus 'Zeus' Silvius's Castle. Immediately intercepted by The Holy Candius fleet, with the rear ship Saint Victor being Commanded by Commodore Vibius Agrippa, the ship further forward and to the right 'Saint Innocent' being Commanded by Commodore Claudius Cornelius Fabius. The ship Directly to its left 'Saint Exsuperius' being Commanded by Captain Bion Diocles and in the front ship 'Saint Constantine' Commanding the entire fleet Third division Captain Amadeus Jullian Ceaser.

As the fleet Approached the stolen battleship Lael's laugh could be head echoing throughout the sees as he took heavy footsteps on to the deck. His hair shined in the sunlight; his body looked as if the gods crafted it, He looked in perfect Condition, shocking Amadeus to his core.

"How did you do it you monster!" Amadeus shouted as he drew his sword.

Lael laughed once more before planting his feet, spreading his arms, and gripping the air. "You're in my way boy," he said as Amadeus dropped his sword gazing at the appearance of a tsunami to his left and as he turned his head another one was quickly approaching to his right. Lael on the other hand could not stop laughing as with the simple movement of his arms he buried four battleships under water. As Lael's crewmates stood in disbelief, the man himself collapsed to one knee vomiting a pool of blood.

"Another shot..." he struggled to say as he hurried a boy carrying a needle towards him. While he started getting injected with a strange serum, his eyes looked up seeing dark clouds form. "He's arrived." he said softly before a lightning bolt struck towards the battleship to being stopped by a shield of water. Whilst the water rained down on his face, Lael shrugged his shoulders looking up at the sky, until his smug face frowned as the clouds parted lowering a lightning coated cloud. "Rare, from what I hear Zeus doesn't bother to fight himself. I'm honoured you half giant freak" he said when he scanned a man twice maybe three times the size of a grown man, with a thick golden beard and long golden hair to match.

Zeus smiled. "Don't disappoint me then," before pointing his finger launching hundred bolts of lightning towards the battleship with Lael quickly returning the favour by launching ice arrows towards the air.

"There's more water than lightning!" Lael shouted whilst he blitzed the sky with ice arrows. Zeus still taking the fight lightly pointed two fingers launching double the lightning bolts to match the ice arrows. But soon he noticed some bolts passing through and thus stopped his attack before quickly bending his head dodging a punch from Lael. Shocked by the moment he touched his ear to feel blood dripping from it. ***How interesting, for a moment he became faster than Milo*** he thought before stretching his arm out watching Lael fall back down with their eyes refusing to look away.

The air froze in anticipation of an impending clash between the human adorned in shimmering azure robes and the giant whose every step now echoed with the low rumble of thunder. A dance of elements was about to unfold, and the air was thick with the scent of charged particles. Lael a master of aquatic manipulation, raised a hand, conjuring a spiralling vortex of water that circled around him like a protective shield. In response

Zues's eyes glowed with an electric intensity as bolts of lightning flickered along its towering frame.

With a swift motion, the giant hurled bolts of lightning towards the human, cracking streaks of energy tearing through the air. The water – elemental responded with agility, weaving through the electrified onslaught, creating walls of liquid to absorb and deflect the bolts. However, Zues' lightning strikes were relentless, forcing Lael to retreat and evade with each electrifying assault.

Seizing the advantage, the giant summoned a storm above, dark clouds started swirling as lightning gathered within them. Thunder echoed ominously, setting the stage for the duel. Undeterred, Lael retaliated, conjuring waves that surged toward Zues with relentless force. Zues, with a booming roar, absorbed the water into its electrified form, converting it into a weapon of immense power.

As the battle unfolded, Zues's control over lightning intensified. Thunderbolts danced across the sea and graveyard of ships, converging with Zues's colossal fists as he unleashed a fury of devastating blows. Lael struggled to maintain composure, drenched and fatigued from the relentless assault.

"This was fun, Lael..." Zues says as he summoned a colossal lightning storm, bolts converging into a single, searing spear of electricity. With a thunderous roar, Zues hurled the electrified javelin towards Lael, who desperately tried to conjure a watery defence. However, the overwhelming power of the lightning engulfed the water, disintegrating it in a blinding explosion.

 The fight lasted a few minutes more, but the news simple wrote how Amadeus fought the leader of 'Justice,' finally capturing him alive with only him left standing from both sides. While he finished reading Alexander grabbed his club tossing it in the air before quickly catching it. He quickly pointed it towards the south, towards Zen, "One year, I will conquer the White Knights."

"Then, get the power and money we need." Stavros added as he approached.

"Create the perfect Kingdom." Ava replied.

"Rest." Basil added before all those around Alex laughed having heard this same proclamation for years. Alex dropped to his back joining in on the laughter.

Alex smiled. "With commanders like you I think it's possible."

"Till we create it that is," Basil added. "I'm not much of a soldier as it is, I think I'll open a school in the kingdom, teach those what I know."

Stavros glanced at his sword. "I know what you mean, I think a family, maybe a small farm will be enough for me."

"I think I'll stick by the future king," Ava said playfully kicking Alex. "I'm afraid of what he would do if I left him alone at this point."

"Your father is a royal knight, so was his, I see you just want to continue the family tradition." Alex teased looking at Ava.

"Though I'd think you would want to be Queen, I mean I see the way you'd look at me."

Ava shrugged her shoulders looking away from Alex. "I'm a warrior, Queens are more Elegant with their dresses and such."

"To be honest it'll be frightening seeing you in a dress, Ava." Stavros said to everyone's laughter.

Eros

Ulfr watched a foreign couple in the streets of Lumina from the top window in the Black Iron bar, his eyes sharpened as his face pressed on the window with his arms crossed. Slowly studding the couple, noticing the wife's fine silk and the husband's flamboyant demeanour.

"Twelve hours," Rose said as she approached beside her brother.

Ulfr smirked. "Five minutes."

"Talk about pessimistic…"

"I'm only speaking reality," Ulfr responded as a group of thugs quickly surrounded the couple. Within moments the wife got stripped and dragged into the dark corners and the husband stabbed to death and taken for all his worth.

Rose sighed. "I guess you were closer."

"I guess…"

"What's wrong?" Rose asked noticing Ulfr's cold aura.

"Just, I promised mother you-"

"Enough you two!" Dafrak interrupted as he placed his hands-on Rose's shoulders. "This one has work to do." He added as he ordered her to the pub's ground floor where another foreigner in fancy cloths sat shaking his leg in joy.

"That's the third one this week, the queen will find out you know." Ulfr added watching over his sister.

Dafrak smiled, quickly putting Ulfr under his wing. "She won't find out even if she did, she owes me a lot of gold now. She won't say or do anything."

"Still, using my sister to break seals. It drains her, she is just a child remember."

"She is also a witch or would you rather I do the right thing and give her to the right authorities?" Dafrak asked with a cold smile.

Ulfr noticing this shrugged him off and as he started walking towards his sister, a loud explosion grabbed everyone's attention. He glanced towards the window once more to see a large woman, pressing her feet towards a rouge thug, with a much smaller woman, pointing her axe towards the rest of the thugs.

"What was that?" Dafrak quickly asked.

"Gavril's place."

"Then go see if your neighbour needs some help." Dafrak commanded.

The land was painted in red by the time Ulfr arrived, he drew his sword marching towards Astrid and her sisters, before a familiar voice stopped him in his tracks. He glanced to see Eros climbing out of the broken window.

"Hanging out with heathens, since when did my little brother believe in the old gods?" Ulfr mocked and he sheathed his sword.

Eros drew an axe as his eyes sharpened. "Since when do you sleep in the same bed as the white knights?" He said as he threw his axe past Ulfr quickly caught by Ser Noham who then simply responded with a short bow.

"Leave, go about your journey away from here," Ulfr commanded him. "You've yet to grab his attention so please."

"Must be the Dafrak guy, right?" Eros asked.

"Do you think axes fall off trees go get that back!" Astrid commanded pointing her finger towards Ser Noham ignoring the clear tension.

"Four beasts..." Dafrak muttered from his window. "So, which one of you became the new King after Gulbrand's unfortunate death... at the hands of a child."

Astrid noticing this quickly pointed her axe towards Dafrak with a cold look in her eye. "Watch your mouth, you rat."

"Come down Princess or should I call you king." Dafrak said as he laughed. "Twenty of you were counted entering my beautiful home, the large angry boy over there, must be Eros Senesto the Awakened sordes. The large girl must be your second sister Ingrid 'The Wall'. Finally, that slender beauty, who my boys have been eyeing all day must be your eldest sister Frigg?"

Ulfr quickly lowered his eyes. "They're just leaving Dafrak, they won't be any trouble. Right Eros?"

"Fine, as a favour I'll let them go just for you my dear son." Dafrak said as he walked away from the window laughing. Eros turned around walking away from the area quickly followed by the sisters and as they reached the entrance, they noticed the sun blocked by a small gang glaring at them.

"How many are with us?" Astrid asked as she drew her axe. Frigg scanned the area to see least a dozen of the White stag approaching from afar. "Ingrid, protect the king. Eros with me in the front. Raijin! I know you are in the shadows, cover our back for us if you would." With all in agreeance with these orders the small group charged at the gang making quick work of them and Raijin took care of all those trying to make sneak attacks. In a far-off building Ser Noham watched diligently, taking notes on each of the white stags, Eros and Raijin.

Eros struck down the last thug, and as he stood Astrid quickly grabbed him holding him under her wing. "The Sordes have not stopped looking at you throughout this fight, Elemental. What do you say shall we bring them to our side and cause hell in this place?"

"No."

"Why?"

"Their gazes are distant; their voices are meek."

"Interesting..." Astrid laughed as she quickly ordered her White stags to move out with her.

At sunset, camping outside the town gate, the scene was set for the upcoming battle. The air charged with anticipation as the small army gathered, clad in weathered armour and bearing banners emblazoned with ancient symbols, converging in the shadow of the town's fortifications. Tents, fashioned from coarse hides and embellished with the marks of battles past, stand resilient against the elements.

The warriors both in chainmail and weathered armour gather around a central fire, its flames casting a warm, flickering glow on the rugged faces adorned with braided beards and distinctive tattoos. The night was alive with the murmur of guttural voices, the clinking of weapons and the rhythmic pounding of metal against anvils as blacksmiths work to sharpen blades for impending conflict.

At the heart of the camp, beneath the sombre light of a crescent moon, the leaders convene around a crude war table. "I see the call was answered by many!" Throar howls through his greying beard.

"At best we have a thousand men and shield maidens!" Astrid snapped.

Durim the eldest of four and leader of 'Ceowulf' chose that moment to appear mockingly shouting "We have the Old Gods little girl!"

Astrid ignored. "I'll take vanguard in the first attack two days from now." She said pointing on a map rendered on aged animal hides. The chieftains, their eyes reflecting the harsh wisdom of seasoned warriors, trace strategic routes and potential points of attack with calloused fingers. The night is filled with muted sounds of tactical planning, the sharpening of blades, the clinking of chainmail and the distant murmur of sagas being recited to boost the warriors' morale.

Suddenly, the tranquillity is shattered by the haunting wail of a war horn, echoing through the night like a dire prophecy. In an instant, the Beast camp is plunged into chaos. A well trained, well armoured army emerged from the shadows, launching a surprise assault. The metallic clash of weapons, the thud of arrows finding their marks and the war cries of the ambushing force shatter the serenity of the Beast camp, leading to a stray arrow striking Throar down.

In the middle of the chaos Astrid roared. "Are you not beasts! Are you not Heathens? Are you not scourges of the west!? Stand and fight!"

Caught off guard, the Beasts scrambled to arm themselves, their armour clinking with urgency. Chaos ensues as the two forces collide in a fierce clash. The ambushing army, disciplined and formidable, threatened to overwhelm the Beasts with their superior numbers and advanced weaponry.

In the midst of the chaos, Raijin and Eros emerge as beacons of resilience. Clad in chainmail, they stood back-to-back, their eyes reflecting the firelight with a blend of determination and ferocity. Against the odds, these two warriors, brothers in arms, weave through the tumultuous battlefield with a dance of skill and precision.

In Dafrak's bar, tabs on Eros and Raijin continued being reported to Dafrak, and with each passing moment Dafrak, felt restless and annoyed. But whilst he continued to think, Rose collapsed and in response Ulfr started to run towards her only to be stopped by Dafrak. "She fine, anyway I have a job for you."

"She's not fine, she's been using magic with a break!"

"Don't raise your voice at me..."

"I'm sorry… but how long do we have to do this. When will you let us go?" Ulfr asked desperately.

Dafrak looked bewildered at the question. "Let you go? You are my son now are you not? As a member of my family, I cannot in good will let you wonder away from me and die by some thug."

Stunned Ulfr looked at his sister being dragged up by the arms then back at Dafrak quickly swinging his fist at him knocking the man off his chair. As soon as he did that Two large man quickly wrestled Ulfr to the ground holding him in place.

Dafrak shook off the punch looking almost proud. "Take him away to cool down. Also tell the white knight to do a better job getting rid of those pests."

"Shields!" Astrid commands as her sisters stand close guarding her blind spots. "Push them north give the champions room to move!" she adds.

Quickly the well-trained adversaries find themselves outmanoeuvred by the agility and unyielding spirit of the duo. Shields clash, swords parry, and the battlefield becomes a stage for an epic struggle between the invaders and the stubborn Beast warriors.

"Count them Eros..." Raijin said holding himself up with his sword. "Fifty dead."

"Fifty Alive..." Eros quickly responded as again he pointed his sword towards his enemies.

"Now the sun is up, they look more like farmers with white knight Sigils..." Eros added.

"Who cares," Raijin quickly responded as he lunged forward followed by Eros. It was simple practice for them, their numbers only slowed them down but, in the end, Eros and Raijin emerged victorious, their blades stained with the blood of their foes. Their triumph a statement to all those who oppose the Thousand Beasts and with the ambushing forces forced to retreat, the Beasts sighed in relief. The sun, witness to the clash, casts a pale shadow on the scene as the victorious warriors, weary yet defiant. Tents, battered by the resent battle, stand as silent witness to the chaos that unfolded moments before. The scent of smoke hangs heavy in the air, a lingering reminder of the skirmish that tested the resolve of the beast warriors. Gathering around the remnants of a dwindling fire, the chieftains engage in a discussion, their voices rising like thunder amidst the quiet of the day. Clad in armour that bears the scars of battle, their faces etched with lines of both wisdom and weariness, the begun to argue intensely about the next move.

"At nightfall we need to move on Dafrak and the White Knights or they will strike us even harder" Astrid spoke.

"How many of us are dead Astrid?" Durim asked as his brothers begun to circle around the fading fire.

"We are still gathering the bodies… you know this."

"Throar was struck down whilst his men panicked, I was cornered whilst yours also fell to the sword."

"I understand" Astrid said with a touch of impatience. " We will bury them, but you saw that attack, this man Dafrak will not let us retreat, build a strategy that makes sense or do anything he deems an advantage to us."

 "Still?" said Durim tapping on the tip of his axe. "We are the Thousand Beasts we do not rely on these Pangean ways; we must honour our dead before anything!" he screamed raising his axe in the air. "So, no I say we gather all the followers of the old gods raise our banners under one name and one King!"

 "Dafrak will not allow that…" Astrid said thoughtfully. " Our best chance of survival will be to raid Lumina at nightfall, he will not expect such a move from such a small force."

"I grow tired of you Astrid."

With the Murmurs growing, most advocate for a swift retreat, gathering the Thousand Beasts under one King. They speak of regrouping, of honouring the dead, of ensuring the safety of their dwindling numbers. Whilst the few loyal to the White Stags, fuelled by the fires of vengeance and pride, argue for a relentless counterattack. Their eyes gleam with the fervour of warriors who have tasted blood and seek retribution against their ambushers.

Amidst the chaos of conflicting opinions, Eros once again drew his sword signalling for Raijin to follow. "The real fight begins now!" Eros said as he set his arms ablaze even engulfing his sword with fire. Raijin coated his body in lightning. They quickly approached the encampment's border quickly calming down letting off a sigh of relief.

As Ulfr limped towards them dragging a sword. His eye blackened, with fresh wounds covering his body, broken the man stopped and as he tried to take a step forward, his body could not hold, and he collapsed forward. Taking short uneven breaths as he tried lifting himself up.

"What fresh hell did you crawl out off?" Eros asked as the rain begun to fall in a gentle cascade from the brooding sky, the three figures stood opposite one another. Their silhouettes blurred by the veil of raindrops. Both wearing rugged attire of mercenaries, with their allegiance known only to the winds that whisper through the storm.

Their footsteps echoed softly against the damp cobblestones, each step a hesitant approach towards the other. Years of friendship echoed with each step, from the raids on the Silver-gey isle, to the first bittersweet taste of ale under in the pale moonlight in Whitburgh, forged in the crucible of shared expe-riences and laughter that all seemed but distant memories now, overshadowed by the bitter divide of opposing loyalties.

As they came within striking distance, Ulfr looked up before dropping to his hands and knees.

"Don't try fake dying, they make sure you know," Eros spoke once again stumbling back as he dropped his arms.

"Fuck you…" Ulfr said as his eyes watered. "Why didn't you just leave… I was fine being his property… At least Rose was safe…"

"Do you need hel-?"

"Fuck you!" Ulfr screamed. "She has a home, she's finally safe, do you have any idea how long we ran how many we lost so rose could sleep in a warm bed!"

"We are brothers, right? That means she's my sister now." Eros said, stunning Ulfr.

Ulfr still on his hands and knees looked up as the rain grew heavy. "Your sister? she's a witch... you have no idea how much weight you carry with her around."

"I'm a fire Elemental... I have an idea."

Ulfr's eyes lowered. "Help me..."

With a resigned sigh, Eros reached out his hand, "You don't have to ask." He whispered, a ghost of a smile playing upon his lips. They brothers stood as one amidst the falling rain, three friends reunited in the midst of conflict, their bond stronger than the forces that seek to tear them apart.

In the black iron, Dafrak sat back on his chair glaring at a tired Rose. He glanced at the window for a second to see the sun at its peak and sighed. With one wave of his hand, he cleared the room, and he dragged his chair closer to Rose. "Go get your fucking brother..." he said softly as he grabbed her cheeks, "If he refuses Muya will deal with him." he added as he blew a loud whistle.

Dafrak watched from his window as Rose marched forward with her hooded cape blowing in the wind and the simple giant Muya following her like a dog armoured from head to toe. Her power was felt as everyone in the streets of Lumina quickly hid from her presence, Men twice the size of her ran in fear when she was near. However, as she neared the gates of Lumina she stopped. Glancing back at Muya and laughing.

"Wait here," she said. "I walk in with a giant, and no one will listen."

Muya quickly plotted himself down. "How long?"

"An hour at most."

As the Trio returned to the camp, the debate showed no signs of resolution, a hush falls over the encampment a tense silence that hangs heavy in the air, Then Duram stepped forward.

"I tire of words," he declares, his voice cutting through the silence like a blade. " Let our actions speak for us."

His challenge is met with a chorus of murmurs, a ripple of uncertainty spreading through the ranks of the warriors. But as the silence stretches on, a sense of resolve settles over the encampment a silent acknowledgement that perhaps this is the only way to find clarity amidst the chaos.

"I accept" Astrid said softly, unsheathing her blade.

On one side stood the towering figure of the Beast King Durim, a colossus of muscle and power clad in armour adorned with the symbols of his clan. His battle axe, gleaming with the promise of devastation, swings through the air with the force of a raging storm, his movements fuelled by raw power and primal fury.

Opposing him is the agile shield maiden, a vision of grace amidst the savage frenzy of combat. Her slender form, adorned in armour that glints with the light of the setting sun, moves with an otherworldly elegance as she wields her sword and shield with lethal precision. Her eyes, ablaze with determination, locked onto her opponent with unwavering focus, a silent challenge issued in the midst of the chaos.

As the brute Beast charged forward with a bellowing war cry, his axe poised to strike, Astrid responded with a dancer's grace, sidestepping his attack with fluid ease. Like a wisp of smoke, she darts and weaves through the brute's onslaught, her movements a mesmerizing display of skill and agility. With each swing of his axe, Durim leaves craters in the earth, yet Astrid remained unscathed, her shield deflecting each blow with the precision of a master craftsman. As the duel unfolded, the battlefield became a symphony of clashing steel and grunts of exertion, the combatants locked in a deadly dance of life and death. Then, in a moment of breathtaking swiftness, the Astrid seizes her opportunity a lightning-fast strike that finds its mark with deadly accuracy. Her sword, guided by the hand of fate, pierced through the chink in Durim's armour, finding its way to his heart with a swift and decisive blow.

"Long Live the Beast King Astrid!" shouted Gautr second oldest of Durim's family. As Durim heard this he staggered backwards, his eyes wide in shock and disbelief. With a final, guttural gasp, he fell to his knees, his lifeblood staining the earth beneath him.

In the background Eros signalled for Astrid to follow into one of the tents.

Nestled within the shelter of a sturdy tent, a wounded Ulfr lay upon a makeshift cot of furs and blankets. The air was thick with the scent of wood smoke and distant sound of steel clashing against shields. At his side knelt Frigg, her hands deftly tending to his injuries with herbs and poultices, her movement practiced and sure. As Frigg worked, Ulfr's gaze wondered, his mind drifting back to a time long before the clash of swords and the roar of battle. He remembered the days when he, his sister and mother fled across rugged landscapes, chased by the shadowy figures of bounty hunters. Theirs was a life of constant movement, of hiding in the shadows and seeking refuge in the most unlikely of places.

In the flickering light of the tent's fire, Ulfr's eyes grew distant, his thoughts consumed by memories of a past he could never forget. He saw his sister, her laughter like music in the darkness and his mother, her eyes filled with both sorrow and determination as she led them ever forward, away from the dangers that pursued them.

But now, as Frigg's gentle touch brought him back to the present, he felt the weight of his past bearing down upon him once more. The ache in his heart was as raw as the wounds that marred his flesh, a constant reminder of the sacrifices made, and the lives lost along the way.

"King, we have some information." Eros said.

"Meet my brother Ulfr." He added as he stepped into the tent.

"King of the Beasts," Ulfr spoke softly. "You need to attack to-night."

"Dafrak will not expect something so straight forward."

"Exactly!" Astrid agreed. "Wait?" She questioned as she turned her head to see Rose comfortably standing at the edge of the tent behind all of them.

"I didn't even sense her..." Eros said in shock.

Rose unbothered looked past Frigg, Astrid and Eros to see her brother bandaged laying down. "You look awful..."

Ulfr glanced back with a smile. "You look scary."

"We need to go back."

"No," Ulfr said softly.

"If you don't Muya will come for you..."

"Then let him come."

"If you don't, I'm not going back..."

"You will, for now..." Ulfr said. "In order for my plan to work you need to."

"Your plan?" Astrid said, grinning.

"I know these lands, I know Dafrak…"

"Fine…" Astrid said with a shrug. "I'll have your head if it doesn't work."

Amidst the flickering flames of torches, a small group of warriors gathered around a makeshift table hastily assembled amidst the ruins. Their faces were grim, their expressions reflecting the gravity of the situation as they watched the injured warrior point at every corner of the map. In a voice rough with pain yet filled with determination, Ulfr began to outline his battle plans. Each word measured; each strategy carefully considered as he sought to turn the tide of the war in their favour. Despite the odds stacked against them his confidence never wavered, his belief in their ability to emerge victorious unshakeable.

As he spoke, the group listened intently, their minds racing as they sought to grasp the nuances of his plan. Every detail was dissected, every potential outcome weighed with the precision of seasoned tacticians. And as Ulfr finished outlining his strategy, a sense of quiet determination settled over the group, their resolve hardened by the fire that burned within their wounded comrade's eyes.

"Your mind is scary, Ulfr of Lumina" Frigg laughed.

"Strategist of the thousand beasts" Astrid smirked. "Sounds perfect to me."

Raijin shook his head. " Risky at best…"

"Yes, but it's our best-"

Rose interrupted. "We'll be hunted again if we do this."

"Yes," Ulfr agreed. "As long as you're not being used like this, then so be it." Hearing this Rose quickly put her hood up leaving the tent and vanishing as quickly as she appeared.

Later, Muya saw Rose approach and quickly stood marching towards her before she lifted her hand to stop him. "They will attack soon," Rose said. "They have a camp filled with Beasts; we should prepare for battle."

As night fell, the black sky was lit up by orange arrows as they quickly landed near the gates if Lumina, setting the huts and wooden houses on fire. Seeing the signal, the frontlines lead by Eros hooked the side wall and quickly scaled it. "The horn now!" Eros commanded as the last of the frontline landed inside Lumina. As the soldier took a large breath to blow the horn an arrow hissed through the air piecing him in the chest. "Shields!" Eros shouted as everyone grouped near each other with their shields held up.

In the front of Lumina, the darkness of the night wrapped the outskirts of the town in an eerie shroud, broken only by the occasional flicker of torchlight and the dim glow of the moon overhead. Along the borders, where fields met forests and civilization gave way to wilderness, two ancient adversaries converged in a class of steel and fury. On one side stood the Thousand Beasts clad in armour forged of iron and leather, their faces obscured by fearsome helmets adorned with horned crests, they moved with the silent precision of predators stalking their pray.

Infront of the gates, the White Knights gathered, clad in gleaming plate armour, stood tall and resolute atop their steeds, their breath visible in the cold night air. Foot soldiers, armed with swords and shield, formed tight ranks, their eyes scanning the darkness for any sign of movement. As the tensioned mounted, the night seemed to hold its breath, awaiting the inevitable clash. Astrid's army three hundred strong, surged forward with a primal roar, their war cries echoing through the night like thunder in the distance.

The White Knights, undeterred by the ferocity of their attackers, met the charge head-on, their ranks holding firm against the onslaught. Swords clashed with the screeching of ringing steel, the clash of weapons reverberating through the stillness of the night. In the chaos of battle, individual duels played out amidst the swirling darkness, illuminated by the flickering light of torches. Knights on horseback thundered through the fray, their lances gleaming in the moonlight as they sought to break the Beasts' lines. But the Thousand Beasts, fierce and relentless, fought with a savage determination that seemed to defy the very laws of nature.

As the battle continued in the outskirts, in the town still pinned down for what felt like a lifetime as arrows zipped and hissed past, Eros laughed. "He is something else right?" He said to the men standing shoulder to shoulder. Which they all agreed. They looked up to see the sky brighten up, the signal had been raised as Raijin's unit continued to set fire to the far east of the city.

"Good, now move forward with your shields up!" Eros quickly commanded.

In the front of the gates Astrid heard the horn and saw the fires spreading, quickly raising her hand for her army to retreat. However, the white Knights stayed in place refusing to follow or brake formation. Astrid spoke once more, "Pick the bows and let lose!" she said with confidence.

In the burning town, a soldier ran into the bar where Rose, Muya, Dafrak and Ser Haman were sat in silence. "They took the gates." the soldier said desperately.

"You have weak men 'Pawn,'"

"You got outsmarted by a child Dafrak."

"You, how many where at the front?" Dafrak asked as he stood grabbing his jacket.

"I couldn't tell in the dark sir, hundred maybe." the soldier quickly responded.

"I can work with hundred. Thug go raise the alarm, tell them to use whatever they want to win its open season!" Dafrak said with a big smile on his face.

"No strategy? You won't even call your clan to fight?" Confused Ser Noham quickly asked.

"You don't understand, do you? I'm fighting me out there, so I know my weakness more than anyone." Dafrak said. "I don't handle random events well, so Ulfr will crumble."

"Then where are you going?" Rose asked.

"I have to show my face do I not?"

"My brother is smarter than you," Rose said. "Once he sees you and the lack of strategy, he will put it together."

"I see he's not the only one who thinks ahead, 'Pawn' you go out there have some fun." Dafrak said as he sat down, and Ser Noham stood quickly exiting the bar and joining what's left of his men. With chaos growing each side from the beasts felt the pressure as rouge arrows flew past, men women children attacked from the shadows only to quickly disappear, Astrid felt the largest hit as one by one her men fell right Infront of her. Eros avoided most attacks but kept being grazed by arrows or knife attacks. Raijin however quickly jumped to the roofs exposing himself but gaining more vision of the area as he made quick work of arrows flying towards him glancing towards their original locations.

"Fuck this!" Eros screamed as he ran forward with his shield up taking arrow after arrow onto his shield to the point it broke but it didn't matter to him as he drew his axe slicing the skull of one man and using his body as a shield till he finally broke through to the main streets where he saw Ser Noham standing with his arms behind his back, and the last of his soldiers with their spears glimmering under the moonlight pointed at Eros. Eros started to move forward as Noham sent out two of his men which Eros quickly delt with. Then Noham raised his hand to no response and as he glanced up, he saw a shadow fall from one of the roofs. He sent out four more of his soldiers which three quickly fell to arrows from Astrid's sisters. Then as the fourth panicked he quickly got struck down by Raijin from the skies.

Noham dusted his long white jacket, before pulling out twin sickles from inside it, dangling them down by thin wires in his left hand. "Two elementals, and several Beasts. I guess I have to be serious against you." He said as he quickly drank a strange blue liquid. "Charge." he ordered as his soldiers quickly lunged at the enemy.

"For the old Gods!" Astrid shouted as her and the remanets of her army responded in kind, Eros and Raijin swiftly slipped past the battle to confront Noham which Noham replied by spin-ning his blades with the strings as a reply. But to his surprise

Raijin quickly ran past and Eros released a ball of fire blinding Noham long enough for Eros to get close and threw a right hook, knocking Noham back. Eros' axe swept through the air aiming for the head. But Noham was nimble, dodging the blow with a dancer's grace and countering with a swift strike from one of his sickles.

The clash of steel rang out through the deserted streets as the two warriors engaged in a deadly dance, their weapons flashing in the moonlight. Eros' strength was undeniable, each swing of his axe sending vibrations through the air, but Noham's agility was a force to reckoned with, his sickles striking with deadly accuracy from unexpected angles. As the duel raged on, the intensity of the battle grew, neither warrior willing to back down in the face of their opponent's ferocity. Then one of Noham's sickles whistled through the air, narrowly missing Eros' chest by inches, while Eros' axe left deep gashes in the Knight's flesh. But then, in a moment of opportunity, the knight saw his chance. With a lightning-fast flurry of strikes, he disarmed Eros, sending his axe clattering to the ground. With a triumphant shout, the knight pressed his advantage, his sickles a blur of motion as he closed in for a final blow. But Eros was not so easily defeated. With a defiant roar, he lunged forward, tackling the knight to the ground and pressing his hand on his face

"Don't!" Noham screamed as Eros released a roaring fire from his fingertips engulfing Noham and lighting up the town.

The explosion was heard even in Dafrak's crumbling bar his grip tightened around his glass, knuckles turned white with the force of his frustration. With each sip, the bitterness of the alcohol seemed to fuel the fire that raged within him, stocking the flames of his simmering resentment.

"I know my brother will do anything to keep me safe. I just can't bear watching him hurt just for me. I think this is the best way don't you Dafrak."

"Shut up and unbind me!" Dafrak screamed. "If I die the world will know you exist Rosaline! You think you were hunted before; you have no idea."

Rose laughed as she tapped her finger on the table. "You've become predictable in your old age Dafrak. I'm not planning on leaving, today will be our last day on this earth you vindictive asshole."

Dafrak realising the situation, stayed stunned unable to reply to Rose.

"What's wrong, all seeing all knowing, can't think of a way out of this?" Rose mocked as she started to shed a tear whilst trying her best to laugh.

"Checkmate I guess," Dafrak said as he lowered his head. "I can't fault a brilliant move; I am a humble player after all."

In the streets as Eros stepped back, Noham's once proud form now reduced to a charred husk laid there. Every movement seemed to cause him agony, his muscles stiff and reluctant to obey his commands. Yet, despite the searing pain that coursed through his veins with every breath, he persevered, his determination evident in the steely glint that flickered within his sunken eyes. In his trembling hand, he clutched a small vial of blue liquid, its contents shimmered with an otherworldly glow. With painstaking effort, he lifted the vial to his parched lips, the glass cool against his blistered skin. As he tilted his head back, a shiver of anticipation rippled through his battered frame.

The liquid poured down his throat like liquid fire, its taste both bitter and sweet, a potent elixir that promised relief from the relentless torment that had consumed him. With each swallow, he could feel its magic coursing through his veins, igniting a flicker of hope within the darkness that threatened to consume him.

And then, as if some miracle, Noham started to stumble to his feet, seeing this Eros lunged forward narrowly missing Noham as the knight started running into an empty building.

But amidst the crumbling bar, just as Dafrak finished his sentence, a figure entered, his strides swift and determined. This was a man of remarkable speed and grace, his every movement a testament to his agility and prowess. With a sense of urgency driving him forward, he dashed through the dilapidated structure, his heart pounding with the weight of impending rescue.

"Why are you here!" Rose screamed.

"I got told to rescue a girl." Raijin replied with a confident smile. Without further hesitation the agile man sprang into action, his movements fluid and instinctual as he raced towards her. With a burst of strength and agility, he lifted Rose and dashed to the top of the staircase. Seeing this Dafrak laughed as he became unbound, quickly running to the back exit.

"No, his escaping, let me go we need to kill-"

"No," Raijin said. "Your brother said he saw a look in your eyes, I guess he was right. Don't worry Rose, whoever is after you has to get through the greatest swordsman now!" He added as he blitzed towards the nearest window. The crumbling building seemed to groan and protest as he crossed its threshold, the floorboards, creaking beneath his feet. Dust motes danced in the shafts of moonlight that filtered through the cracks in the ceiling, lending an ethereal quality to the scene.

Finally, they emerged from the decrepit structure, the moonlight bathing them in its warm embrace as they fell from two stories. As they landed the girl that was clinging to him, struggled out of his grip, watching the bar crumble to the ground.

"You people are insane..." she muttered with a grateful smile.

"I don't see Eros," Raijin said as he gazed upon the smouldering ruins of a war-torn battlefield. Lumina was now shrouded in a heavy silence, broken only by the haunting echoes of clashing steel and the anguished cries of the wounded. The air was thick with the acrid scent of smoke and blood, a grim testament to the ferocity of the conflict that engulfed the once peaceful streets.

As the last of the knights fell beneath the onslaught of Beast axes, a hushed silence descended upon Lumina, broken only by the crackling flames and mournful cries of the wounded. The Thousand Beasts stood victorious amidst the carnage; their triumph tinged with a sense of grim satisfaction.

"Ingrid, on me!" Astrid commanded approaching Raijin. "Capture all those who surrender."

"And those who resist?"

"Do you need to ask?" Astrid quickly questioned as she checked Rose for any wounds.

"Where's Eros?" observed Raijin.

"Your brother is waiting with the Valas" Astrid said.

Rose nodded as she hurried away.

Astrid glanced at Raijin. " "he's in there. Finishing off 'Pawn'" she added as she pointed at an odd building, crafted from the best marble with the eye sign on it.

"What's in there?"

Who knows, 'Pawn' ran in thinking it'll protect him."

As they started walking back to the camp, Raijin watched as the Beasts moved with purposeful intent, their weapons stained with the blood of their fallen enemies. They ransacked homes and businesses alike, their keen eyes searching for anything of value amidst the wreckage.

With his eyes red, hunched over and drooling. Noham was dying only coming back to life as a flash of warm light collided with him. He thought of the days of his youth surrounded by friends playing in the fields of Nero watching the world go by. The war was near its end as the first batch of soldiers came home, beaten hungry and injured. "Mummy…" he muttered as he swung his hand smacking Eros Away dislocating his arm.

Eros bounced his arm off the wall snapping it back in place as he gazed at a mindless brute. His form silhouetted against the backdrop of destruction, he moved with a lumbering gait, each step sending tremors through the earth beneath his feet. His skin, charred and blackened, bore testament to the fires that had ravaged his once mighty frame.

Eros tensed as the brute lumbered closer, his muscles coiled like springs, ready to unleash their fury at a moment's notice. With a guttural growl, the burned brute lunged forward, his fists swinging in a wild frenzy as if driven by some primal instinct. Eros met the onslaught head-on, his movements fluid and precise as he deftly dodged each bone crushing blow. With a swift motion he countered, his axe slicing through the air with deadly accuracy, leaving deep gashes in the brute's charred.

The brute unfazed stepped back gazing into the abyss, remembering the day he became a man. Fighting in the front lines against the Lions and nearly losing his life to the dominating Pier. Later being sworn in as a Knight of the Lions, climbing the ranks with his brilliant mind and afterwards joining under the White Knight's flag and fighting so well the Queen handed him the honour of captain.

He started dragging his feet forward, his movements fuelled by a relentless determination that bordered on madness. With each strike, he seemed to draw strength from the pain, his fists raining down upon Eros with unyielding force. Despite the overwhelming odds, Eros refused to falter, his resolve unshakeable even in the face of certain death. With a primal roar, he pressed on, his axe a blur of motion as he danced around the brute's relentless assault. And then, in a moment of clarity, Eros saw his opening. With a lightning-fast strike ingulfed in flames, he severed Noham's right hand.

Noham screamed as he remembered the scariest day of his life. The day the five armies first assembled surrounding an old castle with Gulbrand being the only person to slowly walk out. With an arm missing but smiling through a full beard. The King of Beasts stood before them as Lancer ordered a charge towards this man and the man responded in kind.

Finally, Noham came to his senses seeing a beat down bloody Eros standing before him, "My heart is slowing…" he says to a confused Eros. "I've never been much of a warrior, so grant me the wish of dying like the greatest man I've ever seen. Grant me the honour of dying like Gulbrand."

Eros felt sharp pains running across his body every time he moved his right arm. He could feel himself fading as his head started to pound. He could feel blood rushing to his mouth, knowing he needed to end this now he smiled as blood dripped from his mouth. "Noham, you were a great warrior, lets end this…" Eros said slowly lifting his hands as he set them ablaze. "Eros I hereby deem you the greatest Fire Elemental of our time!" Noham said as he limped forward, with Eros responding in kind. And so, the unseen fight begun, each trading blows Eros using his fire to burn the skin off Noham, and Noham using his depleting strength to punch Eros in and out of consciousness. Each hit more dangerous than the last, but one thing came to Noham's mind with fire spreading throughout his body and beyond, no matter how much he hit this man, Eros did not go down. This thought scared Noham, not for his sake but for the Queen as he saw before him a beast that could devour the Queen.

Finally, in the last moment of his life Noham saw Eros's fire grow, his Will becoming darker. He laughed as he dropped on his knees being engulfed by Eros' fire finally losing all feeling, he closed his eyes, dying before Eros.

Moments later another explosion shook the ground beneath their feet as Rose turned her head around.

"Even destroying that building..." she said as fire quickly spread and white smoke covered the sky. One man stepped out with eyes bloodshot, his clothes half burned off, His hair red as blood, his chest heaving with exertion as he surveyed the battle-field and a black aura lingering off him. And though the scars of war would forever mark his soul, he knew he had emerged from the crucible of combat stronger than ever, and those who saw this incident, quickly spread the name Eros the awakened Sorde.

Alex

Few days before the attack that rocked the west, in the heart of the recovering village, where thatched roofs kissed the sky and the cobbled streets echoed with the bustle of daily life, there stood Alex covering his face in a brown robe. With his magnetic smile, Alex leaned against the wooden post of a market stall, watching the world go by with a twinkle in his eye.

On this day, as the sun beat down upon the cobblestones, Alex spotted Lady Charlotte Al'Jacques, one of the five commanders of the White Knights army. Dressed in polished armour that gleamed in the sunlight, Charlotte stood proud and tall, her presence commanding respect and admiration. Despite the dangers lurking in the shadows of his past, Alex found himself drawn to Charlotte. With a boldness born of pride, he approached her, his heart pounding in his chest.

"It's a thing called tobacco," Alex said with a sly smile.

Commander Charlotte turned her gaze towards Alex, her expression guarded but curious. " What do you do with it?" she replied, her tone cautious yet intrigued.

"Smoke it."

"I refuse…"

"I understand, it's not very popular around these parts but go south where they grow it, men, women, children everyone smokes it. I've tried it not that nice, but it shows you have money you know."

"South? You mean the Empire of Rodinia?" Charlotte asked with her attention firmly grabbed. "Adam, right?"

Alex took off his hood with a big smile on his face. "Yes, and yes. I can't believe you remembered me."

"You have a unique look..."

"I get that a lot," Alex quickly responded before tucking his hands into his shirt. "So, princess Charlotte, what does this prince have to do to get dinner with thee."

"Princess is correct. Fifteen men have asked for my hand in my life. Some have bought a field of cows, castles, gold. You bring some low-end drug, how insulting."

"Money drives the lady, then?"

"No, power does."

Alex looked around. "Power?" he asked as he bowed walking away from Charlotte.

The following day determined to win her favour, Alex summoned all his charm and charisma, weaving his words like a master storyteller spinning a tale.

"I couldn't help but notice your presence once again" Alex began, his voice soft but sincere.

"It's not often we see a warrior as skilled and noble as yourself gracing our streets." He added approaching Charlotte whilst carrying a bouquet of flowers with each of the construction workers saluting him as he walked past.

Charlotte arched an eyebrow, impressed by Alex's boldness.

"What do you want Adam?" She probed; her voice tinged with doubt.

Alex flashed a charming smile, his eyes sparkling with mischief.

" Only to offer you a moment of rest from your duties, Lady

Charlotte." He replied smoothly. "Perhaps a stroll through the market, or a taste of the finest wine in the nearby tavern."

"There are plenty of high-end restaurants, why not them?" Charlotte asked almost mockingly.

"I'm broke..." Alex quickly answered with a simple smile on his face. "However, a world run by money is so heartless."

"A prince has prestige, why would a poor man call himself a prince."

"Just as every girl wants to be a princess, every boy wants to rule a kingdom as its beloved prince soon to be king." Alex said as he started to back away. "I mean everyone wants to be seen and heard right?"

Another day passed and like clockwork Alex was back in the same shop digging into his pockets for some gold, with the lady of the shop laughing at his misfortune. "It's not my fault, this place is far too expensive!" Alex shouted.

"It's not hers either..." Charlotte interrupted as she saw Alex carrying a small basket. "Since the war between Elizabeth and Logan, money has become a more glaring issue."

"Who cares?" Alex said with a big smile as he raised the basket. "Look I have some fruits and even cheese."

Despite herself, Charlotte felt a flicker of curiosity stir within her. There was something about Alex's easy charm and disarming smile that intrigued her, despite the warnings echoing in the back of her mind.

"I suppose an hour wouldn't hurt," Charlotte conceded, her voice softening slightly. "Lead the way and let me see what adventures await us in this humble place."

With a grateful smile, Alex offered his arm to Charlotte, his heart racing with excitement. As they wondered through the bustling market, the summer sun cast a warm glow over their budding romance, Charlotte seemed to enjoy the simpleness of it all only to be dragged back to reality.

"She loves wars doesn't she."

"What do you mean?" Charlotte snapped. "People won't stop underestimating her keeping this useless charade up."

Alex walked Infront of her with a sly smile. "For someone who abandoned you, you sure have loyalty."

"Abandoned?" Charlotte asked as she stopped.

"I noticed, not one of the white knights where around you the last few days, now everyone and their dog knows you are a high-ranking officer. What if you were attacked..."?

Charlotte stunned for a moment struggled to find her voice. "Enough, let's just get this over with so I can continue my work."

"We are here…" Alex said as he turned around with a sombre tone. "Your Queen will end up dead."

"What?"

"Not by me, by her own actions. Pangea felt the world's hate after they ordered us to destroy an island of innocent people. People who were just searching for the truth."

"Adam, what are you talking about."

"But even them monsters knew when to hold back. Elizabeth doesn't. Thus, this is her reality till her death." Alex said as his sharp gaze pierced through Charlotte who immediately drew her sword.

Charlotte frowned. "I'm so stupid."

Alex raised his hand. "No, you just wanted to forget your life, even for an hour." he said as his men rose through the bushes aiming their arrows at Charlotte. Ava, refusing the take her eyes off Charlotte threw Alex's sword towards him, which he quickly caught.

"Everyone and their dogs know who I am right?" Charlotte said as she pointed her sword towards Alex with a cold look on her face. "Who am I about to send to Ga'Al!?"

"Alexander. The eye of Basilisk." Alex said as he closed his fist, so a fury of arrows flew towards Charlotte but without breaking eye contact with Alex, she threw her sword twisting her hands raising walls to her sides. Grabbing her falling sword and lunging forward clashing swords with Alex.

"A master Earth Elemental. With impressive sword skills... for your age." Alex mocked as he took heavy breaths. "Ava, Orrin, Majus pillar formation! Basil take full command of the archers. Adonis prepare to engage with the rest!"

Charlotte could not stop smiling as she scanned around her. "Basilisk not taking me lightly, I feal honoured!" she screamed. With a wave of her right hand, Charlotte called upon the earth, sending forth branches of soil and stone to ensnare her foes. Basilisk fought valiantly, hacking and slashing at the earthbound branches with swords and axes.

As the battle raged on, Charlotte's control over the earth only seemed to grow stronger. Seeing this Alex smiled as he backed off allowing the Kal twins to hold their ground against her upcoming attack. Charlotte summoned great boulders from the ground, hurling them with deadly accuracy at her opponents. The warriors dodged and weaved, their movements fluid and coordinated, but still they found themselves hard-pressed to evade the relentless barrage.

Alex took a seat crossing his legs and ordering his archers to stand down. "Earth elementals are strong. Able to harness the power of the land itself. However, there's a limit to their fancy rock moulding." hearing this Charlotte panicked looking around for any way to escape, before Stavros and AL'lioe crossed their halberds inches from her neck.

"That's checkmate." Alex said as Charlotte dropped her sword raising her hands and head in defeat.

With Charlotte captured and a few days later the world learning of Noham's death. Alex sat back with a chained Charlotte by his side hearing Logan had defeated Noham and Dafrak. He laughed at the thought as rumours from a demon summoned by a witch laid waste to Lumina all the way to the beasts' rise from the ashes. Arguments quickly broke out to how Lumina actual fell, but as a news hawk dropped the latest news around the world, the arguments stopped. As each one of their faces turned to stone.

The news read like novel. Alex ever the poet quickly gathered his people standing in the middle with the newspaper on hand.

"I can feel the sun from here Amadeus." Lael softly spoke with his legs and arms bound to his wheelchair.

"I failed... I have to admit I didn't expect you to climb from the water and stab me." he added as he slightly coughed.

Amadeus laughed. He looked at himself seeing the new uniform with medals pinned across it. "They call me the Hero of Pangea you know."

"Zeus won't be happy having his glory taken."

"He wasn't."

"At least it's a nice day. I don't mind dying today." Lael said as he glanced up.

Amadeus waved his hand allowing the guards to open the cage pushing Lael from behind. As they made it out Lael's eyes brightened as he saw an endless crowd in his path. The mood of the crowd swirled in unseen currents as not a single person had a smile or filled with rage. The only sound was the wheels turning and the footsteps of the Royal Knights escorting Lael to his last destination. As he got closer, he counted nine kings Including King Lieto Anemoi siting Infront facing the crowd. Above them three generals. General Marcus 'Zeus' Silvius sat on the far left with his hand on his cheek and soar look on his face, wearing nothing but white and red robes and a crown of leaves. To the far right the eldest son of the Dragfier family. General Aegeus "God Hands," Dragfier a man who many believe should have the rank of Brigadier General sitting upright with his arms crossed in full uniform and half his face hidden under a hat. Finally, in the middle in the traditional armour of 'Cicano' with his head under a white thick hooded cape Prince of Cicano and the Thirteen branches 'The strongest swordsman' General Milo Anemoi.

With the stage set and thousands in attendance, Lael felt at peace as he was escorted up the ramp, sat in-between the nine kings and the three generals he looked up at each one of the faces looking back at him and sighed, before turning his head to the executioner. "Can we hurry up; the people are sweating."

"Wait!" shouted a citizen. "Why did you do it!?"

Lael smiled. "Why? I wanted power, money, glory."

Lael laughed; in this moment he felt the Goddess existed as his eyes brightened. "If you want more power than a world breaker! More influence than Pangea itself! More riches than you know what to do with! Find it! Find Eden!"

Finished reading at the proclamation from Lael, Alex fell with a strange look on his face. He tried to continue the article at how the plaza went into chaos with the words that shook the world. But all he could do in the moment was rub his eyes as he raised his fist. "Let's get rid of this queen and get Eden for ourselves!" Alex screamed to a thunderous roar.

Through the infectious celebration, a scout came rushing towards Alex who had just begun drinking. "Sir!" the scout struggled to speak. "The beasts are here with their King!"

"Beasts?" Alex asked as he put his mug of ale down. "Astrid, right? She's a crazy one alright. Basilisk, lets welcome our guests but be ready for war!" Alex added as he grabbed his sword. When they approached with joy in their eyes, Alex quickly drew his sword as he felt a strange presence. ***My hand reacted on its own, Who?*** Alex thought as he scanned the area when he noticed a man who cast a shadow that swallowed Astrid. With leather armour doused in fox pelt that fit him perfectly. His scarred arms exposed under the sun with his left holding a sword almost his size as it balanced on his shoulder. ***Him? A berserker? He seems too slender to be one.*** Alex thought before signalling the rest of his crew to be ready for battle. "What's wrong?" Ava asked softly.

"Them two, are dangerous..." Alex quickly answered pointing behind Astrid.

"Alex!" Shouted Astrid. "My boy wants to fight you!" she added with a bright smile on her face.

Alex gazed with an odd fascination of the creature that stood behind Astrid. ***His Will is almost Animalistic, as if a beast put on a human suite*** he thought before ordering his crew to stand down and walking forward on his own. With the man responding in Kind. There were no words, no stance a simple strike between the two that echoed throughout the field. With their swords locked in place Alex whispered. "How long have you been watching me to block my attack so easily?"

"I'm glad you've never changed, Still leering to the left when you make a strong strike."

Alex stayed silent as his face filled with confusion.

"If you give up now, that will make it two hundred to one, right?" Eros said with a resigned smile.

Alex backed off for a moment, dropping his sword, "Eros is dead..." he whispered, his gaze steady despite the turmoil within.

Eros nodded solemnly, his eyes glistening with unshed tears he dropped his own sword standing tall in front of his brother. "My death was exaggerated." he said as his smile grew larger. Memories flooded in their minds, of a childhood spent free, of days spent training together in the fields and nights spent listening to their mother's endless adventures. Now they stood face to face once more, the wounds of the past reopened with a painful clarity. Alex rushed out tentatively, his hand trembling as it brushed against Eros's shoulder, as if afraid the moment would shatter like glass.

"Eros" Alex chocked out, his voice thick with emotion. " I never stopped searching for you, I never stopped hoping that you were alive."

Eros met his brother's gaze, his own eyes reflecting the pain and longing etched into Alex's features. " And I never stopped longing for the day we would be reunited Alex," he confessed, his voice raw with emotion. With a shared understanding, Alex and Eros embraced, their arms wrapping tightly around each other as if to anchor themselves in the tumultuous sea of their emotions. And as they held each other close, the weight of their shared grief and longing lifted, replaced by a glimmer of hope for the future and promise of resolution.

Alex took a step back and as his eyes grew clearer, he could see his piecing yellow eyes. Strange Red hair and the stupid smile.

"Where have you been?"

"It's a long story."

"I like stories." Alex said as he gained his composure.

So, they travelled back to Logan's camp through the road that did not rise or sink, Alex was riding next to his brother listening to his story, he felt a wave of emotion draining through him, it travelled through every cell till it reached his toes. Strangely enough it was a painful cleanse, a chance for Alex to detox and assess what was hurting the most, instead he bit on the tissue of his cheek and smiled listening to Eros' rise from the ashes. The adventures of his younger brother where more than enough for a lifetime.

"So, you fought sirens whilst Ulfr was bewitched."

"He did make it up to me not long after when a group of pi-rates decided to take our ship." Eros pointed out.

Ulfr hearing this quickly interrupted. "More than that I taught him to read, write and to recognise the beauty of a woman."

"Brother calm down..." Rose quickly said.

"Fine," Ulfr said as he raised his hands. "Remember when they were going to hang us, and you set the ropes on fire?"

"All I remember was you cursing them and their children the entire time." Eros said as he laughed.

Alex spoke gentle, with a sombre look on his face. "When did it start? Was it when mom and sis died?"

"When we were forced to fight a war against the Beasts."

Seeing the mood slowly change Raijin interrupted. "I hated this kid when I first saw him. So weak, such a crier. But time after time he fought, refusing to die."

"You can say that again, he's like a man possessed." Ulfr said quietly.

"This is idle talk!" Astrid said further back. "When are we arriving?"

"We've arrived." said Alex, as they approached over the hill to a large camp of soldiers. Thousands in number with the Lion's Sigel all over it.

As they stepped from the steeds Logan approached with his chest out looking proud as he glanced over at a tied-up Charlotte. "Noham is Dead! Charlotte is captured! This is the power of the Lions" he said as Bern quietly laughed to himself in the background.

Raijin looked over at the laughing man, "Shit..." he said as he turned back to an enraged Eros who firmly grabbed his sword lunging towards Bern. Seeing this Bern responded in kind by open his arms wide and closing his eyes.

"Apollo!" Eros shouted covered in soul crushing bloodlust as he swung his sword down towards Apollo's head with all the force he could muster. Only to stop as the sword touched the tip of Apollo's hair. With the bloodlust fading, logan could finally move his limbs and Apollo's eyes met with Eros.

"Why?" Apollo asked in a raspy voice. "Kill me, have your revenge."

"Don't listen to him Eros, look at him. If you kill him..." Raijin said with his sword drawn blocking people around him from interrupting.

Eros smiled with his eyes bulging from his face before backing away from Apollo. "Sometimes I do believe the Goddess exists. Look at the mighty Apollo." He said as he dropped his sword Taking a few steps back. "For years I've thought how I would kill you. But look at you. For years you've been waiting for me to kill you right?"

Logan looked around still confused. "Bern, why is that crazed man calling you Apollo."

"Soft..." Apollo said as he started to shake. "Even now you are soft. Even with those muscles you are soft Eros Senesto!"

"Have your revenge, right?" Eros said. "It'll be soft to put you out of your misery. I can't think of anything more perfect than watching you crumble beneath your guilt you monster."

In response Apollo dropped to his knees foaming at the mouth. "Coward!"

Elizabeth

Siting upon her throne with several of her knights Infront, Queen Elizabeth watched on as the most important people in the Kingdom, argue to no end. With new paint on the walls, and more jewels surrounding her, the masses wanted some of the gold she was gathering. As the war grew larger the people struggled to keep starvation from reaching them. However, these where not the people Zen, these where the people from the Autonomous zone, Pocasis and Nero.

"Pocasis is going down the route of Therouzen my Queen." Voice of Church Father Gael said. "I am a man of the goddess, but I am also a man of my people. If Pocasis falls, we would be in danger. Thus, spread your influence deeper into their lands like you have for Zen!"

"We are at war father; the Queen cannot be bothered with such trivial things." Lady Delphine St'Louis said. "We need armies, strongholds. My cousin will not make the same mistake a second time. If we are not careful the Golden Lion will walk all over us."

Lady Oceane chimed in with a cold tone. "High taxes, lack of authority, constant war. The police force is struggling my Queen. We understand you need to be careful of Logan's push however raising the Banner of 'King' and sending him to the borders of Nero doesn't make sense 'Bishop' is already stationed around there do you not trust in his power?"

Obeh walked into the Throne room quickly seeing the chaos caused by minor and major lords. He calmly walked past till he reached the Queen's wall, where they let him past. He reached for Elizabeth's Ear and whispered. "They captured 'knight' as well my queen." Hearing this the Queen raised her hand, forcing the lords and ladies to exit the throne room.

Elizabeth frowned as the last Lord left. "What off Isaac..."

"He is still in his room; it seems Noham was of great importance to him."

"No one must know, Find me five suitable replacements for 'Knight and 'Pawn'."

"About that someone is waiting to see you, my Queen." Obeh quickly replied.

"Who?"

"Me!" Dafrak quickly interrupted as he strode into the throne room.

Elizabeth looked up in disappointment. "Logan really won against you. I thought you would be ready. But for Noham to die in your place as well, this is embarrassing."

"Noham was a fool, he relied on his medicine to the end. He was not a tactical Soldier, just a glorified scientist." Dafrak quickly said with a briming smile.

"What do you want Dafrak."

"Revenge."

"Against Logan?" Elizabeth asked.

"Against the beasts, a witch, a fool and Eros Senesto." Dafrak quickly bowed his head as he lowered his knee. "Give me command of 'Pawn's army and I will win this war for you. Even better your dept with me will be cleared."

Queen Elizabeth wondered what had happened for Dafrak to be this obsessed with someone. But against Obeh's clear refusal the Queen agreed to these conditions. "You will be knighted by evening, is… Lancer will welcome you into the great army. You will be the frontlines outside Nero, and thanks to your offer Obeh will send a message for Drominic to raise his banner and march to Pocasis."

"Yes, my Queen." Dafrak replied before promptly exiting the Throne room.

"He's dangerous why give him so much power?" Obeh quickly asked.

"Was." Elizabeth replied. "I don't believe he has the backing of 'E' anymore; did you not hear his voice. The man sounded desperate. Now if you would excuse me, I need to talk to that boy." she added as she stood walking to the door whilst being accompanied by her Knights.

The walk through the hallways was filled with whispers until she reached Lancer's room, within seconds she felt a cold chill running down her spine. She slightly opened his door to see him playing chess with a young girl, who looked around his age.

"Queen to rook five." Lancer said as he moved his chess piece.

"Knight to King." Anna replied to the shock of Lancer as he lowered his head in defeat.

Elizabeth chimed into this peaceful moment. "I never realised you liked chess Lancer."

"I didn't but it's fun."

"I see." she said. "This young lady Anna, right?"

"Yes, my Queen" Anna said as she stumbled to her feet bowing to Elizabeth.

"How is your skin so pale? A new type of makeup?" Elizabeth asked curious.

"She's sickly." Lancer quickly replied still siting watching the chess board as if he were replaying the match in his head.

"Go to Ser Obeh, he will provide you with the best doctors in this kingdom." Elizabeth said with a smile on her face. Hearing this Anna bowed her head one last time with her eyes wide open and quickly ran past the queen. "She's lively, so when am I going to become an aunty?"

"She's weak, always ill." Lancer said. "At first, I found her interesting, but the more I knew of her I couldn't see me and her together."

"Always so cold. So why play chess and be around her so much?"

"Noham asked me to be her friend."

She smiled. "He will be missed. However, we are at war, Logan prepares for another attack. We need to stop him."

"Are you sending me to the front lines?" Lancer asked as he glanced up.

"Not yet, I need you in your best condition, however you need to get back to training."

"Yes, my Queen." Lancer says as he stood up. "You should rest, you look tired." he adds walking past her.

Before she could reply one of her advisers came rushing to her looking distressed. Seeing his face, she frowned "What?" she asked.

"Logan's forces are on the move south. Towards Nero."

"How many?"

"Two maybe three thousand."

Elizabeth sighed before putting on a crooked smile. "Send a message to 'Rook' she loves open battle, right? Then we will give them open battle."

"Yes, my Queen, however we have another problem."

"Is it something that can wait?" Elizabeth asked with a cold stare. "I have to go see my son."

Seeing this the advisor didn't want to irritate the Queen further and promptly bowed his head before asking the Queen if he could leave.

Just north of Pocasis, a few days after the message was sent, Rook's army march out to loud drums. With the sun blazing each member of her army looked possessed chanting and singing as they bashed their axes together with their leader drinking and laughing alongside them.

A young messenger looked frightened next to Hannah Florine Gisele. "Stay calm lad, we will win. Do you know why because I'm the strongest!" Hannah screamed as she raised her axe and her army replied in kind.

Logan

"Sir, 'Rook,' is approc-" Ezekiel said before turning his back to his king. "I did not mean to disturb..."

"It's fine, ladies out. My advisor looks concerned." Logan laughed.

Ezekiel saw the ladies walk past gazing at them coldly. "Thank you," he added before turning back around to his King.

"Speak." Logan said as he confidently stood naked.

"Rook is coming..."

"So? Go meet her in battle. We have more than enough to crush her untrained heathens."

Hearing this Ezekiel nodded as he exited the tent, silently walking past a sleeping Apollo and glancing across to Eros continuously swinging his sword.

"You know," Alex said as he bit down on a hog's leg. "He's not stopped swinging that sword since we reunited. He's like an obsessed animal."

"Strong though," Oliver replied as he sipped on some milk.

"Very."

"Might be strong enough for that obscene Axe, Lord Logan got after his battle with the beasts."

Alex glanced at Oliver in confusion before continuing to eat. Not too far Ulfr was besting Ava in a game of chess with Rose continuously making fun of her when a raging Logan dashed past with the head of a woman in his hands.

"Looks like they're about to fight," Charlotte laughed from her cage in full view of the event.

Eros looked over and as he was about to move charlotte stopped him, "The coward won't start anything. Calm down." she said which he just nodded in response.

The King of the Lions stood right in front of Alex blocking the sun from him with blood dripping onto the ground. "Who is this?" Logan roared.

"An appetite killer?" Alex mocked as he dropped his hog to the floor.

"Appetite killer he says..." Logan muttered as he dropped the head pointing his sword at Alex. "Assassins... is that how you killed my brother? Now you try the same to the Golden Lion!"

"I suppose from your perspective you are right," Alex replied as he yawned. "However, if I wanted you dead Logan. You would be dead."

Shocked, Logan took a step back as he started to snicker.

"Gather the Leaders!" He screamed.

In the heart of the camp, as the sun cast its golden rays upon the bustling scene, the leaders of the Great Lion Army gathered around a sturdy war table set under a canopy to shield them from the midday sun. The table, scarred with battle plans and parchment scrolls, served as the focal point of their discussions. Gathered around were the lords, knights and advisors, each adorned in their respective heraldry, their armour glinting in the sunlight.

Despite the heat and dust of the camp, their demeanour was serious, their minds focused on the task at hand. At the heart of the table stood the commanding general, a figure of authority and experience. With a map spread before him, he begun to outline the terrain and the disposition of enemy forces, his voice carrying across the assembled leaders.

Ser Rupen de Foix was first to be pointed to as he held the largest men under his banner. He stroked his brown beard which pocked through his armour as he listened closely to Logan.

Logan's finger moved across the map, to the once city of thieves, "Take Lord Gabriel with you, and prepare the navy."

"You would use the Trade union's army as a naval force?" Lord Gabriel asked.

"You will have the largest force defending an outpost?" Ser Rupen de Foix asked.

"Yes, according to Ezekiel, Rook is moving on land towards us. Pocasis is already at a weakened state we make a move towards their western ports it'll be easy to take."

"My King, a question." Lord Gabriel asked with a small voice, his eyes lingered as he scratched his head in confusion. "What of 'Knight' sire?"

"The queen would rather take her by force as the boy predicted."

"And she will wipe the trade union off the face of Kindraill if you push south now." Alex interrupted.

Logan's eyes sharpened. "Tomorrow, we make our move. The rest of the forces shall head for Colmar castle. Where we are lightly to engage in battle with one of Elizabeth's army leaders."

Alex smirked as he nodded. "How many are they?"

Ezekiel leaned forward whispering in Logan's ear.

"A few thousand Logan repeated."

"That's too low…"

Ezekiel nodded. " We are missing important information here."

"Silence!" Logan Roared. "Alexander and his band of heathens will be in the front lines."

"The main body will secure the outposts near Colmar before joining Basilisk." He added.

"You make life difficult Logan, but I have a small request for going on this dangerous mission."

"Fuck you and your request." Logan Roared!

"You see, my brother's birthday was not too long ago, and I hear you have a nice Axe with you."

Ezekiel interrupted seeing a lot of people around Alex and Logan in standstill with their hands wrapped around their weapons. "We do, since we are not using it, he is welcome to it. However, I'll have to take some of your reward for being hired by us for the Axe. Only the asking price of course."

"Good, give it him when you have the chance, I was having a nice conversation with young Oliver here so if you will." Alex added with Ezekiel nudging his King's shoulder forcing them both to walk away from the situation.

As they arrived in Logan's tent, the King quickly lashed out throwing a chair into the ground, breaking it to pieces. Ezekiel, standing outside ordered one of the soldiers to hand the Axe to Eros before joining his King in the tent.

"You need to control yourself my King." Ezekiel scorned. "We need Alex, you saw his bounty. You saw how many people flocked to our side because of Alex's name alone."

Logan dashed towards Ezekiel beathing heavily. "That's why I didn't kill him right there and then. But to send an assassin after me? Heathens the lot of them they have no honour just wastes of air."

The following day as the first light of dawn began to streak across the sky, the Lion's camp stirred with purposeful activity. The blacksmiths and armorers worked feverishly to ensure that every sword was sharpened, every shield sturdy, and every suit of armour gleaming in the morning light. The clang of metal on metal echoed through the camp as weapons were repaired and inspected, while squires curried to assist their knights in donning their armour.

Outside the armoury, the camp's horses whinnied and stamped their hooves impatiently, as grooms and stable hands readied them for battle. Warhorses were outfitted in elaborate barding, while packhorses were loaded with supplies and provisions for the long day ahead. In the mess tent, cooks bustled about preparing hearty meals to fortify the soldiers for the challenges ahead. The smell of cooking meat and freshly baked bread filled the air, mingling with the aroma of hot mulled wine to create a comforting atmosphere amidst the tension of impending conflict.

At the western most point of the camp, two of Logan's soldiers came carrying the great Axe presenting it to Eros. Which he grabbed with both his hands, clenching his teeth with veins instantly popping out. The weapon, freshly honed and polished, caught the light of the morning sun, casting dazzling reflections across the camp. With a grin of anticipation, Eros swung the axe in a wide arc, testing its balance and heft. The blade sliced through the air with a menacing whoosh, its edge keen and deadly.

Around him, fellow warriors paused in their preparations, casting admiring glances at the impressive weapon. Some offered nods of approval, while others exchanged knowing smiles, recognizing the power of their comrade and the fearsome reputation he carried.

"Calm down, you'll need your energy today." Ulfr spoke amidst the noise of the camp, men and women adorned themselves in armour and battle gear, preparing for the day's battle. Leather straps were tightened, helmets secured, and shields displayed with fierce symbols of their clan.

"Shut it old man, he's happy for once." Astrid said as she came with a ball of paint. "Now stand still whilst I put this on you."

"Dirt?"

"Body and blood of the fallen." Astrid corrected, before forcing Eros to take his shirt off. "My people, wear this before battle, its stronger than any armour. It's a forgotten tradition even Gulbrand stopped using it." She added as she scanned the scarred boy.

She started painting him. "However, my father continued it, taught all of us and look, me and my sisters are still here. Gulbrand is dead."

As she finished painting markings on Eros, she flinched for a moment before stepping back to marvel at her work as Eros put on a leather vest and chainmail on top. His arms and face with war paint all over reminded Astrid of her Father.

"What's that tattoo on your back?" Rose asked as she ap-proached.

"Your brother has the same. So does Raijin. Its proof of our bond our brotherhood." Eros said before swinging the Axe once more, its blade catching the sunlight in a dazzling display, a sense of camaraderie and shared purpose filled the air.

"Where is he anyway?" Astrid asked.

"Stretching."

Hearing this Astrid made way to Raijin, past Alex who was in the middle of instructing his men of battle formations and Charlotte who was sleeping soundly next to the other captured enemies. As she arrived, she saw Raijin doing what many thought was a ritual, every morning he would sit on his knees before using standing erect, putting his dominant leg forward and striking his sword into the air. Before any food he would do this a thousand times.

"A master still stuck on the basics?" Astrid asked as she approached. Raijin slowly opened his eyes as he turned over to see Astrid in warpaint and light armour ready for battle.

"Did I disturb you?" She asked. "I won't take too much of your time."

Raijin stopped sheathing his blade. He was already in his leather as he looked around in confusion. "The army is yet to move, so why disturb me?"

"Eros is hurt."

"I know, but he still wishes to fight," he said trying not to sound annoyed. "You know him, it's hard to stop him."

"You will be closest to him in this fight, my unit will be supporting the flanks, protect him if you can." Astrid said as she tightened her chest plate.

Raijin glanced at her long brown hair and green eyes. He ponded for a moment if this was truly the Beast King. "Fine, then you and the beasts make sure Ulfr lives. He is part of your Unit this time around."

"Don't Doubt my skills, Trainee swordsman" Astrid jeered.

"Well, I need to head to my Unit for any last-minute Ideas from Ulfr."

The sound of horns echoing throughout the camp interrupted the idle chatters as the rest of the army started to fall into formation, their banners fluttering in the breeze as they prepared to march towards the field of battle. The air crackled with energy and determined, as every man and woman in the camp braced themselves for the trials ahead knowing that the fate of Zen and the Lions hung in the balance.

Alex marched at vanguard quickly followed by the rest of Basilisk. The man looked majestic in the white and grey armour that once belonged to Pier, all the members of Basilisk looked calm and composed they moved as one. A sea of leather and steel followed closely behind led by Astrid. Wearing animal pelts over their leather and chainmail, covered in warpaint with rounded shields on to their right and axes to their left. Standing as part of the Berserker unit Eros marched out with a great Axe strapped to his back, Ulfr riding a horse to his left and Raijin to his right in light steel and leather on top resting his arm on a sheathed sword. Right behind these three the giant Muya in the thickest of armours walked beside the petite Rose in thin robes with a large scroll strapped to her back. In total they were four thousand and behind them the Great Lion Army with King Logan St'Louis leading the thousands slowly following the front lines with some distance in-between.

"History will write how the great Golden Lion marched to battle behind heathens." Apollo mocked riding next to Logan. Ezekiel quickly chimed in from the left. "History will never know of these heathens Apollo."

Logan Roared. "Focus, our next stop will be Infront of the great heathens themselves."

"The armour is its usual gold, but I like the red cape. Brings out your eyes." Isabella O'Alencon yawned as she learned forward on her steed.

"Don't speak to our King so casually." Geoffrey scorned. "Using these heathens as fodder is brilliant. We are ten thousand strong, and we get to destroy Hannah's irritating forces without losing much."

"I heard last time the Lions fought Hannah it didn't end well." Isabella added as she laughed.

"Enough." Logan roared. "The past stays in the past. I will not repeat the same mistake this time."

As the sun shined brightly on their heads, the sound of faint drums being hit rung louder by the second. Everyone Knew Rook's forces had arrived. Alex stretched his arms as he saw the White Knights approach over the horizon. However, as he prepared to ride forward Hannah's absence was noticed surprising everyone including Alex.

"She's not there..." Astrid said softly grabbing Eros's attention.

"She is their leader they follow the Old Gods. Why not battle?" Ulfr smiled. "Well, it's not her idea. Eros do you know how to ride a horse?"

"Why?"

"Be it the Queen or an advisor, their battle tactic includes Alex."

"Ok. I understand"

"Their waiting." Ingrid said as she drew her Axe. "Sister, what's your call." Before Astrid could answer the war cry of thousands of Rook's armies forced their hand as they began charging towards the castle in the distance.

"Don't let them have that!" Logan shouted. "Charge Basilisk stop their push!"

Not wanting to disobey orders, Alex sighed as he opened and closed his fist three times. Forcing Eros to pull a soldier from their horse struggling to sit on it.

"What are you doing?" Raijin asked as he jumped on his own horse preparing to charge. "You are berserker unit remember."

"And he ordered shock tactic, look at their numbers, my brother is insane if he thinks I will let him bash into them without me to help." Eros quickly answered as he finally sat on the back of the horse, holding tight to the saddle confusing everyone around him. Before they could react, the Basilisk charged forward in tight formation followed by the few stragglers from the Beasts, Raijin and a quickly approaching Eros.

"Stick to the strategy, we flank the left, move the Beasts now!" Ulfr screamed before lifting his sword signalling the Beast archers to loss at will.

Astrid smiled before bashing her axe to her shied. "Icei! Skwroga! Igvrodwla!" she screamed leading the beasts into a full charge.

As Alex slowed his horse standing on top of it drawing his sword and spreading his arms apart, his smile quickly disappeared as at the corner of his eye he saw Eros sat on a speeding horse.

"They're brothers!" Stavros said as he started to laugh uncontrollably.

"Slow down brother or you will fly off!" Alex shouted as his eyes focused on the enemy. While they came close to engaging with the enemy like usual Alex jumped into the air seeming to fly for a moment distracting the white knights nearby him, whilst Eros clumsily rolled from his horse quickly getting his footing as he unsheathed the great Axe charging on foot with a Calvary unit surrounding him. The sudden ram, the flying man and now the crazed Berserker, caused a lot of the White Knights to panic in fear and confusion. Alex seeing this ordered the regroup. But as he looked past his soldiers his joyful smile quickly disappeared when he saw too few heads coming to their aid.

Eros continued to swing his axe when all the strength went from his body as pain shot into his chest and arm. Seeing this Raijin unsaddled from his horse slicing through opponents and finally blocking a strike from an enemy aiming for Eros' head. "She was right… you're injured…" Raijin said as he deflected strike after strike.

"Ava!" Alex said before striking down a white knight. "Order everyone into the castle!" He shouted as Ava quicky signalled without hesitation. As they began to retreat Alex glanced over to see his younger brother, looking like a possessed beast hunched over fighting alongside Raijin.

With raindrops dripping down Eros' cheeks, all around was nothing but a whirlwind of disorder and violence. Raijin's arms started to weaken as he tried his best to cover Eros' back. The Beasts finally clashed bringing hope to Raijin, as they made quick work of the White Knights cutting from their flank as they crushed war hammers and axes into a wavering enemy. Men could be heard weeping and whinging whilst the Beasts showed their strength. When a rouge sword slash from the enemy grazed down Raijin's chest freezing the man as his mind went blank. "Raijin…" Eros Muttered, holding his chest in pain as he dropped to knee.

When suddenly a strange horn forced the white Knights to retreat, with a small sigh of relieve, the first arrow landed slowly panning his eyes up, Eros saw a flood of arrows heading to their direction. In a moment of surrender Eros closed his eyes and the next time he opened them his sight was blocked by a giant of a man wearing this armour holding a large shield in front of both him and Raijin.

"Say thank you when we make it into the castle!" Rose shouted interlocking her hands in a strange way with her eyes glowing. Eros Tapped Raijin bringing him back to reality as Raijin repaid the dept by helping Eros move towards the castle.

"Shields!" announced King Logan as the brunt of Hannah's army stood opposite him, while sitting on horseback watching his enemies, he chuckled recalling back to the ending of the hundred-year war. The last days where him and his brother won against two nations. His confidence in victory only grew larger when he looked around.

Ezekiel concerned about the upcoming open battles quickly spoke up. "Look around my King, the men look concerned, we just watched the basilisk, and the Thousand Beasts raid the castle for defence. Remember Alex is the bind for this army we cannot afford to lose him."

"Goddess have mercy, shut up Ezekiel." Logan responded with a cold tone. "If they live or die who cares, what we need to do is win these battles for them to have a chance."

"What off th-"

"Enough, prepper the men, rotations of night and day. We fight till Rook falls!"

Eros

"There he goes again..." Ava said staring at Eros awakening in a pool of his sweat.

"You get used to it." Ulfr said with a sombre tone.

"And there he goes again..." Ava added as Alex rushed over to his brother with a large smile and two swords in his hands.

"They're like a broken clock. One wakes up from a nightmare, the other instantly tries to calm him by fighting him."

Rose with her eyes still closed trying to get back to sleep. "It works doesn't it."

"I guess." Ava quickly replied.

It had been five days with several attacks from Rook's forces trying to gain the castle. With water low the Thousand Beasts would bring a sense of grim determination to their defence of the castle. Their reputation as fearless warriors would bolster the morale of the defenders. However, the people living in there hardly came to the grounds. The invaders had made the castle their home, but their numbers alone had made food scares. The slaves that had been bound there where beyond thrilled quickly helping the invaders in any ways they could, some even asking Eros to calve the tattoo on his back on them.

"How long till the food goes?" Astrid softly asked to her sister.

"A few more days, but food is not the concern. We need water soon." Frigg quickly answered.

Astrid grunted as she glanced around the castle's throne room. She could tell the place was ancient with moss clung into the walls and even the seat she sat on, crooked, and weak. "If you think Hannah will surrender if we hold these people hostage you are lying to yourself. If you think we can fight through her hordes, you are lying to yourself. If you want to survive there is only one way."

"Risking your life over these people." Frigg moaned.

"I am the King of the Beasts. I follow the true gods. Thus, if Hannah is one who follows the same gods, she will fight me for the one true crown."

"Eros won't allow you." Raijin said as he approached.

"Eros is not the king." Astrid said.

"He owes his life to you and will not watch you throw it away."

"And you?" Frigg asked.

Raijin held his chest trying to calm down. "I have yet to thank you for saving us."

"Don't worry about it, we are allies after all scared swordsman." Ingrid mocked to a short laughter from those around.

"Enough!" Astrid roared. "Raijin, the next time you freeze it might mean death. The large man and the witch won't be there to save you every time."

"I know."

Astrid's eyes flicked from Raijin to Eros pondering for a moment. "Send the letter Ingrid. Eros and Frigg will be my left and right when the time comes."

"Sure," Ingrid said reluctantly.

As the day went by a flying sparrow landed by Astrid's side with a note attached. She quickly read it and as she sighed, she nodded to her sisters getting up from her chair she looked over at Eros talking to his brother quickly grabbing his attention. Travelling throughout the castle to the front gates, with her overseers beside her, everyone could see in Astrid's eyes a growing fear. As Astrid herself kept remembering all that was said about the 'Civilised Beast.'

"Open them." she said as her eyes met with Rook's forces stalking them like pray.

"This way." One said with large smile. "She's been itching for a fight you know. She might let you live longer than usual."

The thick smell of blood and the gloomy sky grabbed Astrid's attention for a moment. "What happened..."

"Logan is something else. Five days and nights this man has not moved an inch. Boss has not been allowed to enjoy such a battle as well, so she's pissed."

"Orders from your Queen?"

"I think so," The man quickly replied as they arrived at Hannah's camp, one could barely hear their thoughts as they marched through music, screaming, fighting and fucking. The collection of madness ended as they made it to the middle of the camp where Hannah's hand was up a girl's dress with her smile fading as her eyes locked with Astrid.

"Hannah liked the letter you gave. Hannah knows of our ways little lady."

Astrid shook her head as she begun to calm down. "You are smaller than they say."

"Silence!" Hannah shouted as the entire camp looked as if time had been paused. "Grab Hannah a shield and Axe." She added as she stood tall, towering even Eros himself.

As the circle became made, Hannah started to hop stretching her neck with a wide smile on her face.

"The last time I saw her this restless was when her father agreed to the proposal." a Knight said close to Frigg Ear.

"Proposal?" Frigg quickly asked.

"It was simple, the one to defeat her gets her hand in marriage. That was when she was sixteen." The Knight said in fear. "She's thirty now."

As the drums begin, Astrid and Hannah begin to encircle each other, Astrid reading her opponent down to the twitch on her finger. And Hannah dancing to the beat of the drums barely paying attention to Astrid. Seeing the opportunity, Astrid lunged forward with the shield protecting her and hiding her axe in it, but Hannah quickly responded by swinging her axe cutting the shield in half and sending Astrid flying.

"Fast..." Eros said quietly.

As Astrid fell Infront of Eros she quickly smiled as she asked for another shield. Hannah seeing this became all the happier as she started to advance, before quickly stopping and looking down at her hand, to see blood dripping from it.

"The counter hitter strikes..." Frigg said as she saw Hannah's expression change. "Hey Eros, I bet you've always wondered why a petite tanned girl with long hair is the King of beasts. She is smaller than Ingrid, has less battle experience than me. Physically weaker than most men who follow her. It's simple Spawn of Amon, she is the best hand to hand fighter the Beasts have ever seen."

Seeing this Hannah dropped her shield demanding another Axe, again they circle each other this time with Hannah's eyes sharpened and as Astrid lunged forward Hannah responded in kind showing great speed. Thus, as they met in the middle with Hannah swinging her Axes wildly, Astrid used her agility and reflexes to dodge each attack, "If your plan is to tire me out, good luck little girl!" Hannah shouted as her speed increased. Again, Hannah connected by bashing Astrid away breaking her second shield but this time also cutting through her chest plate.

"Astrid!" Frigg shouted before being held back by a focused Eros.

"Look..." Eros said referring to the many cuts all over Hannah's body. "They're small, but enough will make her fall..."

A silence fell in the camp as Hannah begun to take large breathes shaking her left leg. For a moment Eros thought she was composing herself but from the way her stance loosened he quickly spoke up, "Air Elemental..." he said to the surprise of those around him.

"Astrid, you can't out speed her, you can't out agility her force this into a fight of power or you will lose." Eros said confidently and in response Astrid stood with a cocky smile on her face dropping her axe and raising her fists.

Hannah laughed as she followed suit dropping her axes and approaching Astrid. This was no longer a battle but a one-sided slaughter as Hannah quickly overpowered Astrid hitting her with her fists and bursts of wind. Astrid in response landing odd punches and kicks to no effect. Finally, as Hannah shuffled Infront of Astrid going for a final punch Astrid kicked her one more time to the back of her knee forcing Hannah to buckle. Then as an act of defiance threw all her weight into a punch to Hannah's left temple dazing her for a moment and again to the opposite temple forcing Hannah to her Knee. Then bawling her fists and throwing a hook to Hannah's chin forcing the unmovable mountain on her back. Without a moment to lose Astrid grabbed her axe throwing it to the side of Hannah's face.

"A moment for a kill and you won't take it King?" Hannah asked with a dazzled but blank look on her face.

"I missed." Astrid said wiping the blood from her one good eye. "But I won't next time."

"Missed... Then come here a steady hand will be more effective than a throw." Hannah responded.

"I'm not stupid," Astrid said as she grabbed another Axe from one of Hannah's soldiers. "Move and trust me you will feel this one right between your breasts."

Hannah sighed. "Hannah gives up. Little King is too smart for her." The second she said this Astrid buckled to her knees taking heavy breaths as her sister quickly came to comfort her. Hannah set up with a large smile on her face. "All hail my new Fiancée!" she said to most of the camp roaring. But some looking around gripping the swords and shields harder.

"What does this mean Hannah?" asked one with a cold stare.

"Well, we fight with whoever she wants to fight." Hannah said as she slowly got up. Eros quickly rushed over to Astrid grabbing her axe and dashing it inches from Hannah's head hitting a knight lunging at Hannah. Noticing this Hannah stood as her smile faded. "Hannah is disappointed. Where is the loyalty to our ways!".

The fight quickly ended as they led their horses back to the castle word spread around of Hannah's lose and her betrayal of the White Knights. Astrid with a broken nose and swollen eye felt uncomfortable as her once enemies continued watching her and with each person that got closer, they would bow their head to her. Alex watched from the walls with a blank stare as a row of warriors followed Astrid and Hannah stood next to her walking alongside like a proud wife she was going to be.

Frigg next to Eros looked concerned. "Elizabeth will come at us worse than before."

Eros whispered. "I hope she does."

Frigg was stunned at Eros's excitement. She had always kept an eye on the young man much like Astrid, but each day she saw him grow more obsessed with the white knights. She could feel he was slowly losing his mind over it. "Think about girls or your future a little more will you."

"Like you said, Elizabeth will throw everything at us now, meaning death will be closer than ever." Eros looked up. "Her death will push me through whatever she throws."

Alex

The following day tensions where still high, even with the new members of the Beasts feeding and giving water to everyone that was trapped in the castle. Blood had been drawn on both sides but none of this was a concern for Alex as he once again stood on top of the castle walls stretching his hand out to the horizon. Only to be interrupted by Eros as he hastily placed his Axe next to him.

Alex looked up at Eros. "I can't believe you are taller than me."

"Meat and milk are the secret."

"He jokes." Alex said. "What are your plans after the white knights fall?"

"Justice is next." Eros quickly replied.

"After?"

Eros seemed puzzled for a moment. "What are yours?"

"The money I get, ill build the Basilisk to the point they can attain Eden. Then create the perfect Kingdom." Alex said proudly as he glanced at Eros. "Join me, you will be my second of course. We will travel the world. We will change the world."

"What about -"

"They don't matter, this will change the world so that people like Fanisse will never have to die young." Alex interrupted.

Eros lowered his eyes, glaring at his Axe.

"Don't say no because I'll have to follow you till you say yes..." Alex said jokingly before Basil screamed for his attention.

"They're coming!" Basil shouted.

As Alex walked towards Basil, he noticed Astrid a day after her battle franticly putting on her chainmail. "Are we going to battle again?" Alex said jokingly before Hannah placed a drum of ale in front of him and slamming a map of the land with concern in her eyes.

"Before you ask, Logan has been informed we meet with him in an hour." Ava said as she gathered all the leaders in the castle.

"Alex, an endless number of White Knights are coming from the south led by Drominic and the new 'Pawn'."

Alex was confused. "They replaced Pawn that quick?" he asked.

"Also, an army that large to go unnoticed that long would have had to move when Rook attacked..." when Alex finished his sentence he stumbled back as he sighed.

"Who is the new Pawn Hannah?" Ulfr asked with intent.

Hannah, stealing looks at Astrid only said one word. "Dafrak," shocking Ulfr to his core.

"Who ordered you to not fight?" Ulfr asked again frightened.

"The Queen did, well Dafrak did but I told him to go fuck himself then the Queen said the same thing, so I was like whatever."

Ulfr frowned as he looked at Eros. "Basil, right? What about the north?" he asked with a sharp voice.

"Well, that was my next bad news, the full brunt of 'Knight's forces are marching down and will arrive sooner than the southern forces."

Ulfr sighed. "Freak of nature set the events perfectly..."

"This Dafrak is a smart man," Alex said as he begun to walk away. "We move south and fight Pawn's forces."

"I don't understand..." Eros said quietly.

"Dafrak knew Hannah will either betray them or die in battle. Rook's forces where just to tire us out." Ulfr said. "I agree with your brother though. South is our best bet. Dafrak can't share push him hard enough he will clash with Drominic."

Alex hopped on the back of his steed with the bottom half of his armour back on and holding the chest plate in one hand.

"Eros, Ulfr, Ava and Hannah on your horses. We march to Logan. The rest fall under Astrid's leadership. When you are all armoured and ready march south!"

As the command echoed, with no time to lose the five hastily rode towards Logan as the rest of the army peppered to move out. In the distance as they arrived, Apollo was blowing warm air into his hands as Logan smiled looking at the woman who broke his arm.

"You brought me a present Alexander." Logan said coldly.

Alex quickly stopped his steed. "Hannah, Logan. Logan Hannah now that we know each other, I've prepared the army near the castle to move south."

Logan ignored that. "We will move north; Ser Geoffrey's scouts have said there are less soldier's due north. Even our dear Charlotte agreed that their numbers are signifyingly lower there."

"Are you a fool?" Alex said as his tone became colder. "Charlotte will tell you herself her army will cripple us if we fight them."

"You are angry I understand," Logan said. "I did not betray you; we simply could not cut through her forces. However, I am the King, my orders are final."

Alex smiled. "I'm moving south."

"Do that and you can forget your purse."

"We will move north." Ava said reluctantly. "Your forces will be frontlines though. We've not rested even for a moment this past week. I'm sure the Golden Lion would understand."

"I would not trust you heathens against actual soldiers with my life." Logan roared. "Ezekiel, Get the army ready we march out within the hour." As they prepared for battle a quick message was sent to Astrid, who now had to move her soldier's due north, tired and unprepared, the two armies travelled at a distance from each other.

The sky was cloudless as they approached 'Knight's army. The lions' hands grabbed their steel as they gazed at their enemies. The cold breeze blew Logan's cape in the air for a moment as he lifted his bright gold sword into the air. Alex tightened the strap of his chest plate as he shook his head to stay awake. Eros started to hop and stretch his head before grabbing his Axe to his side. Astrid looked around her army before drawing her Axe and shield. Before Logan could order an attack, the sky was darkened by an ocean of arrows, "Shields!" Logan shouted as his army took the first attack From the White Knights. Suddenly as their eyes cleared, five large units from the White Knights started slowly marching.

Tangi, calm and collected raised his hand continuing the barrage of Arrows as his forces slowly marched forward. Logan trapped in one spot, with his army starting to panic continued holding ground with their shields high. "Send a message tell the Basilisk to bash into them create space for us to move forward!" Logan ordered as Oliver struggled through the cramped army. Barely missing arrows flying towards him he finally reached Alex who was ready to charge.

"This is a bad idea," Ava said to Alex with her shield raised up. Alex ignored her. "Flank right!" he ordered as he charged out first.

"These heathens..." Tangi said quietly watching Logan's back forces move forward. "So strong yet so predictable. Send out the Calvary we cannot allow the main force to be slowed." he put on his helmet as he charged forward with the brunt of the Cavalry unit. "For the Queen, For the White Knights, For the Kingdom!"

Alex saw the approaching Cavalry unit, knowing this would be a hard battle he quickly drew his sword and gripped on the saddle of his steed peppering for impact. As steel and horses clashed Alex and Tangi's eyes met both releasing the same level of Will, surprising everyone including Alex.

Seeing this Astrid knew their battle would last far longer than needed and ordered the beasts to charge forward with Logan responding in Kind with no other plan in mind. As the two armies crashed into each other a ball of fire exploded in the distance as an enflamed Eros swung his Axe through a soldier, taking his time and throwing an attack when necessary. And Raijin close by slicing through opponents keeping them at a sword's distance.

"Back-to-back!" Eros shouted as the two had found themselves deeper into the enemy forces fighting off each attack as they held their ground. In the chaos and fury of the battle, amidst the clash of swords and the thunderous roar of war cries, Astrid finds herself locked in combat. Amidst the chaos, she catches Ingrid fighting valiantly nearby, her sword flashing in the sunlight as she engages the enemy with fierce determination. Suddenly, a rogue arrow streaks through the air, finding its mark with deadly accuracy. In an instant, the trajectory of the battle shifts as the arrow strikes true, piercing through Ingrid's armour and bringing her to her knees. Time seemed to slow as Astrid's heart clenched with anguish and despair. She watched in horror as her siter fell, blood staining the ground beneath her, her once vibrant spirit extinguished in an instant.

With a primal roar of grief and rage, Astrid abandoned all thoughts of self-preservation, her vision clouded by tears she charged toward her fallen sister's side. Ignoring the dangers that surrounded her, she fought through the melee, her axe swinging with unstoppable force as she cut down any who dared to stand in her path. Finally reaching her sister's side, Astrid kneeled beside her, cradling her in her arms as she struggled to stem the flow of blood from her wound. Desperate cries for help echoed through the chaos of battle, "Frigg! ingi got hit..." she screamed turning her head to see a knight deliver a fatal blow that pierced her sister's defence.

As Astrid witnessed another shattering sight. Her sister Frigg's eyes widened in shock as the knight's sword found its mark, a chocked gasp escaping her lips as she staggered backwards, with blood staining her armour. Hannah seeing this quickly picked up a stunned Astrid waving her hand for the Beasts to retreat.

"The battle is lost..." Ava said as she cut down an enemy. "We have to retreat, look the Beasts are leaving, the Lions are barely holding on."

"And the White Knights still have so many forces." Alex added as he stood tall with his enemy's blood dripping from his face. "Where's Eros?"

"Well find him!" Ava said as she rushed into the main forces. "Head south." she added as the battle came to an end.

The White Knights surrounding Eros and Raijin did not feel victory, but growing fear as two men, continued to cut them down. With corpses of their brothers on fire, they gazed upon a blood drenched Eros, as the monster struck them down with little effort. The fight would have continued till either they all died, or Eros surrendered, luckily for them Raijin noticed forces retreat and quickly told Eros to do the same.

As night fell, mass soldiers found their way to the south, towards Pocasis. As the battlefield laid quiet, Alex sat at the back of a carriage watching the starless sky, with his eyes glancing down at what was left of their army, defeated. He looked behind him with Astrid laying down in shock.

"We have their bodies," Alex said softly. "Once we are far enough, we will bury them."

"Now what?" Kal Orrin said as he marched behind the carriage.

"Regroup and think of another strategy." Alex said confidently. "We still have Charlotte, so we can use her for our next attack." Kal Orrin looked concerned at that statement. "Vague, that's not like you strategist."

"I know."

Elizabeth

Elizabeth sat on her throne reading a letter from Dafrak with joy in her eyes. As if he were a seer, everything he said came true and everything he did led to two victories in a week. The first being able to cut the weakness of the White Knights without angering House Gisele, the second crippling Logan's forces beyond recovery. As her joy continued Lancer entered the room in silence brooding, alongside a concerned Obeh.

"You wished for me?" Lancer asked.

Elizabeth snapped her fingers allowing a horde of maids to enter. "Make him presentable." she said as they rushed towards him surrounding and dragging him out of the throne room.

"What was that about?" Obeh asked.

"Dinner, Al'Gadrood has recovered and ready to get back to work, and we have gained hopefully the final victory against Logan. A lot to celebrate." Elizabeth joyfully answered.

Obeh scanned the Queen, quickly clearing his throat. "The lower class are protesting in Pocasis. Pulling the forces of Drominic and Dafrak, has only raised tensions in the country." Elizabeth glanced at her son as he approached in the hands of one of her maids. "Dafrak is on route back there. Drominic is due north after dinner, so if their brave enough to revolt. Both armies have their banners already raised."

"Understood, what off the growing expenses my Queen?"

"Five years from now war, dept and revolts will be a distant memory." Elizabeth answered as she played with Alfred. "The young prince will live the most peaceful life and once I am dead, he will be crowned as King of a peaceful land."

"I see, what do I tell the advisors, the finan-"

"Tell them what you want," Elizabeth interrupted. "I made my mother's dream come true. Now I will make my son's destiny absolute."

Obeh lowered his voice. "What about you?"

Elizabeth was stunned for a moment. But as her personal guard entered the throne room ready to take her to her changing room. She shrugged it off caressing Alfred as she walked past Obeh. Some of her closest people surrounded her, Drominic flirting with one of the chefs at the far end. Al'Gadrood pulling out a seat for the Queen. Lancer silently listening to Anna's ramblings. Lady Delphine St'Louis siting opposite them with a cold stare and finally Obeh quickly grabbing his seat next to the Queen opposite Al'Gadrood. The Royal guards raised their Halberds as a salute as the Queen sat down to a feast. With everything you could think off from roasted pig to slices of cow and goats still smoking as if they had just been taking away from the fire. An ocean of breads, vegetables, cheese and the finest wine in the west overflowing. This was everything she imagined being Queen surrounded by her closest people, in a huge castle with mountains of food.

As they started eating the conversation flowed, all avoiding the topic of war till Anna spoke. "How did you do it, I mean sticking to a dream for so long and actually achieving it's amazing." few words but enough to silence the room, as everyone else on that table knew the correct answer but wondered what Elizabeth would say.

"My mother started it," Elizabeth said before getting a spoon full of rice. "Then I got it to this point, and Alfred with take it further."

"A lineage dream, wow." Anna said as she bit into a pig's leg. "I'm not from nobility, but to think that's how they did things its interesting."

Lancer chuckled surprising everyone but Drominic the most.

"Anna get on one knee you made this walking rock show some emotion. Take the opportunity girl!" Drominic said as he threw his arms around.

Lady Delphine finished her plate of food and finally spoke. "Where are you from Anna?"

"Well Nero originally, but the job opportunities in Zen where far too great so father took us here a few years before the war." Anna said with a large smile on her face.

"Your father fought in the unification war, right?" Lady Delphine asked.

"Till he got injured but he is an assistant blacksmith and I got to hang out with Isaac now so I'm happy."

Elizabeth smirked as she glanced at Lancer. "She's allowed to call you Isaac. I think you are right Drominic, a wedding is soon to happen."

"My wife needs to be strong; Anna is constantly ill. I only keep her around because I can't defeat her in chess." Lancer quickly said with a cold tone.

The Queen frowned. "Ignore him Anna his just stubborn, I'm rooting for you," she said with a joyful tone which quickly left as one of her advisers came rushing into the room whispering to her ear.

Lady Delphine leaned closer to Anna. "He is correct my Queen, Isaac needs a strong wife not some common filth." As she finished that sentence a stray kitchen knife landed inches from her hand and when she looked up Lancer's eyes where sharp with a vain popping from his neck. You could almost taste his bloodlust.

"I apologise Anna, that was rude." Lady Delphine said before standing up. "I have a lot of work if you'll excuse me my Queen."

"Why did you do that?" Elizabeth asked with a cold tone.

"She called me Isaac." Lancer quickly answered in kind.

Drominic scratched his head. "That a lie..." he said before Lancer quickly excused himself and Anna from the table. Drominic quickly followed as he chased after the chef Leaving Obeh and Al'Gadrood siting in silence next to the Queen.

Al'Gadrood could see the queen saddened. "It's only a meal there are plenty of those Elizabeth."

"Revolts have broken out in Pocasis." Elizabeth said.

"I shall order our troops to move in." Obeh said as he quickly got up rushing out of the room.

The Queen took a large gulp of her wine. "I hate this..." she said softly.

Al'Gadrood scanned her for a moment before taking a gulp of his wine, "I know."

"I can't even have a peaceful meal. Without something happening."

"I know."

"But I have to be strong for Alfred. For his destiny."

Al'Gadrood struggled to get up, using a stick to balance himself. "You sounded like your mother then."

Elizabeth forced a smile on her face, "Good she was a powerful woman."

"NO," Al'Gadrood said. "She was an ill woman, who knew her time had come and threw everything at you. I was a fool to follow her so blindly. But now I guess I'm a fool for watching you destroy yourself."

Elizabeth sighed. "Go rest old friend, I know you are still in pain so I will forgive your words."

In Pocasis, tensions had risen to an all-time high. People from the rich to the poor were found on the streets dead. Though it was in small quantity occasionally, the poor would revolt, against the Nobles and rich. The melting pot of the West was becoming more divided by the minute. Due north of the country Dafrak on the back of a carriage was reading a message from Elizabeth, which gave him full authority of the country until Drominic arrived.

"Giotto!" Dafrak said. "Tell everyone we have control of Pocasis you know what to do."

"What about the Nobles left in charge by Elizabeth?"

"Make them fall in line or kill them." Dafrak quickly replied.

Near the Beast's Castle on an uneven hilltop Astrid sat with a cloth around her and paint on her face as she watched her men, gather logs for her two sisters. Hannah stood in the background silent gazing at Astrid. Before the sound of a horn grabbed both their attention, with Astrid's sisters being carried to their final resting place. As the Thousand Beasts, the Basilisk, Ulfr, Eros, Raijin and Rose all stood watching the fire erupt Astrid stripped herself of the cloth marching forward and opening her palm with one of her men cutting it open as she let some of her blood drip on her sisters.

"Thus, part of me will be carried to the other side, where you will never forget about me in your joyful years until we are reunited once more." Astrid said softly.

Ulfr noticed Eros's confused look. "In their culture this life, is like a trial. Only in Death as a brave warrior will their life begin as they will be reunited by all their loved ones and enjoy eternity with them."

"We aim for Pocasis, Nero, Zen!" Astrid shouted as she raised her bloody fist. "My sisters I will see you one day as conqueror of the West!" As she finished saying this the sky filled with clouds and thunder, and as Eros looked over in the distance, he saw the White stag watching over the funeral. Astrid noticed this as well and smiled screaming even louder with the Beasts joining her.

Logan

As the sun dipped below the horizon, casting long shadows across the desolate landscape, the Basilisk and Thousand Beasts returned to their camp, their spoils clutched tightly in their hands. The air cracked with tension; the thrill of victory tainted by simmering discontent. At the heart of the camp, Logan's tent loomed large, its entrance guarded by two towering warriors clad in chainmail. Within, the Golden Lion sat upon a rough throne, his gaze stern and unyielding as he surveyed the gathered throng.

But despite Logan's presence, murmurs of dissent rippled through the ranks. Some spoke of the riches the heathens had plundered from the White Knight outpost, while others grumbled of the losses sustained from the Golden Lion's campaigns. As tensions grew Logan finally spoke. "Again, you move without an order?"

"Again, we return victorious." Alex responded with a cheeky smirk.

"Watch your tone boy."

Alex looked around seeing the brittle spirit in each of logan's men. "Basilisk will move to attack the retook Lumina, those who wish to join we move in two days!"

Before a response Ezekiel grabbed Logan's arm calming him for a moment, but beneath the surface a deep-seated rivalry was brewing, as hours turned to days and the war dragged on, under the brooding sky, two figures astride mighty steeds emerged from the midst of the great Heathen army, their presence commanding respect and awe. One clad in fur-lined armour, the other in glimmering white and grey armour, their faces etched with determination, they rode at the head of their warriors, the ground trembling beneath the thunderous hooves of their warhorses.

As they advanced the air crackled with anticipation, the tension palpable among the ranks of their army. Behind them, a sea of fierce warriors marched in disciplined formation, at the forefront, the two leaders, Alexander the Eye of Basilisk and The Thousand Beasts Queen Astrid, rode side by side, their minds ablaze with strategy and resolve. With a glance exchanged between them, they began to discuss tactics, their voices low but commanding amidst the din of the approaching battle.

"Ulfr has not led us astray, we can march into Lumina and simply take it" Astrid said, emphasising the need for a swift and decisive strike, aiming to overwhelm the enemy with sheer force and ferocity. Her words were like thunder, resonating with the power of a raging storm.

"This is not a simple raid; we need more information." Alex quickly responded. With a keen mind, he emphasized the importance of cunning and guile, urging patience and precision in their approach to ensure victory with minimal losses.

As they rode, their voices melded into a symphony of strategy, weaving a tapestry of plans and manoeuvres to outmanoeuvre their foes. They analysed the terrain, the enemy's possible strengths and weaknesses and devised a plan that played to the strengths of their warriors. Finally, Alex orders the horn to be blown to separate the Basilisk from the main army.

Ava, stuck by Eros as they rode forth leading the Thousand Beasts with Astrid. The two warriors could hear his name being whispered with reverence among the clans, spoken in hushed tones, his presence had started to command respect and awe.

"These brothers… One a strategic King the other an unhinged animal." Ava chuckled.

"Do not call my Greip an animal."

"He's not agreed to follow you, let alone be your right hand, Queen."

"And he has not agreed to captain your Basilisk, Ava."

"Who has trained with him, talked with him, after the war he will join us."

"We'll see."

A horn is sounded and with a smirk Astrid drew her axe as the White Knights marched over the horizon. The open field stretched out before them; a vast expanse of grasslands bathed in the golden light of dawn. On one side stood the Thousand Beasts, their ranks bristling with anticipation and promise of plunder. Across from them, the town militia gathered, their faces set in grim determination as they prepared to defend their home and loved one.

With a thunderous roar, The Thousand Beasts surged forward, their war cries echoing across the battlefield like a chorus of raging beasts. Axes gleamed in the morning sun, swords flashed in the air, and shields formed an impenetrable wall of steel as they charged towards their foes. However the White Knights stood their ground, their ranks bolstered by farmers, black-smiths and tradesmen turned warriors in the face of impending danger. Armed with spears, bows, and whatever makeshift weapons they could find, they braced themselves for the on-slaught, their hearts pounding with a mixture of fear and re-solve.

As the two forces collided, the air filled with the clash of steel on steel, the sickening thud of blades finding flesh, and the anguished cries of the wounded. Bodies fell on both sides, mingling blood and sweat with the churned earth beneath their feet. And again, Amidst the chaos of another battle, Eros stood as a tempest amidst the fray, his presence commanding attention as he waded into the ranks of the town militia with deadly intent. Clad in battered armour adorned with the marks of countless battles, he wielded his axe with a fluid grace, each swing a proof to his skill and ferocity.

With a roar that echoed across the battlefield, Eros charged forward, his eyes ablaze with the fire of conquest. His movements were a blur of motion as he cut through the militia ranks with ruthless efficiency, his axe biting deep into flesh and bone with every strike. Each swing of his weapon sent men tumbling to the ground, their cries of pain drowned out by the clash of steel and the thunder of battle. The air was thick with the metallic tang of blood, mingling with the acrid scent of sweat and fear.

And when the dust finally settled and the cries of the battle faded into the distance, Eros stood victorious amidst the carnage, his axe stained with the blood of his foes. "Carry the dead! Help the wounded!" Astrid screamed before ordering the rest of the army to move forward.

"I'll help here…" Eros muttered as he gazed at a now silent and still battlefield. The once vibrant grass was now stained with crimson blood, littered with the fallen bodies of warriors from both sides. Above, dark clouds hung low in the sky, casting a sheet of gloom over the scene below. Despite the toll of battle, his eyes remained sharp and alert, taking in the devastation that surrounded him. In the distance, a murder of crows circled overhead, their harsh caws cutting through the eerie silence like a knife. With a sense of morbid curiosity, Eros watched as they descended upon the fallen, their dark forms picking at the corpses with a relentless hunger.

In Lumina, the Basilisk started burning the White Knight flags as they celebrated with wild abandon, their faces alight with the flickering glow of torches and bonfires. They danced and sang, their voices raised in raucous chorus, as mead flowed freely from horn to lip, warming the hearts and spirits of all who partook. As the night drew closer the Thousand Beasts arrived to a joyful welcoming. And with them tales of bravery and daring deeds were spun each more embellished than the last "He struck down twenty, no thirty men!" one screamed "his body was covered in flames and his eyes blank a monster I tell you". Another said.

And in the heart of the conquered town, amidst the smouldering ruins of what once stood, the Great Heathen Army leaders feasted in the bar once belonging to Dafrak. Seated at the head of the table, Alexander and Astrid led over the partying.

"Thirty men?" Alex mocked.

"He is a berserker a lover of battle. Thirty is nothing to him." Astrid quickly replied with pride.

"Lumina fell in minutes with few deaths surely that is as impressive."

"These are warriors, only the scholars will care of how you gained your victories Alexander 'Eye of basilisk'."

Alex nodded, "well my brother wastes to much energy, he should be thinking bigger aiming bigger not some glorified farmers."

Hearing this from the stairs above Eros drank what was left of his mead and started to stumble away only to be stopped for a moment by Ava. "You did well today, have a good sleep train-ing resumes in the morning."

Eros saluted with a smirk as he continued to stumble away.

As summer's fervent embrace began to wane, the world's un-derwent a subtle transformation, a gentle segue from the sun-drenched days of abundance to the crisp, golden hues of au-tumn. The air, once heavy with the scent of blooming flowers and freshly cut grass, now carried a hint of earthiness, tinged with the promise of cooler nights to come. And gathering what was left of his army after a string of victories and defeats, Logan wasted no time and started marching towards Pocasis. With temperatures changing, sickness sweeping the forces the idea of another defeat, Soldiers deserting, all this weighed heavy in Lo-gan's mind as he kept his head low marching forward with no tactic or plan. Ezekiel scanned the King for a moment, saw the hope fading from his eyes he quickly grabbed his attention.

"My King, if you would allow me and a few men I can turn this war to our favour once again." Ezekiel said.

"Do what you wish..." Logan muttered. He pulled his hair from his eyes, as he gazed at his army behind him. With Ezekiel marching forward with a few men, Logan ordered his remain soldiers to stop. He stepped of his horse, glanced at the direction of Pocasis one last time before sighing.

"My name is King Logan St'Louis but most of you know me as the Golden lion. What I'm about to say is not meant to deter you but to light a fire in your hearts. For years now some of you have stood by my side, from the Battle of Bamier which forced the peace treaty between us and Nero. To the end of the Hundred-year war to the Campaigns against the Heathens. To the Lion's War of the best. To the war now, which has had many names but only at its end will we know what history decided to name it! I ask you all, what side of history do you wish to be in. The side that ran with their tails between their legs against the White Knights, the side that could not stop them or my side. The side of Honour and Victory, under the Goddess's eyes!" Logan hastily jumped on his steed pointing his sword towards Pocasis. "All those who still want to follow me. Advance!" The final order lit a fire in the hearts of his people, as the sombre looks faded replaced with hope and passion. There were no more than a few thousand left under his command, but each one of them marched as if they were a million strong. With Logan taking led, the soldiers marched with red in their eyes.

In the dimly lit tavern of Lumina, the air thick with the scent of ale and the sound of laughter echoing off wooden beams, a group of strategists huddled around a rough-cut table, deep in discussion. Tankards of ale sat before them, untouched, as they delved into the intricacies of their plan.

Seated at the head of the table was Alexander, as his piercing eyes surveyed the group as he spoke. " We've disrupted their trade, taken key outposts," Alexander began, his voice carrying the weight of authority. "The White Knights grow weaker. We know how quick Elizabeth can recover. We only have this one opportunity to take Pocasis."

Across from him sat Ulfr, a shrewd tactician with a mind as sharp as any blade. "Agreed," he replied, his voice cool and measured. "We have the uniforms, locations and bombs. What else do we need?" Ulfr asked.

Astrid, with a keen eye for detail, leaned forward eagerly. "Our resources are also stretched thin, and our men weary from con-stant skirmishes."

Ulfr nodded thoughtfully, "Thats why this is the only way."

"It's a huge risk." Alex weighed in.

Rose chimed in. "We have the locals on our side, entering would be the easy part."

The strategists exchanged nods of approval, recognizing the ingenuity of the plan. "Let's take Pocasis" Alexander declared, his voice ringing with determination.

"Theres one more thing Alex." Astrid interjected.

"My brother?" Alex quickly answered as he sat back.

"You know him, he does dumb shit like this all the time." Ulfr said.

Rose chimed in. "He seems too reckless for this plan so it might be beneficial."

Astrid sighed. "What off Raijin."

"He will return when the time is right," Ulfr interrupted.

Alexander tapped his finger against the table, lost in thought.

"Go rest, we'll meet again tomorrow to finalize the details. Until then, let's prepare for the upcoming battle."

Once a bustling hub of prosperity, Pocasis stood as a testament to the wealth and ingenuity of its inhabitants. Situated at the union of two major rivers, its strategic location made it a vital route of trade, attracting merchants from distant lands and fostering a thriving economy. The town's skyline was dominated by towering spires and sturdy stone walls. Market squares bustled with activity, merchants hawking their wares beneath colourful banners fluttering in the breeze. The aroma of exotic spices mingled with the scent of freshly baked bread, filling the air with an intoxicating blend of scents.

But as the winds of war swept across the West, Pocasis's fortunes began to falter. The streets grew quieter, shops shut their doors and the once vibrant marketplace fell silent. Gone were the days of prosperity and abundance, replaced by a grim determination to hold fast against the encroaching threat of invasion. However, Pocasis looked like heaven to a rough looking boy as he ran through stopping short of the soldiers as they did their daily marches. "Came to salute us again Oscar?" to which the boy nodded before arching his back and placing his hand on his chest. Placing his three fingers out for the three kingdoms that made the White Knight Kingdom.

"Brother, do we have to do this every day?" a child asked through her gap teeth holding a branch of grapes.

"One day your big brother will be one of these I have to at least get the salute right." Oscar quickly answered with a wide smile on his face as the last of the soldiers went past.

"Mom said its more likely to end up as those." The child responded as she pointed her finger as a group of injured homeless former soldiers chatting amongst themselves.

"Michelle! Your brother will be the Hero of the White Knights. The greatest White Knight!" Oscar shouted at the top of his lungs as he jumped backwards colliding with a soldier falling on his knees.

"Hey, watch where you're going " Michelle shouts instantly going to her brother's defence. The tall, soldier with a bandaged eye crouched to the kids' eye levels revealing long red hair and yellow eyes. He went to grab Oscar's knee noticing it had just sustained a small injury from the fall but suddenly stops as his eyes lower.

"I'm sorry I'll be more careful from now on," Eros says.

The little girl handed Eros some grapes. "Don't look so down Mister, I'm sure it'll get better."

"Thanks," Eros said with a sombre tone. "Hey kid... never mind."

Eros soon disappeared into the crowd glancing past the shop keepers haggling with their customers, soldiers drinking and gambling. It seemed sweet he ponded sordes where well respected if they could fight, but as he looked ahead, he saw, the ones who couldn't, cast aside or enslaved, he laughed at this before vanishing into an alleyway.

Alex inched closer to Ulfr in the crowded streets. "Tonight." he said as he picked up an apple.

"Ten Cuni!" the vender said grabbing Alex's attention.

"That's extortion!" Alex quickly responded. "Right?" referring to Ulfr who had his attention elsewhere as one of the stalls had people in cages.

"Stick to the plan..." Alex said with a cold tone.

"Ignore this like I had to ignore Charlotte being caged?"

Alex leaned closer to Ulfr. "I love your moral code sometimes but, we had to ignore Mrs Knight or the army that belonged to Logan would have branded us as traitors and killed us."

"She is still with him, in chains. Even though we've seen the Queen has a new Knight."

"I don't know Ulfr, maybe Logan thinks she's still useful. Now you tell me brother, how are those people useful to us?"

Ulfr shook his head. "They outnumber the entire country, I'm sure if you gave them a sword they will fight."

Alex was surprised by that answer. "That's why we play by the plan. No heroics ok."

"But -"

"Nothing, one wrong move and we lose this amazing advantage."

"Il make it quick".

"Then we will have to fight a horde of White Knights forcing everyone into an unstable battle." Alex pointed behind him.

"Risking your sister's life unnecessary."

"Fine!" Ulfr grumbled as he sat back down watching as the town guard marched ready for the approaching enemy army. As the sun dipped below the horizon, casting long shadows across the cobbled streets, the heathen villagers took their positions, blending seamlessly into the bustling evening activities. The aroma of hearty stew wafted from the tavern, where soldiers disguised as jovial patrons gathered around rough tables, their laughter masking the tension that hung in the air.

Meanwhile, in the city square, dancers twirled to the lively tunes of a fiddle, their colourful costumes a stark contrast to the sombre mood that gripped Pocasis. Little did the enemy know that these dancers were skilled fighters, their nimble footwork concealing the deadly precision with which they wielded their weapons. As night fell and the moon cast an ethereal glow over Pocasis, a lone rider galloped into the town, bearing news of the enemy's approach. With a nod from Astrid, the villagers sprang into action, their movements swift and purposeful as thy prepared for the coming battle.

From the rooftops and hidden corners, archers took aim, their arrows poised to strike with deadly accuracy. Meanwhile, the brunt of the Beasts armed with swords and axes melted into the shadows, their eyes trained on the approaching enemy forces. Finally, a single torch held aloft from the tallest tower of the city's castle. "Now!" Ulfr screamed with a fierce battle cry, the villagers unleashed their fury upon the unsuspecting White Knights.

Arrows flew lie a deadly hailstorm, finding their mark amidst the chaos of battle, while the Thousand Beasts emerged from their hiding places, striking with ferocity born of desperation. The White Knights, taken by surprise, scrambled to mount a defence, but the villagers fought with determination.

"So predictable, now we know they're in the country we can call Dafrak." Jon said watching from his window.

"Ser, what about the Golden Lion army." The Knight asked as he saluted.

"That useless old man? Don't worry about him, just send the order and trust in mine and Dafrak's process."

As the Knight opened the door, he was welcomed by a knife digging across his neck, the guard in panic held his neck falling on his back as he took his last breath. "Found you…" Eros said coming out of the shadows whilst ripping the bandages from his eye.

Eros

In the prosperous study of Lord Jon, the air was heavy with tension as he faced Eros who had just dispatched his loyal bodyguard with chilling efficiency. The room was adorned with antique furniture, a stark contrast to the grim reality of the situation unfolding before them.

"You are one slippery guy; I have to respect that." Eros said as he leaned over dragging the knight's body deeper into the room. The scent of rich mahogany mingled with the aroma of fine wine as Jon and Eros sat across from each other, a table laden with glasses and a bottle of aged wine between them. The body of Lord Jon's slain bodyguard lay motionless on the floor, a silent testament to the danger before him.

Lord Jon, his demeanour a careful blend of calm and caution, poured two glasses of wine with practiced ease, his hands steady despite the gravity of the situation. "It's a spy's duty to be good at disappearing…" he remarked, his voice betraying none of the unease that churned within him.

"I was convinced you were an architect now. You designed that plaza and all." Eros replied glaring down Jon as he accepted the proffered glass with a nod of thanks, his movements fluid and precise.

"That's how…"

"How what?"

"How you found me, my hobby sold me out in the end."

"Like I said slippery guy, I went to Lumina first, but no one had ever heard of Jon, imagine."

"Well, my papers say Benoit…"

"Why?"

"Stop people like you finding me, part of the agreement me and Elizabeth had. How did you find me?"

"You slipped up." Eros said as they sipped their wine, the air between them crackled with tension, each aware of the delicate balance that hung in the balance . "I knew you were in Pocasis but to be one of the people that gives soup and bread to home-less veterans. Such a saint."

"How long have you been here?"

"About three months." Eros said with a slight smirk. "I became good at playing the role of the castaway."

"I looked for you… After I heard about Sarrah's unfortunate death." Hearing this Eros slammed his fist onto the table spilling some wine whilst holding his chest trying to compose himself.

"Never say her name. Any of their names!" Eros said through the gaps of his teeth.

Seeing this Jon composed himself guzzling down his glass of Wine, even spilling some on his white shirt. "Why am I still alive Eros?"

"Why did my mother and sister have to die Jon?" Eros asked, calmly with a cold look in his eye.

Jon poured another glass of wine, sighing before sipping a small amount. "About ten maybe eleven years ago, Lael came to Elizabeth she was a well-known mercenary leader at that point, and I was nothing, just fodder. They employ us for this job, but the pay was insane. I was just transporting some dirty laundry when I hear Elizabeth foaming at the mouth in her tent, seeing an opportunity I took it. There where twenty of us, some still work for her some are dead anyway my part was easy enough, give back information every now and then. Simple spy stuff."

A few seconds go past as Eros crashed the glass of wine. "You didn't answer my question."

"I don't know, it wasn't personal."

"Until it did become personal." Eros said as he guzzled from the glass. "She got raped to death you know; I saw her body… what was left of it. She was so kind and died in such a painful way. Why did she have to die that way, Jon?"

"I'm sorry, but I didn't have anything to do with that."

"My sister died in my arms; I carried her dead body for almost a mile to my mother!" Eros Roared as fire seeped from his fingertips.

"I was just… doing my job…" Jon said as he lowered his head.

"Your information led to the White Knights being successful, the Vassilles setting base in Utopia. My brother being transported miles away. My family dead… my Sarrah… murdered that way."

"You can't put all that on me Eros, I couldn't see the future no could I see making friends with you, and everyone else." Jon said, noticing Eros starting to calm down.

Eros inclined his head in acknowledgement, his eyes gleaming with predatory glint. "Indeed, "he said.

"If you gaze long into the abyss, the abyss also gazes into you."

"Very well," Eros said at last, his voice tinged with resignation.

" But I won't stop until all my enemies are dead."

Before Jon could respond, Eros was upon him, his hands closing around Lord Jon's throat with a vice-like grip. Panic surged through Jon as he struggled against Eros' iron grasp, his vision growing dim as the world began to fade.

In the final moments before oblivion claimed him, Jon's last thoughts were of the betrayals and plots that had led him to this fateful encounter. And as the darkness closed in around him, Eros leaned in and whispered. "Every…Last…One." As Jon stopped struggling.

Alex

The gates of Pocasis begun to edge open, as ghosts begun to hunt the country. Hiding in the shadows killing all who bared the White Knight Sigel, Ava stood among them as he grabbed a White Knight firmly placing the edge of his dagger on their neck. "Where are slaves?" she asked.

"The pits, The pits!" The knight said as he pointed, Rose and Astrid nodded in the background. Fading into the alleyways. The second they disappeared Ava sliced the Knight's throat and started moving. On the rooftops Alex waited patiently as he looked across seeing everyone was in position until the first flamed arrow lit up the sky. The second signal had been made and the sky brightened with thousands of flamed arrows.

The sight was beheld for a moment as even a white knight captain, stood near his window watching as the arrows fell on each rooftops.

North of Pocasis, at the edge of Lumina Logan looked ahead raising his fist in the air "The retake of Pocasis starts now!" he screamed to a roaring response. "All cavalries take to the walls!" He screamed once again before an Arrow flew past his head, as if time had slowed, he watched as each of his man get shot down from their horses. "Shields!" halting the cavalry charge.

"Your scouts said light defence!" Logan screamed as he jumped of his horse charging towards Geoffrey.

"My scouts will never lie…" Geoffrey said shamefully.

Logan grabbed a young scout screaming for him to check the area and as the scout ran into the open and arrow pierced through his eye.

Isabella O'Alencon smiled as she finally arrived. "Looks like we met that monster sooner than later…"

"Have you ever fought him?" Logan asked as he leaned on a large rock.

"My father did during the great war," Isabella O'Alencon said as she started to pray.

Logan tightened his belt looking at all his soldiers crouched waiting for an order. "How many horses do we have Ser Vauquelin?"

"About 300…"

"How many men?"

"Two thousand." Ser Jeremy Pierre quickly answered.

Logan sat down with his hands clasped together. He felt the presents not only of everyone before him but everyone who had died under his command. He looked up seeing all their faces waiting for an order. "I wish Ezekiel where here…" he sighed before standing.

"Ser Rupen de Foix of House Fox, Isabella O'Alencon of house Alencon, Ser Vauquelin, Ser Jeremy Pierre and Ser Geoffrey… If I ordered, you to die would you, do it?"

Confused Isabella stopped praying and began to slowly glare at Logan. "What do you mean?"

"Our opponent is Drominic, one of the best Marksmen in the world, His army would be tailor made for him. We basically have no cover and no intel on the enemy."

Ser Rupen de Foix dropped on his knees in despair. "So, you want us to die?"

"Yes."

"What if we retreat… Gather ourselves and come back." Ser Geoffrey asked in desperation.

"Drominic is no fool. He's a strategic mastermind, we walked into his trap… if we run, he will kill us anyways." Isabella O'Alencon said as she begun to sob.

"If we charge forward using all the Cavalry as bait, the remaining soldiers can scale the walls and have a better chance of winning. If I'm correct most of his army are archers, so they should be wearing light armour." Logan said as he stood tall.

"So, in the end our lives where useless?" Ser Jeremy Pierre asked with a deranged look on his face.

"No, our fallen houses, our invaded kingdom. We showed the world who we are! Warriors till the end!" Logan screamed as he raised his fist. "I'll give you a minute to decide." He added whilst he walked away.

Losing vision from the rest of the army, Ser Vauquelin finally caught up grabbing Logan's shoulder.

"I sounded cool right?" Logan asked as he started snivelling.

"You did my king… And I will lead the charge… You don't have to fall here…" Ser Vauquelin stated.

"I'm not like Ezekiel, he could do the most mysterious things. Even now I don't know what his doing but I'm sure it's to help me…" Logan said as he dried his tears. "If I don't lead, no one will follow…"

"What?"

"After I die, please make sure a Lion sits on the throne. And at least make a statue of me I want it to read here lies the greatest hero in the west. Logan 'The Golden Lion' St'Louis."

"My king, you don't have to do this all these Knights want you on the throne more than anything else!"

"No… All my life I wanted to be a hero and now I have the chance to do so…" Logan said as he started heading back. "I know I'm pathetic, I didn't even think I would need to die to become a hero. But there is no other way my friend."

Unable to respond Ser Vauquelin marched back with logan as they both gazed upon the dread stuck on everyone's faces.

Sat on their horses the drums of a calvary grew louder as Logan held his family's sword proudly in the air. "Advance!" Logan ordered recklessly as Drominic smirked simply pinning them down as a wave of arrows kept bashing into them. "For Zen!"

Logan said as arrow after arrow cut down each of his Knights. "For Freedom!" He shouted as an arrow struck Ser Jeremy Pierre throwing him from his horse. "For honour!" He shouted as Isabella O'Alencon's body bounced around before hanging of the edge of her horse with multiple arrows sticking out. "For the Lions!" He screamed one last time as an arrow struck him sending him tumbling off his horse.

"What a fool…" Drominic said before squinting his eyes as he slowly turned his head to see the sky brightened. "That's in the direction of Pocasis…"

"You there boy," Drominic commanded still glaring at Pocasis burning. "Order the chariot archers to move forward and grab me mine." He ordered before grabbing the boy's bow and pushing him away. "We have to end this quickly Pocasis is burning!" he shouted before launching an arrow in the air, which whizzed past Logan striking Ser Geoffrey in the eye socket of his helmet forcing the Lord to scream in pain. As the bodies pilled, Drominic was left in shock witnessing this unending charge from Logan's army.

In the country of Pocasis the raid continued, as Beasts and Basilisk alike stormed through the homes causing as much violence as they could. But what people found odd is they aimed for the rich, the nobility and left each commoner's household un-touched. These simple steps and movements snowballed as Alex stood Alone on top of a house watching chaos grow pretending to play a violin to the sound of screams. He looked at peace as his plan was working perfectly, Commoners, villagers and the like took arms and went to the streets allowing the Beasts and Basilisk to blend in. Soon after the white knights led by Dafrak had formed their units and knew their mission quickly marching out into the streets. As dozens cut through the people relentlessly.

Alex stood tall before drawing his blade. "Up too you now brother, bring this song to its climax." he said before jumping off the roof joining his people in battle.

In house Pan'therr, Ser Onfroi Pan'therr the third sat huddled in his chair as he heard the chaos just outside his doors. "They will come after me next Ser Ezekiel!" he said in pure fear as Ezekiel calmly poured himself a glass of wine.

"No," Ezekiel said before sipping on the wine. "They will rape your wife and kill your sons, before they even pay attention to you."

Ser Onfroi was startled. Ezekiel's cold stare as he said those words shocked the man to his core, immediately he got on his knees praying to the Goddess. "Enough of that…" Ezekiel said softly before sitting down opposite Ser Onfroi.

"Do you know how pathetic you Lords and Ladies of the south are." He added. "A while ago I came asking, begging each of you to raise your banners when the time came. Each of you agreed so easily. The time has come, only half have agreed to go to war in the morning."

"If I fight by these Heathens' side, will my family be safe?" Ser Onfroi squeaked.

"You mean will you be safe." Ezekiel corrected. "Send out a letter to each of your captains in the morning all three hundred who fight under your name will raise their banners and aim their swords at the White Knights. If you don't do so, the Heathens, the Commoners hell even Logan himself will have your head Ser Onfroi."

Ser Onfroi sank deeper into his seat. "I… I understand" he said before struggling to stand, writing a rough note and tying it to a sparrow. The second the bird flew out of the window, a slight whistle from Ezekiel, brought in everyone including Stavros.

"How did they all get in here?" Ser Onfroi asked. "Where are my guards?"

Ezekiel made another glass of wine handing it to Ser Onfroi. "You look far too heavy to be going into battle, so send one of your most trusted man to fight as your vessel."

"What would have happened if I refused your of-"

"Remember we move at dawn, now if you'll excuse me my lord. I have a meeting with the Eye." Ezekiel said as he stepped out of the room leaving his men to protect Ser Onfroi.

As the battles, riots and looting continued, Ezekiel quickly made it to Rose, who was being defended by Muya as she broke the slaves of their collars. "Lady Rose, have you seen Alexander anywhere?"

"In the streets fighting," Rose quickly answered continuing to break the enchantment. "You sound calm Ezekiel, are you not surprised of all this carnage?"

"Not in particular, you see when I recruited the young man, I knew he would not follow Logan's orders. But it's not until he made a remark on Ser Lancer that I understood what type of person he was." Ezekiel said as he picked up a crooked chair sitting next to Rose. "I should have seen it coming. No decent man would call themselves the eye of Basilisk and lump to-gether people worth millions as part of him."

"You sound a lot like Dafrak..." Rose said softly.

"I'll take that as a compliment," Eziekiel said as he scanned the area. "And these word I keep hearing, Yuelan?"

"It's what they call him, even now hundreds, no thousands of these free slaves are swearing loyalty to the man." Rose said. "Also, rumour is he killed one of the Queen's trusted men by himself."

"You don't sound remotely surprised."

"Admired by slaves and Sordes alike, plus a witch's and a world breaker's blood runs through his veins." Rose said with a sombre tone. "If anything, I'm jealous."

"Eros and Alexander," Ezekiel said curiously. "I didn't realise they were so special. Then again, the signs where there. Young lady don't tell another soul of this, you being a witch will be minor compared to what you just told me."

Rose glanced at Ezekiel for a moment. "What are you planning old man."

"Nothing major, it's just making friends with those brothers will truly help us." Rose ignored this and continued doing her work, as the riots continued.

"Speak of Amon himself. Here comes the man of the hour." Ezekiel said as the warrior passed by. A hushed respect fell upon the gathered crowd as they watched Eros stride through the midst. His presence demanded attention, his every movement imbued with a sense of strength and purpose that left onlookers spellbound. Among the flock, a group of castaway Sordes stood at their edges, their eyes alight with admiration and awe as they beheld the figure before them. These were men and women who had known the sting of oppression, and now they looked upon him chanting, "Yuelan…"

As Eros passed by, their gazes followed him with a mixture of gratitude and reverence, their hearts swelling with admiration for the one who had become their herald. They had heard tales of his bravery, of his victories on the battlefield, and his dominance in the arena. As Eros disappeared into the crowd, leaving behind a trail of whispered accolades and whispered prayers, the former slaves and castaway Sordes exchanged knowing glances. In the north as the moon cast its pale light over the desolate battlefield, Logan found himself alone, a solitary figure amidst the wreckage of his once proud army. The war cries of his charging Calvary had long since ceased, replaced by an eerie silence broken only by the occasional groan of the wounded and dying. With each laboured breath, Logan felt a piecing agony of the arrow lodged in his shoulder. The shaft protruded ominously, a grim reminder of the brutality of war. He gritted his teeth against the pain, his jaw clenched in determination.

In the darkness, Logan could barely see beyond his reach. Shadows danced ominously, concealing unknown dangers lurking in the night. Yet, despite the uncertainty that enveloped him, Logan knew he could not afford to falter. Summoning every ounce of strength left within him, Logan reached for the arrow shaft with trembling hands. With a sharp intake of breath, he yanked it free, a wave of agony washing over him as blood gushed from the wound. Clutching his injured shoulder, he fought to stay upright, his vision swimming with pain.

"Why did I survive..." Logan muttered as he forced himself to his feet, his sword clutched tightly in his free hand. Though his body screamed for rest, his spirit remained unbroken as he warbled forward watched on by the remnants of his army.

"My king," one spoke. "We need to rest."

"The caravans will be heading for Pocasis today. Maybe arriving by tomorrow. We need to take the city for them, we rest then." he said as he continued to limp forward followed in kind by what was remaining of his army.

As the first light of dawn began to streak across the horizon, casting a golden hue over Pocasis, the invaders stood vigilant, their breath hanging in the crisp morning air. They had fought through the night, and now as the sun rose, they awaited the inevitable response from the defeated defenders. Pocasis lay before them, its once- proud walls breached and its streets littered with the remnants of battle. Smoke still smouldered from burning buildings, a testament to the devastation wrought by the heathen's onslaught. With the rising sun came a sense of anticipation, a tense energy crackled in the air like static before a storm. They all knew this conquest would not go unanswered, that the defeated White Knights would soon rally and seek to reclaim what had been lost.

Suddenly, a low, mournful horn sounded in the distance, its hunting melody echoing across the battlefield. "More Knights?" Adonis asked in fear. Instantly Alex's allies tensed, their hands tightening around the hilts of their weapons. They exchanged wary glances, their minds racing with thoughts of the approaching enemy. ***Dafrak? Drominic? The new Knight? Whose approaching*** Alex pondered as the heathen army sprang into action, rallying to defend their hard-won conquest.

Ezekiel pulled Gaston to the side whispering in his ear. "Tell them to raise their banners now!"

"Bring them on, each moment more and more people flock to us!"

Astrid could see Alex troubled and stuck in thought and took it upon herself to take command. With shouts of defiance, The Great Heathen Army formed ranks, their shields interlocking to create an impenetrable wall of iron. Eros took vanguard boosting the moral of all that follow him.

"Maybe Logan's army is not too far away." Alex muttered.

"Who cares, they are approaching Astrid is taking command your brother is ready to fight again" Ava yelled as she cleaned a cut on her arm. "What's your order!" She said as she saw Alex's concerned look.

"Keep the wounded away from the frontlines I want our archers ready to strike." Alex commanded as he gained his confidence.

Through the swirling mist of dawn, they glimpsed movements on the horizon, shadows emerging from the gloom. Hearts pounding with adrenaline, they braced themselves for the impending clash, their eyes fixed on the approaching figures. But as the mist began to dissipate, revealing the true source of the sound, a wave of confusion swept through the Heathen ranks. For instead of the enemy army, it was what's left of Logan's army some limping along, their movements hampered by wounds that oozed blood and throbbed with every heartbeat. Others leaned heavily on their comrades, their strength drained by the relentless onslaught of the enemy. Shields lay discarded, armour dented and torn, the scars of battle evident on every man.

"The King has returned!" Ezekiel roared as the Great Heathen army let out a sigh of relief.

Eros

"The snow settled in quick this year." Apollo said as he watched the sun rise.

"Leave before I make you leave," Eros quickly responded as he saw Apollo approaching.

"Kill me, then I won't annoy you." Apollo said jokingly before wrapping his blanket tighter. "Will you be there later on?"

"He asked for us personally..."

Apollo glanced at Eros, seeing the scars down his arm, the bloodshot eye, the cold blank look on his face. "Keep going, you shall inherit my legacy."

Eros ignored that.

"Your fate mirrors mine, a sombre affair don't you think?" Apollo asked with a concerned look.

"You should be proud; you've always wanted to make a warrior out of me." Eros answered as he begun to walk away.

"The only time you were a true warrior is when you decided to let me live..." Apollo said stunning Eros for a moment before he disappeared into the thick fog.

In Nero a small village that stood outside of the great walls stood a solitary school. Where in the grand courtyard of the school, clash of blades echoed like thunder and the air cracked with anticipation, strode an eager Raijin. With dreams of mastery fuelling his every step, he entered the halls of learning, his heart briming with ambition. ***The Hattori school a master that dwells in the shadows lives here. A monster in the great war that kept the rebel forces fighting for Nero.*** Raijin smirked as he walked in. When he witnessed it the Hattori style of fighting as two students inches from each other stood like statues not breaking eye contact. In an instant the first student went for a strike before the second quickly parried and placed his sword on his enemy's collar.

Raijin eyes glimmered, standing firm. "I seek to challenge Hattori Hanzo!" He screamed at the top of his lungs. Training instantly stopped before an old man let out a sombre sigh.

"Why?" An old man asked.

"To prove I'm strong."

" Boden, fight him." The old man said as he laid on his side. As Raijin stood matched against a fellow student, a towering figure whose muscles ripped like coiled serpents beneath his taut skin. And so, it begun, Boden glided towards Raijin showing how his every movement was poetry in motion, a symphony of fluidity and finesse. With each clash of steel, Raijin's shortcomings were laid bare, his clumsy strikes effortlessly parried and countered by his opponent's precise and calculated manoeuvres.

"Don't kill him" the old man muttered as in a flash Boden had his sword an inch from Raijin's neck. Humility washed over Raijin like a gentle tide, as he realised the vast chasm that separated him from his peers. His pride wounded, he swallowed his ego and embraced the hard truth.

"I'm still weak."

"Calm your self-boy, you just went toe to toe with the next head of the Hattori school." Hattori struggled to his feet. "You are rough but strong, stand proud."

"Teach me…" Raijin asked with renewed determination, resolved to learn from his defeat, to hone his skills with the same dedication and discipline from the Hattori school.

In Ser Onfroi's house at the edge of Pocasis, dozens of Lords and ladies sat surrounding Logan, as they wait for Ser Jose to finish introducing them. Just outside Astrid stood trying to warm her hands as Eros approached, he stood watching for a moment before cupping his hands and creating a small ball of fire, resembling a large candlelight.

Astrid smirked. "Thank you... Sometimes I forget how beautiful your fire is."

Eros shook his head for a moment. "Where's Hannah, you two are always together these days."

"Months of endless fighting, and the fact I keep rejecting her proposals. I think she might hate me right now." Astrid said as she reached out her hands warming them in the fire.

Eros nodded. "Shall we?"

"We shall." She quickly responds as the two enter the house doors, instantly slipping into the background watching Logan's small coronation. With Pocasis firmly in their hands and the rest of the loyal houses' Lords here, Ezekiel for a moment remembered life before the White Knights.

Ser Vauquelin Philippe stood with a large smile growing from his thin brown beard proudly bragging of his family's reach as the most powerful in Pocasis before declaring King Logan

St'Louis as his one true King. Though short this speech quickly inspires all the Lords in this house to declare their undying loyalty to the rightful King. With cheers all around Logan finally stood.

"Some of you, I know, some I have yet to personally meet. But all who stand in this room have fought for the last two months to their last breath for more than Zen, Nero, Pocasis. They have fought for true Justice; they have fought to drive the invaders from our Lands. I the Golden Lion, Hero of Bamier, Uniter of the West, the rightful King say we end this. We end the White Knights and leave in the Utopia they took. In this room there is no Beasts, No Basilisk and No 'Legion of Hati.' We are all Lions!"

Most of the room erupted in joy, as they drew their swords raising them in the air. Eros could not look less entertained watching from the background. Alex stayed sitting with a brooding look on his face as he glared at Logan. Astrid kept glancing at Eros with a stern look on her face and Ezekiel kept clapping behind the King even though his smile looked forced. The festivities continued throughout the night, with sixteen individuals including the King missing. These few where the leaders of the

New Lions as they stood around a table as Logan moved his finger Along the White Knight's map.

"Nero's surrender was a god send." Logan said with a smile as he pointed at Bamier. "We march through and take my city."

Ser Thibault Gael looked concerned before he placed a stone on the map directly south of the border of Nero and Zen. "They're religious people in Nero, and the idea of the Queen pushing their Goddess away slowly. I'm sure it never set well with them."

"And the stone?" Logan quickly asked.

"We attack on both ends, they expect us to move to Bamier, because of your well recorded history with the village. But what if we take an equal army and take the city of Cularo."

"A city with the nickname fortress of Zen?" Alex interrupted. "How do we take such a thing?"

Ser Thibault smiled. "You took an entire country with barely any men. I'm sure you'll figure it out."

"Alex will head to Bamier," Logan said Confidently. "They're the strongest force we have, we need them for this battle. Eros with his slave army will be vanguard for the Beasts to Cularo. And the main forces will head for Duntingport take both the castles and split due north and south to secure the other two cities."

Alex glanced at Logan for a moment. "I'll get the Basilisk ready for battle."

"No," Logan corrected. "You will lead House Pan'therr, the trade union's remaining militia, House Philippe and House Francois. How many men is that, Ezekiel?"

"Roughly eight thousand My King." Ezekiel quickly answered.

"You will win, I trust in that." Logan said with a bright smile. "When it comes to impossible feats Alexander is the greatest in that."

Alex smirked as he felt his ego being stroked. "Ava will be your second then, she is almost as good as I am Afterall."

"I'll have to agree Sire, with Ava being the second victory will be almost certain, but what of Eros and Astrid's army?" Ezekiel asked. "They are children Afterall leading into such a force might be too much for them."

"Children he says," Laughed Lady Daniela Vernon as she cracked some of her white face powder. "You forget I was in Pocasis when these Kids, slaughtered White Knights with little effort."

"See, Ezekiel, they will be fine." Logan added before pushing the stone off the map. "Now we leave in the morning get some good sleep, tomorrow we end this."

As the sun dimmed behind the clouds, Eros and Alex hugged each other promising to return to each other once this battle is over. Ava propped herself on top of a horse, surrounded by few of the Basilisk, and a large force of the Lions. Astrid, painted Hannah as she had done for Eros an hour ago, chanting as she blessed her with as much protection as she could give. Ulfr at the far side near the beasts kept relaying the plan to Rose, making her repeat every scenario to him. Finally, Damon and Fini Spoke to Oliver for the first time bragging about their undefeated combination and how it would finish this war. The Horn sounded as the three armies started marching out, quickly dividing as they entered the borders of Nero.

"You got comfortable riding a horse." Astrid mocked as their army marched due south. "A berserker on horseback, would never be allowed in my culture."

"I'm sure I saw someone ride that white stag once," Eros said softly. "A few years ago, now… you might not remember."

Astrid sat stunned for a moment. "Thanks for not shooting me that day?"

"Thanks for not cutting my head off." Eros quickly answered with a smile on his face.

"Good memory."

"Like wise."

Astrid cleared her throat before letting out a forced laugh. "I'm not nervous for your information. The White stag blessed me, it's my destiny to win."

Eros scanned Astrid for a moment, before nodding his head. He could have told her he also witnessed the White stag on more than one occasion, but this was her moment. Her motivation for heading towards a suicide mission. However, she could cope Eros respected that before Hannah barged into the middle of the two. Acting as if it was by mistake but glaring at Eros at every moment.

Due north Alex watched as his brother slowly disappeared, he started to breath heavily and for a moment he thought to rush by his brother's side fearing they would be separated once more.

"Clam down, I know it must be a lot to be separated from your brother once again." Kal Orrin said as he nudged Alex.

Alex laughed it off. "I'm being childish, he's so strong now he doesn't need my protection."

"Not only strong, but more Sordes and freed slaves follow him day by day," Kal Orrin said. "For two months I just watched him grow and being heralded as a Sordes savour. Incredible."

"Not to mention his skills in battle are unmatched I swear!" Kal magus interrupted.

AL'lioe started to wonder. "If anything, it sounds like the Eye is falling into Eros's shadow."

"Enough you idiots." Alex said laughingly. "He's been reckless since he was young. That's why I'm concerned."

"Since he was young. I mean sure but he only became so because of everything that happened." Kal Orrin added.

Alex sighed. "Even before, I remember the last time I saw him before going to camp. He was obsessed with this one clown."

"He never got to see it though..." Alex added as he cleared his throat, siting in silence for a moment. The rest of the trip was in silence. And with the sun rising and setting, they finally made it to the Border of Bamier. A land full of silence not a single soul in the village roads. Alex quickly understanding the situation and drew his sword as he put on his helmet.

"Archers! Lose!" Alex shouted and as the arrows flew over Bamier he quickly ordered the Cavalry to march forward. The warhorses raced across the ground covering as much land as they could before a mass of boulders came flying from the horizon. "Spread!" Alex ordered as his Cavalry quickly separated still charging forward.

Held back for a moment from the surprise attack, Tangi quickly ordered his soldiers onto their steeds, and the rest without to march forward. "He knew!" Tangi said as he unstrapped his helmet taking it off. "We are going to close combat be ready for impact!" Tangi ordered as he drew his sword and shield ordering his Cavalry to march forward. As the ground begun to shake louder the two units finally faced each other. The rest of their armies still approaching from behind Alex pointed his sword "Advance!" he ordered taking of his helmet to match his opponent. Beneath a leaden sky heavy with the weight of winter, the two cavalry units thundered towards each other across the snow-covered plains, their hooves pounding out a rhythm that echoed like thunder. Winds danced in the air, swirling around the charging warriors like a cloak of icy mist. As they drew closer, the ground trembled beneath the thunder of hooves, the air crackling with anticipation of the clash to come. With each passing moment, the distance between them closed, until finally, they met in a discord of steel and fury. Swords flashed like lightning in the dim light, shields clashed with the force of a winter gale and screams of battle drowned out by the howling wind. The snow-covered plains became a battlefield of chaos and carnage, as horse and rider alike fought tooth and nail for supremacy.

They were too organised... Alex thought as he fended off each strike from Tangi's men. ***A mole...*** Alex thought as he came to a sudden realisation. He glanced back for a moment before a wild swing of a sword almost cut his head off. In response Alex shoved his sword into the eye of his enemy's steed forcing it to panic jumping in place knocking off the soldier but also knocking Alex off his own horse as a result. Tangi not too far saw this as opportunity and as he tried to bash through the forces to reach Alex Orrin blocked him hitting his shield with endless strikes before breaking it.

As Tangi fell to the ground Orrin jumped of his horse going for a final strike on the Knight before Tangi Forced his Will out paralysing Orrin for a second but long enough for Tangi to pierce Orrin's heart with a perfect sword strike. Seeing this Kal Magus panicked using strengthen to lounge from his horse landing feet away from his brother not wanting to be interrupted the Earth elemental quickly bent the ground to his will creating mass spikes and launching them in all directions killing all those close by. But before he could reach his brother a set of boulders clouded the skies and as all those in the area looked up Magus desperately held his still brother as the boulders crashed onto the ground creating a mist in the area.

Seconds, minutes, hours Alex pondered as he stood in a daze. When he felt around his body for any missing parts, he could feel part of his chest plate crumbling, so he quickly took it off leaving only a leather shirt underneath. He ran his fingers up the side of his head to feel blood pouring from it. And as he turned around be it the fog or the faintness, he could not see his army approaching and as he turned back, he could see hordes of shadows becoming more solid.

"Why am I here..." Alex said as he picked up a rouge sword, barely pointing it at the shadows. "I am Alexander the Eye of basilisk!" he screamed as he stumbled back for a moment before grabbing hold of the club on his left side and glancing at it for a moment. "I will be the one to rule this world!" he added as some of the white knights got close enough for him to strike them down. Each moment each attack Alex used the fog to cut down endless amounts before it began to fade revealing tangi dead on the ground with half his body cashed by a boulder his eyes pale glaring at the sky. Alex laughed as he looked up to see Dafrak slowly approaching surrounded by endless knights. Nodding, the knights quickly charged into Alex who again used his skills to parry, counter, and block each of their attacks until a rouge attack from Dafrak's sword ripped through Alex's stomach cutting his intestines and piercing through the other side.

As Alex's mouth flooded with blood, Dafrak put a finger on his lips. "Shhh," he said as he struggled to keep his smile from appearing. "Convincing your idiot leader to send you here was so easy its almost unfair." Dafrak said as he pressed his hand on Alex's cheeks with Alex slowly falling onto his knees.

"Don't worry Alexander, bastard of Adira Senesto, killing you will ruin my plan. You will live, for my revenge you need to live." He said as called over a doctor. "But damn, it took so much just to take down the human Senesto, I wonder what I'll have to do to take down the Awakened Sorde."

"Sir some escaped!" a white knight said as he quickly approached from Alex's side of the battle.

"Good, then Mr Eros will be convinced his brother is alive. And will do anything to get him back." Dafrak said as he started uncontrollably laughing.

In the south Eros and his camp finally reached the outskirts of Cularo, A walled city that could be seen miles away Eros gazed at it from a distance wondering what it would take to enter it. At first, he thought of sneaking in like Pocasis, but Hannah quickly laughs of the idea. Then he suggested a raid like in Lumina. Which Ulfr disagreed stating they would die before they could scale the walls. Out of ideas the few leaders of this army pondered for a moment before their attention got quickly grabbed.

"Looks like it's time," Eros says pointing at a flaming arrow in the far distance.

"Hannah, you back Astrid. Eros catch up with the rest and wait for the signal. Then push the east." Ulfr smiled looking at the endless wall before him. "I now know how we can invade this city."

"How long?" Hannah asked as she began riding back.

"An hour max, I'll start heading back and bring the ladders." In an open field west of Cularo Astrid stood as she continued counting the flying arrows. "Five…" She said lifting her hand summoning her army who stood with a possessed look ready for battle.

"It's been a while since we had an open battle, Astrid!" Hannah screamed in joy racing towards Astrid.

She jumped from her horse as she got closer smacking her chest. These actions only further fuelled the excitement felt throughout the army. The beasts felt at home in open battle and being starved for so long made them rabid.

"The ground is moving..." Rose said softly before snapping her head at Astrid who was already tightening her armour. "Is it the Knights? No too many horses." She muttered.

"Red banner…" Hannah said softly. "It's King…"

"That's not possible the spies confirmed King to be in Zen!" Astrid screamed as she started to realise the situation, they had been put in. "Fuck!"

"Last Arrow!" Hannah roared as she drew her axe and grit her teeth.

"Icei!" Astrid Roared drawing her axe and shield planting her feet in the ground. "Skwroga!" She shouted rallying the beasts who stood behind her. "Igvrodwla!" she screamed charging forward into a tsunami of Cavalry.

The impact shook the ground as horses and Beasts died alike. Astrid could not tell in the middle with fog rising from horses stamping on the ground. Heads flying across her. Each time she saw a horse she jumped in the air aiming as high as she could in hopes of killing the rider. She tried to look further and as she looked across the valley, King's immense Will emerged. Seeing this monster approaching sent a chill down her spine, her teeth clenched to keep her jaw still, as adrenaline flooded her system waking her up. Before she could react though, Hannah jumped into the mix throwing all her weight into her element dashing it directly at King, who grabbed the nearest of his soldiers and used them as a human shield to take this attacking ripping them apart and tearing part of Ser Andre's helmet.

Andre looked up seeing four arrows fly in the air. "Three is retreat… four is SOS, right?" He said gazing down at a shocked Hannah before dashing his dead ally and lunging towards her. And as he swung down a hand grasped his sword stopping in its place. "The living golem Muya." He said as pressure around the area grew. Hannah took steps back getting in formation by Astrid's side.

Muya now free to do as he pleased, charged forward with a primal roar, his fists swinging like hammers. He sought to overwhelm his opponent with sheer brute force, to crush him beneath the weight of his relentless assault. But Andre remained unfazed, his movements deft and agile as he dodged and weaved through the onslaught of blows. With each strike that fell short, he countered with devastating precision, exploiting every opening with ruthless efficiency. Seeing his efforts failing Muya retreated.

"Protect Rose…" Astrid muttered making sure Andre didn't realise.

Andre intrigued ripped through Beasts trying to catch Muya slowly growing in frustration, when finally, his eyes flicked towards a shield wall. "Found you!" He screamed as he changed his direction heading straight for Rose. Then to be cut off again this time by Astrid holding him in place.

"Protect Rose with your life!" she commanded kicking Andre back.

Andre scanned the area for a second raising his sword and gathering his soldier's attention then with a single point the entire army knew their target. Not paying attention Hannah jumped in throwing pressurised air and knocking Andre's helmet clean off and Muya jumped from the other side putting all his wight into a right straight knocking Andre's head to the side. Seeing this Hannah kicked the back of Andre's leg, and both begun confronting the Crimson Knight. As the attackers descended upon him like a pack of hungry wolves, he remained steadfast, his gaze unyielding, his fists clenched in determination.

Astrid struck with a vicious swing of her axe, aiming for the head, but Andrew deftly sidestepped the blow, his movements fluid and precise. Undeterred, Muya pressed on, launching a barrage of punches in a desperate attempt to overwhelm their target. Andrew starting to feel overwhelmed, quickly encased himself in an earth egg forcing Hannah and Muya to fall back. Seeing this opportunity, the beasts gathered together getting time to rest. Surprisingly Andre's army also took a step back seemingly resting. And so, the egg begun to crack with green hands seeping through crushing the rest of the egg. As a drooling creature with red eyes and an inflamed body stepped out. Muya charged forward to intercept this creature but before he could reach it, the creature blitzed forward smacking Muya and sending him flying back towards the Beasts. Knocking him out on impact.

Rose starting to feel the effects of using blood magic. Begun to vomit slurring her words as she tried to compose herself.

"That… thing… is… Mixed breed…"

"We know Rose. Well at least I know." Hannah said as her leg begun to tremble. "Whilst Wind Elementals like me get wings when we mix, Earth elementals turn into some grotesque mix of a human and a troll. Well at least he does, look at him he only has one horn meaning he has an incomplete transformation. If there was a chance to kill him its now before he fully transforms."

Dozens of Beasts rushed forward before being quickly overwhelmed by Andre. The bloodbath was clear as day no matter the blades launched in him, or the arrows impaled into him, the monster kept moving forward reaching within feet of Rose, and as she tried to form another blood contract to bind this monster, it went to grab her only for Astrid to jump forward protecting Rose with her life. "Live! And win this war!" she screamed before Hannah jumped in front of Astrid resulting in her insides being ripped apart as Andre's hand carved its way through her chest. Hannah forced a smile before grabbing hold of Andree's hand.

"Now..." she said.

And with a streak of lightning trailing behind, Raijin's blade sliced through the monster's arm. Hannah dropped to her knees as the horn sounded signalling the second army's entrance. Eros burst forward holding his Axe in one hand screaming at the top of his lungs. This one act broke everyone's paralysing fear as the Beasts and the Hati charged Blindly forward following Eros, screaming as loud as they could. Reaching the frontlines Eros planted his feet into the ground grabbed his axe as hard as he could, ignited fire on both his arms and legs and swung with all his might, ripping apart the head of a charging horse planting his axe deep in a Knight's chest. Knocking the surprised soldier onto the ground. Moments like this were sung around the campfire and seeing this inspired everyone to charge blindly into the white knights despite some falling to a raging monster.

Ser Andre suddenly felt a sharp blade carve him up.

"What…you…assassin?" Andre asked in his deep raspy voice as he starred Raijin.

He tried to keep up with Raijin's speed to no avail as the swordsman showed his prowess. With Raijin coated in lighting he went into a stance sharpening his glowing eyes as he blasted forward barely being seen by the naked eye. With a thunderous impact, the blade met its target, the force of the blow sending shockwaves rippling through the air. But as the metal clashed against Andre's skin, sparks ignited in a shower of brilliance as Andre parried the blow away. And as the tide of battle turned against him, Raijin found himself face to face with a foe of unimaginable strength.

With a roar that shook the very earth, Andre charged forward, muscles bulging with raw power. In a split second that seemed to stretch into eternity, Raijin raised his blade to parry the incoming blow. Before he could react the force of Andre's punch crashed into the sword with the fury of a thunderbolt. The sound of splintering steel echoed across the battlefield as the sword shattered into pieces, fragments of metal flying in all directions like shards of glass.

He parried that? Andree thought seeing Raijin reeling backwards. With no weapon to defend himself, Raijin stood defiantly. His spirit remained unbroken, a testament to the indomitable will of warrior who refused to yield. ***Dying on your feet how poetic*** Andre thought before marching forward to finish him off and as he approached, he jumped back barely missing an attack from Muya then raised his arm blocking a second attack from an enraged Astrid. Again, King created distance looking at his opponents as his eyes reddened.

Astrid void of reason launched a fury of attacks and as her fury grabbed Andree's attention Muya went to cut his head only to be stopped by Andree's hardening. Feeling the growing pressure Andree kicked the earth creating a wave that forced all his enemies back. Andre now in full control of his body glanced at the sky, feeling light-headedness "My daughter, I won't be able to save you…" he muttered gritting his teeth.

As the day continued, Andree's army had all but fell and the monster stood refusing help. As swords flashed and axes swung as lethal blows rained down upon him, each strike intended to cleave through flesh and bone. Andree seemed to weather the storm of steel with an iron will. But time and time again, The Lions's weapons found their mark, leaving deep gashes in Andree and drawing blood from his wounds. Yet still he fought on, his determination unshaken by the pain, his spirit burning bright with defiance.

Until the monster in question stopped his retaliation for a moment gazing up at the sky with his one good eye. "If I'm too die, so will you." he said softly before releasing an ungodly amount of Will, large enough for Ulfr to clench his chest remembering Octavius's Will. In an instant he vanished appearing before Rose and as he went to strike a beast gave his life taking the brunt of the attack.

"Keep him still!" Rose shouted as once again she made a blood contract binding Andree in place and Eros forced all the fire, he could from his hand blackening his arm as it exploded out.

Pure one... Andre thought before being engulfed by flames, in one last valiant effort Andre reached through the fire with his burning moulting hand and Raijin blinked in and sliced it off. After a few moments Eros screamed in pain as he collapsed to the ground, Ulfr ran forward cutting through Andre's chest and Raijin wanting to make sure this monster stayed dead got into a stance "First-hand…" He muttered again blasting forward as he cut Andre's head off. Marking the end of the battle.

Elizabeth

The fires stayed lit as the mass funeral begun, again the Queen had to stand strong in black as she watched more of her people be laid to rest forever. She shivered for a moment before Drominic quickly placed a fur jacket over her dress. The wind sang as the priest blessed the funeral whilst Elizabeth stared blankly.

"War is war…" Drominic said softly snapping Elizabeth from her trance. "Both tangi and Andree, their men, fought for your dream."

"It's not my dream." Elizabeth corrected. "I'm at least glad that traitor fell with him."

"Our battle only lasted less than an hour before that coward retreated." Lancer said as he glanced at a crying Anna. "At least one of us can still cry."

Elizabeth smirked for a moment before composing herself. "Years of fighting does that I guess..."

The battle for Zen was theirs, a definitive victory on two of the three sides, however Elizabeth could tell her soldiers had grown tired. The people's eyes had grown dry unable to cry anymore for the fallen. She crushed her foot deeper into the snow, as she scanned around. "We only, have Zen and less than half our soldiers. Can we hold it?"

Drominic sighed. "Yes, without the Basilisk, Logan is like a headless chicken."

"He still has the beasts and that slave group, Hati or whatever." Elizabeth added before bending down to grab a handful of snow. "Maybe we only need Zen."

"What do you mean?" Al'Gadrood spoke up as he stood strong without the help of a walking stick.

"It's time, we call for an end. I'm sure the Golden Lion would like that as well." Elizabeth told him. "Then we can focus on Zen, and forget the other two, expending was a mistake now that I think about it."

"Did you forget their favourite quote; a Lion must always sit on the throne of Zen." Al'Gadrood said. "Do you think Logan will even accept giving up Zen."

"Either that or we fight till our last breath." Lancer interrupted. "The White Knights have too much to protect in Zen to give it up to such a man." He added as he glanced at Anna once more. Elizabeth noticed this and simply smiled. Before carrying on with the funeral in silence.

In Nero at the grand Cathedral of Colonz Father Gael finished his service, blessing all those who fell in the last battle as Logan sat in the front silent. Many surrounded him glaring at him, and he could feel it. He himself could not tell who gave the information for the attacks but he knew they blamed him once more until one of his soldiers hurried towards him handing him a Letter, with the White Knight' Sigel.

"That look, get used to it they will show you that look till..." Apollo stopped in his ramblings as he also noticed the Sigel.

"What do they want?" he quickly asked with a concerned look in his eye.

Logan slowly read the contents of the letter. "Terms of surrender." he said as he laughed.

"No," Apollo said. "You surrender now and everyone and I mean everyone will go for your head."

"The terms are good though..." Logan quickly responded.

"Look Logan, I love you as a brother but right now people hate you, Eros is out there losing it and if he hears you are surrendering, he will kill you."

"We get Nero and Pocasis, we just have to give up on Zen and Charlotte, I told you she would be useful."

"Logan, stop." Apollo said desperately, before he looked into Logan's eyes. In that moment he could see no amount of words could convince him, the man stood patting Logan on the shoulders before limping out of the church. Logan could be seen hastily scribbling a note and handing it to a soldier.

The soldier bowed. "As you say my King." He stood quickly going to send the message. The day went on as Logan walked around the city of Colonz he scanned each of the men, that had fought relentlessly till this moment, until he glanced over at a grieving Astrid surrounded by her friends. He tried to listen in to their conversation from afar but all he could gather was Astrid saying she never got to say goodbye again. Logan sighed as he clenched his chest, **maybe my children or grandchildren will get the throne,** he thought as he walked away. The exchange of letters was quick, as once again one of Logan's men came rushing in handing him the location of the meeting, "Call Ezekiel to me," he said softly as the soldier left his site. The man closed his eyes while he relaxed on a bench listening in to the sounds of people, not fighting, screaming, dying, no strategies, no cramped areas or fear of attack, nothing just people living their lives, in that moment, in that daydream he knew this was the correct decision before he opened his eyes to Ezekiel's look of concern.

"How many know of this?" Ezekiel quickly asked.

"You and Apollo."

"Cancel it."

"It's the best way Ezekiel."

"It's the best way to have your head taken yes."

"There's always the future my friend," Logan said.

Ezekiel froze for a moment as he looked at his King. "What about now, the soldiers that laid their lives down, the ones that remain with fallen comrades?"

"Don't forget I am still the King," Logan warned. "My decision is final." Frustrated Ezekiel stormed off not too be seen again until the next day, as Logan alongside some of his most loyal Knights hastily announced the surrender to a deafening silence.

Logan looked at Ezekiel with hope in his eyes, "Will you accompany me one last time old friend."

Ezekiel still angry simply shrugged. "If you let me punch you."

Logan laughed, "Not in front of everyone they would also try to do the same."

Ezekiel ordered one of the Knights to move from a steed as he jumped on it. "Shall we, my King?"

"We shall."

In Bamier, in the heart of a vast, sunlit meadow, surrounded by a tapestry of wildflowers and embraced by the serenity of nature, two oppositional factions met for a meeting of peace talks. The grassy region stretched out endlessly. At the centre of the meadow stood a worn and weathered table its surface bearing the etchings of battles' past. On it lay maps and scrolls, a tangible representation of the territories that had fuelled the enmity between the two nations. The emissaries, draped in garments that bore the symbols of their representative houses, approached the meeting grounds with cautious steps. The leaders, their faces etched with the lines of war, eyed each other warily as they took their places on either side of the table. Swords, now sheathed, hung at their hips.

"Theres no need for introductions between us is there".

Eros nodded. "I hope these talks fail or killing you would be much harder."

"So much hate for one so young." Elizabeth adds.

"Whose fault is that?" Eros responded sounding perplexed.

"Eros this is your doing, be proud o hero of the lions." She said mockingly. "You have his eyes, but I can tell you have a gentle heart."

Elizabeth glanced down to see Eros' hands, once at ease, now found refuge in subtle, repetitive gestures. A tapping finger, a restless drumming on the tabletop. "Are you so tired you can't even control your anger?" She teases.

"There will be no bloodshed today, I promised".

Ulfr, Mula and Rose watched close by as gusts of wind swept across the field, sending spirals of powdery snow into the air, as if nature itself participated in the solemnity of the moment.

"It was nice of Logan to include us in this." Rose said mockingly.

"We have to find Alex and adding him to the negotiations would have helped us." Ulfr quickly replied as he rubbed his eyes.

Rose scanned her brother for a moment. "How many days has it been since you slept."

"How many days has it been sine Eros has. The Kid is losing his mind I can see it, he hides it well, but I caught him talking to some guy named Ake. Imaginary friend of his I think."

"And Dafrak?" Rose asked with a stern look. "Does he just get to walk away with everything he did to us. To you?"

Ulfr trembled for a moment. "Patience, we will have his head even in times of peace."

As Logan his men and Ezekiel travelled along the long road, they started to talk like old times about Pier, about the parties Phillip used to throw. About the first battle against Andree, where Ezekiel became the King's most trusted advisor. Though still feeling bitter Ezekiel added to the conversation talking about how history will tell this story both laughing and hopping history will at least show their good sides.

"Are you sure you wish to do this my King," Ezekiel asked hoping Logan had changed his mind.

"What do you mean?" Logan asked him. "We are already going there to sign the papers."

"Then me and you need to go into hiding after because our heads will roll if we stay around here."

"We are attached, I guess we could migrate into Pangea Open up a shop." Logan quickly answered before the horses got stopped. "Gaston?" he asked stepping off his horse as he does so, all ten of his men draw their swords pointing at him. "What's the meaning of-" before finishing his sentence Ezekiel drew a dagger pressing it against the King's throat.

"You as well?" Logan said as he his reality started to settle in. Ezekiel with a sombre tone leaned towards Logan. "I made you a promise. That I will see the White Knights dethroned. I keep my promises." he said before slashing Logan's neck slowly backing off as the Golden Lion struggled to breath whilst his eyes wondered around looking for one person to help him. Each time he tried to speak a pool of blood flooded his mouth. His legs became heavy, and his thoughts ran towards the past Logan fell to the ground. As his warmth faded into the Snow's cold embrace his eyes could not look away from his dearest friend standing above him. With the snow turned red, Logan's eyes whitened, in that moment the Golden Lion died.

"Go send the message, I'll stay with him." Ezekiel said as he dropped the dagger. It seemed like he had to force the words from his mouth as he stood unable to move while snow slowly covered his King, his friend's body. Ten minutes had passed from that moment and with Gaston walking towards him with slow heavy steps, he knew the plan was set I'm motion and for the first time in his life Ezekiel left the future towards the Goddess's hands.

A sparrow flew from the shoulder of Ser Vauquelin, he quickly dropped the Note drawing his sword with tears flowing from his eyes. "Fucking White Knights!" He screamed in pain, "They betrayed Logan!"

Eros instantly lunged towards Elizabeth clashing his axe with Al'Gadrood's sheathed sword. Ulfr confused quickly drew his sword and in retaliation the White Knights opposite them all did the same. "What happened?"

"Logan's dead, assassinated on his way here by the White Knights!" Ser Vauquelin franticly said as he started pacing back and forth. "Attack Kill their bitch!" he screamed once more as the rest of the lions standing guard drew their weapons. Al'Gadrood edged back for a moment his hand on his sheathed sword as he counted twenty Lions, with twenty horses. Whilst twenty of the White Knights stood on the opposite side. He quickly grabbed the soldier to his closest left, "Get the Queen and escape..." he ordered quietly. "Rest of you, the Lions have betrayed us be ready to fight!" as the words left his mouth both sides charged into each other and while their swords clashed, Al'Gadrood glanced behind him to see Elizabeth being escorted to a horse. their eyes met, "leave Lizzy, I'll catch up once I'm done with these idiots!"

Elizabeth unarmoured, nodded. "Don't you dare die!"

"I order you to not die!" she added as she jumped on the back of a steed riding off with one of her Knights. In the fight, with Elizabeth safely away, Al'Gadrood strengthened himself, immediately feeling pain in his knee, but smiling it away when he begun to fight his enemies. Though being able to make quick work of some of his enemies his age crept up on him as he went for a swing of his sword wildly missing and being struck through the chest by Ser Vauquelin. He punched Vauquelin away. Stepping back for a moment before remembering the picnic him, Drominic, Lancer and Elizabeth had, many years ago before this mess started. He smiled even louder as he lunged into his enemy. "I will go to Ga'Al with a smile!" he screamed as he struck a Lion, lifting him above his head and throwing him over his shoulders. Everyone including the remaining White Knights froze for a second, admiring this man's strength before Ulfr struck another sword through his chest. "Gi dri fo su..." Ulfr said softly looking down.

"Ga... Al...su..." Al'Gadrood responded before numbing his body, dying on the spot. Ulfr looked up at Al'Gadrood's faded eyes before stepping back.

"Surrender, your Captain is dead!" he shouted at the remaining White Knights who immediately dropped their weapons.

Alexander

The castle loomed ahead; its familiar silhouette etched against the crimson sky. Queen Elizabeth stumbled across the threshold, her breaths shallow and ragged, her heart pounding like war drums in her chest. Behind her, the remnants of her retinue marched warily. The air within the castle walls was heavy with grief and fear, mingling with the cutting scent of smoke and blood. Elizabeth's eyes swept over the courtyard, which was eerily silent, save for the faint echoes of distant screams still ringing in her ears.

Her heart clenched with grief as she remembered the faces of her fallen soldiers, the ones who had fought valiantly by her side. But the image that haunted her the most was that of her dearest friend, Al'Gadrood, standing in-between her and death. Tears threatened to spill from Elizabeth's eyes, but she refused to let them fall. There would be time to mourn later. Right now, she needed to be strong for her people, for her Kingdom.

She continued making her way through the castle, her steps faltering but determined. She knew what she had to do, what her duty demanded of her. She would not let Al'Gadrood's sacrifice be in vain. She would fight, tooth and nail, until her Kingdom was safe once more. Reaching the armoury, Elizabeth's gaze fell upon the suits of armour that lined the walls, relics of battles long past. Memories flooded ger mind, of victories won and losses suffered, of comrades fallen and heroes risen. And amidst it all, she saw herself, a queen transformed into a warrior, ready to face whatever darkness lay ahead.

With a steely resolve, Elizabeth donned her old armour, each piece a testament of her strength and resilience. The weight of it settled upon her shoulders like a familiar embrace, grounding her in purpose once more. But as she fastened the final buckle, a voice broke through the silence, halting her movements.

"Liz…"

She turned, her heart skipping a beat at the sight of her friend, Sir Drominic, standing in the doorway, his expression sombre and grave.

"Drominic," she breathed, relief flooding her veins at the sight of him. "Be ready for battle."

"Is it true, is the old man…" he said softly, his voice heavy with regret. "Is he dead Liz?"

A cry tore from Elizabeth's throat, raw and primal, as she stumbled backwards, her vision blurring with tears. She reached out blindly, grasping for something, anything to anchor her to reality. But there was nothing, only the emptiness that stretched out before her, a void where once there had been light, laughter and love. And then, with a trembling hand, she reached for her sword, her fingers closing around the hilt like a lifeline. The metal was cool against her skin, a stark contrast to the fire that raged within her soul.

"I can't do this," she whispered, her voice choked with grief and despair. "I can't… I can't bear to lose anyone else."

But even as her words left her lips. She knew they were a lie, a coward's excuse to hide from the pain that threatened to consume her. She was a Queen, a leader, and her people needed her now more than ever. With shuddering breath, Elizabeth straightened her spine rigid with determination. She would not falter now, not ever. For Noham, for Lachlan, for Al'Gadrood, for all those who had fallen in defence of her Kingdom.

"What are you doing?" Drominic asked struggling to gather the words.

Elizabeth ignored him quickly turning towards Lancer. "Gather our army we end this today."

"I asked you a question." Drominic hissed at her.

Startled, Elizabeth franticly turned away from Drominic, as she marched out of the armoury. She did not look back, she could not bare to see the pity in his eyes, the sympathy that would only serve to weaken her resolve.

"Cursed..." he said softly. "This place, cursed."

"Its war people die," she replied. "Well avenge him..."

"Do what you wish," Drominic said starting to stumble away. "I'm done. I only stayed to protect you, Elizabeth. But fuck man, look at you, protecting you has... Let them have their cursed fucking Kingdom or don't. I'm going for a drink."

"Where?"

"Away from here." Drominic quickly answered as he walked away leaving Elizabeth alone once more in suffocating silence. For a moment, she lay there, stunned and numb, the echoes of Drominic's departure ringing in her ears. And then with a gut-wrenching cry she let go of her pain, of her guilt, of the walls she had built around her heart. Her sobs echoed through the empty halls, a lament for all that had been lost and all that could never be regained. But amidst the tears and the anguish, there was a glimmer of hope, as Lancer stood across from her. While he watched her clench her chest. Having a difficult time trying to form words, crying like a new-born baby.

"I'll find Dafrak," Lancer said confidently, "I'll bring him back and us two will win this war for you." He added before Elizabeth grabbed his trousers shaking her head franticly. He knew he couldn't leave her in such a state and opted to embrace his Queen as she cried into his chest.

In Nero, the feeling of despair was nowhere to be found some of the soldiers felt rage at their King's death, some felt relief. Ezekiel could see it in all their faces from his tower as Gaston entered the study with a stern look on his face.

"We found him…" He said grabbing Ezekiel's attention. "A castle due south."

"He was in Nero…" Ezekiel said puzzled. "Doesn't matter go bring our vanguard for the good news."

Gaston scanned Ezekiel for a moment. "Why are you so sure he will fight in this final battle if we give him his brother?"

Ezekiel was quiet but firm as he glared at Eros from afar. "Give a dog a treat and he will thank you. Give a dog food and he will be loyal."

Gaston gave Ezekiel a sorrowful look. "You want to use him to win this war?"

"Yes. He has the most loyal people, he's strong brave. Simple. Anyways he gets his brother back and his beautiful revenge, if I gave you all that would you not want to do anything for me?" Gaston could not answer he simply nodded and exited the room before Ezekiel walked closer to the study's main table knocking off a chess piece. As he glanced at the door, minute by minute he waited with a cold dead stare. And when the nob started to turn, he cleared his throat trying to compose himself. His and Eros's eyes met and all he could think about in that moment was an abyss. He shook his head as he reached out his hand. "We will gather everyone everything to get your brother back."

"No," Eros said, surprisingly. "I'll go myself."

"It is personal business," Ezekiel responded. "Will you lead our armies into Zen for the final battle, Ser Eros Senesto?" Ezekiel asked with a desperate look in his eye.

"Thank you, Ezekiel." Eros said grimly. "You gave us 'King' at his most vulnerable, you gave me my brother like you promised now, you give me a chance to be destroy the White knights. You are a true friend."

In castle Mae-Dura, South of Nero, in the depths of its forsaken dungeon, where the echoes of despair lingered like ghosts in the shadows, there hung Alex. His form, once proud and bold, now dangled limply from chains that bound his wrists, suspending him above the cold, stone floor. The flickering torchlight cast macabre dances upon his tortured frame, revealing a look marred by unspeakable agony.

His flesh, once whole and unblemished, now bore the cruel testament of torment. Strips of skin peeled away from his body like parchment left too long in the sun, exposing raw ligament and quivering muscles beneath. Each breath heaved with the effort of enduring the unbearable, his chest rising and falling in a rhythm of suffering. Mice, emboldened by the scent of decay, scuttled across the damp stone floor, their tiny claws clicking against the ground as they gnawed voraciously at the exposed flesh. They feasted upon his torment with a relentless hunger, their sharp teeth sinking into his tender flesh, leaving trails of crimson in their wake.

But it was not only the vermin that inflicted pain upon him. No, the true cruelty lay in the absence of his tongue, torn from his mouth by hands as cruel as any executioner's blade. In its place remained only a gaping, bloody void, a silent testament to the brutality that had befallen him. Within his voice, he was rendered mute, his cries for mercy stifled by the darkness that enveloped him. Yet, amidst the horror that surrounded him, there lingered a flicker of defiance in his eyes. They blazed with a fierce intensity, a spark of resilience amidst the suffocating despair. Though broken and battered, his spirit remained unbroken, a beacon of hope in the abyss of suffering.

Memories danced like phantoms through his fractured mind, images of a life once lived, now obscured by the fog of pain. *I should have told him to not go...* He wondered, as he started to think back on the last day, he saw his mother and sister as he remembered the laughter, warmth and love. *Goddess if you can hear me, why do you forsake me so much? I did not kill my sister; I did not seek vengeance. Everything I did was to better your people yet I'm the one in chains.*

Time lost all meaning in the dungeon's embrace, its passage marked only by the steady drip, drip, drip of water echoing through the chamber. Days bled into nights and knights into days, until boundaries between them blurred into a seamless stitching of suffering.

But yet he endured. For in the heart of a tortured soul, there burned the flame that could not be extinguished, a flame fuelled by defiance and resilience as he continued to linger in his thoughts. *He is a spawn of Amon... Your true enemy yet I'm the one who doesn't have the strength to move. He fought with heathens, yet I'm the one tortured every day. Not for my wrong doings but for his. I loved my brother the small curious boy with a life ahead of him, this man now is a shell that I must protect because his obsession destroyed our small family. Am I cursed because I wanted Eden? Do you even hear me goddess?*

Eros

Al'Gadrood's death was felt across the world In the Vassille Isles with tensions at an all-time high as the crowned Princess Gaia Vassellet sat in a heavily protected Villa south of the main castle, reading through the newspapers.

"My dear nephew the standing King, thinks he can stop my rise to the throne." She said stretching the leather of her trousers as she crossed her legs.

"Another Al falls and all you can think about is the crown my child." Hestia Vassellet scorned sipping on some tea making sure her lipstick did not smudge. "You have yet to make a move on Amon's spawn, how do you think we will win favour for the crown?"

"How do we kill someone who seems to be surrounded by a terrifying army?"

"Have you tried assassins?"

"The man killed the King and successfully hid for nearly seven years; no assassin is killing him." Princess Gaia roared. "No… Only the best will be able to cut down that monster."

"Shall we make preparations for your voyage future Queen?" Gaia smiled as she nodded.

In Lefki-thyra the country west of the city of Pangea, Octavius crunched the newspaper enraged. "The foolish Queen is bound to lose everything now!" He screamed interrupting Amadeus Jullian Caesar's wedding before quickly excusing himself out.

"It's wrong to interrupt the Hero's special day," Northern Chancellor Frida Heldegerd interrupted as she joined him.

"It's a sham wedding anyways."

"It's important," Frida Heldegerd corrected brushing the greys of her hair from her eyes. "This is the first step in establishing Utopia as the twentieth Kingdom for Pangea."

Octavius sighed. "Hero becomes king, the revolutionary army are finally making moves, attacking our south base. Another anomaly appeared in the middle of the desert. And a crazed patriot seems to be taking over Sun-En-Lio. Amos' spawn still lives! This is too much for an old man."

"Milo is on his way to convince the Brigadier General to take care of the desert Anomaly. So that's one problem gone."

"Will it work?"

"You should know Octavius; the old man only listens to Milo."

In the outskirts, at Pangea's borders Miriam sat lowering her face from the newspaper.

"What's wrong with you," a hooded man said as he rested his hand on her shoulder.

"Our old friend Al'Gadrood passed away…" Miriam said in a sombre tone.

"Justice, take care of our guest… I have something to do." She ordered standing.

Justice observed the creature on top of the hill landing on a pile of dead or dying clansmen. "Have you found the next piece?"

"No, but I think it's time we retrieved the first piece don't you think?"

"Then the G'AL'Rodinia Empire?"

"Yes."

In Nero Eros' allied forces had finally arrived. "Past the village, the castle sits on the hilltop." announced Ulfr as he read the map on horseback, "But to think Eros marched forward with the scouts, his eager." He added as he turned to Rose, wrapping the map up and putting it on the saddle's bag.

Rose looked uneasy as she gripped her sword, seeing this Ulfr put it down as her rage growing as they got closer to Dafrak.

"Remember the plan." Ulfr said softly.

"Using 'E's disgusting weapons?" Rose muttered.

"Using them will put us in an advantage," Ulfr added as he bit his teeth. "As we speak Eros, and the scouts are evacuating the Village. Making an interesting entrance to this battle don't you think?" he added looking at both Rose and Astrid who simply ignored Ulfr's words.

As Eros arrived at castle Mae-Dura's solitary village, he instantly drew his axe as he climbed of his steed. It was silence peaceful, unnerving. "Set them up!" Eros ordered as the scouts climbed from their horses running from house to house placing small balls near them. He again ordered another of his scouts to march forward and give a signal if he saw something odd. The wait felt like an eternity, with the Beasts and Hati quickly ap-proaching and the silence from the village adding more pressure to Eros. Until finally a flaming arrow flew in the air, *the signal...* Eros thought before shouting for the remaining scouts to move from the area.

I don't know how far the army is, Eros thought as he held tightly on a string. He looked around as he saw the young scouts in a panic. He lifted his head over the small rock he was hiding behind and stayed in that position for a few minutes until he saw shadows peeking through the snow's fog. ***They're already attacking...*** Eros thought as he sat back down counting back from twenty in his head. ***Three, Two, One...*** The second he reached zero he ignited his hand setting the string on fire it was silent for a second before a blinding white flash covered the area, sending Eros flying forward into the ground knocking him in and out on consciousness.

As Eros looked to his burned arm with some of its skin pealed of, he finally gathered his senses as an endless shrill from the explosion echoed throughout his body. He struggled to stand as he looked around hearing faint screams whilst holding on to his injured arm. Through the billowing smoke and the glare of the flames, Eros caught sight of faces twisted in terror, their eyes wide with shock and disbelief.

A sense of profound sorrow washed over Eros as he knelt amidst the ruins, his hands trembling as he reached out to touch the cold lifeless bodies of the fallen. The faces of the dead stared back at him, their eyes empty and accusing, as if silently asking why their lives had been cut short by the cruel whims of fate. With his trembling hands he reached out to touch the charred remains of a child's toy. The innocence of youth, snuffed out in an instant by the merciless hand of war.

"Villagers?" A scout muttered.

" He turned us into monsters…" Another wept.

"He did this…" Eros said softly.

"Who?" the scout asked as he saw a kid approaching Eros with a cold look in his eye.

"Dafrak... White Knight…"

With trembling hands, the young boy Oscar approached the weary figure of Eros, his gaze fixed upon the man who bore the weight of his sins upon his shoulders.

"You," Oscar said, his voice trembling with anger and grief, " I will never forget what you've done."

"It was a mistake…"

The boy's eyes blazed with fury at Eros' wors, his fists clenched tight with resolve born of pain and loss. "I'm going to kill you!" He screamed stumbling backwards as his face faded in colour.

"Every last one of you!" he added before collapsing the ground.

As dusk turned to night Ulfr and the rest of the army finally arrived to see the horror before them. "Eros... What happened..." Astrid said softly as she struggled to keep her eyes up. Hours before they arrived on the scene Eros had dragged himself and the young scout into an open field. His eye sharpened as a stray arrow hissed past his face striking the scout down.

Snow danced in the light, As Eros took a cold breath gripping his axe and slashing it through the fog painting the wind the blood of his enemies. ***How many this time...*** Eros thought as he lunged into the fog gliding his axe across the fog ripping the skull of one from their body. "Am I a Warrior now!" Eros screamed swinging his Axe downwards ripping an enemy in half. The snow bed continued to flood with the unburied, the dance of bloodshed continued as the dim lit sky vanished and a cloudy night took its place. Finally, Eros stopped moving his legs asking him to rest, to find somewhere warm and safe. To simply stay there. His body could feel every muscle twitch and twist, but his mind still raced as he saw the dead before him, hearing them speak their last words. "Where is my… Axe" Eros muttered as he glanced around. A familiar voice finally spoke to him, "You killed them all. Each one of them had lives, dreams and hope. Some had children some had wives, some had people they needed to take care of. Eros Senesto… You took all that from them, you took their lives…" The voice edged closer whispering in Eros's ear one last time. " How far are you willing to go… Monster…."

Ulfr and his allies finally arrived to see a sceptical. A painting of death with Eros standing in the middle. Ulfr slowly approached

"I don't understand what's he doing?"

"Careful," Rose said. "Something is not right."

"Eros can you hear me?" Ulfr asked as his hand slowly reached out.

"Give me a sword and shield" Eros said softly gazing at Dafrak slowly smiling in the distance.

"What's the plan boss?" one of Dafrak's men asked him.

Dafrak laughed. "Plan? Its already in motion."

"Let's end this play shall we…" Dafrak said as he drew his sword watching Eros start to Limp towards him and his allies follow in silence. Like undead, Eros and his allies walked forward with their shields in the air, blocking each of the unorganised archer attacks. Seeing they could not even make a single dent in their forces, Dafrak's Men grabbed their swords and shield and rushed forward screaming at the top of their lungs. As sword and shield clashed from both sides. Eros felt heavy, unable to help but stand in the background watching. But as they finally made it into the castle. Him and Dafrak looked at each, "That look suits you better…" Dafrak said coldly. Eros approached him, "My brother, where is he" Eros responded.

"Downstairs in the dungeons." Dafrak said as he opened his arms closing his eyes, only to soon realise he was still alive and as he turned back, he could see Eros limping into the castle's hallways. Before he could settle in his stunned expression, the sound of steel hitting the floor beneath him forced him back to reality as he turned back to the cold gaze of Ulfr's eyes.

"Children, really?" Ulfr asked in rage.

Dafrak picked up the sword. "I'm not much of a fighter my son. I'm not much of a killer either. You know me I'd rather break someone than kill them." He said as he swung his sword being easily deflected by Ulfr.

"You lost, accept it." Ulfr said before cutting into Dafrak's arm. "My mother, my sister, my friends all of them all who suffered under you, today I avenge them." Ulfr said as he carefully cut each of Dafrak's tendons.

Ulfr shook his head as he kicked Dafrak to the floor placing his sword on the man's chest. "I win!" he shouted as he slowly cut into his skin.

"Mr Nobody is coming..." Dafrak said as his mouth slowly flooded with blood, shocking Ulfr and Rose to their core.

As Eros cautiously infiltrated the depths of the accursed dungeon, his heart pounded with a mixture of dread and determination. The flickering torchlight cast eerie shadows upon the damp stone walls, and the air was thick with the stench of decay. With each step, the echoes of his own footsteps reverberated through the desolate corridors, a haunting reminder of the perilous journey he had embarked upon. Finally, he reached the chamber where his older brother was held captive, and what he witnessed within chilled him to the bone.

There, suspended by chains from the ceiling, hung his beloved brother a mere husk of the man he once was. His body was frail, his skin stretched taut over protruding bones like parchment stretched over a weathered frame. But it was not just the boniness of his form that struck Eros with horror. No, it was the sight of Alex's mutilated flesh, stripped away in cruel increments to reveal the raw, pulsating tissue beneath. His lung was exposed, a grotesque display of suffering that bore testament to the unspeakable torment inflicted upon him.

Tears welled in Eros' eyes as he approached, his voice catching in his throat at the sight of his sibling's agony. "Brother," he whispered, his voice chocked with emotion. Alex's head lifted slowly; his eyes glazed with pain yet still alive with recognition. Despite the anguish etched upon his features, there remained a flicker of resilience. With trembling hands, Eros reached out to his brother, his fingers brushing against the cold, clammy skin. Each touch seemed to scorch his very being, a reminder of the horror that had befallen his brother.

Gently, he began to unbind the chains that held his brother captive, his movements slow and deliberate as if afraid to cause further harm. With each link that fell away, he could feel the weight of despair lifting from his brother's weary soul, replaced by a glimmer of hope. At last, the chains fell away, and Alex flumped forward into his sibling's arms, his body trembling with exhaustion and relief, and his hand stretching out as it approached Eros' face. Eros seeing this quickly caressed his brother's hand as he begun to lift him up. Together, they made their way towards the dungeon's exit, their steps faltering but resolute.

Elizabeth

Another loss... Elizabeth thought as again her forces were pushed closer to the city. ***It's only been a month since his death yet if feels like I'm going to join him soon.***

Lancer saw the blank look on Elizabeth's face as she sat on the throne. He approached her casually, as the last of the Knights saluted. There was no noise, the fire was gone, the chefs, maids and anyone who wanted to live had left. Leaving only the most loyal to defend the city's walls. "All sides are surrounded right?" Elizabeth asked softly as she lowered her eyes from the sky. Lancer didn't bother to bow but remain standing. "What is your order my Queen?"

"If Alfred did not exist, I'd say surrender and let them take my head." Elizabeth said as she looked down at her lap to a sleeping Alfred. "If I did not care for what remains of the White Knights, I'd say fight till the last breath. So, Commander of the White Knights, what will it be?"

Lancer could see the hopelessness in Elizabeth's eyes. He quickly lifted his sword. "All those who are willing to lay their life for Elizabeth I Isaac request you do so when they next attack!" Though short Elizabeth's eyes lit up as all her Knights lifted their weapons up in solidarity.

"Well, if they're human," Elizabeth said with a tear in her eye. "I hope they spare Alfred."

Isaac nodded. "Now if you excuse me, I must do something. Anna will be with you shortly."

Confused Elizabeth nodded as Isaac quickly left the throne room.

As the sun went down, the fires in Lion's war camp lit up the sky. Eros sat on a hilltop watching over it as he crunched a letter in his hand. He stopped for a moment as his eyes sharpened before he quickly sighed. "Make it a clean cut please, I think I've suffered enough" he said as he felt the coldness of a blade gently placed on his shoulder. He made a quick glance to see it was Charlotte before he laughed turning back to the site of the lit war camp.

"The one I freed is the one to kill me," Eros said as he continued to laugh. "So many names yet..." He stopped as he bent his head making the area of his neck more visible.

"What do you see?" Eros asked.

"A war camp, power? What else?" Charlotte quickly answered with a stern tone.

"Dreams, I see dreams. You know Stavros wants to be a teacher and Ava wanted to follow her family's tradition." Eros added as he smiled. "Raijin vowed to me; he will never lose again. Imagine a week in a coma to come out of it with such confidence. And Alex, well even though all he cares about these days is that club, even he wanted something before Dafrak crippled him."

"Very well. I want to kill the man who destroyed this peaceful land." Charlotte answered as she clenched her sword.

"A monster like me should have never been allowed to live in the first place." Said Eros. "You might become a saint when you take my head."

Hearing this Charlotte sighed as memories of the bloodshed, the pain and the loos flooded her mind. She remembered the weight of her armour, the toll of endless battles and the emptiness that consumed her soul. In that moment, she saw not a foe before her, but a fellow human, weary and worn by the cruelties of this world. And so, with a heavy heart, Lady Charlotte withdrew her sword, letting it fall to her side.

Eros turned to her, surprise and confusion etched on his face. But before he could speak, she spoke with a voice filled with sorrow and resolve.

"I owe you nothing now." She said, her words carrying the weight of a thousand regrets. "And I hope all those people you left behind come and take your head."

With that, Lady Charlotte turned away, her footsteps echoing in the silence of the night. She chose to walk her own path, leaving behind the cycle of violence and vengeance and as her presence vanished from Eros's senses, he looked down at the note one last time before standing up, strapping his axe to his back, grabbing a bag cradled next to a tree and walking away from the war camp.

The next day, Raijin took lead as they began their invasion of the castle. No one had seen or heard from Eros most mentioned his silent demeanour the night before he walked up the hilltop. But the disappearance of one man would not stop the Lions, Beasts, and his own faction's attack on the White Knight's final stronghold.

Over in the Montven forest Eros sat with his legs crossed meditating. "You took a while." Eros said as he slowly opened his eyes.

"Your 'Will' got stronger..." Lancer quickly responded as he approached from the trees. "More than that you got stronger since our match in the Coliseum."

"You even wore what you wore during our match..." Eros said as he stretched his head.

"And you seem to have adopted the style of the Beasts fluently." Lancer said as he sat down. "I have never met a man with such destructive emotions. I honestly want to pick at your brain."

Eros rubbed his fingers in the cold grass, scanned the area and smirked, the forest was filled with all colours and the ground was brittle. He looked up at the skyscraper like trees. The wind was ice and felt sharp on his scars. The forest's smell was fresh, the peace on this land was soothing to the soul. Eros felt dread grow as soon him and the man before him would stain this serene world.

"Sins of our fathers, know no bounds." Lancer said grabbing Eros' attention.

"And shall be rested upon the sons; Leang Zhue." Eros interrupted. "You learned that from Jon I'm guessing. Not a wise way to make me give up on this journey."

Lancer snorted. "Anna suggested I talk it out." Silence fell in the area for a moment.

"Was it worth it?"

"Not anymore…"

"Charlotte is free if you were wondering." Eros said.

Lancer pondered for a moment. "Was she still as command-ing?"

"Surprisingly, even from a cage she kept shouting and acting like she was in charge."

"I'm glad she's safe…"

Eros sharpened his eyes Letting out a burst of Will and Isaac responded in kind.

"Elementals are truly blessed." Lancer said as he stood up with Eros mirroring him.

Unarmed they both marched to within feet of each other. Eros hunching over with his right hand at a distance. And Lancer lifting his hands with the feet shoulders' width apart, and toes facing inwards. At the slight gust of wind, they began trading blows, each dodging in quick succession with Eros being tagged forcing him to take steps back as he felt his jaw.

Eros bounced on his toes, with Lancer carefully watching. Eros then used his height to his advantage throwing a jab with his right hand whilst pulling his body back, seeing this Lancer weaved past the punch stepping in and receiving a left hook from Eros forcing him to wobble back as he felt his jaw.

So, as they stepped in once more, the fight truly begun with lightning reflexes, Lancer danced around Eros' heavy strikes, sidestepping each blow with the precision of a seasoned dancer. Their movements were a symphony of controlled aggression, a testament to years of fighting. Eros' fists pounded the air with thunderous force, aiming to overwhelm his opponent with sheer strength. But Lancer was elusive, slipping through the gaps in Eros' defence like a shadow in the night.

Eros grunted with frustration, his attacks meeting only empty air as Lancer danced around them like a ghost. But Eros was undeterred, launching a barrage of punches that thundered through the forest with bone shaking force. Lancer deflected the blows with deft blocks and parries, his movements fluid and efficient. He ducked under a swinging fist and delivered a punishing kick to Eros' midsection, causing him to stagger back with a grunt of pain.

Sensing an opening, Lancer closed the distance between them. He locked arms with Eros, their bodies pressed together in a deadly embrace. With a twist of his wrist Lancer applied pressure to Eros' joints, eliciting a grunt of pain as Eros struggled against the hold.

"Yield!" Lancer screamed but Eros was strong, and he fought back with a primal ferocity. With a surge of brute force, he broke free from Lancer's grip and retaliated with a vicious elbow strike to the ribs. Lancer winced in pain as he broke away. The forest rang with the sound of flesh meeting flesh as the two combatants traded blows with relentless intensity. Each strike was a testament to their skill and determination, each impact sending shockwaves through the air. But as the fight wore on, Lancer knew he needed to change tactics. With a quick glance to his left, his eyes fell upon his lance. With a burst of speed Lancer disengaged from the brawl and darted towards his weapon. Eros sensing the shift in momentum, charged to his right with a primal roar aiming to grab his axe.

The battlefield crackled with tension as Lancer and Eros squared off, their weapons gleaming in the in the fiery glow of the midday sun. The air was thick with the scent of smoke and anticipation as the two adversaries locked eyes, each assessing the other with a mixture of caution and determination. Lancer stood tall on resolute, his weapon held firmly in hand, its gleaming tip poised like a deadly spearhead. Across from him, Eros wielded a massive axe wreathed in flames, the fiery aura casting an ominous glow upon their rugged features.

With a fierce battle cry, Eros charged forward, flames dancing in his wake as he closed the distance with lightning speed. But lancer was ready, as again with his fluid movements he sidestepped the oncoming assault. With a swift thrust of his lance, he aimed for Eros' exposed flank, but Eros was quick to react, deflecting the blow with a swing of his blazing axe. The clash of metal echoed through the battlefield, a symphony of steel and fire that reverberated in the air.

Undeterred, Lancer pressed his advantage, launching a flurry of rapid strikes in a relentless assault. Each thrust was met with a wall of flames as Eros countered with a series of sweeping arcs, his axe leaving trails of fire in its wake. The heat of the flames licked at Lancer's skin, but he gritted his teeth and fought on, his determination unyielding. With a deft twist of the wrist, he parried Eros' attacks and retaliated with a series of calculated thrusts aimed at exploiting weakness in their opponent's defence.

But Eros was no mere brute as he fought with cunning ferocity, his movements unpredictable and wild.

"What a monster…" Eros muttered whilst glaring at Lancer. "Had you been born an elemental; no man would be able to stop you. Lancer 'The beast slayer'!" Eros roared as he unleashed a torrent of fire, engulfing the battlefield in a blazing inferno that threatened to consume everything in its path. Feeling Eros' true will Lancer grit his teeth. "Disgusting…" He muttered as he pressed through the flames. With each step, drawing closer to Eros, his lance held steady and true. As the inferno raged around them, the two adversaries once again clashed with a ferocity that seemed to defy the very elements themselves. Lancer's strikes were precise and calculated, aimed at finding weakness in Eros' defence. And Eros fought with a primal rage, with each swing of their axe, he unleashed waves of heat and flame, forcing Lancer to dance on the edge of danger with every step.

In the midst of the chaos, Lancer saw his opening a brief moment of hesitation in Eros' movements, a split second where their guard faltered. With a swift and decisive thrust, Lancer aimed at Eros' hear, their lance piecing through the flames w3ith unstoppable force. Eros' eyes widened in shock as he staggered back, the lance barely missing his heart and ripping though the side of his chest. **Mother… Fanisse…** he thought before letting out a defiant roar.

"Even now you have no chance in defeating me." Isaac said as he gathered his thoughts releasing an unreasonable amount of

'Will' forcing Eros to pause and snaping back to reality. "Elizabeth's ways gave birth to a lot of enemies. But her idea of a perfect nation is what drives us White Knights. What would it take for you to leave this place Eros?"

"All of you dead," Eros struggled to get his words out.

Lancer sighed taking his stance. And so, their final stage was set, a Fire Elemental devoured by rage and a Human fighting for more than himself. In the first move both release their Wills at full power clashing into each other blowing the surrounding fire away. As their eyes met, they lunged at each other Eros using his strength to swing his widely, Lancer wisely remembering this monster's strength and deflecting each attack whilst sending one back. Seeing this Eros let out a ring of fire forcing Isaac to jump back to avoid being burned. But when his eyes focused, he saw Eros closing the gap momentarily forcing Lancer to grab Eros's fist stopping the momentum. Unfortunately, this wasn't enough as Isaac clenched his teeth while he could feel the overwhelming power from Eros and immediately being launched deeper into the forest.

Isaac finally landed quickly grabbing his footing, he jumped to the side dodging a ball of fire lunging forward with a high kick cutting Eros's cheek before Eros stepped back for a moment.

Both recognising their opponent's strengths, Isaac pulled out a vile of liquid quickly drinking it as Eros's mind went back to his fight against Noham. Only for him to be brought back to reality as he blocked an attack from a blitzing Isaac. "To match your ungodly strength, I had to coat my body in my Will and use Noham's final gift. You are a monster Eros!" Isaac said as he smiled disgustingly, vanishing from Eros's sight for a moment before slicing the side of his chest.

Both blood-drenched and exhausted. Isaac looked lost for a moment, before reaching into his pouch grabbing and drinking another vile of liquid. He clenched his chest for a moment before letting out a bright smile.

"I bid you," he said with veins quickly growing across his body. "Eros 'Herald of Amos'" he added as he ran forward breaking the ground with each step. Eros could see him clearly running towards him, but his heart could not bear to back off from this attack. And like the warrior he was he firmly ignited his arms and legs before the fire begun to consume his entire body with his eyes turned bright yellow running towards Isaac.

With a thunderous roar, they collided in a flurry of fists. Each strike was met with a counter, each blow parried with a devastating counterattack as they danced on the razor's edge between victory and defeat. Their faces were set in grim determination, their eyes locked in a fierce gaze as they pushed themselves to the brink of death. They fought with a primal intensity, each blow fuelled by a roar, untamed energy that seemed to surge through their very veins.

In the end Lancer took a step back instantly vomiting blood as Eros struggled to stay on his feet.

"Your name…what is it." Eros asked.

"Isaac…"

Eros smiled through the blood, before his arm set ablaze and as he tightened his back going in for a final punch, a timid voice stopped him in his tracks. "Enough!" it said. And as Eros stepped back to see a young girl standing behind Isaac as the fire on his arm quickly disappeared.

"Is she safe?" Isaac asked still gazing at Eros.

"Yes…" Anna responded with tears flooding her eyes when Isaac dropped to the ground. Though it took a moment Eros quickly limped past Isaac as Anna ran into him. Feeling his legs drag into the ground. His vision distorting and with warmth hugging him, he slumped heavily against a gnarled tree, he fought to catch his breath. Blood seeped from his wounds, staining the ground beneath him. The forest around him seemed to close in, its shadows whispering secrets of both danger and sanctuary. He gazed upon Isaac laying in Anna's lap before 'The beast slayer's arm lumped over and as Eros looked up taking heavy breath, he saw Ake at the corner of his eye. "Bring… me…a…blade." He muttered waking himself from his delusions. And with a grunt of effort, Eros pushed himself upright, his muscles trembling with the strain. Drawing upon the last vestiges of his strength, he resumed his journey, each step a testament to his resilience. The forest offered no mercy, its tangled undergrowth and twisted paths testing his resolve at every turn. But still, he pressed on, driven by a primal instinct to survive. With every agonizing step, he left behind the echoes of the fight, seeking solace in the embrace of the wilderness.

And at the castle of Zen 'the Lionic wars,' where quickly coming to an end with Raijin and Astrid leading the vanguard, as they breached the towering walls of the enemy castle. Their swords clashed against the gates, their war cries echoing through the empty courtyard. But as they spilled into the heart of the fortress, they were met not by the fierce resistance they had expected, but by an eerie silence. The enemy, it seemed, had abandoned their stronghold, leaving only the echoes of their presence.

Confused ripped through the ranks of the Lions as they cautiously advanced, their senses alert or any sign of danger. They passed through deserted halls and empty chambers, their footsteps echoing in the stillness of the abandoned castle. The air was heavy with the scent of dust and decay, the remnants of a once proud stronghold now left to crumble in the wake of their victory. Torches flickered dimly in the darkness, casting long shadows across the stone walls.

As they explored further, they discovered signs of a hasty retreat, discarded weapons, hastily packed supplies, and hastily extinguished fires. It became clear that the enemy had fled in the face of their advance, leaving behind their fortress as a hallow shell.

Was it minutes, seconds, hours for Eros it felt like an eternity as his heart swelled with relief as he approached a small shed nestled among the trees. With trembling hands, he pushed open the creaking door and stepped inside. There, in the dim light filtering through the cracks in the wood, sat his brother. Though unable to stand or fight like other warriors, his brother's spirit remained unbroken, a beacon of resilience in the face of adversity. Alex glanced at him with a blank look and a warm smile spread across Eros' face, banishing the shadows of pain and exhaustion. Despite the injuries and the hardships, they had endured, they were together once more, bound by blood and brotherhood.

End of prologue